LOOP

By Koji Suzuki

Ring
Spiral
Loop

Dark Water

LOOP

KOJI SUZUKI

Translation
Glynne Walley

HARPER

This novel is entirely a work of fiction.
The names, characters and incidents portrayed in it are
the work of the author's imagination. Any resemblance to
actual persons, living or dead, events or localities is
entirely coincidental.

Harper
An imprint of HarperCollins*Publishers*
77–85 Fulham Palace Road,
Hammersmith, London W6 8JB

www.harpercollins.co.uk

This paperback edition 2007

First published in Great Britain by
HarperCollins*Publishers* 2006
1

First published in the USA by Vertical Inc, 2005

Originally published in Japan as *Rupu*
by Kadokawa Shoten, Tokyo, 1998

Copyright © Koji Suzuki 2005

Koji Suzuki asserts the moral right to
be identified as the author of this work

A catalogue record for this book
is available from the British Library

ISBN-13: 978 0 00 717909 1
ISBN-10: 0 00 717909 X

Set in Meridien

Printed and bound in Great Britain by
Clays Limited, St Ives plc

PART ONE

At the End of the Night

1

He opened the sliding glass door, and the smell of the sea poured into the room. There was hardly any wind—the humid night air rose straight up from the black water of the bay to envelop his body, fresh from the bath. The resulting immediacy of the ocean was a not-unpleasant feeling for Kaoru.

He made a habit of going out onto the balcony after dinner to observe the movements of the stars and the waxing and waning of the moon. The moon's expression was constantly, subtly changing for him, and watching it gave him a mystical sort of feeling. Often it would give him ideas.

Gazing up into the night sky was part of his daily routine. He'd slide open the door, feel around in the darkness below until he found his sandals, and step into them. Kaoru liked it up here on the twenty-ninth floor of the apartment tower, on this balcony thrust into the darkness. It was where he felt most at home.

September was mostly gone, but not the heat of summer. The tropical evenings had arrived in June, and while the calendar now said it was autumn, they showed no sign of faltering yet.

He didn't know when the summers had started getting longer. All he knew was that coming out onto the balcony like this every evening never cooled him off. It just brought him face to face with the heat.

But then the stars rushed right down to him, so close that he felt like he could touch them if he only stretched out his hand, and he forgot the heat.

The residential part of Odaiba, facing Tokyo Bay, boasted an overgrowth of condominium towers, but not many residents. The banks of windows only gave off a limited amount of light, little enough in fact to allow a clear view of the stars.

An occasional fresh breeze took the sea out of the air some, and his hair, just washed and still clinging to the back of his neck, began to dry.

"Kaoru, close the door! You'll catch cold!" His mother's voice, from behind the kitchen counter. The movement of the air must have told her that the door was open. She couldn't see the balcony from where she was, though, so Kaoru doubted she realized that he was outside, fully exposed to the night air.

How could anybody catch cold in this heat, he wondered, exasperated at his mother's over-protectiveness. Not that it was anything new. He had no doubt that if she knew he was out on the balcony, she'd literally drag him back inside. He shut the door behind him so he couldn't hear her anymore.

Now he was the sole possessor of this sliver of space jutting into the sky a hundred yards above the ground. He turned around and looked through the glass door into the apartment. He couldn't see his mother directly. But he could read her presence in the milky band of fluorescent light that shone from the kitchen onto the sofa in the living room. As she stood in front of the sink, cleaning up after the meal, her movements caused slight disturbances in the rays of light.

Kaoru returned his gaze to the darkness and thought the same thoughts he always did. He dreamed of being able to elucidate, somehow, the workings of the world that surrounded and contained him. It wasn't that he hoped to solve a mystery or two on the cutting edge of a particular field. What he desired was to discover a unifying theory, something to explain all phenomena in the natural world. His father, an information-engineering researcher, had basically the same dream.

When they were together, father and son discussed nothing but the natural sciences.

But it wasn't quite right to call them discussions. Basically, Kaoru, who had just turned ten, shot questions at his father, and his father answered them. Kaoru's father, Hideyuki, had started out as part of a team working on an artificial life project. Then he'd elected to move his research into a university setting, becoming a professor. Hideyuki never blew off Kaoru's questions. In fact, he maintained that his son's bold thinking, unrestrained as it was by common sense, sometimes even gave him hints he could use in his research. Their conversations were always deadly serious.

Whenever Hideyuki managed to get a Sunday afternoon off, he and Kaoru would spend it in heated discussions, the progress of which Machiko, Hideyuki's wife and Kaoru's mother, would watch with a satisfied look on her face. Her husband had a tendency to get so involved in what he was saying that he would forget his surroundings; her son, on the other hand, never neglected to be mindful that his mother was probably feeling left out because she was unable to join in the debates. He'd explain the issues they were discussing, breaking them down into bite-size chunks, in an effort to allow her to participate. It was a kind of consideration Hideyuki would never be able to imitate.

She always wore the same look of satisfaction as she watched her son, full of gratitude for his effortless kindness and pride that at age ten he could already discuss the natural sciences at a level so far beyond her own understanding.

Headlights flowed along on Rainbow Bridge far below. Kaoru wondered expectantly if his father's motorbike was in that belt of light. As always, he couldn't wait for his father to get home.

It was ten years ago that Hideyuki had gone from mere team member on the artificial life project to university professor; ten years ago that he'd moved from the Tokyo suburbs to this condo in Odaiba. The living environment here—the tall apartment buildings on the water's edge—suited his family's tastes. Kaoru never got tired of looking down from on high, and then when night came, he'd pull the stars down close, using them to bolster his imagination concerning the world whose ways he couldn't yet fully grasp.

A living space high above the ground: the kind of thing to foster a bird's eye. Kaoru fell to wondering. If birds represented an evolutionary advance from reptiles, it meant that living spaces had gradually progressed skyward. What effect did that have on human evolution? Kaoru realized that it had been a month since he'd set foot on soil.

As he placed his hands on the balcony railing, about his own height, and stretched, he felt *it*. And not for the first time, either. He'd felt *it* from time to time for as long as he could remember. Only never, oddly enough, had the feeling come over him when he was with his family.

He was used to it by now. So he didn't turn around, even though he could feel someone watching him from behind. He knew what would be there if he did: the same living room, the dining room beyond it, the kitchen next to it, all unchanged. And in the kitchen, his mother Machiko washing dishes just like always.

Kaoru shook his head to chase away the feeling that he was being watched. And the sensation seemed to take a step back, blending into the darkness and disappearing into the sky.

Once he was sure it was gone, Kaoru turned around and pressed his back against the railing. Everything was just as it had been. His mother's shadow, flickering in the band of light from the kitchen doorway. Where had they gone, those countless eyes watching him from behind? Kaoru had felt them, unmistakably. Innumerable gazes, fastened on him.

He should have felt those inky stares on his back when he was like this, staring into the apartment, his back to the night. But now those eyes had disappeared, assimilated into the darkness.

Just what was it that was watching him? Kaoru had never thrown this question out at his father. He doubted even his father would be able to give him an answer.

Now he felt a chill, in spite of the heat. He no longer felt like being on the balcony.

Kaoru went back into the living room and peeked into the kitchen at his mother. She'd finished washing the dishes and was now wiping the edge of the sink with a dishcloth. Her back was to him, and she was humming. He stared at her thin, elegant shoulders, willing her to notice his gaze. But she just kept humming, unmoved.

Kaoru came up behind her and spoke.

"Hey, Mom, when's Dad getting home?"

He hadn't intended to startle her, but there was no denying that his approach had been a little too silent, and his voice when he spoke a little too loud. Machiko jumped, her arms jerked, and she knocked over a dish that she'd placed at the edge of the sink.

"Hey, don't scare me like that!"

She caught her breath and turned around, hands to her breast.

"Sorry," Kaoru said. He often accidentally took his mother unawares like this.

"How long have you been standing there, Kaoru?"

"Just a few seconds."

"You know Mom's jumpy. You shouldn't startle me like that," she scolded.

"I'm sorry. I didn't mean to do it."

"Really? Well, you did it all the same."

"Didn't you notice? I was staring at your back, just for a few seconds."

"Now, why should I notice that? I don't have eyes in the back of my head, you know."

"I know, but, I . . ." He trailed off. What he wanted to say was, *People can feel someone staring at them even if they don't turn around.* But he knew that would scare his mother even more.

So he went back to his original question. "When's Dad getting home?" Of course, he knew it was pointless to ask: not once had his mother ever known when his father was coming home.

"He'll probably be late again today, I imagine." She gave her usual vague answer, glancing at the clock in the living room.

"Late again?"

Kaoru sounded disappointed, and Machiko said, "You know your dad's really busy at work these days. He's just getting started on a new project, remember?" She tried to take his side. He got home late every night, but never did she betray the slightest hint of discontent.

"Maybe I'll wait up for him."

After she'd finished putting away the dishes, Machiko went over to her son, wiping her hands with the dishcloth.

"Do you have something you want to ask him again?"

"Yeah."

"About his work?"

"Unh-uh."

"How about I ask him for you?"

"Huh?" Kaoru couldn't stop himself from laughing.

"Knock that off! You know, I'm not as dumb as you think I am. I did go to grad school, you know."

"I know that. But . . . you studied English lit, right?"

Machiko hād indeed belonged to a department of English language and literature at the university, but to be exact her focus had been on American culture, rather than English literature. She'd been particularly knowledgeable about Native American traditions; even now she kept up on it, reading in her free time.

"Never mind that, just tell me. I want to hear what you have to say."

Still holding the dishcloth, Machiko ushered her son into the living room. Kaoru thought it was a little odd: why should she suddenly take an interest tonight, of all nights? Why was she reacting differently?

"Wait a minute, then." Kaoru went to his bedroom and came back with two pieces of paper. He sat down on the sofa next to his mother.

As she glanced at the pages in Kaoru's hand, Machiko said, "What's this? I hope these aren't full of difficult figures again!" When it came to mathematical questions, she knew it was time for her to admit defeat.

"It's nothing hard like that this time."

He handed her the two pages, face up, and she looked at them in turn. A map of the world was printed on each one.

"Well, this is a change. You're studying geography now?"

Geography was one of her strong suits, particularly North American. She was confident that in this field, at least, she knew more than her son.

"Nope. Gravitational anomalies."

"What?" It looked like she'd be out of her league after all. A faint look of despair crept into her eyes.

Kaoru leaned forward and began to explain how these maps showed in one glance the earth's gravitational anomalies.

"Okay, there's a small difference between the values you get from the gravity equation and those you get by correcting gravitation acceleration for the surface of the geoid. Here we have those differences written on maps in terms of positive or negative numbers."

The pages were numbered, "1" and "2". On the first map were drawn what seemed like an endless series of contour lines representing gravitational anomalies, and each line was labeled with a number accompanied by a plus sign or a minus sign. The contour lines looked just like the ones found in any normal atlas, where positive numbers equaled heights above sea level and negative numbers depths below sea level.

But in this case, the lines showed the distribution of gravitational anomalies. In this case, the greater the positive number, the stronger the gravitational force, and the greater the negative number, the weaker the gravitational force at that particular location. The unit was the milligal (mgal). The map was shaded, too: the whiter areas corresponded to positive gravitational anomalies, while the darker areas corresponded to negative ones. It was set up so that everything could be understood at a glance.

Machiko stared long and hard at the gravitational anomaly distribution map she held in her hands, and then looked up and said, "Alright, I give up. What is a gravitational anomaly?" She'd long since given up trying to fake knowledge in front of her son.

"Mom, surely you don't think that the earth's gravity is the same everywhere, do you?"

"I haven't thought about it once since the day I was born, to be honest."

"Well, it's not. It varies from place to place."

"So what you're saying is that on this map, the bigger the positive number, the stronger the force of gravity, and the bigger the negative number, the weaker, right?"

"Uh-huh, that's right. See, the matter that makes up the earth's interior doesn't have a uniform mass. Think of it like this: if a place has a negative gravitational anomaly, it means that the geological material below it has less mass. In general, the higher the latitude, the stronger the force of gravity."

"And what's that piece of paper?"

Machiko pointed to the page marked "2". This, too, was a map of the world, but without the complex contour lines: instead it was marked with dozens of black dots.

"These are longevity zones."

"Longevity zones? You mean places where people tend to live longer?"

First a map of gravitational anomalies, and now a map of longevity zones—she was growing more confused by the minute.

"Right. Places whose residents clearly live longer than people living in other areas. This map shows how many of these spots there are in the world," Kaoru said, indicating the black dots on the map. Four of them were actually marked with double circles. The Caucasus region on the shores of the Black Sea, the Samejima Islands of Japan, the area of Kashmir at the foot of the Karakoram Mountains, and the southern part of Ecuador. All had areas famous for the longevity of their inhabitants.

Kaoru seemed to think the second map needed no further explanation. Machiko, though, was looking at it for the first time. She urged him on.

"So?" The real question now was, of course, what the two maps had to do with each other.

"Put one on top of the other."

Machiko obeyed. They were the same size, so it was easily done.

"Now hold them up to the light." Kaoru pointed to the living room chandelier.

Machiko raised them slowly, trying to keep the pages aligned. Now the black dots of the one were showing up in the midst of the contour lines of the other.

"Get it?"

Machiko didn't know what she was supposed to get.

"Stop putting on airs. Tell me what I'm supposed to see."

"Well, look—the longevity zones correspond perfectly to the low-gravity areas, don't they?"

Machiko stood up and brought the pages closer to the light. It was true: the black dots representing longevity zones only showed up in places demarcated on the first map by low-gravity lines. Very low gravity.

"You're right," she said, not bothering to disguise her astonishment. But she still cocked her head as if not entirely convinced. As if to say she still wasn't sure what it was all supposed to mean.

"Well, maybe there's a relationship between longevity and gravity."

"And that's what you want to ask your father about?"

"Well, yeah. By the way, Mom, what do you think the odds were of life arising on earth naturally?"

"Like winning the lottery."

Kaoru laughed out loud. "Come on! Way smaller. You can't even compare the two. We're talking a miracle."

"But someone always wins the lottery."

"You're talking about a lottery with, like, a hundred tickets and one winner, where a hundred people buy tickets. I'm talking about rolling dice a hundred times and having them come up sixes every time. What would you think if that happened?"

"I'd think the game was rigged."

"Rigged?"

"Sure. If someone rolled the same number a hundred times in a row, it'd have to mean the dice were loaded, wouldn't it?" As she said this, she poked a finger into Kaoru's forehead affectionately, as if to say, *Silly.*

"Loaded, huh?"

Kaoru thought for a while, mouth hanging open. "Of course. Loaded dice. It had to be rigged. It doesn't make sense otherwise."

"Right?"

"And humanity just hasn't noticed that it's rigged. But, Mom—what if dice that aren't loaded come up with the same number a hundred times in a row?"

"Well, then we're talking about God, right? He's the only one who could do something like that."

Kaoru couldn't tell if his mother really believed that or not.

He decided to move on. "By the way, do you remember what happened on TV yesterday?" Kaoru was referring to his favorite afternoon soap opera. He loved the soaps so much that he even had his mother tape them for him sometimes.

"I forgot to watch."

"Well, remember how Sayuri and Daizo met again on the Cape?"

Kaoru proceeded to recount the plot of yesterday's episode almost as if it involved people he knew personally. Sayuri and Daizo were a young couple in their first year of marriage, and a series of misunderstandings had brought them to the brink of divorce. They were still in love, but coincidence had piled on coincidence until they were hopelessly tangled in the cords that bind men and women: now they were in a morass they couldn't find their way out of. So they'd separated. And then, one day, by pure chance, they'd run into each other on a certain point of land on the Japan Sea coast. The place was special to them—it was where they'd first met. And as they began to remember all the wonderful times they'd had together there, their old feelings for each other had been reawakened. They cleared up their misunderstandings one by one, until they were sure of each other's love again.

Of course, a heartwarming twist lay behind this trite tale. Both of them were under the impression that it was purely by chance that they'd run into each other on this sentimental promontory, but they were wrong. They had friends who were desperate to see them make up, and those friends had colluded, taking it upon themselves to arrange it so that each would be there at that moment.

"Get it, Mom? What are the chances of a separated couple running into each other like that—being in the same place at the same time on the same day? Not exactly zero. Coincidental meetings do happen. But in some cases, when the chances of something happening are really small, and then it actually happens, you tend to think that there's somebody in the shadows pulling strings. In this case, it was Sayuri and Daizo's nosy friends."

"I think I see where you're going with this. You're trying to say that even though there was almost zero chance of it happening, life actually did arise. After all, we exist. In which case, there must be something somewhere pulling the strings. Right?"

Kaoru felt that way constantly. There were

times when the idea that he was being watched, manipulated, insinuated itself into his brain for no apparent reason. Whether this was a phenomenon unique to himself, or whether it was in fact universal, was something he hadn't yet figured out.

Suddenly he got chills. He shivered. He looked at the sliding-glass door and found that it was open a crack. Still seated on the sofa, he twisted his body until he could close the door.

2

Kaoru just couldn't get to sleep. It was already thirty minutes since he'd crawled into his futon after having given up on waiting for his father to get home.

It was customary in the Futami household for both parents and their son to sleep in the same Japanese-style room. With its three Western-style rooms, one Japanese-style room, and good-sized living room, plus dining room and kitchen, their apartment was more than large enough for the three of them. They each had their own room. But for some reason, when it came time to sleep, they'd all gather in the Japanese-style room and lie down together. They'd spread out their futons with Machiko in the middle, flanked by Hideyuki and Kaoru. It had been like that ever since Kaoru was born.

Staring at the ceiling, Kaoru spoke softly to his mother, lying next to him.

"Mom?"

No reply. Machiko tended to fall asleep as soon as her head hit the pillow.

Kaoru wasn't what you'd exactly call agitated, but there was a faint pounding of excitement in his chest. He was sure he'd discovered something in the relative positions of gravitational anomalies and longevity zones. It couldn't be just a coincidence. The simple interpretation was that gravity was somehow related to human longevity—perhaps even to the secret of life itself.

He'd discovered the correlation purely by chance. There'd been a documentary on TV about villages where people lived to extraordinary ages, and it just so happened that at that moment his computer screen had been displaying a map of world gravitational anomalies. Lately he'd come across a lot of information about gravitational anomalies while fooling around on the computer; he'd gotten interested in gravity. Between the TV screen and the computer screen, something triggered his sixth sense, and he'd overlaid the two maps. It was the kind of inspiration only given to humankind.

No matter how prodigious its ability to process information, no matter how fast its calculation speed, a computer has no "inspiration" function, reflected Kaoru. It was impossible for a machine to bring together two utterly disparate phenomena and consider them as one. Were such an ability to arise, it would be because human brain cells had somehow been incorporated into the hardware. Human-computer intercourse.

Which actually sounded pretty intriguing to Kaoru. There was no telling what sort of sentient life form that would bring into the world. Endlessly fascinating.

Kaoru's desire to understand the workings of the world manifested itself in a lot of different questions, but at the root of all of them was one basic unknown: the source of life.

How did life begin? Or, alternatively: *Why am I here?*

Evolutionary theory and genetics both piqued his curiosity, but his biological inquiries always centered on that one point.

He wasn't a single-minded believer in the variation on the coacervate theory which held that an inorganic world developed gradually until RNA and DNA appeared. He understood that the more one inquired into life the more the idea of self-replication became a big factor. It was DNA that governed self-replication; under the direction of the genetic information it carried came the formation of proteins, the stuff of life. Proteins were made of alignments of hundreds of amino acids, in twenty varieties. The code locked away within DNA was in fact the language that defined the way those acids aligned.

Until those amino acids lined up in a certain predetermined way, they wouldn't form a protein meaningful to life. The primordial sea was often likened to a soup thick with the prerequisites for life. Then some power stirred that thick soup up, until it so happened that things lined up in a meaningful way. But what were the odds of that?

To make it easier to comprehend, Kaoru decided to think in terms of a much smaller, neater number. Take a line of a hundred amino acids in twenty varieties, with one of them turning into a protein, the stuff of life. The probability then would be twenty to the hundredth power. Twenty to the hundredth power was a number far greater than all the hydrogen atoms in the universe. In terms of odds, it was like playing several times in a row a lottery in which the winning ticket was one particular hydrogen atom out of a whole universe full of them, and winning every time.

In short, the probability was infinitesimal. Essentially impossible. In spite of which, life had arisen. Therefore, the game had to have been rigged. Kaoru wanted to know just how the wall of improbability had been surmounted. His uttermost desire was to understand the nature of that dice-loading—without resorting to the concept of God.

On the other hand, sometimes there arose the suspicion that maybe everything was an illusion. There was no way to actually confirm that his body existed as a body. His cognitive abilities may have convinced him that it did, but there was always the possibility that reality was empty.

As he lay there in the dim room, illuminated by only a night light, the stillness was such that he could hear his heart beat. So it would seem that right now, at this very moment, it was no mistake to think that he was alive. He wanted to believe in the sound of his heart.

The roar of a motorcycle sounded in Kaoru's inner ear. A sound he shouldn't have been able to hear. A sound that shouldn't in reality have been able to reach his ears.

"Dad's home."

In his mind's eye Kaoru could see his father on his off-road bike skidding into the underground parking area a hundred yards below. He'd bought that bike new less than two months ago. Now his father got off the bike and looked at it with satisfaction. He used it to commute to work, probably because otherwise he'd have no time to ride it. And now he was home. The signs of it communicated themselves to Kaoru intensely. There was no mistaking them. Separated though they were, Kaoru's sixth sense enabled him to follow his father's movements tonight.

Kaoru imagined his father's every little movement, tracing each one in his mind. Now he was turning off the ignition, now he was standing in the hall in front of the elevator with his helmet tucked under his arm, now he was looking up at the floor indicator lights.

Kaoru counted to see how long it took him to

get to the twenty-ninth floor. The elevator door opened and his father strode quickly down the carpeted corridor. He stood in front of the door to apartment 2916. He fished his card-key from his pocket and inserted it . . .

Imagined motions and sounds were replaced by real ones starting with the *click* of the front door opening. He felt a palpable moment of precariousness, caught between imagination and reality, and a cry rose within his breast.

It was Dad after all!

Kaoru wanted to jump up and go to greet his father, but he forced himself to hold back. He wanted to try and forecast what his father would do now.

Hideyuki seemed to be walking down the hall in the apartment with no care for who might be trying to sleep. The helmet under his arm banged loudly against the wall. His humming was nothing short of its normal volume. At the best of times, Hideyuki seemed to make more than the usual amount of noise when he moved. Maybe it was because he radiated so much energy.

Suddenly Kaoru found himself unable to read what his father would do next. All sound stopped, and he had no idea where his father was. His mind was a blank, but then the sliding door to the room where he slept was flung roughly open. Without warning, light from the hall flooded the room. Not that it was that bright, but still Kaoru

had to narrow his eyes against it. He hadn't foreseen this. Hideyuki walked onto the tatami mats
until he was right next to Kaoru's futon. Then he
knelt and brought his mouth close to his son's ear.

"Hey, kiddo, wake up."

Kaoru pretended he'd just this minute woken
up, saying, "Oh, Dad. What time is it?"

"One in the morning."

"Huh."

"C'mon, wake up."

This happened a lot to Kaoru—getting dragged
out of bed in the middle of the night so he could
keep his dad company over beer, conversing till
dawn. Kaoru would always end up missing school
the next day, sleeping the whole morning away.

Last week he'd been late for school twice on
account of his father. Hideyuki evidently didn't
think much of what his son was studying in
elementary school. Kaoru often found himself
exasperated at his father's lack of common sense:
to a kid, school wasn't just a place to study, it
was also a place to play. His dad didn't seem to
get that.

"I want to go to school tomorrow."

Kaoru whispered so as not to wake his mother,
sleeping next to him. He didn't mind getting up
to talk—in fact, he'd like nothing better—but he
wanted to make it plain that it shouldn't go too
late.

"Pretty responsible for a kid. Who do you take

after, anyway?" With a devil-may-care tone in his voice, he ignored Kaoru's efforts to keep the noise down. Frustrated, Kaoru leapt out of his futon. If he didn't get Dad out of the room now, he'd wake Mom up.

Yeah, who did he take after? In terms of facial features, Kaoru and his father sure didn't have much in common. In terms of personality, too, Kaoru was a lot more sensitive—high-strung, even—than his rough-and-tumble father. Of course, he was still a child, but still, Kaoru was sometimes puzzled by how little he and his father resembled each other, outwardly or inwardly.

Kaoru put his hands on his father's back and pushed him across the room into the hall. Then he kept pushing him until they'd made it to the living room, at which point he sighed and said, "Boy, you're heavy," and stopped.

If his son was going to push, Hideyuki was going to lean back, which he did, putting up a playful resistance which he supplemented with a forceful fart and a vulgar laugh. Then he noticed that where Kaoru had shoved him to was right next to the kitchen counter: as if he'd just remembered something, he walked over to the refrigerator and opened it.

He took out a beer, poured some in a glass, and held it out to the still-panting Kaoru.

"You want some too?"

Hideyuki hadn't stopped for a drink on the

way home. He was stone-cold sober. This was the first alcohol he'd seen today.

"No thanks. Mom'll get mad at you again."

"Stop being so responsible."

Hideyuki took a showy swig and wiped his mouth. "I guess when a kid's got a dad like me, he's got to have his shit together, huh?"

With an audible gulp Hideyuki drained his second glass, and in no time he'd finished the bottle.

"I'll tell you, this stuff tastes best when I'm looking at you, kiddo."

For his part, Kaoru didn't mind keeping his father company when he was drinking. His father took such obvious pleasure in his alcohol that Kaoru had fun just watching him. As the fatigue of the day's work left his father, Kaoru's mood, too, lightened.

Kaoru went to the fridge, got another bottle, and filled his father's glass.

But instead of saying "thanks," Hideyuki issued his son an order.

"Hey, kiddo, go wake up Machi."

Hideyuki was referring, of course, to Kaoru's mother.

"No way. Mom's asleep. She's tired."

"So am I, but do you see me sleeping?"

"But you're up 'cause you want to be."

"Never mind that, just go wake her up."

"Do you need her for something?"

"Yeah. I need her to drink beer."

"Maybe she doesn't want to drink."

"'s alright. Tell her I want her and she'll come running."

"We don't need her. We're okay, just the two of us, aren't we? Besides, there's something I want to ask you."

"Gimme a break. I'm asking you here. We don't want Machi to feel left out, do we?"

"This always happens . . ."

Kaoru headed for the bedroom, dragging his feet. For some reason it always fell to Kaoru to wake his mother. Supposedly his father had tried it once a few years ago, and she'd reacted very badly; now he was gun-shy.

In the Futami household, Dad always got his way in the end. Not because Hideyuki exercised his patriarchal authority, but rather because, of the three of them, he was the most juvenile.

Kaoru respected his father's talent as a scientist. But he couldn't help noticing that he was distinctly lacking as a grown-up. Kaoru wasn't sure exactly what his father was missing, but his child's mind figured that if growing up was a process of eliminating childishness in favor of adult wisdom, then it was precisely that function that his father lacked.

3

He hated to disturb his mother's peaceful slumber. Kaoru went to the bedroom door and hesitantly slid it open. But Machiko was already sitting up in her futon, running her fingers through her hair. Kaoru didn't need to wake her up—his father's noisy homecoming had taken care of that.

"Oh, Mom. Sorry." He was apologizing for his father.

"That's alright." The expression in her eyes was as gentle as ever.

Kaoru's mother almost never scolded him. Probably because he never asked for anything unreasonable, she'd always given him what he wanted. Though he was still a child, he could tell from her words and actions how absolutely she relied on him; it made him happy, but also gave him a feeling of grave responsibility.

The Futami Family Three-Way Deadlock, was

how Kaoru thought of his and his parents' relationship. It was just like a game of rock-scissors-paper—each of them had someone they could always beat, and someone they'd always lose to.

Kaoru was strong against his mother, but weak when it came to his father. So he'd always end up going along with his father's unreasonable courses of action, doing whatever he was told. Hideyuki was strong enough vis-à-vis his son that he could treat him high-handedly, but somehow he couldn't manage such a firm front with his wife. When his wife was in a bad mood, he seemed to pale and shrink.

So he had to fob the task of waking his sleeping wife off on his son. Kaoru's mother, meanwhile, was lenient with her son's demands, but could at times respond severely to her husband's impossible behavior, scolding him as she would a child.

His father would sometimes boast about how this marvelous balance of power maintained harmony in the family. He'd joke about their relationship pseudo-scientifically, calling their family a "self-sustaining structuralization of chaos". The peculiar situation wasn't the result of intent on anybody's part—it had arisen naturally through the interaction and altercations of the three parties involved.

"What's Hide doing?" Machiko scratched her neck and ran her fingers slowly through her hair.

"Drinking beer."

"At this late hour? He's hopeless."

"He wants to know if you'll join him."

Machiko stood up, laughing through her nose. "I wonder if he's hungry."

"I don't know. Probably he just wants to see you, don't you think?"

Kaoru said it with a straight face, but Machiko just laughed, as if to say, *You don't know what you're talking about.*

But Kaoru was already quite aware of his parents' erotic side.

One night three months ago—a night in mid-June, a rare dry night in the middle of the rainy season, hot enough to forebode the tropical nights to come—Kaoru had been shocked to run into his father in the kitchen in an unexpected state.

That night Kaoru had been shut in his room using his computer, when his thirst finally became too great to ignore. He'd gone to the kitchen to get some mineral water. His parents had apparently shut themselves in their separate rooms, saying they had work to do, and the apartment was quiet. His parents often went to their rooms to work and fell asleep like that. Kaoru had expected it to be the same that night. He didn't realize they'd been in the same room after all.

He didn't turn on the light. He stood there in the darkness and poured some mineral water into a glass, and then popped a piece of ice into his mouth.

Then he opened the refrigerator door again to put the plastic bottle back in, and that was when he found himself facing Hideyuki, who had suddenly entered the kitchen. The light from the refrigerator shone on his father's naked body.

Hideyuki jumped, but in surprise, not embarrassment.

"I didn't know you were there," he said, and with no thought for his nakedness he grabbed Kaoru's glass from him and gulped down its contents.

What surprised Kaoru was not only that his father was completely unclothed, but that his genitalia was larger than it normally was. It was covered with some sort of thin bodily fluid, and it gleamed slickly. It always hung limply when Kaoru and his father were in the bath together. But now it arched and pulsed, exuding the confidence of having fulfilled its role as a part of its owner's body.

The whole time his father was drinking the mineral water, Kaoru couldn't tear his gaze from it.

"What're you looking at? Jealous?"

"Unh-uh."

Kaoru's reply was blunt. Hideyuki bent over a bit and placed the tip of his right index finger on the tip of his member. With it he took up a single drop of semen and held it out before Kaoru's eyes.

"Look, kiddo, it's your ancestors," he remarked, with mock seriousness. Then he wiped his fingertip on the edge of the sink against which Kaoru was leaning.

"Eww," said Kaoru, twisting away, but he kept staring at the white droplet on the edge of the sink.

He didn't know how he should react. Hideyuki turned his back on him and disappeared into the bathroom. After a while, from the open door came the sound of urination, forced, irregular bursts.

Sometimes Kaoru didn't know if his father was stupid or clever. Sure, he was an excellent computer scientist, but sometimes he did things that were worse than childish. Kaoru respected his father alright, but watching him made him nervous. He could understand his mother's sufferings.

So ran his thoughts as he stared at what his father had called his "ancestors".

The sperm swimming in the tiny droplet gradually died as the stainless steel stole heat from them. They were, of course, invisible to the naked eye, but Kaoru found himself quite aware of the actions of the herd—he could quite easily imagine the faces of each one of them as it died and contributed its corpse to the growing layer of dead.

These sperm, born of meiosis inside his father, held, as did his mother's eggs, half the number of chromosomes contained within the cells of his body. Together they made a fertilized egg, only then supplying the total number of chromosomes necessary for a cell. But it didn't follow that a sperm was merely half a person. Depending on how you looked at it, the sperm and the egg were the body's basic structural units. Only reproductive cells could be said to have continued uninterrupted since the inception of life—it wasn't too much of a stretch to say they possessed a kind of immortality.

All that aside, to have a chance to leisurely observe his father's sperm was something he'd never dreamed of. Right here in front of him was the source of the life form that he knew as himself.

Was I really born from something this tiny?

He stood there mystified and mute. These sperm hadn't existed anywhere until they'd been made within his father's body. Created from nothingness by means of that mysterious power only life possessed.

So caught up was he in his examination that Kaoru didn't notice when his father finished urinating and rejoined him.

"What are you doing, kiddo?" He seemed to have already forgotten his own prank.

"Observing your . . . things," said Kaoru, not looking up. Hideyuki finally realized what his son was looking at and gave a curt laugh.

"What kind of idiot would stare at a thing like that? Shame on you."

Hideyuki grabbed a dishtowel, wiped up the semen, and then dropped the dishtowel in the sink. As he did so, the image of life that Kaoru had been constructing fled with its tail between its legs.

He suddenly had an awful premonition, as he imagined his own body being wiped up with a rag and tossed away.

So his parents' secret life, something not for him to come in contact with, became, under the influence of his father's attitude, something subject to no taboo whatsoever. Kaoru remembered that incident three months ago as if it were last night.

Of course, Machiko had no way of knowing what mischief her husband had worked on her son as he went about opening the refrigerator and using the bathroom. Had she known, her embarrassment would no doubt have lit a bonfire of anger within her; no doubt she would have refused to speak to her husband for some time. Probably tonight she would have been in no mood to get up and fix him a snack.

"What am I going to do with him?" she muttered again and again; still, she fixed her hair with a will, and refastened her misaligned pajama buttons. Kaoru found it a pleasant, warm sight.

4

Kaoru's mother put on slippers and headed for the living room, and he followed her.

"Sorry to get you out of bed," Hideyuki said to Machiko.

"That's okay. I'll bet you're hungry, aren't you?"

"A little."

"Why don't I make something?"

Machiko was already heading for the kitchen, but Hideyuki stopped her, holding out a glass of beer.

"Have a drink first."

Machiko accepted the glass and took a few sips. She didn't like carbonated beverages, so it was impossible for her to down a beer in one gulp. That didn't mean she wasn't a drinker, though— she was above average when it came to holding her liquor.

When he'd seen that his wife had settled down with her beer, Hideyuki finally loosened his necktie.

As a researcher, he was under no special requirement to wear a tie to work. Still, every day he put
on a suit and buttoned the top button of his shirt
before getting on his motorcycle to go to the lab.
No doubt the sight of him in a suit riding an off-
road bike struck people as peculiar, but that didn't
bother Hideyuki in the least.

Kaoru's mother poured some oil into a frying
pan and started warming up some sausages, and
his father stood next to her and began reporting to
her on his day in the lab. Oblivious to the fact that
she hadn't asked him, he recounted the day's events
with brio, mentioning coworkers by name, sometimes with a disparaging comment. Kaoru began
to feel bored as his parents receded into their own
world, seeming to forget his presence beside them.

Then Machiko noticed him, and in her consid-
erate way changed the subject. "By the way,
Kaoru, why don't you show your father what
you showed me?"

"Huh? What?" He'd been taken by surprise.

"You know, those gravitational anomaly thin-
gies."

"Oh, those." Kaoru took the two pages out of
the dish cupboard where he'd put them away
and handed them to Hideyuki.

"You'll be amazed at what he's discovered," his
mother said, but Kaoru didn't feel it was that
great a discovery.

"What's this?" said Hideyuki, holding the printouts up to his face. He gazed at the first one, with its contour lines and their positive and negative numbers, and within a few seconds had grasped its meaning.

"I get it, this is a map of the earth's gravitational anomalies."

He turned his gaze to the second page, and this time he didn't have such an easy time figuring it out. He frowned. Hideyuki already had a geological map of the earth stored in his brain, but try as he might he couldn't figure out what the black marks on this map meant. He tried several guesses connected with gravitational anomalies, such as subterranean mineral deposits, before giving up and turning to his son.

"Alright, you got me. What is this?"

"The earth's longevity zones."

"Longevity zones?" No sooner had he heard the words than Hideyuki placed the maps over one another and looked at them anew.

"Would you look at that. The longevity zones are only found in places with high negative gravitational anomalies."

Kaoru was impressed, as usual. His father's mental quickness was one of the reasons why he enjoyed their discussions so much. "That's right!" he said, his excitement lending his words added emphasis.

"I wonder why that is," Hideyuki asked himself, raising his eyes from the maps.

"Is this, like, common knowledge?" It had worried Kaoru to think that people had already noticed this correspondence, that it was only he who'd been ignorant of it.

"Well, I for one wasn't aware of it."

"Really?"

"So, what? Does this mean that perhaps there's some sort of relationship between people's life-spans and gravity? The data's so clear and specific, it's hard to think it's just a coincidence. By the way, kiddo, how do you define a 'longevity zone'?"

It was only natural for Hideyuki to stick at that point. Kaoru felt the same way. How exactly should he define a longevity zone? Was it an area with lots of long-lived people in it? Perhaps an area where the average lifespan was longer than in other areas? If that was what he meant, there was nothing to prevent him from seeing all of Japan as one big longevity zone.

He had to use a more limiting definition. It would be more exact, at least, to stipulate that a longevity zone was an area clearly delineated from the surrounding territory, a high percentage of the inhabitants of which were a hundred or more years in age.

But in reality, no such mathematical definition existed. The villages that he'd seen talked about on TV were simply places that had been found, statis-tically and experientially, to have lots of long-lived people in them, and they were known for it.

"I'm not sure there is a mathematical definition."

He found it more and more curious that the villages mentioned on TV, defined as impressionistically and sentimentally as they were, should match up so nicely with gravitational anomalies, so clearly visible as numerical values. Kaoru and Hideyuki both were impressed by this.

"Too vague. Still, I wonder why it came out like this?" Hideyuki said this under his breath, as if bothered.

"Have you heard anything about the relationship between gravity and life, Dad?"

"Well, they did an experiment where they had a chicken lay eggs in a zero-gravity environment, and they turned out to be unfertilized eggs."

"I've heard about that. That was ages ago."

Somewhere in the corner of his mind he recalled the sight of his father's sperm three months ago. He remembered reading an article about the chickens, which had laid unfertilized eggs in spite of the fact that they had copulated. He'd forgotten exactly what the experiment had been trying to prove. He'd read about it in a mass-market weekly, which had seized on the results of what was actually an old experiment in order to make some point about modern sexuality.

His imagination started to run away with him. Suppose an egg started to undergo cellular division without fertilization, growing through birth to maturity—what kind of human being would result? Kaoru got a mental image of a woman with a smooth, egg-shaped face. He shivered. He tried to banish the image, but the woman's slippery face wouldn't leave him.

"Well, nobody's made a logical connection yet, I don't think. But anyway, why did you think to compare gravitational anomalies and longevity?"

"Huh?" Sometimes the images taking shape in his brain undermined Kaoru's ability to think, and he couldn't hear what was being said to him.

"Stop making me repeat myself." Few things annoyed the impatient Hideyuki more.

"Sorry."

"What gave you the idea, in other words?"

Kaoru explained how a TV special on longevity villages had been playing in the background while on the computer he'd been looking at a map of gravitational anomalies, and how he'd had a flash of intuition.

"I think it was just a coincidence."

"Meaningless coincidences produce nothing. Take jinxes, for instance."

"Jinxes?"

Kaoru actually had something of an idea why his father would bring up something unscientific like that now. He was trying to give Machiko an entry into the conversation.

Having pretty much finished fixing snacks to go with the beer, Machiko had joined them at the dining room table, where she sat listening to the conversation without offering up a word. Not that she'd looked particularly bored, but she did lean forward just a bit when her husband mentioned jinxes.

Her reaction didn't escape Hideyuki's notice.

"Hey, Machi. Know of any interesting jinxes?"

"Why ask me?"

"You like that kind of thing, don't you? Fortune-telling, charms, stuff like that. Don't think I haven't noticed you reading the horoscopes every week. Plus, you know a lot about folk-tales from around the world."

"Okay, jinxes. How about the one that says if you give a handkerchief to your lover as a present you'll break up?"

"Everybody knows that one. Don't you know anything, you know, weirder?"

Kaoru thought he could guess what kind of thing his father was looking for. He was probably trying to find an example of a belief that connected, seemingly at random, two disparate phenomena.

"Something weirder? Okay, how about this? If you see a black cat swimming in a river, someone close to you will die."

Kaoru immediately pursed his lips. "Really?"

"That's what they say. You've heard it, haven't you, dear?" She looked at Hideyuki for support. But he just laughed and cocked his head.

"Don't you have any that are just way out there?"

"How about the one that says, when you leave the house, if a chair has its back to the window, you'll drop your wallet?"

Hideyuki clapped his hands.

"Okay, we'll go with that one. Now, it may be true or it may be false, but let's just take it as a given that such a superstition exists."

"It does!" Machiko frowned.

"Alright, alright!" Hideyuki said, putting his palms together. "Now, we have two phenomena brought together. A chair having its back to the window when you leave the house, and dropping your wallet. Scientifically, these two phenomena have no relation to each other. There are lots of superstitions in the world, and no doubt different kinds come about for different reasons. But what I find fascinating is when you have the exact same superstition existing in two distant places, isolated from each other. If this crazy superstition that Machi just told us about happened to exist in different places on the globe, it'd make you wonder, wouldn't it? Of course it would."

"So, are there superstitions like that? That exist in different places in the world?" Kaoru looked back and forth between Machiko and Hideyuki.

Hideyuki prompted his wife. "How about it, Machi?"

"Of course there are. The jinx I just told you about is one. It exists in Europe and in the Americas, too."

Kaoru and Hideyuki exchanged skeptical looks.

"By the way, Machi, have you ever thought about why superstitions arise?"

"No," she said, curtly.

"What about you, kiddo?"

"I guess it has something to do with human psychology. I'm not real sure, though."

By this point there were five empty beer bottles sitting in front of Hideyuki. His conversational engine was finally getting warmed up.

"Ask yourself: what is a superstition? It's an oral tradition that if you see something or experience something, a certain thing will happen. With a jinx it's something bad, but of course a superstition can involve something good, or even something that can't necessarily be categorized as good or bad. To cut to the chase, a superstition is something that connects one phenomenon with another phenomenon. Sometimes science can explain the connection. For example, the superstition that when clouds move from east to west it means it'll rain can be explained very easily by modern meteorology. There are others that you can understand intuitively, like the one that says being photographed takes years off your life. Or ones about breaking chopsticks or sandal thongs, or seeing black cats or snakes—those aren't too hard to understand. Those things are just eerie somehow. There's something about black cats and snakes that makes people the world over uneasy.

"The problem is superstitions that aren't reasonable. The ones that strike you as totally arbitrary, like, 'Why in the world do people believe *that*?' The jinx Machi told us about is a good example. What could having a chair back toward the window when you leave the house possibly have to do with dropping your wallet?"

Hideyuki stopped and looked Kaoru in the eye.

"Maybe it's based on experience."

"No doubt it is. Maybe people found out through experience that the chances of dropping your wallet are greater if a chair's back is to the window when you leave your house."

"But there's no statistical necessity that it has to be that way."

"We're not talking strict accuracy here. Let's say when you drop your wallet, it just so happens that the chair's back is to the window. And let's say that the next time you drop your wallet, the chair's back is toward the window again. So you tell someone about it, suggesting that the two phenomena are related somehow. Now the important thing is whether or not the person you tell about it has had a similar experience—whether or not they can nod and say, 'yeah, you're right'. If the idea is dismissed by a third party, then chances are it won't be handed down. But once it becomes established as a jinx, then by the mere fact of people's being aware of it, it can influence their actions, and so it stands a good chance of surviving. Once the relationship is established between the two things, the fact that people are aware of the relationship strengthens the bond even more, see. Reality and imagination begin to correspond to one another."

"So you're saying that the phenomenon of a chair having its back to the window when you leave the room and the phenomenon of dropping your wallet exert some kind of invisible influence on each other?"

"You can't rule out the possibility that they're connected on some level, deep down."

What was his father trying to say, using the superstition as an example? Kaoru had the feeling that he could substitute "life" for "superstition" and the argument would still stand up.

"Life," Kaoru muttered. As if that word were a cue, the three exchanged glances.

"It reminds me of the Loop."

It was Machiko who brought up the subject. It seemed she felt it was a natural progression from the word "life".

Hideyuki had started his college career in pre-med. He'd switched fields, to logic, in graduate school, studying the concepts of metamathematics, but one thing led to another and he found his old abandoned interest in the world of living things rekindled. He decided it would be interesting to see if the language of mathematics could explain life. His original interest in biology was reanimated as it found expression in numbers.

Thus it was that when he'd finished his doctorate and received an offer to join a joint Japanese-American research project on artificial life, he'd accepted without a second thought. To create life within a computer? Hideyuki couldn't think of anything he wanted to do more.

He was still young, in his late twenties, married but childless. Five years after he took the appointment, the project was brought to a halt in an entirely unforeseen way. It wasn't a failure, having achieved a certain manner of success. But it never felt like success to Hideyuki because the way it all ended stuck in his throat.

This project into which he'd poured all his youthful passion, only to see it miscarry, was known as the Loop.

5

Hideyuki presented a new question to Kaoru, forcefully steering the conversation away from the Loop.

"So do you think life emerged by chance or by necessity? Which side are you on?"

"The only answer I can give to that question is, 'I don't know'."

It was all he could say. He couldn't affirm the necessity argument just because he himself existed. In the absence of confirmed life anywhere else, it was possible that life on earth was an utterly random gift, unique in the universe.

"I'm asking you what you think."

"But Dad, aren't you always saying that it's important to recognize what modern science doesn't know? To be willing to say 'I don't know'?"

Hideyuki chuckled at the question. A look at his face revealed the alcohol taking effect. The number of empties was up to six.

"You don't have to tell me that. Think of this as a game if you have to. We're in the world of play. I want to know what your gut tells you, that's all."

Machiko had gone into the kitchen to fry up some noodles; now she stopped what she was doing and fixed her gaze on Kaoru, a gleam in her eye.

Kaoru thought about himself. Things like the emergence of life and the universe were beyond the reach of his imagination, when he got right down to it. It was better to take the emergence of one individual as an example, and work up from there.

First and foremost, what about the inception of his own life? When was that? When he'd crawled out of his mother's womb and had his umbilical cord cut? Or when the egg, after insemination in the fallopian tube, had been safely embedded in the wall of the womb?

If he was going to talk about inception, then he figured he should probably take insemination as the first step. His nervous system had taken shape by around three weeks from insemination.

Now, he thought, just suppose that a fetus of that age had consciousness, the ability to think. To that fetus, the mother's womb would be the whole universe. *Why am I here*, the fetus asks. Immersed in amniotic fluid, he begins to wonder about the mechanism of conception. But as he knows nothing of the world outside the womb, he can't even imagine that his own conception was preceded by reproductive acts. All he can do is make guesses based on evidence he finds within the womb.

So he begins to think of the amniotic fluid itself as his parent—a natural conclusion. He begins to think of the amniotic fluid as the primordial soup covering the primeval earth, churning until twenty kinds of amino acid join hands in brotherhood to make life-enabling proteins; these then begin to replicate themselves . . . The probability of which is, of course, the same as the monkey at the typewriter, banging keys at random, coming up with a passage from Shakespeare.

A probability so low that even with trillions of monkeys banging away for trillions of years, it was still virtually nil. And if a passage from Shakespeare should appear anyway? Would people still call it a coincidence? Of course not—they'd suspect some kind of fix. A man in a monkey suit sitting at one of the typewriters, or an intelligent monkey . . .

But the fetus immersed in amniotic fluid thinks his conception was by chance—he can't make his imagination comprehend the mechanism behind it. And that's because he doesn't know about the world outside.

Only when he crawls out of the birth canal after roughly thirty-six weeks in the womb does he for the first time see the outside of the mother who bore him. Only after growing and increasing in knowledge yet further does he come to understand with exactness why and how he was conceived and born. As long as we're inside the womb—inside the universe—we can't understand the way it works. Our powers of apprehension are blacked out on that point. They have to be.

Kaoru decided to apply the example of the fetus in its universe—the womb—to the question of life on earth and the universe it occupied.

In most cases, the womb comes pre-equipped with everything necessary to nurture a fetus after insemination. But does it always host a fetus? Of course not. The phenomenon of insemination itself is controlled largely by chance. And many women choose not to have children.

And even if a woman has a couple of children, the length of time in which her womb holds a fetus is still less than two years total. In other words, equipped for a fetus though it may be, the womb is usually unoccupied.

Kaoru decided to take a step back and think about the universe again. Given that we are actually existing within it, it seems reasonable to say that the universe is equipped with what is necessary to sustain life. In which case, life arose out of necessity, right? But, no, remember the womb: it may be capable of sustaining the life of a fetus, but it's usually without one. So life arose by chance, then? The universe is not constantly filled with life—indeed, a universe that does not beget life may indeed be more natural.

In the end, Kaoru couldn't come up with an answer after all.

But there was Hideyuki, drinking his beer and expecting a reply.

"Maybe we're the only life in the universe after all," said Kaoru.

Hideyuki grunted. "That's what your gut tells you?"

Hideyuki stared at his son fascinatedly, then shifted his gaze to his wife.

Machiko was sleeping peacefully, her head pillowed on her hands on the table.

"Hey, go get a blanket for Machi, will ya?"

"Okay." He immediately went to the bedroom and brought back a blanket, which he handed to Hideyuki. Hideyuki draped it over Machiko's shoulders and smiled at her sleeping face before turning back to his son.

The eastern sky had begun to whiten without them noticing, and the temperature of the room had dropped. Night in the Futami household was over, and it was just about time to sleep.

Hideyuki's eyes as he drank the last of the stale beer were hollow.

Kaoru waited until his father was finished drinking, then said, "Hey, Dad. Can I ask you a favor?"

"What?"

Kaoru lay the gravitational anomaly map in front of his father again. "What do you think of this?"

Kaoru's pinky was pointing at a particular spot on the map, a desert region, the so-called Four Corners area of the western North American continent, where the states of Arizona, New Mexico, Utah, and Colorado met.

"What about it?" Hideyuki brought his eyes close to the map, blinking.

"Look closely at it. Now take another look at the gravitational anomaly figures for this area."

Hideyuki rubbed his eyes again and again, as the numbers swam in his tired eyes.

"Hmm."

"See, the space between the contour lines gets smaller and smaller the closer they get to this point."

"That's what it looks like."

"That means an extreme gravitational anomaly."

"I see. The negative values are quite large here."

"I think there has to be something there, geologically speaking. It's like there's something deep under the earth's surface there with extremely little mass."

Kaoru took a ballpoint pen and made an X where the four states met. He didn't have a gravitational figure for that exact point, but the contour lines surrounding it certainly pointed to a spot with particularly low gravity.

For a while, Kaoru and Hideyuki looked at the map in silence. Then Machiko raised her head a little and broke in, drowsily, "I'm sure there's nothing there, dear."

Evidently she'd been listening to their conversation the whole time, only pretending to be asleep.

"I didn't think you were awake."

His mother's words were provocative. Kaoru tried to imagine a space filled with nothingness deep beneath the desert. If the earth there concealed a huge cavity, it could easily explain the extreme gravitational anomaly.

And in that huge limestone cavern lived an ancient tribe of people . . . Kaoru could see it now, a close-up look at an extreme longevity zone.

Even more than before, Kaoru wanted to go there.

Machiko yawned and mumbled, "That sounds strange though—if it's nothing, how can it be there?" She got up from her chair.

"See, Mom, you're interested in the place, too. If low gravity and longevity are connected, then maybe there's a city of ancient people there, cut off from civilization. It's at least possible, right?"

Kaoru was fishing for a response, based on his knowledge of Machiko's interest in North American folk tales, especially Native American myths. He figured that he stood a better chance of getting what he wanted if he got Machiko to go to bat for him than if he just blurted it out himself.

Just as he'd hoped, Machiko's interest seemed to grow suddenly. "Well, it is close to a Navajo reservation."

"See?"

Kaoru knew—Machiko had told him—that there were tribes who had made their homes in the wildest deserts and ravines, and whose lives today were not all that different from the way they'd lived in ancient times. He hadn't heard of any noted for their longevity, but he knew that if he suggested it without really suggesting it, he could pique Machiko's curiosity.

"Hey, kiddo, what are you trying to pull here?"

Hideyuki had evidently guessed what Kaoru was going for. Kaoru shot a meaningful glance at his mother.

"It'd be interesting to go there," Machiko said.

She sounded less like she was pleading Kaoru's case than like she'd become interested herself.

"Yeah, let's go!" Kaoru said, expectantly.

"Four Corners, eh? Talk about coincidences."

"Huh?" Kaoru looked at his father.

"Well, in a little while—next summer, maybe, or the summer after that—it looks like my work is going to take me there."

Kaoru yelped in delight. "Really?"

"Yeah, I'll have to be at some laboratories in New Mexico, in Los Alamos and Santa Fe."

Kaoru clapped his palms together as if in prayer. "Take me! Please?"

"Want to come too, Machi?"

"Of course."

"Well, then I guess we'll all go."

"That's a promise, okay?" Kaoru held out paper and pen. If he was bound by a contract, Hideyuki couldn't turn around someday and pretend he'd never said it. This was just a little insurance. Kaoru knew from experience that his father's promises stood more chance of being kept if they were backed up by writing.

Hideyuki filled out the contract in his sloppy handwriting and waved it in Kaoru's face. "There, see? It's a promise."

Kaoru took it and examined it. He felt satisfied. Now he could sleep soundly.

Dawn was breaking and September was ending, but still the sun as it climbed was brighter than at midsummer. A few stars still shone evanescently in the western sky, looking now as if they would disappear at any moment. There was no line dividing light from dark—Kaoru couldn't say just where night ended and morning began. He loved with all his heart this moment when the passage of time manifested itself in changing colors.

Kaoru remained standing by the window after his parents disappeared into the bedroom.

The city was starting to move, its vibrations

reverberating in the reclaimed land like a fetus kicking in the womb. Before his gaze a huge flock of birds was circling over Tokyo Bay. Their cries, like the mewling of newborns, asserted their vitality under the dying stars.

At times like this, staring at the blackness of the sea and the subtly changing colors of the sky, Kaoru's desire to understand the workings of the world only increased. Taking in scenery from on high stimulated the imagination.

The sun rose above the eastern horizon, pushing the night aside; Kaoru went into the bedroom and curled up in his futon.

Hideyuki and Machiko were already asleep in their different positions, Hideyuki with arms and legs akimbo and no blanket atop him, Machiko curled into a ball hugging the rumpled blanket.

Kaoru lay down beside them, hugging his pillow and clutching the paper holding the promise that they'd go to the desert. Curled up like that, he looked something like a fetus.

PART TWO

The Cancer Ward

1

Recently Kaoru had begun to look older than his twenty years. It wasn't so much that his face had aged as that his unusually large frame projected a robust presence. He exuded an air of adulthood. People he met tended to tell him he was mature for his age.

Kaoru thought that was only natural, considering how he'd been forced to become his family's pillar of strength at the age of thirteen. Ten years ago, in elementary school, he'd been skinny and short, and people had often thought him younger than he was. Supposedly he'd been something of a know-it-all, tutored as he'd been in the natural sciences by his father and in languages by his mother. His main job had been to give his imagination free reign, to wonder about the structure and workings of the universe, rather than to involve himself in mundane chores.

Ten years ago—it felt like another world altogether. Back then, playing with his computer, sitting up talking with his parents into the wee hours of the night, the road ahead of them had been clear and without shadow. He could remember how he'd started thinking about longevity and gravity, and how that had turned into a family plan to visit the Four Corners region of North America. He'd even gotten his father to sign a pact to that effect.

Kaoru still kept that contract in his desk drawer. It had never been fulfilled. Hideyuki still wanted to honor it, but Kaoru the medical student knew better than anybody how impossible that was.

Kaoru had no skill that could tell him when or by what route the Metastatic Human Cancer Virus had infiltrated Hideyuki's body. No doubt the virus had turned one of his body's cells cancerous years before he first complained of stomach problems. Then that newborn cancer cell had probably undergone its first cellular division not long after he'd promised that trip to the desert. And those cancer cells had silently, steadily reproduced themselves until the family trip had become an unattainable dream.

Hideyuki's initial plans to visit some laboratories in New Mexico had been delayed; only three years after the initial promise had he been able to finally work the visits into his schedule. He'd arranged for a three-month stint at the Los Alamos and Santa Fe research centers. He'd planned to depart for New Mexico two weeks early, so he and Machiko and Kaoru could visit the site of the negative gravitational anomaly that still fascinated Kaoru so.

And then in early summer, two months before they were scheduled to leave—after they'd already bought the plane tickets and the whole family had their hearts set on the trip—Hideyuki suddenly complained of stomach pain.

Why don't you see a doctor, Machiko said, but he wouldn't listen. Hideyuki decided it was a simple case of gastritis, and made no lifestyle changes.

But as the summer wore on, the pain became worse, until finally, three weeks before their departure date, he vomited. Even then, Hideyuki insisted it was nothing. He kept refusing to be examined, reluctant to cancel the plans they were so excited about.

Finally, though, the symptoms became unendurable, and he agreed to go to the university hospital and see a doctor who happened to be a friend of his. The examination found a polyp in his pylorus, and he was admitted to the hospital.

Naturally, the trip was cancelled. Neither Kaoru nor Machiko was in any mood to travel. The doctor in charge informed them that the polyp was malignant.

Thus did Kaoru's thirteenth summer turn from heaven into hell: not only did the trip fall through, but he and his mother ended up spending most of the sweltering summer going back and forth to the hospital.

Don't worry, I'll get better next year, and then we'll go to the desert like I promised, just you wait and see, bluffed his father. Their one comfort was Hideyuki's positive attitude.

Machiko believed her husband, but, at the same time, whenever she let herself imagine what might happen, she became despondent. She grew weaker emotionally, and physically.

And that was why it fell to Kaoru to take a central role in the family. It was Kaoru who stood in the kitchen and made sure his mother ate enough when she couldn't bring herself to think about food; it was Kaoru who swiftly absorbed enough medical knowledge to plant thoughts of an optimistic future in his mother's head.

There was an operation in which two thirds of Hideyuki's stomach was removed, and it went well; if the cancer hadn't metastasized, there was every chance he'd get well. By the beginning of autumn Hideyuki was able to return home, and to his laboratory.

It was around that time that a change began to appear in Hideyuki's attitude toward Kaoru. On the one hand, as a man he had a new respect for the dependability his son showed while he was in the hospital, but on the other hand he began to be stricter with his son out of a new determination to make him into a stronger man.

He stopped calling him "kiddo", and encouraged him to spend less time on his computer and more time exercising his body. Kaoru didn't resist, but went along with his father's new expectations: he could detect a certain desperation in his father, as if he wanted to transfer something from his own body to his son's before it disappeared.

He knew his father loved him, and he felt special, as if he'd inherited his father's will; pride coursed through him.

Two years passed uneventfully, and Kaoru's fifteenth birthday came around. But changes had been taking place inside his father's body. Those changes were revealed by a bloody stool.

This was a red light signaling the spread of the cancer. With no hesitation this time, Hideyuki saw the doctor, who gave him a barium enema and x-rayed him. The x-ray showed a shadow on the sigmoid colon about half the size of a fist. The only conceivable course of action was surgery to cut it out.

There were, however, two possibilities for the surgery. One option would leave the anus; the other would remove more tissue and require the insertion of an artificial anus. With the former, there was the fear that they would miss some of the invading cancer cells, leaving the possibility of a recurrence, while the latter option of removing the entire sigmoid colon allowed for more surety. The doctor's opinion was that from a medical standpoint the artificial anus would be preferable, but because of the inconvenience and lifestyle changes that would bring, he had to leave the final decision up to the patient.

But Hideyuki didn't flinch as he coolly chose the artificial anus. *If you open me up and can't say with certainty that the cancer hasn't spread that far, then I want you to cut it all out without hesitation*, he'd volunteered. He intended to bet on the option with the best odds of survival.

Once again the summer found him back in the hospital for surgery. When they cut him open, the doctors found that the cancer hadn't invaded as far as they had feared; normally, in this situation, leaving the anus in would give at least even odds of success. But the surgeon in charge decided, in view of the patient's expressed wishes, to remove the sigmoid colon entirely.

Once again autumn found Hideyuki checking out of the hospital. For the next two years he'd lived in fear of signs of a relapse, as he strove to get used to life with a colostomy.

Exactly two years later there was another sign, this one a yellow light, as it were. Hideyuki became feverish and his body took on a yellowish cast, symptoms that got worse day by day. One look at his jaundiced condition told the doctors that the cancer was attacking his liver.

The doctors hung their heads. They thought they'd made sure, over the course of two previous surgeries, that the cancer hadn't spread to the liver or lymph nodes.

It was at this time that Kaoru began to suspect that what they were seeing was the emergence of some unknown illness, something that was indeed a kind of cancer, but one different from those previously known. His interest in basic medicine intensified. In the summer of his seventeenth year, having graduated from high school a year early, he entered the pre-med program in the same university that his father had attended.

The third time he lay down on the operating table, Hideyuki lost half his liver. He subsequently checked out of the hospital, but neither Kaoru nor Machiko could make themselves believe now that the battle with cancer was over. The family watched for enemy movements with bated breath, wondering where the cancer would invade next; the return of a peaceful, happy home life was something hardly to be hoped for.

That cancer won't rest until every organ in his body has been plucked out, Machiko insisted, and she wouldn't listen to any of Kaoru's medical knowledge. If she heard about a new vaccine, she'd scramble to get her hands on it even before it was fully tested. Hearing vitamin therapy was effective she tried that; she pressured the doctors into trying lymphocyte treatment; she even sought salvation in charismatic religion. She was willing to try anything—she couldn't swear she wouldn't sell her soul to the devil if it would save her husband's life. It depressed Kaoru to see his mother running around like a woman possessed. It was beginning to look like his father's death would also mean the collapse of his mother's psyche.

After that, Hideyuki spent most of his time in his hospital bed. He was still only forty-nine, but he looked like an old man of seventy. His hair had fallen out as a side-effect of the anti-cancer drugs, he was emaciated, his skin had lost its luster, and he was constantly running his fingers over his whole body and complaining of itchiness. But even so, he never lost his attachment to life. As his wife and son sat by his bedside he'd hold their hands and say, "You listen to me, next year we're going to that desert in North America." And he'd force a smile. It wasn't exactly false cheer—he obviously fully intended to fight this illness so he could keep his promise. The sight was both reassuring and painful.

As long as his father showed such a positive attitude toward life, Kaoru never entertained thoughts of giving up. No matter how bad the cancer got, Kaoru believed his father would conquer his illness in the end.

At around this time, a type of cancer with the same progression as Hideyuki's began to be identified, first in Japan, then worldwide. At first the

true cause of this new strain could not be identified, as if it lay wrapped under a veil. A few medical
professionals supported a theory that it was the
work of a new virus that turned cells cancerous,
but they couldn't explain how this cancer virus
differed from others, and besides, there had been
no reports of such a virus being successfully
isolated. But the vague suspicion spread.

It can take several years after a new disease
has been identified to pinpoint the virus that
causes it. The lag was especially understandable
in the case of the cancer that had afflicted
Hideyuki and millions of others, because at first
it looked just like any other cancer: nobody realized they were dealing with a new disease. But
gradually the world came to be gripped by fear
that a terrible new virus had been unleashed.

Finally, one year ago, the new cancer virus had
been successfully isolated in a laboratory at the
medical school of Fukuzawa University. With that
they had proof: a virus was the cause of this
metastatic cancer.

The new virus was named the Metastatic
Human Cancer Virus, and it was thought to have
the following characteristics.

First, it was an RNA retrovirus that actually
caused normal cells to become cancer cells. Thus,
anyone infected with the virus ran the risk of
developing cancer, regardless of whether or not
they had been exposed to carcinogens. However,

there was room for individual variation: there were confirmed cases, though only a few, of infected people who were mere carriers, never developing cancer themselves. It took on average three to five years from the time of infection for the cancer to grow large enough to be detected clinically, although the degree of individual variation in this was great.

Second, the cancer was contracted through the direct introduction of virally-infected lymphocytes into the body. That is, it was not spread through the air, but through sexual contact, blood transfusions, breast-feeding, and similar contact. Thus, it was not what would be called highly contagious. But there was no definitive evidence to say that it would not at some point in the future become transmissible through the air. This virus mutated with frightening speed.

Due to the similarity in the manner of its transmission, some scholars speculated that the new virus was the result of some sort of mutation in the AIDS virus. Perhaps the AIDS virus had sensed that it was about to be eliminated by vaccines, and so had colluded with an existing cancer virus, skillfully changing its appearance. And indeed, there was a nasty resemblance between the two viruses, not only in how they spread, but in the way they nested in cells in the human body.

When the Metastatic Human Cancer Virus,

carrying reverse-transcription enzymes, merged with human cellular tissue, the RNA and reverse-transcription enzymes were released to synthesize the double helix of DNA.

Then, this synthesized DNA mingled with normal cellular DNA, turning the cell cancerous. Which was bad enough. But it didn't end there. The cell could now no longer tell the difference between its own DNA and the viral DNA, and so it kept manufacturing the cancer virus and releasing it outside the cell. The released virus made its way into the bloodstream and the lymph stream, where it deviously fought off attacking immune cells while awaiting the chance to move into a new host.

The third characteristic: when the cancer started, almost without exception it metastasized and spread throughout the body with frightful strength. This, of course, was why it was called the Metastatic Human Cancer Virus.

There are benign tumors and malignant ones, and the difference between them lies in the thorny questions of invasiveness and metastasis. A person may develop a tumor and still have no reason to fear, as long as it doesn't spread through the surrounding area, move into the blood and lymphatic vessels, and metastasize.

But this metastatic cancer spread through rapid reproduction and extreme invasiveness, and was highly resistant to the immune-system attacks it experienced as it circulated through the lymph and blood streams. It was much more likely than normal cancer to survive in the circulatory system.

As a result, anyone who came down with this cancer had to assume a 100% probability that it would metastasize. The question of whether or not one survives cancer can be restated in terms of whether or not one can prevent that cancer from metastasizing. With a 100% chance of metastasis, it was essentially impossible to hope for a complete recovery from MHC.

The fourth characteristic was that the cancer cells created by this virus were immortal—they would live forever if their host didn't die.

Normal human cells have a limit to the number of times they can divide over the course of their existence—just like humans themselves, they have a certain span of life allotted to them at birth. For example, by the time a person becomes an adult, his or her nerve cells have lost their ability to reproduce themselves, so that they are no longer replenished. It might be said that nerve cells have the same lifespan as humans do.

In this way, the aging and death of cells is intimately connected with the question of human lifespan. But these cancer cells, when removed from a host and sustained in a culture fluid, went on dividing infinitely—they would never die.

There were certain religionists who pointed to this and spoke of it in a prophetic vein, saying,

If we could harness the power of these cancer cells and transfer it to normal cells, we would be able to achieve immortality—we'd never grow old.

But of course these were nothing but amateurish delusions. It was paradoxical that cells which had achieved immortality would then kill their human hosts, assuring that they themselves would die. But it was a paradox that, by and large, people managed to accept.

2

It was the rainy season, early summer of the year before Kaoru was to take his national examinations, and every day was a busy one for him. Visiting his dad and working a part-time job took up so much of his life that he barely had time to look after his mother's mental state—much less study.

If left to her own devices, his mother would try to get her hands on anything that claimed to be effective against cancer; Kaoru had to keep a constant watch so it didn't get out of control.

Hideyuki didn't approve of his son spending so much energy on his part-time job. He felt that his son should concentrate on studying, and that splitting his time between that and working was essentially a waste. The idea that Kaoru was doing it on account of his own illness irritated him even more: Hideyuki insisted that he could pay for Kaoru's school expenses, that they had enough money in savings. As far as talking big went, he was as healthy as ever; but the optimism in his words was Kaoru's salvation.

In reality, Kaoru was the one who held the family's finances in his hands, and he knew that they didn't have much to spare. He had to keep his job. But of course he wasn't about to complain to his father about their budgetary straits. There was nothing to be gained by letting his father know things were tight. So Kaoru lied to Hideyuki, telling him that he worked because he wanted more spending money.

When they were together, Kaoru wanted to set his father's mind as much at ease as possible. It wouldn't do to betray the fact that because his illness had decreased the family's income, Kaoru and his mother were having to squeeze by. Luckily, as a medical student Kaoru had no trouble hanging out his shingle as a tutor, and in fact he made quite a bit of money that way. The hospital connected to Kaoru's medical school had a lot of child patients whose parents didn't want them to fall behind in their studies when they went back to school; tutors were always in demand.

One day early in his summer vacation, Kaoru visited the hospital to tutor a junior high schooler in math and English, and then had a light lunch in the cafeteria. His father was a patient in this very hospital. Kaoru had just heard that there was a possibility that the cancer had spread to his father's lungs; his mood was black. His father had recently gone into his annual litany. *This year*, he said, *we're going to see those longevity zones in the North American desert*. But the words had rung hollow. And then came—as if on cue—the indications that the cancer had spread.

Kaoru was sitting in the cafeteria, sighing over his father's illness and his family's future, when he saw Reiko Sugiura and her son Ryoji.

The cafeteria was on the third floor of the hospital, surrounding a courtyard on three sides; the walls facing the courtyard were of glass. There was a fountain in the courtyard, and sitting at a table in the cafeteria one was eye level with the top of its spray. The cafeteria was so carefully decorated, and its food so pleasant to the taste, that it felt more like a stylish outdoor café than part of a hospital. Gazing at the water from the fountain had a truly relaxing effect.

Kaoru's eyes were drawn naturally toward the beautiful woman being shown to an empty table.

Her tanned body was sheathed in a summery beige dress, and her face was so nicely formed that it was eye-catching even without the aid of cosmetics. If it weren't for the child at her side, she could have passed for ten years younger than what Kaoru guessed she had to be.

The woman and boy sat at the table the waiter indicated, which happened to be diagonally adjacent to Kaoru's. Kaoru watched them seat themselves, and, after that too, he found his attention drawn to the woman, his eyes riveted to the legs stretching out from beneath her minidress.

He realized this was the same mother and child he'd seen at the hotel pool two weeks ago. One of his students' grades had gone up so much that the kid's parents had given Kaoru an all-summer free pass to that pool. On the first day he'd gone to swim there he'd encountered this pair, sitting poolside in deck chairs.

From the first moment he'd laid eyes on the woman in the green bathing suit, he was sure he'd seen her somewhere before, but when and where he couldn't say. Kaoru was normally confident in his powers of recall, but poke about as he might in the recesses of his memory he couldn't place the woman. The experience left him with an unpleasant aftertaste that wouldn't go away. A woman as beautiful as this he wouldn't expect to forget, and yet evidently he had. At the time, he'd tried to put her out of his mind, telling himself he was mistaken, but then something about her finally triggered memories of the star of a soap opera he'd watched as a child. He wondered if it was the same woman.

The boy made an odd impression, particularly his physique. The blue swim cap that he wore pushed back on his head, the goggles, the check-pattern shorts that Kaoru could tell at a glance weren't for swimming in, his skinny bowed legs, and most of all his abnormally white skin. He resembled an "alien corpse" Kaoru had seen on some fake TV show a long time ago. Everything about the boy looked strangely off-kilter. The pair stuck in Kaoru's memory: this woman he'd seen somewhere before and this weird-looking boy.

And now they were sitting at the next table over. Kaoru, sitting by the window so he could gaze down at the fountain, found he could catch their reflection faintly in the glass. He observed this instead of staring at them directly.

After a few moments, Kaoru figured out why his first impression of the boy had been of unbalance. It was his hair, or rather his lack of it. When Kaoru had first seen the boy poolside, his swim cap had been missing the bulge that would normally have told of a full head of hair.

Today, too, the boy was wearing a hat when he sat down at the table, but after a few moments he took it off, revealing his head to be perfectly devoid of hair.

Kaoru realized what that meant. The boy was here to be treated for cancer. He'd assumed mother and child were both here to visit a patient, but now it turned out that the mother was accompanying her son to chemotherapy. Hideyuki was undergoing chemotherapy, and his hair too had fallen out, but somehow seeing a child suffer that side effect was even more heart-rending. Kaoru thought about that day at the pool, that swim cap hugging the boy's bare scalp directly—no wonder he'd left such a peculiar impression.

Kaoru rested his head on his hand and watched the beautiful thirty-something woman and her son, who was probably a fifth or sixth grader, eat their lunches without talking. Without being conscious of it, he was comparing them to his father, hospitalized here. His father was forty-nine, while this boy had to be eleven or twelve. Both were taking anti-cancer medication.

The mother in her airy beige dress looked too bright and cheerful for a hospital. Once in a while she raised her head and glanced out the window. She didn't look like she was tasting what she ate—she was just eating to eat, looking at no one in particular with an expression that could have been a smile or the equivalent of a sigh.

She paused with her spoon in the air, then returned it to the plate, then started to bring it to her mouth again, and then suddenly shot a glance in Kaoru's direction. At first her gaze was sharp, as if to ask, *What are you looking at?* But as her eyes met Kaoru's her gaze softened. Kaoru found himself unable to look away.

It seemed she recognized him from the pool. She looked like she wanted to say something. Kaoru bowed his head slightly, and she answered with the same gesture.

And then her attention was taken up by her

son, who chose that moment to toss aside his chopsticks and spoon and throw a tantrum. The sight of Kaoru fled her mind.

Even then Kaoru continued to watch the two. He was powerless to resist—it was as if his consciousness had been uprooted and physically carried to where they were.

Several days later, in the courtyard this time, Kaoru had the opportunity to speak to this mother and her child. By some lucky chance they ended up sitting side by side on the same bench, making it possible for a conversation to start naturally without either one making the first move.

The mother introduced herself as Reiko Sugiura and her son as Ryoji. Ryoji's cancer, which had first appeared in his lungs, now looked like it had spread to his brain, and his days were filled with tests preparatory to radiation and chemotherapy.

Not only that, but it seemed that the agent that had turned his cells cancerous was none other than the recently isolated Metastatic Human Cancer Virus—the progress of the illness, from first appearance through subsequent metastasis, was nearly identical to Kaoru's father's case.

Kaoru felt a sense of kinship. A sense that they were comrades fighting the same enemy.

"Brothers in arms."

The expression was Reiko's, but it echoed Kaoru's thoughts. However, Kaoru doubted her words, having observed their expressions in the cafeteria the other day. It was resignation he'd seen then, wasn't it? At the very least, their faces hadn't been those of people dedicated to battling an illness. Kaoru still remembered the affectless way she'd eaten.

He took this opportunity to clear up the doubt that had been nagging at him since their first encounter.

"Haven't we met somewhere before?" It embarrassed him as he said it, it sounded so much like a pickup line, but he couldn't think of any other way to ask it.

Reiko responded with a laugh whose import escaped him. "I get that a lot. I'm told I look like an actress on an old TV show," she said shyly.

It sounded like a lie to him. She didn't just look like the actress—he couldn't help but think they were one and the same. But if she was the actress, and was lying so she could escape her past, then he didn't feel he should press the issue.

When they parted, there in the courtyard, Reiko gave him their room number and said, "Why don't you come visit us sometime? Please."

Three times they'd met, he and Reiko Sugiura. Now more than ever, he couldn't take his eyes off her.

3

It was the very next day that Kaoru took Reiko at her word and knocked on the door to Ryoji's room.

Reiko greeted him, with a smile that might have been a bit overdone, and showed him into the room. Ryoji was sitting up in bed reading a book, his legs dangling over the side. As a medical student, Kaoru knew how much the room cost the moment he entered. It was a private room with a private bathroom complete with bathtub. The daily rate was five times that for a normal shared room.

"Thank you for coming," Reiko managed to say. Evidently she'd only invited him as a social courtesy, not really expecting him to come. Now that he was actually here she couldn't disguise her happiness. She turned to Ryoji and tried to stir his interest. "Look who's come to see you!"

It hit Kaoru that Reiko had invited him up as

someone for her son to talk to. He should have realized it before.

It was Reiko, not Ryoji, who had piqued Kaoru's interest. Kaoru didn't know much about women, but he'd sensed something sexual, some kind of desire, in her unwavering gaze. She had full lips and wide, alluring eyes that drooped a little at the corners; her breasts weren't especially large, but still there was something undeniably feminine in her five-foot frame. She had a refined air about her that he hadn't found in women his own age, and it aroused something within him.

In comparison with that, there was nothing for him to hold onto in Ryoji's gaze. As he sat down facing the boy in the proffered chair, he was astonished at how little light the boy's eyes held. Ryoji didn't even try to meet Kaoru's gaze. He was looking in Kaoru's direction, but plainly he wasn't seeing anything. His eyes looked right through Kaoru, their gaze wandering across the wall behind. For a long time, they wouldn't focus.

Ryoji set his book down on his knee with a finger still stuck in between the pages. Trying to find something to talk about, Kaoru leaned forward to see what the boy was reading.

The Horror of Viruses.

Patients want to know as much as possible about their illness. Ryoji was no exception. Naturally he was concerned about this foreign thing that had invaded his body.

Kaoru informed the boy that he was a medical student, and asked him a few questions about viruses. Ryoji answered him with a level of accuracy and detail astonishing in a sixth grader. Clearly he understood a great deal about viruses. Not only did he understand how DNA worked, he even had his own views on matters at the farthest reaches of current knowledge about the phenomenon of life.

As they went back and forth, questioning and answering, Kaoru began to imagine he was looking at a younger version of himself. He looked on this child, armed with scientific knowledge, the same way his father had looked on him. Kaoru felt like an adult.

But it wasn't to last long. Just as they had warmed up to each other, just as the conversation was really taking off, Ryoji's nurse showed up to take him to an examining room.

Kaoru and Reiko were alone now in the small sickroom. Kaoru was suddenly fidgety, while Reiko, who had been leaning on the windowsill, now coolly came over and sat down beside the bed.

"I had no idea you were twenty."

Kaoru had mentioned his age during his conversation with Ryoji; Reiko had noticed. Kaoru was always being told he looked older than he was; he was used to it.

"How old do I look to you?"

"Hmm. Maybe about five years older . . . ?"
She trailed off apologetically, afraid she'd offended him.

"You mean I look old?"

"You look mature. Really . . . together." To say he looked old might hurt him; to say he looked "mature" would sound like a compliment, she evidently figured.

"My parents got along well when I was growing up."

"And that makes kids look older than their age?"

"Well, they always looked like they'd be happy enough to be left alone, just the two of them, so I had to learn to be independent pretty early."

"Ah." Reiko's expression said she wasn't convinced. She looked at her son's empty bed.

Kaoru found himself thinking about Reiko's husband. Something about Ryoji suggested that he didn't have a father. Maybe there had been a divorce, maybe he'd died, or maybe he'd been absent from the start. In any case, Kaoru had the impression that Ryoji's relationship with his father was, at the very least, extremely attenuated.

"In that case, maybe my son will never become independent," said Reiko, still staring at the bed.

Kaoru braced himself and waited for her next words.

"It was cancer . . . "

"Oh." He had expected that.

"It was two years ago. Ryoji didn't mourn his father's death one bit, you know."

Kaoru could understand that. The kid probably hadn't let her see him cry once.

"That's how it is sometimes."

But he didn't mean it. When he imagined his own father's death an uncontrollable sadness came welling up from the depths of his heart. He wasn't sure he'd be able to overcome it when he faced the actual event. He realized that, at least in that sense, maybe he wasn't all that independent yet himself.

"Kaoru, would you mind . . . " Reiko trailed off again, fixing him with a clinging gaze. "Would you mind watching over his studies?"

"You mean, as his tutor?"

"Yes."

Teaching children was his specialty, and he had time for one or two more students. But he wasn't sure Ryoji actually needed a tutor. Just from their brief talk together it was obvious that Ryoji was far more capable than other students his age.

But it wasn't only that. If the cancer had already spread to his lungs and his brain, Kaoru knew that all the tutors and all the studying in the world wouldn't make any difference in the end. There was no chance that this kid would return to school. But then, maybe that was precisely why she wanted to hire a tutor, in the hopes that letting him prepare to go back to school and resume his studies would restore his faith in the future. Kaoru knew how important it was for those surrounding the patient to show by their actions that they hadn't given up hope.

"Sure. I have time to come by twice a week, if that would do."

Reiko took two or three steps toward Kaoru and placed her hands demurely in front of her, one over the other. "Thank you. Not only will it benefit his schoolwork, but I'm sure he'll be happy to have someone to talk to."

"Okay, then."

No doubt Ryoji didn't have a friend in the world. Kaoru could understand, because he'd been the same. He'd been just a little of a social outcast at school. But in his case, he'd had a good relationship with his parents that had saved him from feeling lonely. Crazy as his father could be, he'd been the best possible conversation partner for Kaoru. With his father and mother around, Kaoru hadn't been inclined to wonder why he'd been born into this world. He'd never had doubts about his identity.

What Reiko sought in Kaoru was a father figure for her son. Kaoru didn't have a problem with that. He was confident he could play that role, and do it well.

But, he wondered: *Does she also want a husband figure for herself?*

Kaoru's imagination began to run away with

him. He wasn't as confident on that score. But he wanted to at least try to be the man Reiko needed.

They arranged a date and time for his next visit. Then Kaoru left Ryoji's hospital room.

4

Kaoru and Ryoji ended up talking with each other a lot, even outside their scheduled lessons. Usually their talks ended up focusing on general science topics. Kaoru was reminded of his own childhood, when his desire to understand the world had led him to delve deeply into natural science.

At one time, Kaoru had desired to formulate a system or theory that would encompass and explain things normally dismissed as non-science—paranormal phenomena. But the more he learned, the more he came to see that no matter what unified theory he came up with, there would still be phenomena that couldn't be accounted for within it. That realization combined with his father's illness turned his exploring impulses into an interest in a practical field of study, namely medicine.

Kaoru snapped out of his reverie and looked

at Ryoji, a younger fellow-inquirer into the workings of the universe.

Ryoji was sitting cross-legged on his bed as
always, rocking gently back and forth. Reiko was
in a chair by the window, watching them talk,
and she must have been fairly sleepy, for she'd
started moving her head back and forth in time
with her son's movements.

"So is that what you're interested in right
now?"

Ryoji had been peppering Kaoru with questions about genetics.

"Yeah, I guess so."

Ryoji turned his normally hollow gaze forward
and began to stretch where he sat on the bed. He
was smiling like he always did, although there was
nothing funny about what they were discussing. It
wasn't a healthy smile. It was the desperate grin
of someone at the end of his own life scorning the
world. Kaoru thought he'd gotten used to it, but
it could still annoy him if he looked at it long
enough. If his father smiled like that, he'd give him
a good talking-to—he'd rip into him, father or not.

There was only one way to wipe that smile off
Ryoji's face: goad him into a passionate debate.

Kaoru changed the subject. "So what are your
thoughts on the theory of evolution?" It was a
natural progression from genetics.

"What do you mean?" Ryoji squirmed and
rolled his eyes at Kaoru.

"Okay, how's this for starters? Does evolution move randomly or toward a predetermined goal?"

"What do you think?" This was one of Ryoji's less pleasing habits. He always tried to ferret out his interlocutor's thinking first, instead of coming straight out with his own opinion.

"I think evolution moves in a certain direction, but always with a certain latitude for choice." Kaoru couldn't bring himself to give a ringing endorsement of mainstream Darwinian evolutionary theory. Even now that he was taking his first steps toward becoming a specialist in a natural science, he couldn't completely abandon the idea that there was a purpose behind it all.

"The direction theory. That's pretty much what I believe, too." Ryoji leaned toward Kaoru, as if he'd accomplished something.

"Shall we start with the emergence of life?"

"The emergence of life?" Ryoji looked truly astonished.

"Sure. How you look at the emergence of life is an important question."

"It is?" Ryoji furrowed his brow and looked like he wanted to get out of this question but quick.

Kaoru didn't appreciate this attitude of Ryoji's. For a kid like him it should be fun to play around with questions like this. The question of why life on earth was able to gain the ability to evolve was intimately connected with the question of how life first emerged on earth. Kaoru, at least, had gotten a lot of enjoyment out of debating this with his father.

"Well, let's move on, then. Let's grant that life emerged, by some mechanism we don't yet understand. So, next . . . " Kaoru stopped to let Ryoji step in.

"I think the first life on earth was something like a seed. That seed contained the right information so that it could sprout, grow, and eventually become the tree which is life as we know it, including humankind."

"Are there no variations?"

"Yes and no. The biggest tree grows from the tiniest seed. The size of the trunk, the color of the leaves, the type of fruit—all that information is already contained within the seed. But of course the tree is also influenced by the natural environment. If it doesn't get sunlight it'll wither, if it doesn't get enough nutrients the trunk'll be thin. Maybe it'll be struck by lightning and split in two, maybe its branches will break in a gale. But no amount of unpredictable influence of that kind can change the basic nature of the tree as contained in the seed. Come rain or snow, a ginkgo tree will never bear apples."

Kaoru licked his lips. He didn't mean to contradict Ryoji. He basically agreed with him, in fact.

"So you're saying that if sea creatures learn to walk on land, if giraffes develop long necks, it's all because they were programmed that way from the start?"

"Well, yeah."

"In that case, we should assume that there was some kind of will at work before life began."

Ryoji responded innocently. "Whose will? God's?"

But Kaoru wasn't thinking about God per se, just an invisible will at work both before life began and during the process of evolution.

He found himself imagining a school of fish fighting with each other to get to land. There was an overwhelming power in the thought of all those fish, enough of them to dye the sea black, jumping around as they sought dry land.

Of course it was possible that sea life had never intended to go on land, but had simply succeeded in adapting to it after orogenic processes had begun to dry up the water. That was how the mainstream evolutionary thinker would explain it.

But the image that came to Kaoru's mind was of those hollow-eyed fish, yearning day in and day out for the land, dying at the water's edge and making mountains of their corpses. Mainstream evolution had it that a certain fraction of them had simply been lucky enough to adapt. Kaoru simply couldn't believe that. The transition from a marine to a land-based living environment involved changes in internal organs. Their insides had to be remade to allow for the transition from gill breathing to lung breathing. What kind of bodily trial and error had resulted in those changes? One kind of organ had been reborn as another. It was pretty major, when you thought about it.

Right in front of Kaoru was Ryoji's bald head. Because Ryoji was hunched over, the top of his head came up to the tip of Kaoru's nose. At this very moment, within that emaciated little body, a violent cellular conflict was being enacted. As it was within Kaoru's father Hideyuki. He'd lost most of his stomach, part of his large intestine, and his liver. And still, more as-yet-unknown cancer cells had taken up residence in some new spot in his body and were writhing there even now.

An unexpected inspiration came to Kaoru.

Cancer cells invaded a normal organ, changing its color and shape and constructing new bulges, until the normal functioning of the organ was impaired and it died. The obviously negative aspects of this were what stood out, but at the same time it was possible to detect in the cancer's actions a certain groping towards something. By infiltrating the blood and lymph to penetrate cells elsewhere, it was experimenting with transplanting its immortal nature bit by bit. But to what end?

To create somewhere within the body a new organ adapted to the future. Maybe the Metastatic

Human Cancer Virus was nothing but a sort of trial-and-error attempt to create a new organ.

In the process, large numbers of human beings would die, just as most of the fish had died at the water's edge. But just as after a hundred million years sea life had finally made it onto the land, someday, after countless sacrifices, maybe the human race would find itself with a new organ. Humanity would have evolved. Maybe an evolutionary leap comparable to the movement from the water to the land was impossible without something like a new organ. When would it happen?

Human cancer deaths were surging upward, but without knowing when the cancer cells had started their work it was impossible to know if the human race had just begun its fumbling toward evolution, or was about to complete it. The only thing certain was that the pace of evolution was accelerating. The time it took for apes to evolve into humans was shorter than what had been needed for sea creatures to evolve into amphibians, so much shorter that there was almost no comparison. So it was possible. The intervals in the evolutionary process were gradually getting shorter, so maybe it wasn't too soon for this to be evolution, too.

Kaoru wanted to think so. He wanted to turn his attention to anything that would afford him hope. He wanted to believe that his father would be the first one to successfully evolve, rather than just another sacrifice.

To be reborn. Kaoru would have wanted that, if it were possible. No doubt everybody wanted to live again. The gift of eternal life.

Since it was a property of the MHC virus to create immortal cells, it was only natural to fantasize about human immortality. Maybe even Ryoji had a chance.

Kaoru almost said so, but bit back the words. Anything that sounded like an affirmation of the illness might have the effect of loosening the boy's attachment to living.

He heard faint snoring right behind him. Reiko, who had been nodding off for some time, had finally lowered her face to the table and gone to sleep. Kaoru and Ryoji looked at each other and giggled.

It was still early, not even eight o'clock. Outside the window, the evening cityscape was starting to emerge from the summer dusk. From below the window came the sounds of highway traffic, suddenly loud.

Reiko's elbow twitched, knocking an empty soda can to the floor, but she didn't awaken.

Kaoru spoke cautiously. "Your mom's asleep. Maybe it's time I was leaving." The lesson had ended long ago.

"Weren't you about to say something to me just now, Kaoru?"

Ryoji looked discontented, as if he hadn't had his fill of talking yet.

"We'll pick up where we left off next time."

Kaoru stood up and looked around the room. Reiko had gone to sleep with her right cheek pillowed on her hands and her face turned in his direction. Her eyes were closed but her mouth was half open, and the back of her hand was wet with drool. Fast asleep, she looked quite cute.

It was the first time he'd thought that about a woman ten years older than him. Kaoru felt affection for her entire body, and harbored a momentary desire to touch her.

Ryoji reached out and shook her shoulder. "Mom, Mom." She still didn't wake up.

"It's no good. She's out like a light."

Ryoji trained his innocent eyes on Kaoru, and then on the extra bed provided for relatives accompanying the patient. "Mom gets tired taking care of me, so I like to let her sleep when she can. She'll have to wake up in the middle of the night tonight anyway," he said, as if he weren't making a veiled entreaty.

Kaoru felt an unaccustomed warmth in his body, as if Ryoji had managed to peek inside his heart. He realized that what the boy was really saying was, *Would you pick her up and move her to the extra bed real gently so she doesn't wake up?*

If he could manage to pick her up, it was only about six feet to the bed. Reiko's knees beneath her short culottes were pressed tightly together as if to fend off any attempts to touch her. Carrying a woman to bed was nothing for someone of Kaoru's physical strength, but his guard went up at the thought of touching her—he wasn't sure he'd be able to control his desires in the face of that stimulus.

"When she's like this you couldn't move her with a lever." Ryoji's expression as he said this was suggestive; then he pointedly turned his face away from Kaoru, even as he seemed to be looking right through him. It was as if he knew Kaoru was interested in his mother as a woman, and was egging him on.

Look, I know you want to touch my Mom. It's okay. You have my permission. I'll even give you the opportunity.

Ryoji was provoking him, biting back laughter while he did it.

Kaoru wordlessly set up the extra bed. It wasn't so much that he was caving in to Ryoji's challenge as that he was eager to yield to whatever he felt on touching Reiko. If his feelings were going to deepen, let them. As yet he didn't understand the effect physical contact with her would have on his psychological state.

Kaoru placed his arms behind Reiko's neck and under her knees, and in one motion lifted her up and placed her on the bed.

As he laid her down, her lips brushed against

his neck, just for a moment. She opened her eyes slightly and flexed her arms so as to hug him closer, then loosened her grip with a contented look on her face, and fell back to sleep.

Kaoru stayed silent and motionless for a little while, afraid she'd wake up if he moved. For several seconds, his body covered hers. With his face between her chest and belly, he could feel the resilience of the flesh of her abdomen; his eyes were trained on her face. He was looking up at her face from below, essentially. He could see the fine lines of her jaw, and above it the two black holes of her nostrils. He'd never seen her face from this angle before.

At length he stood up again. As he separated himself from her body, he asked himself, repeatedly: *Am I falling in love with her?*

The touch of her lips was still vivid on the skin of his neck.

"Well, then, I'll see you next week."

Kaoru put his hand hesitantly on the door-knob, so as not to reveal the pounding of his heart.

Ryoji still sat cross-legged on his bed, rocking back and forth, cracking his knuckles. Unlike a few moments ago, his face held no look of provocation or mockery now—he'd stifled all expression.

"Good night."

Kaoru slipped out of the room. He could feel

Ryoji's unnatural smile fixed on the door as he shut it behind him.

Kaoru had a flash of intuition. This meeting was not mere coincidence. His future would be intimately tied with Reiko and Ryoji.

5

Among Kaoru's pleasures in life were his visits to the office of Assistant Professor Saiki in the Pathology Department. Saiki had been a classmate of his father's in this very university, and now, with his father in this unfortunate condition, Saiki was always ready to lend an ear or some advice. Officially, he wasn't Kaoru's advisor, but he was an old friend of the family, someone Kaoru had known since childhood.

These days there was a specific purpose to Kaoru's regular visits. Cells from the cancer torturing his father were being cultured in Saiki's lab, and Kaoru liked to come by to look at them under the microscope. To adequately fend off this enemy's attacks, he felt he needed to know its true visage.

Kaoru left the hospital proper and entered the building containing the Pathology, Forensic Medicine, and Microbiology laboratories. The university hospital was a motley collection of new and old buildings; this was one of the older ones. The Forensic Medicine classrooms were on the second floor, while the third housed Pathology, where he was headed.

He climbed the stairs and turned left into a hallway lined with small labs on either side. Kaoru stopped in front of Professor Saiki's door and knocked.

"Come in," Saiki called out. The door was open a crack; Kaoru stuck his head in. "Oh, it's you." This was Saiki's standard response on seeing Kaoru.

"Is this a bad time?"

"I'm busy, as you can see, but you're welcome to do what you like."

Saiki was involved in examining cells taken this afternoon from some diseased tissue; he barely looked up. That was fine with Kaoru; he'd rather be left alone to make his observations in freedom.

"Don't mind if I do, then."

Kaoru opened the door of the large refrigerator-like carbon dioxide incubator and searched for his father's cells. The incubator was kept at a constant temperature and a nearly constant level of carbon dioxide. It wouldn't do for him to keep the door open long.

But the plastic Petri dish in which his father's cells were being cultured was in its usual place, and he had no trouble finding it.

So this is what immortality looks like, he thought. It mystified him, as it always did.

His father's liver had been removed—having changed from its normal reddish-pink to a mottled hue covered with what looked like white powder—and was now sealed in a glass jar, preserved in formaldehyde, in another cabinet, where it had been stored for three years now. Sometimes it seemed to squirm or writhe, but maybe that was a trick of the light.

The liver was dead, of course, pickled in formaldehyde. Whereas the cancer cells in the Petri dish were alive.

The dish contained cells grown from Kaoru's father's cancer cells, cultured in a medium with a blood serum concentration of less than one percent.

With normal cells, growth stops when the growth factor in the blood serum is used up. And within a Petri dish, they won't multiply beyond a single layer no matter how much growth factor is added, due to what is called contact inhibition. Cancer cells not only lack contact inhibition, but they have an extremely low dependence on the blood serum. Simply put, they are able to grow and reproduce, layer upon layer, in a tiny space with virtually no food supply.

Normal cells in a Petri dish will only form one layer, whereas cancer cells will form layer upon layer. Normal cells reproduce in a flat, orderly fashion, while cancer cells multiply in a three-dimensional, disorderly manner. Normal cells have a natural limit to the number of times they can divide, while cancer cells can go on dividing forever.

Immortality.

Kaoru was fully aware of the irony in the fact that immortality, the object of man's deepest yearnings from time immemorial, was in the possession of this primeval horror, this killer of men.

As if to demonstrate their three-dimensional nature, his father's cancer cells had bubbled up into a spheroid. Every time Kaoru looked they had taken on a different shape. Originally, these had their source in normal cells in his father's liver, but now it might be more appropriate to see them as an independent life form. Even as their erstwhile host faced his crisis, these cells greedily enjoyed eternal life.

Kaoru set this dish full of concentrated contradiction into the phase contrast microscope. Its magnification only went up to x200, but it allowed easy color imaging. He could only use the scanning electron microscope when he had time to spare.

The cancer cells, these life forms which had gone beyond any moderating influence, presented a peculiar sight. Perhaps there was something actually, objectively grotesque about their appearance, or perhaps they only looked grotesque to him because of his preconceptions about them as usurpers of human life.

Kaoru struggled to abandon this bias, his hatred of the agent of his father's suffering, as he observed the sample.

Raising the magnification, he could see that the cells were clumping together. The long, spindly, translucent cells grew as a thicket, stained a thin green. This wasn't their natural color; the microscope had a green filter attached.

Normal cells would have been evenly distributed in a flat, orderly fashion, with no one part sticking out, but these cancer cells revealed, here and there, a thicker green shadow.

He could see them clearly: a multitude of points, bubbling up roundly, shining. These were cells in the process of dividing.

Kaoru changed the dish under the microscope several times, comparing the cancer cells to normal cells. The surface difference was readily apparent: the cancer cells displayed a chaotic filthiness.

But the surface of the cells was all he could examine: an optical microscope wasn't powerful enough to show him their nuclei or DNA.

Still, Kaoru gazed on untiring. His heart was heavy with the knowledge that he was wasting his time: just what was he going to learn looking at them from the outside? Still, even as he cursed himself for doing so, he examined the external part of each and every one of them.

The cells all looked alike on the surface. Thousands of identical faces, all in a row.

Identical faces.

Kaoru raised his face from the microscope.

Totally out of the blue, he had compared the cells to human faces. But that was what they looked like: the same face thousands of times over, gathering and sticking together in a clump until they formed a mottled mass.

Kaoru had to look away for a while.

That image came to me intuitively. Was it for a reason?

That was the first question to consider. His father had taught him to pay attention to his intuition.

It often happened that Kaoru would be reading a book or walking down the street and suddenly a completely unrelated scene would present itself to his mind's eye. Usually he didn't inquire into the reason. Say he was walking down the street and saw a movie star on a poster: he might suddenly remember an acquaintance who resembled the movie star. If he didn't register having seen the poster, which was entirely possible, it would seem as if the image of his acquaintance had come to him out of nowhere.

If it was a kind of synchronicity, then Kaoru wanted to analyze it to find out what had synched up with what. He'd been looking at cancer cells under x200 magnification, and something had been triggered so that the cells looked to him like human faces. Now: did that mean something?

Pondering it brought no answer, so Kaoru returned his gaze to the microscope. There had to be something which had elicited the comparison in his imagination. He saw narrow cells piled up in three dimensions. Little glowing globes. Kaoru muttered the same thing as before.

No doubt about it, they all have the same face.

Not only that, but it was clearly not a man's face, not to his imagination. If he had to choose he'd say it was somehow feminine. An egg-shaped, regular face, with smooth, even slippery, skin.

This was weird. In all the times he'd looked at cells through the phase contrast microscope, he'd never thought they looked like human faces.

6

Kaoru was in a hospital room face-to-face with Ryoji, but his mind was on the sounds coming from the bathroom. Reiko had been in there for some time, with the water running. She wasn't showering; maybe she was washing underwear. While tutoring Ryoji he'd seen Reiko hurriedly gathering up underwear that had been hung up to dry in the room.

Distractedly, Kaoru set about answering Ryoji's questions about his father's condition.

He gave him a brief rundown, but Ryoji's body language said he wanted to hear more. Maybe he wanted to sketch in the future of his own illness based on what he could learn of Kaoru's father's.

Kaoru stopped the conversation before Ryoji could start to guess that the cancer had spread to his father's lungs. Partly he hesitated because he thought the knowledge might have a negative influence on Ryoji, but partly he simply didn't want to say it out loud.

When the cancer had become heavy on his lungs, Hideyuki's face had started to betray weakness; he'd started to talk about what would happen after he was gone—to talk about entrusting Kaoru with his mother's care.

Look after Machi, okay?

At the sight of this weakness, Kaoru was seized with a desire to deliver the full force of his anger upon his father. *And just how am I supposed to comfort Mom after you die*, he wanted to say. *Quit laying these impossible tasks on me!*

Now as he sat talking about his father's condition with Ryoji, also lying flat in a hospital bed, his father's image came to him, and he had a hard time speaking. Not noticing that Kaoru had fallen silent, and insensitive to the reason why, Ryoji produced a forced-sounding laugh.

"Now that I think about it, Kaoru, I talked to your father once."

They'd both been in and out of the hospital with the same illness. No matter how big the hospital, it wasn't unlikely that they'd come into contact.

"Really?"

"He's the tall guy in 7B, right?"

"That's him."

"He's pretty strong. He's always frisky, slapping the nurses' butts and stuff like that."

That was Hideyuki alright. He'd achieved a certain notoriety among the patients for the cheerful way in which he battled his illness, never seeming to lose heart. They said that seeing him act so cheerful, so unafraid of death, made it possible for them to hang on to the hope necessary to gamble on long odds. He'd lost his stomach, his large intestine, and his liver, and now it looked like the cancer had spread to his lungs: his time, it appeared, had come. But regardless, in front of other people he put on a display of high spirits he couldn't possibly feel. The only exception was when he was alone with Kaoru: then he allowed his weak side to show . . .

"What about your Mom, Kaoru? How's she doing?" Ryoji asked, without much evident concern.

Reiko came out of the bathroom, spread the laundry out on the extra bed, and then disappeared back into the bathroom.

Kaoru followed her with his eyes, but the expected sound of running water never came. It seemed that Reiko just didn't want to be there. Maybe because the topic of Kaoru's mother had come up.

The Metastatic Human Cancer Virus can also be spread through contact with lymphocytes, the attending physician had said. Kaoru's first fears had been for his mother. He imagined they'd ceased sexual relations as soon as they'd been made aware of the risk, but there was a good chance she'd already contracted it by that point. Recently, Kaoru had finally been able to prevail on his mother to have her blood tested.

The results were positive. She had yet to manifest any symptoms, but it was a fact that the MHC virus had already attached itself to her DNA. In other words, the retrovirus's base sequence had been incorporated into the chromosomes in her cells.

At the moment, the process was paused at that step, but at any time her cells might begin to turn cancerous. In fact, there was every chance that it had already begun, and it just wasn't yet apparent on the surface.

The mechanism that determined when and how the provirus attached to the chromosomes would turn the cell cancerous was not yet understood, so the disease's progress from this point could not be predicted with any accuracy. But if it moved on to the next step, then his mother's cells would start producing new copies of the MHC virus.

Even if I get sick, I don't want to have surgery, she'd proclaimed, as soon as she'd heard the results. Since there was no way to head off metastasis, surgery was doomed from the start. All it could do was slow the progress of the disease, not cure it. After watching her husband suffer, she had a strong aversion to seeing her own body carved away piece by piece.

But what bothered Kaoru most was seeing his mother stray into mysticism, thinking that if modern medicine couldn't cure her, she'd try to find her own miracle elsewhere. The person she really wanted to save was not herself, although she knew she'd someday come down with cancer, but her husband, in the last stages of his.

With a passion that wouldn't blink at selling her soul to the devil, she started reading old writings on North American Indians. Her desk was stacked high with primary sources sent from who knew where.

The mythical world holds the key to a cure for cancer, she insisted, almost deliriously.

Again from the bathroom came the purposeful sound of running water. Ryoji reacted by glancing toward the bathroom.

"My mother's a carrier," said Kaoru in a low voice.

"Oh. So are you . . . ?"

Ryoji asked his question with no emotion whatsoever, and Kaoru slowly shook his head. He'd had his blood tested two months ago, and the results had come back negative.

Hearing this, Ryoji actually laughed. Not necessarily out of relief that Kaoru was uninfected, though. Rather, it was a scornful, even pitying cackle. Kaoru glared at him.

"What's so funny about that?"

"I just feel sorry for you."

"For me?" Kaoru pointed at himself, and Ryoji nodded his head twice.

"Yeah. You're strong and healthy, so you're probably going to live a long time. Just thinking about it . . . "

Under his motorcycle-loving father's influence, Kaoru had taken up motocross, and under Hideyuki's tutelage he'd improved his showing with every race he'd entered. He'd grown up muscular and fit in a way that nobody could have predicted from a childhood spent on a computer from morning to night. Kaoru's muscles were visible even through his T-shirt, and yet this scrawny kid was pitying him. To Kaoru it sounded like he was laughing at something Kaoru had inherited from his father, and he fought back vigorously.

"Living's not as bad a thing as you seem to think it is."

Part of him could understand Ryoji's feelings, of course. Kaoru didn't know when or how he'd been infected, but here he was at age twelve—between surgery, chemotherapy, and repeated hospitalizations, his life had been nothing but an endless round of suffering. Kaoru could see why he'd want to generalize from his experience and believe that everybody must be feeling the same way.

"Yeah, but everybody dies." Ryoji turned his hollow gaze toward the ceiling. Kaoru no longer felt like arguing with him.

Death filled everything, everywhere. There in front of him was that bald little head. It was a solemn fact.

Nobody who hasn't experienced it can understand the misery of chemotherapy. Overcome with violent nausea, you lose your appetite, and anything you do manage to eat, you bring up again soon enough; you can't get any sleep. That was Ryoji's life, and that was how his life was going to end in the not-too-distant future. Kaoru knew it. What could he possibly say in the face of that?

Kaoru felt tired. Not physical fatigue. It was like his heart was blocked and screaming. He wanted to soar; he wanted to laugh, freely and from the heart. He wanted to spend time in close bodily contact with another human being.

"I never wanted to be born in the first place," Ryoji said, ignoring Kaoru's unresponsiveness. At that very moment, Reiko stepped out of the bathroom and into the reverberations of Ryoji's statement. Without the slightest change in her expression she crossed the room and went out into the hall.

Why did you have me? Perhaps she left because she couldn't bear her son's accusations, or perhaps she simply had an errand to run. There was no way of telling.

But Kaoru had been paying attention to her movements. And now two questions raised their heads. First of all, was Reiko infected with the MHC virus? And, second, by what route did Ryoji become infected with it? These were questions Kaoru couldn't come right out and ask, as they touched on private family matters.

"Well, I think I'll be on my way now." He couldn't be by Ryoji's side any longer. Plus, he wanted to follow Reiko.

Kaoru left the boy's bed and opened the door to the hallway. He wanted to come into closer contact with Reiko, both bodily and with what was inside her. Maybe his interest in her amounted to a kind of love; he couldn't tell. He felt that she was urging him out of the cramped hospital room and into the world outside.

Compelled by this stimulus, Kaoru wandered the long corridors of the hospital, looking for Reiko.

7

He had an idea where she was, or at least he thought he did.

My only peace these days comes from going to the very highest point in the hospital and looking out over the city.

A few evenings before, Kaoru had seen her standing outside the restaurant on the top floor of the hospital, nose pressed against a window, and he'd asked her what she was doing. She'd explained her actions with those words.

The sun would be setting soon, silhouetting the skyscrapers in this subcenter of the city, bringing them into beautiful relief. Kaoru knew that this was her favorite time of day for gazing at the city.

He got off the elevator on the seventeenth floor, and when he stepped into the hallway and looked left he could see a woman standing there, leaning against a pillar. Kaoru approached her without speaking, until they were standing side by side.

The setting sun streaked Reiko's face with crimson. Her cheeks glowed seductively as they reflected the sky's shifting hues.

She knew as soon as he came up to her; she could see his reflection in the glass. She addressed his reflection with a faint smile.

"I'm sorry."

Kaoru couldn't figure out what she was apologizing for. Maybe she was recognizing his skill in tutoring her difficult-to-deal-with son, but in that case a thank-you would have been more appropriate. Kaoru was embarrassed for a response.

He decided not to ask why she'd apologized. "You really like high places, don't you?"

"I do. Maybe it's because I've lived my whole life hugging the ground."

Did she mean she'd always lived in one-story houses? If so, it was a stark contrast to Kaoru's own living environment. He still lived with his mother in their apartment tower overlooking Tokyo Bay.

Reiko changed the subject in an effort to dispel the oppressive atmosphere; in an enthusiastic voice she started talking about dreams. She started right in, like a shot, with what she wanted to do first when her son had recovered from his illness. The precondition itself—her son recovering—

being utterly impossible, she was free to dream whatever unrealistic dreams she felt like. Among the more realistic ideas she mentioned was taking a trip overseas.

So when she changed tack and asked Kaoru, "What's your dream?" he was able without hesitation to come up with the family trip to the North American desert that they'd planned ten years ago.

Kaoru gave Reiko a brief account of what they'd talked about that late night ten years ago— the relationship between gravity and life, the mysteries of life itself, and how those led to the possible existence of longevity zones.

He then explained in simple terms how his father's promise to take him to the desert had fueled further interest in global longevity patterns. Then came his father's cancer, which had prompted him to deeper research, and the belief that there had to be a relationship between longevity zones and the number of cancer victims.

This last point piqued Reiko's interest, and, still leaning against the glass, she turned to face Kaoru.

"What kind of relationship?"

"I'm not entirely sure yet, but the statistics show certain peculiarities that can't be ignored."

Kaoru warmed up to his explanation, as he could see that Reiko had pricked up her ears.

"It was not just coincidence that led me that night into associating gravitational anomalies with longevity. I had a flash of intuition. Most scientific discoveries are the result of intuition. Inspiration comes first, then reason. It might not be far off to think that I was responding to some kind of suggestion that night.

"When my father's cancer spread to his liver, I started researching longevity zones worldwide. It wasn't just my imagination. It's been confirmed: there are spots on the globe where people live longer. I analyzed all kinds of data. If they had something in common, I was going to find it.

"I finally narrowed it down to four particularly well-known longevity zones: Abkhazia, an area of the Caucasus on the shores of the Black Sea; Vilcabamba, a sacred valley on the border between Peru and Ecuador; Hunza, a mountainous region surrounded by the Karakoram Mountains and the Hindukush and cut off from the surrounding area; and Sanaru Island, in the Samejima archipelago of Japan. I wasn't able to visit these places myself to investigate, so I read everything I could get my hands on that related to them, and compiled my own statistics. When I did that, one thing stood out. It's a bit too early for me to make a definitive judgment, but it would seem that these places have not seen a single death from cancer. Doctors and biologists from around the world have investigated longevity zones, and they've left countless reports. None of them record deaths from cancer.

"The reports all agree in pointing to diet as a possible cause for this low cancer rate. But this is nothing more than a guess, seeing as how we haven't yet fully explained the mechanism that produces cancer. There's no denying that people in these areas live on a simple diet consisting mainly of vegetables and grains, but data suggests that their consumption of tobacco and alcohol may even be higher than other areas. At the very least, we aren't able to say that their exposure to carcinogens is lower than normal.

"All of this makes me wonder. Why is it that these longevity zones have so few people suffering from cancer? And then . . . Listen to this. Cancer cells have the ability to make normal cells immortal. Is that somehow related? And how are we to account for the fact that these longevity zones match up perfectly with areas of unusually low gravity?

"There's got to be a satisfying explanation, but I haven't been able to come up with it yet."

Kaoru paused for breath. His excitement had risen to a peculiar pitch as he talked.

Reiko was silent for a time, looking at Kaoru. Then she licked her lips and spoke.

"This MHC virus that's suddenly everywhere—where did it come from?"

Her question struck Kaoru as beside the point. "Why ask me?"

Reiko's eyes were open wide and her expression

was serious: she evidently really wanted an answer. At that moment Kaoru found her unbearably adorable. He forgot all about the fact that she was ten years older than he; he wanted to place his hands gently on her cheeks and draw her to him.

"Don't laugh. It's just that I wondered, for a second, if the MHC virus might just possibly have come from one of these longevity zones of yours."

Kaoru could guess at her train of thought. He'd read a novel once about someone whose entire body had been overrun by cancer; only, instead of dying, the cancer had made him immortal.

Maybe people in those areas have learned to coexist with cancer, and that's why they live so long. Most likely Reiko's imagination had moved along those lines. *Maybe it's not that those areas are free of cancer. Maybe they're full of it, in fact. Maybe it's just that nobody dies from it. Maybe the cancer virus started there . . .*

"Maybe a virus somehow picked up these people's cancer chromosome and the result escaped into the world as the Metastatic Human Cancer Virus. Is that what you're saying?"

"It's all much too difficult for me to understand, I'm sure. It was just a thought. Forget about it."

Reiko turned her gaze to the world below. Over the last few minutes the sky had changed color dramatically, and that change was reflected even more vividly in Reiko's expression. Deep shadows pooled in the hollows of her eye sockets. The darker it got outside, the more the window began to function as a mirror. Against the backdrop of skyscrapers Kaoru saw Reiko's face reflected in the glass as if it was floating disembodied in the darkness.

"Metastatic cancer victims are especially numerous in Japan and America."

It was true: the geographical distribution of the victims showed marked variation. Japan and America each had roughly a million patients with the disease, and the advanced nations of Europe had several hundred thousand, while remote areas of the type where the longevity zones were located had hardly reported any cases at all. Kaoru was trying to imply that her hypothesis had holes.

"What about the desert area you mentioned, in North America? It has abnormally low gravity, so it wouldn't be surprising if people there lived longer, would it?"

"It's just a guess."

"So you have no proof."

"I suppose you could say all this has just been a game for me."

The word seemed to come as a shock to Reiko: she became visibly discouraged. "Oh." Now her discouragement turned into a frown; she made as if to turn away from Kaoru.

"What's wrong?"

Kaoru was a bit taken aback by this sudden change in her.

"I was hoping for a miracle. It's all we have left," she said, still looking away.

A miracle, Kaoru thought in disgust. Reiko was about to fall into the same trap as his mother.

"I think you'd better stop hoping for a miracle."

"I won't stop."

"You have other things you need to be doing."

He wanted Reiko to keep her wits about her. But she wasn't listening to him now.

"I was just thinking, maybe all the inhabitants of those longevity zones get viral cancer at some point. But before the cancer cells incapacitate their internal organs, some factor turns their cells immortal, and the cancer becomes benign. Its bad side disappears, and the cancer is able to coexist with human beings. Their cells are able to undergo mitosis more times, with the result that they live longer. How's that for a theory?"

He'd never seen Reiko go on like this before. She wasn't making reason the arbiter of truth and falsehood anymore: she was judging subjectively, based on how much hope the result would allow her. You could find two or three pieces of evidence to support any hypothesis if you allowed your judgment to be swayed by your desire for a particular result, Kaoru knew. This wasn't going to help her son. He understood the desire to cling to a god. But how was he to deal with her clinging to what she knew was nothing more than idle speculation? It might make for good fiction, but Kaoru didn't have time to take such fancies seriously if he wanted to make it as a doctor.

For her part, Reiko was prepared to believe in her imagined world with all her might. Kaoru knew he'd sown the seeds for this. He wished he'd never mentioned any of it.

"Please, just forget everything I told you."

"No way. I can't. That place you were trying to get to has something, some factor that can eliminate cancer's negative properties, that can change it from something malignant to something benign."

Kaoru held up his hands as if to calm her down, but to no avail. She was more enthused than he'd ever seen her.

"I think you need to go there after all—you need to get your hands on whatever it is that can turn death into life."

"Now hold on a minute."

Her face was close to his now, and she'd grabbed hold of his hand.

"Please!" The soft touch of her hand reinforced the message.

"I'm tired of living like this. Ryoji's going to start his fourth round of chemotherapy soon."

"I'm sure that's tough on you."

"I'd go with you if I could."

In that moment, what had started out as a

family trip suddenly turned into something different. Imagining a journey to the North American desert alone with Reiko made Kaoru feel hot inside. That low-gravity point at the Four Corners area—it felt like a deep crevice, a vortex, sucking everything in. He was being pulled in by low gravity . . . No, at this moment Kaoru was being pulled in by this pair of eyes right in front of him.

She wore no makeup except for a very little lipstick, and she gave off a perfume that seemed to be the natural scent of her skin. Kaoru and Reiko were enveloped in the shadows where the fluorescent lights of the hallway were blocked by a large pillar. The window was now a perfect mirror, reflecting the occasional passerby in the corridor.

Before he knew what was happening, Kaoru was returning her grip on his hands. Hand toyed with hand, fingers intertwined with fingers, and eyes checked each other's intentions.

The last sound of footsteps disappeared from the hallway, and as if they'd been gauging the moment when silence would grace them, they drew each other close in an embrace. They seized the moment when the seventeenth-floor corridor was empty.

Arms encircled backs in embrace, body communicated to body the pulsating of blood vessels. The individual rhythms of their blood synchronized, cells were stimulated through thin cloth layers. Kaoru became erect, his swelling pressing against Reiko's midriff.

Kaoru needed her lips, so he pulled his head back and tried to turn her face up towards his; Reiko didn't respond, but only dug her fingers deeper into his back. She pressed her forehead into his jaw and forced his head sideways—she seemed to be actively rejecting his kiss. After several tries and several rebuffs, Kaoru finally understood.

She's infected too.

The MHC virus was known to have been transmitted via saliva. Reiko must be rejecting him out of fear for his safety. He began to understand her unexplained course of action that evening. Earlier, when Ryoji had said, "I never wanted to be born in the first place," she'd left the room without a word. Maybe Ryoji had been infected while still in his mother's womb. He'd finally let these recriminating words escape, and she'd found she couldn't bear to remain.

However, the fear of infection did nothing to cool Kaoru's ardor. He gently parted his body from hers, cradled her cheeks in his hands, pleaded to her with his eyes that he'd understood the situation, and then placed his lips on hers in a way that brooked no refusal.

This time, Reiko didn't even try to reject him. He placed one hand on the back of her neck, the other on her bottom, and pulled her toward him. Such was the force of their coming together that their teeth collided softly, with a lascivious sound composed equally of the softness of lips, the hardness of teeth, and saliva.

They pressed their mouths together until they'd sucked out all their breath and could no longer sustain the intensity. Then their lips parted and they touched cheek to cheek, listening to each other's tortuous gasps. Reiko stretched up to her full height so she could bring her lips close to Kaoru's ear.

"Please," she said, between ragged breaths.

He couldn't tell if the vibrations at his ear were gasps or sobs.

Reiko wanted to save not only her son, but herself.

"Please . . . help."

"I'm not God."

It was all Kaoru could do to say that much. The only thing he understood clearly at this moment, with his organ engorged with blood and his mind not behaving rationally, was that he had taken his own first steps into Death's territory. He felt no confusion, no regret over having obeyed his body's commands and held Reiko and kissed her. He felt that no matter how many chances he had to live this moment over, he would always make the same choices. Reiko's body emanated a power that could not be opposed.

"Please. I know you'll go there."

Now even Reiko was spurring him on to visit the low-gravity zone. The fiction whose seed he himself had planted, to which Reiko had given form, was now taking root within Kaoru.

8

As Kaoru entered his father's hospital room, he found Professor Saiki just getting up from the chair by his father's bed.

"Hey," Saiki said on seeing Kaoru. He raised a hand and made as if to leave the room.

"That's alright, stay a while." If he was leaving because he felt bad about disrupting Kaoru's visit with his father, then Kaoru felt a duty to press him to stay.

"I can't. As you know, I'm quite busy." And it didn't seem like mere politeness: Saiki was twitching as if he did indeed have pressing business.

"Oh. Well, then."

"That's right. I just popped in by special request," Saiki said, glancing at Hideyuki. Then he raised his hand again, said, "Later, then," and left. Kaoru watched him walk away, then went to his father's side.

"How are you feeling, Dad?"

Kaoru gazed down at his father for a moment, studying his color and the set of his jaw, before taking Saiki's place in the chair.

"Annoyed," Hideyuki said in a monotone, eyes raised to the ceiling.

"What happened?"

"Saiki. He brings nothing but bad news."

Saiki was an old classmate from med school, but as he'd elected to go into research rather than clinical medicine, he wasn't directly involved in Hideyuki's case. Which made Kaoru wonder all the more what sort of bad news he could have been bringing.

"What do you mean?"

"Do you know Masato Nakamura?"

Hideyuki's voice was hoarse.

"One of your friends, right?"

Kaoru recognized the name Nakamura. He'd been a coworker of Hideyuki's on the Loop project; Kaoru believed he was currently a professor in the engineering department of a provincial university.

"He's dead," said Hideyuki, curtly.

"Really?"

"He had the same illness as me."

Kaoru had heard people say that when someone your own age dies it invariably comes as a shock, making you feel it might be your turn next.

"You're still alright, Dad."

Kaoru couldn't think of anything to say that

didn't sound commonplace. Hideyuki slowly shook his head where he lay, as if to say that meaningless words of encouragement wouldn't do him any good.

"Do you know Komatsuzaki?"

"No." Kaoru had never heard this name.

"He joined the Loop project after me."

"Oh?"

"He's dead, too."

Kaoru swallowed hard. Death's shadow was creeping ever closer to his father.

Hideyuki proceeded to list three more names, summing up with a simple "They're all dead."

"Doesn't it make you wonder what's going on?" he continued. "All those names I mentioned belonged to people I worked with on the artificial life project, or who were at least connected with it in some way."

"And all of them died from MHC?"

"How many people in Japan have been infected with this virus?"

"About a million, maybe?" That included people like Reiko and Kaoru's mother who had been infected but hadn't yet gotten sick.

"That's a whole lot, but it's still no more than one percent of the population. Whereas, me, I don't know anybody who's not infected."

Hideyuki cast a sharp glance at Kaoru; at first he seemed to be searching Kaoru's soul, but then his expression relaxed into one of prayer.

"You're okay, right?"

Hideyuki brought a hand out from under his sheet and touched Kaoru's knee through his jeans. No doubt he wanted to hold his son's hand, but was afraid of skin-on-skin contact. With his wife already infected, all it would take to rob Hideyuki of the will to fight the cancer would be knowing that Kaoru had contracted the virus too.

Kaoru averted his eyes from his father's weakening gaze.

"Were there any problems with the test results?"

Kaoru felt like his father could look right through him, but he forced himself to speak through his fear. "I told you there's nothing to worry about." True, two months ago his test results had been negative, but there was no telling what next month's test would reveal.

Kaoru turned away, pretending to be reacting to the sound of footsteps in the corridor. He flashed back to the scene in Ryoji's room yesterday afternoon; the mental images brought with them stirrings of the blood and of the flesh, resurrecting the sensory fluctuations that had rocked his body.

The evening before last, he'd been forced to limit his contact with Reiko to kissing. They'd been in a hallway, and they'd only been vouchsafed a few minutes. Considering they were in a hospital, it was about as much as they had any right to hope for.

The next afternoon—yesterday—he'd gone back to Ryoji's sickroom to retrieve the pathology textbook he'd left there, and he arrived just after Ryoji had been taken off to Radiology for some tests. Kaoru hadn't known it was time for his tests; Reiko hadn't told him. But to all appearances it looked as if he'd timed his visit to coincide with the boy's absence.

He knocked softly, and immediately Reiko opened the door, but just a crack. Her face was wet and she was holding a towel—she must have been washing her face when he knocked. There was a sink next to the door, and the ten-watt fluorescent bulb above it was lit. She'd been taking off her makeup there, rather than in the bathroom.

Patting her face with the towel, she spoke in a quiet, controlled voice.

"You forgot something yesterday."

"Sorry, I should have called first." Kaoru lowered his voice in response. There was no sign of Ryoji.

"Come in."

She took his hand and guided him into the room, then shut the door. They stood in front of the sink, in front of the mirror, facing each other. She finished wiping her face. She was letting Kaoru see her features unadorned by cosmetics.

There were crows' feet around her eyes, appropriate to her age, but they only made her look more attractive to him.

A partition stood between them and Ryoji's empty bed; Kaoru nodded toward it, as if to ask why he wasn't in it.

"The nurse just took him away."

"Tests?"

"Yes."

"What kind?"

"A scintigram," she said in a shaky tone that suggested she was unfamiliar with the word.

A scintigram, a precursor to chemotherapy, took two hours at a minimum, since it involved injecting a contrast medium into the subject's veins. Nobody would be coming in until the test was finished. For that brief interval, Reiko and Kaoru had been left with a private room all to themselves.

With Ryoji's test regimen reaching this point, Reiko found herself face to face with the prospect of her son entering chemotherapy. She was dejected. A bitter battle was beginning. Anticancer drugs harm normal cells in the process of attacking cancer cells. She knew she'd have to watch her son suffer from lethargy, loss of appetite, nausea, and the prospect hurt her more than anything, especially as she knew that his enduring this suffering wouldn't guarantee the extinction of his cancer cells. All it would do would be to slow their rate of reproduction, and thereby delay the final moments. This cancer was destined to metastasize, and there was no way to prevent it.

Kaoru didn't know what to say to this mother whose son had been taken away from her. Platitudes would only make it worse.

But Reiko looked him in the eye and said, "The miracle will come if we wait for it."

She enfolded Kaoru's hands in hers; it seemed to be a habit of hers.

"I just don't know."

"I'm sick and tired of living like this."

"Me, too."

"Well, do something! Please! Help us! I know you can."

Like I can do anything! Kaoru felt like screaming, but managed to keep himself from saying anything.

Reiko's bangs were still wet and several strands clung to her forehead. Beneath them her eyes were moist and pleading. Her mouth quivered as if she might break out into sobs at any moment; Kaoru's heart went out to her. If only he could help. He wanted to, badly. He couldn't stand by helplessly and watch this magnificent body laid low.

The faucet next to them hadn't been shut off all the way—a little trickle of water came out of it. The sound filled the room and stimulated his desire. The noise of the water itself was what urged him into action.

Reiko looked at the faucet, and tried to free one hand to turn it off. But Kaoru only gripped her hand tighter, pulling her toward him with great force.

At first she made as if to resist, a complex series of emotions clouding her features. Conflicting feelings raged within her—Kaoru knew this by the touch of her skin. Her obligations as a mother, and her desires as a woman.

Still holding her to him, he shifted positions and tried to lay her down on the bed. But she resisted slightly, so that she ended up sitting on the floor with her back pushed up against the edge of the bed.

Pinned against a sickbed missing its owner, hunched over with death a burden on her shoulders, Reiko tried to confront the sexual impulses pressing in on her. The specter of death was assaulting her from everywhere, except the direction from which lust came, boiling up as if to prove that she was still alive. Then she thought of how her son at this very moment was undergoing cruel tests, and the knowledge enervated her desire. Her maternal instincts began to crowd out her sexual needs.

But not Kaoru. He was beyond reining in now, as his mind and body came together in pursuit of a single goal.

He didn't care that Reiko was infected with MHC. He was aware of the data showing that the virus spread even more easily through genital contact than oral, but for the moment that knowledge was clean gone from him.

He sat down next to her, intertwined with her, on the floor of the sickroom. He placed his mouth over hers, nimbly undid the buttons of her blouse. These bold, playboyish actions surprised even him: he was relatively inexperienced at romance.

While Kaoru basked in his memories of the previous afternoon, Hideyuki obstinately hammered away on the dangers of exposing oneself to the virus.

. . . *Your blood test came back negative? . . . I was your age once—you've got to be careful with women . . . You can't let yourself get careless . . . Don't give in to momentary temptation . . .*

The words went right over Kaoru's head. He couldn't look his father in the eye. The pure, simple act of loving a woman had become a betrayal of his father's expectations.

"Hey, kiddo! Are you listening to me?"

Hideyuki threw a monkey wrench into the workings of Kaoru's reverie. It had been ages since he'd called Kaoru "kiddo". Kaoru gradually let himself be pulled back to the present moment.

"Don't worry, I said."

Hideyuki still showed no signs of softening his suspicious gaze.

They stared at each other in silence for a while.

They exchanged more information that way than they'd been able to communicate in words. Then Hideyuki reached out and touched Kaoru's knee once more.

"Don't you get it? You're my greatest treasure."

Kaoru placed his hand over his father's.

"I know, Dad."

"I don't want you giving in to this. You've got to fight it. You've got to concentrate all your intelligence on confronting this enemy that wants to destroy your body, your youth."

Reiko was imploring him to *help*; his father was ordering him to *fight*. He felt pressure from both sides. But if he had been infected with MHC, if he was at risk of developing metastatic cancer, then those imperatives would cease to be things external to him. He'd have to rouse himself to action in order to protect his own body.

Hideyuki returned to his previous topic. "When Saiki was here he was telling me how all my old colleagues were succumbing to this disease, one after the other, and it struck me. I know a lot of cancer victims."

"I guess so," Kaoru grunted. He, too, knew a lot of carriers of the MHC virus.

"Maybe there's a reason."

"Like, maybe researchers are particularly susceptible?"

"This should be right up your alley. You're the one who ferreted out those longevity zones from the gravitational anomaly map. Listen to me. I want you to make a distribution map of people with MHC in Japan and America. Or a breakdown of infected people by occupation. Anyway, just gather all the data you can and come up with some statistics."

"Okay. I'll give it a try."

"I've got a feeling about this. I don't think it's a coincidence that we have so much sickness around us."

Still looking up at the ceiling, Hideyuki stretched his hand out to the sideboard and groped around as if searching for something. Kaoru noticed a stack of printed matter there, dozens of pages. He picked them up first and showed them to his father. "Is this what you're looking for?"

The first page contained the following sequence of letters:

<pre>
        10   20
AATGCTACTACTATTAGTAGAATTGATGC

30   40   50
CACCTTTTCAGCTCGCGCCCCA   .   .   .
</pre>

Kaoru recognized it at a glance: it was a chromosomal base sequence.

"Saiki left those."

"What chromosomes was he analyzing?"

"This, of course," Hideyuki said, tapping his

own chest. Now that the daily wash of tests was suggesting that the cancer had spread to his lungs, all he had to do to indicate the cancer virus was to point, with contempt, at his chest.

This is the complete base sequence of the Metastatic Human Cancer Virus.

Moved, Kaoru looked at the sequence of letters again. The dozens of pages he held in his hands contained the base sequences for nine genes; they held thousands, even tens of millions of letters; they held the blueprint for the virus that bedeviled them.

9

First off, Kaoru decided to visit the lab that maintained the massive memory banks of the Loop. The history of the imaginary universe known as the Loop was stored in 620 terabytes of holographic memory; even now, twenty years later, it was safe and sound.

To get to the lab, it was faster to take the New Line than the old subway system. Kaoru left the university hospital and headed for the station.

He only walked for a few minutes, but by the time he boarded, his T-shirt was wet with perspiration. It being early afternoon, there were few passengers. As a result, the air conditioning cooled the air a little too efficiently for Kaoru. In no time, his T-shirt felt clammy and cold against his skin.

He had a seat and took from his briefcase the stack of printouts he'd just gotten from his father, containing the entire base sequence of the MHC virus. The sequence consisted of the letters A, T, G, and C, representing the different varieties of nucleotides. He could, he knew, stare at it forever and it still wouldn't get him anywhere in particular. But he had nothing to do. If he'd had a paperback he'd be idly flipping through it right about now, but as it happened his briefcase contained nothing else to pass the time with.

A gene is essentially a unit of information, and the MHC virus had a mere nine of them. By way of comparison, a human being has something like 300,000 genes—so the virus's total was fairly small.

Each gene can be represented by a sequence of a few thousand to a few hundred thousand bases; three bases form one amino acid. So, for example, a string of three thousand letters (ATGC . . . and so on) means that a thousand amino acids have all joined hands to create a protein.

Kaoru scrutinized page after page, and when his eyes got tired he lifted his head and gazed out the window at the scenery. The print was so small that trying to focus on it through the jostling of the train was making him queasy. Above each row of letters was a series of numbers in multiples of ten, allowing the viewer to tell at a glance what number in the sequence each letter was.

By scanning these numbers it was an easy matter to figure out how many bases constituted each of the nine genes. They ranged from a few thousand to hundreds of thousands. In order, they were:

Gene #1: 3072 bases
Gene #2: 393,216 bases
Gene #3: 12,288 bases
Gene #4: 786,432 bases
Gene #5: 24,576 bases
Gene #6: 49,152 bases
Gene #7: 196,608 bases
Gene #8: 6144 bases
Gene #9: 98,304 bases

Kaoru stood up and moved over to the door. The breeze from the air conditioner had been hitting him on the left side of his body. He especially disliked this kind of unnatural chill; if the cost of sitting was freezing, he'd just as soon stand.

As he leaned against the door he idly pictured Reiko's face. But visions of his father's attenuated features kept coming to mind.

The research center where he was headed was a partial leftover of the place where his father had once worked. Kaoru knew that twenty-five years ago, upon finishing his doctorate, his father had been invited to join the Loop project, and that his father had devoted the next five years to researching artificial life. He didn't, however, know the specifics of what his father had been researching. It had all been before Kaoru was born.

Every time he tried to ask, his father became close-mouthed. But the project hadn't ended well: that much Kaoru had been able to guess. Hideyuki was the type to jump up and down and celebrate when his work was successful, but he'd clamp his mouth shut tight in the wake of failure. Once Kaoru recognized the signs, he realized it wouldn't do to keep rooting around.

But this time—maybe it was his age, or maybe his illness had softened him—when Kaoru had made to leave his father's sickroom with the sheaf of papers in his hand, Hideyuki had stopped him with a word.

"Kiddo."

Then his father, on his own initiative, had brought up the topic of his research some two decades before.

"My area was to come up with a computer simulation of the emergence of life."

His explanation was simple: for years it had been his dream to elucidate how life had first appeared on earth. But, as Kaoru had guessed, the experiment had come to an unforeseen conclusion, and it had been put on ice. His father didn't use the word "failed". As far as he was concerned, the experiment as an experiment could be considered a resounding success. But he still couldn't figure out why it had come out the way it had.

"The Loop . . . well, you might say it turned cancerous."

By which he meant that all the patterns in the program had been assimilated into one set pattern: all diversity vanished, and the program ground to a halt.

To Kaoru it sounded like his father was rambling. He didn't know what to make of all this. And it was no wonder: he knew nothing about the project's methodology, and he couldn't see it as a whole.

But he did have a desire, first of all, to understand what it was his dad had been working on. And, second, he wanted to find out whether or not it was a coincidence that most of his father's colleagues from the lab had died from the MHC virus.

So it had been Kaoru's idea to visit the research center. His father had given him the name of a surviving colleague and done what he could to ensure that the visit went smoothly.

Word from his father would doubtless have reached somebody at the research center by now. Kaoru had every expectation that he'd be received courteously.

He glanced down at the paper again.

There was something about the total number of bases in each gene that was tugging at him.

The top page held nine numbers, ranging from four to six digits, each number representing the bases in one gene.

3072
393,216
12,288
786,432
24,576
49,152
196,608
6144
98,304

Kaoru had a special ability when it came to numbers; it was this ability that was sending up a red flag now. But he couldn't put his finger on exactly why. He felt like there was something these numbers had in common. Yes, he was sure of it. His intuition on that point was strong.

To clear his mind he gazed at the scenery outside the window. On both sides of the tracks tall buildings clustered; the streamlined train threaded its way between them silently.

The train slowed down as it approached a platform. He saw a building under construction, and beyond it another painted in bright primary colors.

The station was in a cluster of four skyscrapers, each a thousand feet tall, organically connected into a single city-within-a-city. It had an English name; everybody knew it.

The Square Building.

"Square." He knew what it meant: a quadrilateral with each side the same length. But it had another meaning, as well.

Kaoru looked down again at the printout, concentrating on the nine numbers.

"It couldn't be," he murmured. He recalled that the English word "square" also referred to the process of multiplying a number by itself. And with that, it came to him.

$$
\begin{array}{rcl}
3072 & = & 2^{10} \times 3 \\
393{,}216 & = & 2^{17} \times 3 \\
12{,}288 & = & 2^{12} \times 3 \\
786{,}432 & = & 2^{18} \times 3 \\
24{,}576 & = & 2^{13} \times 3 \\
49{,}152 & = & 2^{14} \times 3 \\
196{,}608 & = & 2^{16} \times 3 \\
6144 & = & 2^{11} \times 3 \\
98{,}304 & = & 2^{15} \times 3 \\
\end{array}
$$

It was astonishing: each number equaled two to the power of n times three.

Kaoru made some quick mental calculations as to the probability of nine random four to six digit numbers all turning out to equal $2^n \times 3$. There were only eighteen such numbers in all the possible figures up to six digits.

Kaoru didn't need to come up with the exact probability, though: it was breathtakingly close to zero.

Why do this virus's gene sequences come out to $2^n \times 3$?

The chances of it happening were basically zero, and yet it had happened. These nine numbers had surmounted that wall of improbability. It couldn't be a coincidence. He had to proceed under the assumption that it meant something.

He could remember coming to the same conclusion during that debate with his father ten years ago. That time the topic had been the emergence of life. Oh, and superstitions, jinxes . . . It was best to think that behind every amazing coincidence was some entity pulling strings.

An announcement came on to say that the train had reached Kaoru's station. The voice sounded to Kaoru like it was coming from far, far away.

Kaoru was expelled from the train doors onto the platform. If his father was to be believed, it was only a ten minutes' walk from the station to the research center.

Kaoru wandered the hot platform, looking like an apparition. The sudden transition from the chilled train interior to the oppressive heat outside had left him tired.

He placed the stack of papers back into his briefcase and followed his father's directions to the research center.

10

The center was indeed not far from the station, but the road was hilly, and by the time Kaoru arrived he was drenched in sweat again. He stood in front of an old-fashioned building behind an embassy and compared the address to what he'd written down. No mistake. The fourth and fifth floors of this building held the laboratory maintaining the Loop data.

Kaoru took the elevator to the fourth floor, where he asked the receptionist to page a Mr Amano. This was the name Hideyuki had given him.

When you get to the lab, have them page a guy named Amano. I'll let him know you're coming.

Hideyuki had stressed this step a number of times.

The woman at the desk picked up her intercom receiver. "There's a Mr Kaoru Futami to see you, sir." Then she smiled at Kaoru and indicated a couch in the hall. "He'll be with you in a few moments."

Kaoru had a seat and waited for Amano to show up. While he waited he surveyed the place, taking in the fact that this was where his father had worked before Kaoru was born. Had he walked past this very reception desk every morning on his way to his lab?

"Sorry to keep you waiting."

The voice came from a completely unexpected direction. Kaoru had been expecting Amano to appear from the main section of the floor, behind the receptionist, but instead he approached Kaoru from the elevator landing. Kaoru stood and bowed slightly.

"Pleased to meet you. I'm Kaoru Futami. My father's always saying how much in your debt he is."

"Not at all, not at all. I'm in his debt, actually."

Amano took a business card from his card case and handed it to Kaoru. As a mere medical student, Kaoru of course didn't carry business cards, so he had to take Amano's without offering one in return.

Beneath the name of the research center was the man's title, Professor of Medicine, and his name: Toru Amano.

Kaoru was puzzled to find a medical professor in what seemed to be a computer research center. But come to think of it, his own father had a medical background. Perhaps it wasn't so surprising after all.

"What's your specialty, if I might ask?"

Amano smiled, showing the dimples in his cheeks. "Microbiology."

He was a small, slender man. He'd been junior to Kaoru's father by two years, so he had to be in his late forties, but he certainly didn't look that old. He could easily have passed for mid-thirties.

"Well, I know you must be busy, so . . . "

"It's nothing. Why don't I show you around?"

Amano guided Kaoru to the elevator and pushed the UP button.

The upper floor had a similar reception area; Amano led Kaoru past it without stopping.

He brought him to a large private room. Two walls were filled entirely with books, and several computers sat on the desk.

Amano sank into his chair, motioning Kaoru toward the chair for guests.

"I'm told you'd like a detailed explanation of Dr Hideyuki Futami's research."

"That's correct."

"How is he, by the way? How's his health holding up?" It didn't appear that Amano was just asking to be polite: he seemed sincerely worried. If it was proven that the cancer had spread to Hideyuki's lungs, the situation would be essentially hopeless, but Kaoru glossed over that.

"About as well as can be expected."

"He taught me quite a lot, you know." Amano got a look of nostalgia on his face and continued. "Things have changed these last few years. It's gotten . . . quiet."

Kaoru assumed he meant the research center. Now that he thought about it, he hadn't seen anybody here besides the receptionist and Amano. He suspected the reason had something to do with the virus.

"My father told me that many of you who participated in the Loop research have died of cancer."

"Very many indeed."

"Is there a specific reason?"

"Well, I don't believe there's been any statement to that effect."

Kaoru couldn't believe it was a mere coincidence, though, and if some kind of cause-and-effect relationship could be established, it would be epochal. It might lead to the discovery of a new way of treating viral cancer.

"Do you know where the first victim was discovered?" As a microbiologist, Amano should know a lot about that sort of thing.

"It's been hard to get exact data, because it's hard to distinguish it from previous varieties of cancer, but the MHC virus was first discovered in an American patient."

Kaoru had heard rumors to that effect, that America had been the birthplace of the disease.

"Where in America?"

"The victim was a computer technician living in Albuquerque, New Mexico."

Amano frowned, as if he'd just noticed the curious commonality. The MHC virus had been first discovered in the body of a computer technician. The infection rate among researchers at this facility, a computer-research center, was much higher than average. Of course, it wasn't totally beyond the realm of coincidence, but . . .

Amano's frown only lasted an instant. The coincidence struck him, but he immediately decided it wasn't worth assigning a special explanation to, and so he erased the frown.

And then he stood up quickly, as if in confirmation of what Kaoru guessed to be his thought process.

"Oh, yes. There's an old, old videotape you might like to take a look at."

"A videotape?" Kaoru felt himself tense up; he didn't know why.

"It's something Futami-sensei's staff put together. A sort of introduction to their research aims and methods. Part of their job was to elicit budgetary contributions from various sources. The video was just a promotional tool, but it's the best and quickest explanation of the purpose behind the Loop."

Amano went through the door first, urging Kaoru to follow. "This way, please."

The hallway snaked through several turns as it led through the complex of laboratories. Finally, Amano showed Kaoru into what looked like a reception room. It had a table and sofas.

There were no windows; the room had to be in the middle of the building. The furnishings put Kaoru in mind of an art gallery—framed pictures adorned the walls.

What was strange was that there was exactly one picture on each wall, at exactly the same height, at exactly the same distance from the corners, in exactly the same size frame—as if they were icons hung to keep away evil spirits or something. Each frame contained a modernist painting incorporating photography.

Kaoru's eyes were riveted to the pictures. They seemed to have captured in photographs some rectangular piece of modern art from four sides and then distorted it; as he looked around the room he got the feeling that he was inside some kind of angular construction. Modern art *objets* usually gave a cold, hard impression. And what about the aesthetic sense that had placed, not the object itself, but pictures of it at the same point on all four walls? It was as if the fact that they were pictures was emphasizing a certain obsessiveness.

Kaoru looked closely at one of the pictures to see if he could make out the name of the artist. There was a signature, a foreign name, but it was hard to make out. A "C . . . " and an "Eliot . . ."

"Please. Have a seat."

At the sound of Amano's voice behind him, Kaoru remembered where he was. He sat on the couch to which Amano was pointing, and noticed a 32-inch television facing him. Amano must have pulled it out of the cabinet while he wasn't looking.

Amano opened another cabinet and took out a videotape. The tape had a label on its spine, and the label had a title written on it in large characters.

LOOP

There was no way he could miss it.

11

The video began by explaining the concept of artificial life. The program was aimed at a general audience, and its makers had assumed they needed to nail down the basics first.

Amano glanced at Kaoru and laughed. "Shall we skip this part?"

He felt it was safe to assume that any son of Hideyuki Futami would have a precise grasp of what artificial life was. Kaoru nodded, and Amano fast-forwarded.

The screen displayed a succession of geometrical patterns, appearing, changing, flickering, and disappearing.

Artificial life did not mean a biotech lab with people cutting and pasting DNA to create man-made monsters. Nor did it involve cloning technology. It was a computer simulation: man-made life forms appearing and disappearing on computer monitors.

It was fair to say that the idea behind artificial
life had come from the Life Game, a computer
game in general circulation toward the end of the
last century.

In its earliest forms, it was rather like playing
on a chess board. The computer screen was
filled with intersecting lines in two dimensions,
like a chess board, only with a far greater
number of squares. Each square was known as
a cell. A cell could be either alive or dead: a
"living" cell was black, while a "dead" cell had
no color. A glance at the board showed only
the "living" cells, colored black. Each cell
bordered eight other cells on the top, bottom,
left, right, top right, bottom right, top left, and
bottom left. Rules were determined for the cells.
For example, it might be decided for a "living"
cell that if it bordered on two or three "living"
cells, and neither more nor less, it would
survive to the next generation; if it bordered
on no "living" cells, only one, or four or more,
it would "die".

At the beginning of play, living and dead cells
were randomly determined, and play proceeded
from one generation to the next, time advancing
digitally, with cells living or dying in each generation. If a cell had two or three cells adjacent to
it, it would be sustained by these neighbors and
live on, while if it had one or no cells nearby, it
would die of loneliness, and likewise, if it had

four or more neighbors, it would die of over-crowding.

Since the living cells were represented by black squares, with each passing generation the mono-chromatic pattern on the display changed.

The principle behind the game was quite simple, but in actual play a wide variety of patterns was possible, with highly suggestive results. One pattern found squares spreading slantwise after a certain number of generations. Another pattern saw what looked like repeated tremors. Some patterns were stable, with no change at all. Some patterns negotiated with each other, changing shape on the board like living beings. These changes continued until all the cells had died out, or the patterns all became fixed, with no further movement.

As they developed the concept of the Life Game, researchers started to detect what seemed like signs of life within their computers. The first element of the definition of life is that it can reproduce itself. As soon as self-propagating patterns were discovered in the Life Game, researchers from many disciplines began to lend their expertise, in the hopes that keys to the beginning and evolution of life on earth might there be found.

It was this chain of events which led to Hideyuki Futami, with his background in medi-cine, to work with computers on the artificial life project. No doubt Amano the microbiologist had similar reasons for joining the center. Science had progressed to a point where it could go no further without breaking down the walls between disciplines and enabling a more dynamic exchange of ideas.

Amano stopped fast-forwarding at an appropriate place and pressed *PLAY*.

"There. Now it gets into the aims of the Loop research."

Hideyuki's face was onscreen now. Kaoru felt a tightening in his chest as he saw his father's youthful countenance—this had been filmed not long after his marriage. His hair was still thick, his whole being suffused with passion and confidence. The firmness of his muscles was evident even through his clothing.

Come to think of it, this was the first time Kaoru had seen video of his father from before Kaoru's birth. He hadn't been expecting it—it was surprise as much as anything that shook him.

The image changed to a vast desert in America, to a superconducting super accelerator some thirty miles in diameter, part of a project long since abandoned. Aerial shots showed the exterior, and then the scene cut to the interior. The huge ring-shaped research facility, once a useless hulk, was now filled, the video revealed, with a huge number of massively parallel supercomputers. The numbers were incredible. Six hundred and forty thousand computers buried beneath the desert sand: a truly overwhelming sight.

Then the scene made another abrupt shift, this time to the skyscrapers of Tokyo. The camera went underground again, into a maze of abandoned subway tunnels branching out like a spider's web. Here, too, were installed 640,000 massively parallel supercomputers. Underground, where the humidity was low and the temperature was relatively constant year-round, was the ideal place for the computers.

This joint Japanese-American collection of massively parallel supercomputers—a staggering 1.28 million in all—was there to sustain the Loop.

Hideyuki reappeared onscreen. Having shown off the hardware that drove the Loop, it was time to explain the software.

Hideyuki pointed to a computer screen and narrated in precise, well-chosen words while the process of cellular division was demonstrated through symbols. The Hideyuki Kaoru knew was inclined to speak quickly and animatedly, but the Hideyuki on the video averted his eyes from the camera and spoke somewhat shyly, although not without confidence.

Kaoru already understood what Hideyuki was explaining now. Although it had been research in progress then, from a standpoint twenty years on, it was fairly easy to comprehend. But what was their methodology? These were the first detailed images Kaoru had seen of the project, and his interest was captured.

The monitor Hideyuki was pointing at showed the development of the cell of some organism, and next to it the same process recreated artificially and represented symbolically. A natural cell and a man-made one, side by side. Over time, they both took roughly the same shape. The process by which the real organism formed was translated into symbols and manifested in the computer simulation. Upon the incorporation of various algorithms, the shape of an organism appeared on the monitor.

The idea behind the Loop project, a joint Japan-U.S. undertaking, had been to create life within the virtual space of the computers, pass on DNA from generation to generation, and incorporate the mechanisms of mutation, parasitism, and immunity, thereby to create an original biosphere to simulate the evolution of life on earth. In short, to create another world exactly like the real one, on computers.

At this point, Amano paused the videotape and turned to Kaoru.

"Do you have any questions thus far?"

"Well," Kaoru spoke up. "What field, exactly, was this research supposed to be useful to?" This had been nagging at him for some time. Where did the funding come from? What kind of practical application would this research have had?

Judging by what he'd seen, the budget was probably big enough to require government support. Solving the riddles of life on earth, the mechanism of evolution, would be sure to satisfy academic curiosity, but he doubted it'd make money for anybody.

"We were taking the long view. We knew that at first it would be of only limited use. But once we opened up the field, there was no telling what kind of developments would pop up later. The number of possible applications was literally infinite. Fields like medicine and physiology for starters, but also microbiology, physics, meteorology . . . And not just science: we expected it to have implications for everything from understanding movements in stock prices to figuring out social-science problems such as population increases."

Amano paused and laughed.

In fact, the fruits of the Loop research had proven useful on a wide variety of fronts. It became possible to know the point at which earth's environmental and ecological balance would be destroyed, allowing for the development of management strategies; there were epochal advances in the study of at what point in the brain's development consciousness appeared. The contribution to medicine was huge, as treatments for several serious illnesses came to light.

The rest of the video was spent mostly on methodology. Hideyuki used diagrams to explain how through the application of chaos theory, nonlinearity, L-systems, genetic algorithms, and the like, the program was able to learn and evolve.

As an example, fragmentary images of cellular division were interspersed into the narrative. A shot of a cell dividing and redividing until it grew into an organism pulsated its way across the screen as if on fast-forward. The network developed dynamically, rather like a cancer cell growing capillaries. Even though Kaoru knew it was a mechanical simulation, it looked remarkably alive.

Having concluded its explanation of the methodology and thus its introduction to the project, the video ended with an invitation to the viewer to follow the real-life progress of the experiment.

Kaoru found it a pretty convincing promo.

Creating a computer simulation of the beginning and evolution of life wasn't a particularly unusual thing: it had been done several times in several different places. What amazed Kaoru was the scale of this project: the minute level of detail, the innumerable parameters that had been fed into the program. He figured it had to be the first time anything like it had been attempted.

What the experiment did was to take the some four billion years since life had begun and compress them into an accessible digital time frame. Billions of years had been abbreviated on the computers into ten or so years of real time, while still perfectly recreating in the virtual space the complexity of the real world.

Kaoru was curious about the subsequent progress of the research.

"How far did the Loop go?" he asked Amano, who was rewinding the tape.

"Didn't Futami-sensei tell you?"

"He told me that the pattern turned cancerous, that's all."

Amano looked troubled. "Well, that's about the size of it."

"I'd like to know more about the sequence of events, though."

"I'm sure you realize that even if you had the time to look at it, your life would end long before you finished."

Kaoru sighed intentionally.

"Okay, why don't we move to a different room and talk over coffee? I'd like to hear more about your father's condition, actually."

Amano led Kaoru into a larger but drearier room that looked like it was used for meetings or training sessions. It contained steel desks and folding chairs, and instead of modern art the walls held a map of the world; all in all it was an unremarkable room, sort of like a school classroom in miniature.

They sat at a table facing each other, and from

nowhere appeared the receptionist to place cups of coffee in front of each of them.

It looked hot, at least: steam rose from the disposable cups. Amano wrapped both hands around his cup and brought it to his mouth. This room was windowless, too, and the air conditioning was turned up too high. Up to now Kaoru had been so wrapped up in what he was hearing that he'd been oblivious to the cold inside the center. As he watched Amano take advantage of the warmth of the coffee Kaoru finally noticed that his own arms had goose-bumps from the cold.

In between sips, Amano began to relate the history of the virtual world.

He spoke like an old man telling him story-book stories: relating the simulation in the form of a story was probably the most primal, direct way to go about it. In any case, it didn't strike Kaoru as inappropriate. Simulation it may have been, but it was also life, and it was natural for its history to contain storylike elements.

Perhaps that was why Kaoru was able to become comfortably absorbed in Amano's tale. It was fun to reexperience the history of the world. But only until just before the end.

12

" . . . But even after we implanted RNA, which meant the ability to self-replicate, for a while it remained a normal, chaotic world. It put some of the staff in a bad mood—they were afraid it would change nothing at all.

"But there were a few who had a more upbeat outlook. After all, real life had developed along much the same lines. Primitive life began, single-celled organisms, and then just stayed like that for three billion years with very little change, no signs of evolving.

"One day, just as we'd expected, complex life forms began to appear—just as the Cambrian Explosion came along in real life. We have no logical explanation for why varied life forms appeared at just that moment. Extremely simple life forms, similar to single-celled organisms, begat many-celled organisms, through a mechanism that was identical to how it happened on earth, they say.

"The life that emerged then became the proto-type for the natural world that would later develop. Some life retained the same form and became naturally extinct, while some life began to evolve into more complex forms. The family tree branched out, the phenomena of parasitism and symbiosis appeared, life emerged that moved in fascinating ways. Things that moved like worms burrowing their way through the earth. Things that moved swiftly through the seas. Things that soared through the air like birds. And things that stagnated, giving up on evolution and remaining single cells forever. These can probably be likened to bacteria and viruses. There were things whose pictorial representation was large but which didn't move: these took forms like those of trees on earth.

"Of course each living thing had information that corresponded to genes, and every time they reproduced, a certain percentage of errors crept in, mutations that resulted in evolution in a posi-tive direction, stagnation, or extinction. We'd done a good job of incorporating natural selec-tion, the competition to survive.

"Observing this process, we were astonished to see something emerge that could only be gender. In the natural world, too, it's considered a mystery why species branched into male and female. In our world, too, a bifurcation occurred that clearly couldn't be explained except through reference to male and female.

"Some simple life forms were still able to reproduce without coupling with another of their species, but complex life forms now had to mate within their species in order to self-replicate. Just as we'd predicted, once the gender distinction arose, genetic information came to be combined in more dynamic ways as it was passed down to the next generation: this made for diversity, and evolution picked up speed.

"Please don't misunderstand. I didn't actually witness this myself—I heard some older colleagues talking about it. But it's pretty exciting, don't you think? The idea of artificial life forms inside a computer having sex is pretty interesting, is it not?

"With the Cambrian Explosion as a jumping-off point, life changed into complicated patterns with wondrous speed. One minute huge life forms that resembled dinosaurs appeared, and the next minute they were extinct.

"What came next was life forms that incubated the next generation's information inside the parent generation until it had achieved a certain degree of maturity, and only then divided. I'm sure you recognize what I'm talking about: mammals.

"Things went on like this for some time, until the appearance of what seemed to be the ancestors of the human race. I've pulled that scene up and watched it myself. Imagine it, if you can. At first they moved like orangutans. Then, through a long period of trial and error, their walking became smooth, free of the awkwardness it displayed at first.

"At this point the amount of genetic information was extraordinary, and soon thereafter there emerged a life form that we guessed must be humanity. It was obvious that this life form was aware of itself, that it possessed intelligence. Obvious, because these life forms were actually observed making what seemed to be signals to one another.

"By exchanging digital signals, zeros and ones, these life forms were able to manipulate more and more information. As a result, their survival rate went up. It was unmistakable: they'd acquired language.

"By analyzing the clusters of zeros and ones they exchanged, we were able to translate their exchanges of information as language. Of course, the beings within the Loop didn't consider themselves to be interacting in binary code. As far as their awareness went, they were utilizing complex language the same as you and me.

"Once we'd analyzed their language so that we could interpret it using machine translation, it became a much more interesting world, they say. You could call up any scene on the display as a three-dimensional image, and it was just like you were a character in a movie.

"These artificial life forms began making their own history. Similar individuals came together in groups, states fought wars and engaged in political machinations. They advanced their civilization and designed their own world as if it was their own. It's said that watching it was like watching human history itself.

"The price was that as their history advanced the level of information being generated rose, and time began to move more slowly. The computers had a limit to their processing ability.

"The first three billion years from the creation of the earth had only taken a half a year on the computer. But the speed began to slow as life began to emerge, and especially after it evolved into intelligent forms on a level with human beings. At the end it took the computers two or three years to advance the Loop a few centuries.

"The Loop, as a virtual world, was recognizable and knowable to the staff of the research center. But it was utterly impossible for the sentient beings within the Loop to know us, their creators. To them, I imagine we were God Himself. As long as they were within the Loop, they were unable to comprehend how their world worked. The only thing that would have enabled comprehension was for them to get outside of their world.

"The progress of their civilization was marvelous. Their cities contained entertainment districts with flashing neon signs; they overflowed with sound and color. All manner of media sprang up, dramatically broadening the reach of information, and people lived lives filled with the pleasures of the musical and verbal arts. Their lives were no different from ours by this point. They had artists just like Mozart or da Vinci, who played the same historical role as in reality, adding vibrancy to their culture. Their world was beautiful, but at the same time it began to have an air of decadence. Some of our staff members were enraptured, while others began to whisper forebodings of doom. There were signs all over the place that something unpredicted was about to happen.

"And the premonitions were right on target. The Loop, the entire living world, began to turn cancerous . . . "

Amano paused there for a breath, and to bring his coffee cup to his lips. It was empty and he knew it; the gesture was simply something to do with his hands. Had he been a smoker, he would have lit a cigarette at this point.

"What do you mean, turned cancerous?"

Amano shrugged slightly and lifted his hands in a pose of surrender. "The Loop biosphere came to be monopolized by identical genes. It lost diversity and began moving toward extinction."

Kaoru looked at the ceiling, as was his habit. He tried to make sense of what Amano had told him.

They had created a three-dimensional virtual space inside an ultrafast supercomputer system, a world that didn't exist in reality, and they'd named this space the Loop. The space itself was large enough that from the point of view of the life forms within it, it might as well be considered an infinite universe. The experimenters had established conditions of soil, topography, and physics so that the world would be just like the primeval earth. Mathematically speaking, it was a world supported by the same formulas and theories as the real world. Not only the speed of gravitational acceleration and the boiling temperature of water, but the very landscape was identical to that of earth.

Carbon, hydrogen, helium, nitrogen, sodium, oxygen, magnesium, calcium, iron, and the rest of the 111 elements had been deposited, each according to its properties. Rules were laid down so that they would act exactly as they did in the universe enveloping the earth: two hydrogen atoms (H_2) and one oxygen atom (O) when combined would form a water molecule (H_2O), and this would react with a nitrogen molecule (N_2) to form ammonia (NH_3).

Fundamentally, no reason exists in the world to explain why two hydrogen atoms and one oxygen atom, when combined, have to form water: the rules are simply set up that way. And who made the rules? If you had to give it a name, it would be God.

The fact that evolution in the Loop proceeded exactly as it had in the real world was suspected to be due to the first primitive RNA life form that had been caused to be born. Or, rather, since the physical conditions of the Loop had been precisely modeled on those of the real world, evolution there probably couldn't help but follow the path it had already followed in the real world.

One of the purposes of the Loop was to enable researchers to trace the actual process of evolution. If evolution in the Loop followed the same path as it did in reality, then the results of the Loop's evolution would predict the future of the real world.

Suddenly chills ran along Kaoru's spine. The Loop predicted the future of life on earth. All life would turn cancerous.

What in the world? That's exactly what's happening now.

Cancer cells reproduced with no respect for persons, they were sexless, and they were immortal to boot. At the moment there were only a few million victims worldwide, but there was always the chance that the numbers would shoot up due to some mutation or population explosion in the MHC virus. It would be the same as what had happened in the Loop. Was it just a coincidence? Or was the Loop in fact an accurate prediction of the future?

As he sat before Kaoru, Amano was not about to assert a scientific connection between the results of the Loop and reality. And it was no wonder. How many people would believe such a ridiculous story?

Kaoru struggled to mask his shock with rationality as he asked, "What was the cause? Why did the Loop's life forms turn cancerous?"

Amano answered him in clipped tones. "That's easy. It was the appearance of the ring virus. But that emerged in a way we simply don't understand, as if by magic."

"You're saying that a single virus managed to influence all of the patterns in the Loop?"

"Yes. It shouldn't be that hard to believe. Not when a butterfly flapping its wings on one side of the world can affect the weather on the other."

The butterfly effect. Kaoru guessed it wasn't all that strange that the ring virus could change the fate of the Loop world. What he didn't understand was why it had appeared.

"Are there any theories as to the emergence of the ring virus?"

"Theories?"

"You know, like maybe one of the staff members introduced it into the program."

"Security was perfect."

"Well, maybe it was a computer virus."

"That's not impossible. In fact, they say most people took that view."

Something appeared to be bothering Amano; he seemed to sink into thought.

"Excuse me, but is there anybody from the original staff I can contact?"

Amano smiled wanly. "I'm the only survivor," he said, then hurriedly put a hand over his mouth. Hideyuki Futami wasn't dead yet. Kaoru didn't let it bother him, but laughed bitterly.

Amano quickly added, "My participation in the project was limited to the very final stage, just before it was shut down. You'd be better off consulting the father of the whole project, Cristoph Eliot, but he's hidden himself away . . . " Amano fixed Kaoru with a meaningful gaze and then continued. "Oh, I do know of one person who was fairly close to the center of the project. An American researcher. Supposedly an odd duck—he had problems with teamwork."

"Do you know his name?"

"Wait a moment," Amano said, and stepped out of the room. When he returned, several minutes later, it was with a file under his arm. He flipped through it. "Ah, there it is," he muttered, glancing up at Kaoru without raising his head. "Kenneth Rothman."

Kaoru repeated the name. He was an old friend of his father's. He'd visited five years ago: there were photographs of Rothman and members of the family standing on their balcony overlooking Tokyo Bay. Rothman had been in Japan to speak at a conference, and Kaoru's father had put him up for several days.

Those days were deeply etched in Kaoru's memory. Rothman's appearance left quite an impression, from his thin goateed face to the gold chains that flashed around his neck and wrists; his manner, too, was impressive, from the cynical smile he'd flash during scientific discussions to the cutting logic with which he'd announce his pessimistic analyses of the future.

"Has Futami-sensei told you anything about this man?"

"Yes, he's a friend of my father's. I've met him myself once, five years ago. I remember his beard, mostly. Where is he now?"

Amano flipped through the file again.

"According to this, he moved from Cambridge to the laboratories in Los Alamos, New Mexico, ten years ago."

New Mexico. The name sent a jolt through Kaoru's brain. He looked around the room, then stood up and took a close look at the world map on the wall.

Los Alamos, New Mexico. He held down the spot with his finger: it wasn't far at all from the Four Corners of New Mexico, Arizona, Utah, and Colorado, where his family had been planning to go.

Kenneth Rothman had moved there ten years

ago. The first MHC victim had been in New Mexico. The coincidences were piling up . . .

Kaoru shut his eyes tightly. He couldn't help but feel that an important clue lay hidden there. Hoping against hope, he asked, "Is it possible to contact him?"

Amano's answer was brusque.

"I sincerely doubt it."

"Why is that?"

"The last I heard from him was six months ago. What I heard then grabbed me, but I haven't been able to contact him since."

"Grabbed you how?"

"Something about having figured out the MHC virus, and that Takayama held the key . . . Tantalizing, isn't it?"

"Takayama? That's someone's name, I take it? Whose?"

"I'll give you the short version. The cancerization of the Loop came about through the emergence of an unknown virus and a series of events linked to it. At the center of those events were three artificial life forms: one called Takayama, one called Asakawa, and one called Yamamura. It's been determined that these three life forms played important roles in the cancerization of the Loop."

"The artificial life forms have names?"

"Of course."

"So Kenneth Rothman disappeared, leaving behind nothing but the name Takayama?"

"Yes. I didn't think much of it—in this day and age, when I lost contact I simply figured that the cancer must have gotten him, too." Amano threw up his hands. "Especially in his case. He had his own laboratory in a remote town called Wayne's Rock. It was the kind of situation where he could slip out of touch at any time and nobody would be too surprised."

"Wayne's Rock?"

"Wayne's Rock, New Mexico. Basically a ghost town in the middle of the desert."

Kaoru sighed and turned back to the map, placing his fingertip on one particular spot.

Wayne's Rock, New Mexico.

He had the feeling Rothman was waiting for him there, in his lab.

His finger still on the map, Kaoru turned back to Amano. "Have you watched the whole series of events involving Takayama and Asakawa?"

Amano shook his head. "No. I think only a few staff members watched it. The memory is stored in America, not here."

This aroused Kaoru's interest still more.

"Would it be possible for me to . . . see it?"

"It would take a while, but it wouldn't be impossible. I think you'd be wasting your time, though," was Amano's answer. Kaoru's finger was still on the map.

13

It had been some time since he'd gone out onto the balcony at home and gazed at the night sky. Even from a hundred yards above he could tell that no ripples disturbed the black surface of the bay. It was a hot, windless evening. The humidity bathed him where he stood.

He saw the sky differently this evening—he couldn't help but do so after everything Amano had told him this afternoon about the contents of the Loop. As a child, so full of the desire to understand the universe, he'd stared at the glittering stars with a passion born of the feeling that if he just looked long enough he'd understand.

What's at the end of the universe? That was the kind of naïve question that had presented itself to him. Staring at the cosmos now, it was utterly beyond his imagination what might lie outside the universe.

Kaoru tried to imagine himself as a denizen of the Loop. Assuming he were a being aware of time and space, how would he interpret that universe? It would most likely appear to be expanding. The Loop had gradually grown with the changing passage of time. Before the program had been started, there had been nothing there at all. A mountain of silicon chips, yes, but no time, no space. But from the moment the staff had started the program, space had grown at an explosive rate. The Big Bang.

The Loop space did not exist within the massively parallel supercomputers enshrined beneath the ground, just as a nature scene on a movie screen was not actually contained within that screen. That space existed neither inside nor outside the computers. It was only experienced as space by beings able to recognize it as such. As life forms evolved and their awareness grew, that space must have expanded, as if fleeing before the eyes that sought to recognize it.

Kaoru turned his eyes to the actual sky. The universe he was looking at was expanding, but he wondered suddenly if it wasn't simply trying to get far away from earthly DNA and its powers of recognition. He couldn't discard the possibility that the real universe was a hypothetical space just like the Loop. Would that interpretation cause any inconvenient problems?

No, it wouldn't. In fact, he felt that regarding

the real world as a hypothetical space was getting closer to the truth. Maybe the ancient ways of thinking—the Buddhist idea that form is emptiness, or the Platonic notion of the ideal world—did a better job of capturing the reality of things.

And if one assumed the universe was a virtual space, then there was the possibility that it was being observed through an open window in space, just as humans had been able to peek into the Loop world. Make the right time and space adjustments, and images of a particular moment in a particular place would unfold on the monitor in 3D.

Kaoru placed one hand on his other arm, then moved it to his chest, his belly, and below.

Do I just think I have a body, when really there's nothing at all?

But there was that little organ located just below the center of his body, and there were desires which emanated from it. He couldn't believe those were without reality. As he touched it, stroked it, he thought of Reiko's face.

There was nobody behind the glass door at his back. The television was showing something different from a while ago. His mother was probably shut in her room, absorbed in Native American myths.

Kaoru glanced behind him, and then allowed his organ to tower in the direction of the window that might be there in space somewhere; allowed it to insist on its existence.

Kaoru wanted to shout to the night sky: *This flesh can't be a fictional construct. Reiko's body can't be a fictional construct.*

14

There in the awkward darkness, Kaoru considered the two facts of which he'd just been made aware. Both were pieces of extremely bad news, and it was taking him a while to accept them. He knew they were coming, but now that they'd come he couldn't help but go unnaturally rigid as he looked down at his father.

Up until a few minutes ago Kaoru had been in Ryoji's sickroom. As soon as Ryoji had been taken away for his test, Kaoru had locked the door from the inside and lost himself in passion with Reiko. Afterwards, he'd stopped by his father's room. What he'd heard there felt like a punishment for lewd acts in an inappropriate place. The scent of Reiko's skin still lingered in his nostrils, and he could still feel the soft touch of her skin here and there on his body. On a deep cellular level his excitement had yet to subside.

Now he regretted coming to his father's room while still in the throes of afterglow.

His father seemed to have physically shrunk a size over the last few days—the swelling of the sheet over his chest was pitifully small. When Kaoru was a child his father had been a giant in his eyes. He could beat on his father's muscular chest with both fists and his father wouldn't flinch in the slightest. His physique had been out of place on a scientist, but now it hardly disturbed the flatness of the sheet.

So it wasn't that much of a surprise to hear that the cancer's spread to his lungs had been confirmed. But still it was news he hadn't wanted to hear—he'd been putting off thinking about it for so long—and revulsion was his first reaction, followed by something like anger as the facts sank into his head.

"Don't just stand there. Have a seat." Whereas Kaoru's expression as he stood there was one of rage, Hideyuki's was soft. Kaoru only then realized that he'd been standing ever since hearing the two pieces of bad news.

Kaoru did as his father said and sat down on a stool. Suddenly his anger receded; he felt drained.

"Are you going to have surgery?" His voice sounded hollow to himself.

Hideyuki had the answer ready. "No, not this time."

Kaoru was of the same opinion. Cutting the cancer out of his lungs wasn't going to prolong his life. The end result was all too clear. Chances were, an operation would actually shorten his life.

"Right," was Kaoru's response to his father's determination.

"But never mind about me. This has turned into something really nasty." Hideyuki was referring to the information Saiki had just brought him.

The second piece of news had to do with the results of animal experiments conducted simultaneously but independently in Japan and America. Until this point, it had been thought that the Metastatic Human Cancer Virus only affected humans: only humans could catch it, and only human cells would turn cancerous under its influence. But experiments on mice and guinea pigs had just revealed that animals could contract the disease, as well.

It wasn't yet clear whether this was the result of a mutation in the virus, or whether its ability to infect non-humans was simply something that had been overlooked up until now. What was important was the threat of animals in close contact with humans, dogs or cats or even smaller animals, becoming carriers of the virus. If this happened, it was to be expected that the virus would spread even more explosively than it already had. Events in the real world were taking on an even crueler resemblance to the end stages of the Loop. There, the cancerization had affected all life-form patterns. If the analogy held up, the MHC virus wouldn't cease its attack until all life on earth became cancerous.

Even if Kaoru hadn't gotten the virus from Reiko, it would invade his body somehow, by some route or another. It was inevitable. At least, that was how he tried to rationalize his relations with her, even as he closed himself off to imagining the doom that awaited him.

His father's voice reached him as if over a great distance.

"Huh?"

"Hey, are you listening to me?"

"Sorry."

"You spoke to Amano, right? Tell me your impressions."

It was a vague enough question.

"Well, a few things bother me about what he said."

Hideyuki nodded. "I'll bet."

"Dad, was it really only recently that people started to notice that reality was starting to look like the way the Loop wound up?"

"The Loop project started thirty-seven years ago and lasted for seventeen years. The program was shut down five years after I joined. That was twenty years ago. That world had disappeared from my memory. It's really only in the last few days that I've started worrying about the way the Loop ended."

Kaoru found this statement of his father's totally unbelievable.

Ten years ago, when Hideyuki had steered the conversation away from the Loop, refusing to tell Kaoru how the project had turned out, it had to have been because he was bothered by the way it had ended. All life forms within the virtual space losing diversity, turning cancerous, and going extinct—it wasn't the kind of story to tell a ten-year-old kid. No doubt Hideyuki hadn't wanted his son to project that story onto the real world and thereby fall into an unhealthy obsession with the end of all things.

Because he'd felt that a child's view of the future of mankind should be sunny, Hideyuki had distanced his son from the Loop. Which meant that in at least a corner of his mind Hideyuki had been worried all along about the conclusion of the Loop experiment.

"Dad, about the reason that the Loop turned cancerous . . . "

"It was the appearance of the ring virus."

"Could somebody have introduced it into the program?"

Hideyuki was silent for a while, as if pondering the idea.

"Why do you say that?"

"Because nobody could explain how the virus came to be. It couldn't have emerged naturally. So if it couldn't have been born on the inside, isn't it most natural to think it was brought in from the outside?"

"Hmmph."

"Isn't it?"

"If people could just start introducing things once the program had already started to evolve, it would have nullified the whole experiment. Security was flawless."

At this point, Kaoru mentioned a name. "You know Kenneth Rothman, right?"

Still face up on the bed, Hideyuki turned his eyes toward Kaoru.

"Did something happen to him?" he finally managed to choke out. He was bracing himself to receive another death notice.

"Do you know where he is?"

"I heard he was in New Mexico, still researching artificial life, but . . . "

"Yeah, supposedly he moved to the laboratories in Los Alamos. But nobody knows where he is now. And just before he went missing he mentioned something that sounded pretty important. He said he'd figured out the MHC virus, and that Takayama held the key."

"Takayama . . . "

"Dad, did you watch the scenes in the Loop involving Takayama?"

Kaoru's question sent Hideyuki deep into his thoughts again. His eyes darted around desperately as, with his weakened vitality, he tried to recall something.

He was clearly shaken. It was only natural that his memory should become somewhat opaque after several major surgeries and his long battle with cancer. But still it was setting Hideyuki's nerves on edge that he could find no answer to his probings into the darkness of his memories.

"I . . . I don't think so."

Kaoru decided to ease his father's struggles by changing the subject. "Oh, Dad, another thing. The MHC virus has been sequenced, right?"

"Saiki brought by a printout of it two days ago."

"Well, have a look at these figures."

Kaoru showed the printout to his father; he'd highlighted with a marker the total number of bases in each gene.

"What about them?"

"Look at the number of bases."

3072—393,216—12,288—786,432—24,576—49,152—196,608—6144—98,304.

Hideyuki read the nine numbers off in order. But by the look he turned on Kaoru it was evident he hadn't noticed anything special about them.

Kaoru enunciated clearly as he explained. "Get this, Dad. All nine of these numbers equal two to the nth power times three."

Hearing this, Hideyuki looked over the numbers again at some length, before crying out. "Nice catch!"

The old light returned to Hideyuki's eyes as he lost himself in their scientific back-and-forth; it only lasted an instant, but that was long enough for Kaoru to notice. It pleased him at the same time that it made his chest tighten. How long had it been since his father had praised him like this?

"Do you think it's a coincidence, Dad?"

"It can't be. What are the chances of all nine numbers—some of them six digits—turning out to equal two to the nth power times three? Extremely low. Any time something overcomes that kind of improbability, it means something. You were the one who told me that, that night ten years ago."

Hideyuki gave a weak laugh. Kaoru replayed in his mind his memories of that night and his family's back-and-forth; a summer as hot as this one and a childhood dream fanning anticipation of a trip to the North American desert. That place, once a fun-filled destination for a family vacation, had changed drastically for him, but it still drew him with great force.

As Kaoru and Hideyuki sat there reminiscing about times spent together, the hospital corridor outside burst into a commotion.

Two or three people ran past, creating a sense

of tension not often felt in a non-emergency ward. Apprehensions stirring, Kaoru listened closely.

He heard what sounded like a woman's scream mingled with a male voice barking commands. The woman's voice sounded familiar. He was sure of it: it was Reiko.

"Excuse me," Kaoru said, glancing at his father and getting up.

He opened the door and looked up and down the hall. He saw a woman scurrying down the corridor away from him, following two men in guards' uniforms. She was wearing a casual yellow housedress; the zipper on her back wasn't zipped all the way up. Kaoru himself had fumblingly unzipped that dress not long ago; he knew the white neck above it. This was Reiko.

She wore sandals with no socks; a further glance showed that she was in fact only wearing one sandal. This made one shoulder rise and fall with her strides. She must have been in quite some hurry as she'd left her son's sickroom.

Realizing the situation must be urgent, Kaoru chased her, calling her name.

She didn't even look back, but followed the two guards around a corner and through the door to the stairs, beside the elevator.

She was screaming; just what her screams meant was not clear. It sounded like she was calling out a name, but with all the noise, Kaoru couldn't make it out.

"Reiko!"

Kaoru sped after her, opening the stairwell door as it slammed shut in front of him and rushing in. In the stairwell was a freight elevator, and beyond that the fireproof door to the emergency stairs. This door opened from either side, in case of emergency, but any unauthorized entry by this means would show up on the security monitors, bringing guards at a run. Of course, the system was also designed to prevent people from jumping to their deaths.

Reiko and the guards opened the door to the emergency stairs, and over their shoulders Kaoru could see the child. The outside wall had a window in it, marked with a red triangle: this window opened from the outside or the inside, so that firemen could use it as an entrance in an emergency. The window was open now, and curled up on the windowsill sat Ryoji.

The boy turned a mocking gaze on the panicking adults and continued to kick and dangle his legs in his usual way.

As soon as they saw Ryoji, the guards stopped in their tracks and began trying to talk him down.

"Calm down."

"Don't do it."

"Come down from there."

"Ryo!" Reiko croaked, not at her son but at the narrow square of ceiling above him.

Ryoji seemed to notice Kaoru standing behind

his mother. Their eyes met. Then Ryoji rolled his eyes back in his head until only the whites were visible, and leaned back. Kaoru's last glimpse of Ryoji's eyes showed him something no longer alive.

The next instant, Ryoji threw himself toward the sunset behind him and disappeared.

15

Kaoru sat next to the bathtub with his hand in the running water, adjusting the temperature so that it would be on the tepid side. At first the water felt a bit hot to the touch, but as he grew accustomed to it he decided it was close to body temperature. Then he got in and sank back until the water was up to his shoulders. He soaked a while. Once the last droplet had fallen from the tap, the bathroom was silent. It was unusual for him to take a bath on a weekday afternoon like this.

He lay back until his head rested on the rim of the tub, closed his eyes, and pricked up his ears. He hugged his knees and curled into the fetal position. He had the feeling that his heartbeat was being picked up by the water, making wavelets in the tub.

He tried to empty his heart, but it was no use. The same scene kept replaying in his mind.

It was nearly a week since Ryoji had jumped to his death from the hospital emergency stairs.

Help me. Help Ryoji.

Ryoji had ended his young life before Kaoru's very eyes, forsaking his mother's wishes.

The sight of Ryoji jumping had made a strong impact on Kaoru. The moments just before and after, the empty look in Ryoji's eyes as he leaned backward, Reiko's scream. The images, the sounds, the most fragmentary details were tragically etched into Kaoru's brain. They'd appeared in his dreams every night for the last week.

Immediately after Ryoji had jumped, Kaoru and Reiko and the others had rushed to the window to look out. They could see the boy's body twisted unnaturally from its collision with the concrete. They could see rivulets of blood, all flowing in the same direction, shining reddish-black in the setting sun. Reiko fainted on the spot; Kaoru picked her up. He made arrangements for Ryoji's body to be taken into the emergency ward, but he already knew just by looking that it was too late. The chances of surviving a twelve-story drop onto a concrete surface were virtually nil.

Sometimes he dreamed about the stain Ryoji's blood left on the concrete. The stain was still there, in a corner of the hospital courtyard. The boy's life was gone, but it had turned into a shadow which lingered on the surface of the walkway. Kaoru couldn't make himself go near it.

Ryoji's suicide was an impulsive act, but there was something premeditated about it, too. When he made his move he'd dashed straight for the window in the emergency stairwell. He must have known the windows there were the only ones that opened from the inside. He must have had his eye on them for some time.

The motive for his suicide was obvious. He'd finished the scintigram, and was now facing his fourth round of chemotherapy. He must have been filled with revulsion at the thought of that miserable struggle starting again. And it was a struggle against an enemy he couldn't defeat. Sooner or later, his life would end, and until then there would be only agony. He must have begun to weigh the question of which was better, to prolong his life a little and thereby ensure more suffering for himself, or to cut his life short and spare himself the pain. Perhaps he'd taken into consideration the way his mother suffered watching him.

With the MHC virus ravaging his body, Ryoji had chosen death. Kaoru could understand his feelings—could understand them painfully well. This was something that touched him—a catastrophe that would befall him in the not-too-distant future. This was an enemy Kaoru himself would have to fight. He understood Ryoji's act.

But that didn't mean he wanted to end up the same way.

You've got to concentrate all your intelligence on confronting this enemy that wants to destroy your body, your youth.

Those were his father's words. If he wanted to escape death, he'd have to fight, and he'd have to win. And he had only one weapon, just like his father had told him: his intelligence.

Kaoru sank deeper into the bathtub. Now the water was up to his earlobes. *Do I have that kind of strength?*

The more he thought about it the stranger it seemed. All these events connected with the MHC virus springing from somewhere close to him, closing in on his body as if he'd been assigned to save the world.

You're overestimating yourself.

Unable to stand the heat any longer, he got out of the tub.

Saving the world actually had a nice ring to it. He wouldn't mind looking like a hero, playing at savior. But he had a personal matter he had to attend to first. Nothing world-class—something far more local in scale. This evening, for the first time in a week, he had a rendezvous planned with Reiko.

He wiped himself clean of perspiration and then put on a brand-new T-shirt and jeans.

He hadn't seen Reiko since Ryoji's funeral.

Since then, she'd refused even to meet him. Finally, she'd offered to speak with him for an hour this evening. This would be his only chance. Kaoru would have only tonight to find out why Reiko had closed her heart to him.

16

Reiko's condo was on the edge of a wooded hilltop. The building was an ostentatious one, three stories, red brick exterior.

Kaoru went around to the entrance, pressed the buttons for her room number, and waited for a response. The speaker came to life and he heard Reiko's voice softly say, "Come in." A moment later, the door slid open.

He'd already assumed that Reiko was financially comfortable due to the fact that she'd been able to put Ryoji in a private room at the hospital. As he walked down the carpeted hallway to the elevator, he saw his assumption borne out.

Of course, he'd never tried to find out where the money came from. He never asked, and she never volunteered the information. However, she'd hinted that her husband had been socially successful. He'd been older than her; he'd died of cancer a few years ago.

Hers was a corner apartment on the third floor. Before he could even ring the bell, the door opened. She must have been watching through the peephole, estimating his time of arrival.

It had been a week since he'd seen her. She opened the door a crack and stuck her head out. They were face to face. Her hair was combed back and held in place with an elastic band. He noticed a few strands of white.

"Come in." Her voice seemed to recede within itself.

"Long time no see."

She showed him into her living room, where he sat on a couch. For a while neither spoke. Kaoru felt uncomfortable. He didn't know why she was acting so cold toward him, and not knowing that, he didn't know what he should say or how to start.

Reiko wordlessly placed a glass of iced barley tea before him, and then sat down facing him.

"I've been wanting to see you." He reached out for her, but she avoided his touch. She sank back into the sofa, maximizing the distance between them.

The same thing had happened at the funeral. Flattering himself that he was the only one who could heal the pain of losing her only son, Kaoru had tried to put his arm around Reiko's black-clad shoulders, but she'd rejected the gesture, twisting away from him. Inexperienced with women he may have been, but even Kaoru could get the message if it was repeated enough times. But he couldn't fathom the reason behind her persistent refusals. One day they'd been in intimate physical contact, and the next she recoiled from his touch.

Reiko hugged herself tightly, rubbing her arms with her hands as if chilly. But the air conditioning was at a reasonable level, and the room was far from cold. In fact, it was still too hot for Kaoru.

He observed her exterior, hoping to understand the pain in her heart, hoping that if she'd closed herself off to him out of anguish at losing her son, he might yet find a way to comfort her.

He wanted to say something that would give her courage, ease her heart, but the only words that came to him sounded so weak and forced, even to himself, that he was embarrassed to speak them. "Cheer up"—he couldn't bring himself to say that if his life depended on it. And so there was no way to start a conversation.

"How long do you intend to sit there without saying anything?" She said this coolly, looking at the floor. This bothered Kaoru—she'd made it so he couldn't say anything, and now she was reproaching him for his silence.

"Knock it off already," he finally managed to say.

"You . . ."

She held her head in her hands and shuddered violently. She was crying: every now and then he could hear a sob.

"I want to relieve your sadness somehow, but I don't know how to do that."

Reiko groaned and looked up at him, biting her lower lip. Her eyes were red from weeping, and her cheeks were wet with tears.

"I wish I'd never met you."

Kaoru was shocked.

"So you hate me now?"

That just can't be, he wanted to shout. If she really hated him she wouldn't have consented to meet him. She could have spared herself this awkward scene simply by continuing to ignore his phone calls. And yet she hadn't: she'd set up this tête-à-tête, albeit on the condition that it last only an hour. There had to be something she wanted to talk to him about, some legitimate reason for meeting him.

"He knew." Her voice was suddenly, unexpectedly calm.

"What?"

"About you and me."

"That we're in love?"

"In love? So that's what being in love looks like?" A self-mocking smile appeared on her face.

Kaoru sat bolt upright, startled. *What being in love looks like?*

"What *did* he know?"

"What you and I were doing in that room."

She couldn't go on. Kaoru swallowed and said, "He couldn't have known."

"He was a sharp boy. He picked up on it. We were so stupid. How could we . . . how could we do something like that?" Her heart was starting to crumble.

"But . . . "

"He wrote it in his note."

"Huh?"

"What do you think he wrote?"

Kaoru swallowed again, bracing himself.

Reiko imitated her son's voice. "'I'll be gone, so you two knock yourselves out.'"

Oh, no.

Kaoru thought of Ryoji in his swim cap, smiling, standing by the side of the pool in his baggy trunks, repeating the words over and over. *I'll be gone, so you two knock yourselves out. I'll be gone, so you two knock yourselves out. I'll be gone, so you two knock yourselves out.*

They'd taken every precaution. They'd only been together when Ryoji was gone for two-hour tests. Even then, the act itself had been over in less than ten minutes. After it had been accomplished, they'd spent the rest of the time on the edge of tears, eyeing each other with lethargy or regret. Kaoru would sometimes kiss away Reiko's tears and whisper, "I love you."

Reiko rocked back and forth as if having a

seizure, as if reading Ryoji's suicide note had stolen her reason.

Kaoru let her weep for a while. There was nothing else he could do. She'd calm down eventually, once she'd cried herself out.

He tried to imagine things from Ryoji's perspective. His mother had seized on the occasions of his tests, moments when he'd been in the worst pain, to abandon herself to pleasure. To Ryoji it must have amounted to betrayal. His mother was supposed to be fighting this illness side by side with him, but instead, she'd sent him off to fight it alone while she got her kicks. No wonder he felt disillusioned. No wonder he'd lost the will to fight. Kaoru had assumed that Ryoji's suicide had been a form of surrender to the illness, but the reality turned out to be something else again.

Up to now, Kaoru had grieved relatively little over Ryoji's death, knowing that the poor kid was destined to die soon anyway. His time would come soon enough, so if he wanted to shorten its remaining length himself, maybe it was better that way. Kaoru had almost felt relief.

But if Ryoji's mother's actions had triggered his suicide . . . Ryoji's thinking suddenly seemed a little more complicated than Kaoru had imagined.

No doubt Reiko felt the same. She'd paid extra for a private room, she'd hired a tutor on the assumption that her son would return to school someday, and she'd generally tried to show an enthusiasm for life. When you know somebody's going to die, love is letting that person see that you're willing to fight right by his side. She'd wanted to show Ryoji that she would stick by him until the very last moment, but instead she'd simply sped him on his way.

No wonder Ryoji had despaired. And now Reiko was wracked with remorse for having driven her son to that despair, to his death. She'd turned the brunt of her rage on Kaoru, her partner in crime. Kaoru finally understood why she'd fled when he'd tried to put his arm around her at the funeral. Standing in front of Ryoji's memorial tablet, she didn't want to be seen touching him even for an instant.

What Kaoru needed was time to think. He was still young—he didn't know how to deal with something like this. It would've been easier if he'd wanted to end their relationship. But he had no intention of doing that. He desperately wanted to find some way to fix things, to overcome this seemingly hopeless situation.

"Can you give me some time?" He decided to be honest with his feelings. He wanted to wait a while, then consider rationally what they should do.

"No." She shook her head violently.

"But I don't know what to do."

"Neither do I. That's why . . . "

Therein lay his salvation. She hadn't called him

here today to put an end to their relationship once and for all. She was admitting that she herself was lost, that she didn't know what to do. She couldn't make this decision alone.

He'd promised only to stay for an hour, but outside the window the autumn sunset was already upon them. It had been the rainy season, early summer, when he'd come to know Reiko. They'd only been together for three months. It felt longer to Kaoru.

The majority of their time together that evening was spent in silence. Sometimes the gaps when they couldn't think of what to say lasted ten minutes or more. But still, Reiko never told him to go home. Kaoru thought he sensed something unnatural in her attitude. Several times she'd be on the verge of saying something, only to bite the words back.

"Reiko, you're hiding something from me, aren't you?"

This made up her mind for her, and she looked up at him. Her expression challenged him.

"I think I'm pregnant."

It took him a few seconds to process what she was saying.

"You're pregnant?"

"Yes."

Their eyes met, and he knew she was telling the truth.

The shock ran up and down his backbone. He

simply couldn't grasp this. Death and birth had been almost literally bumping elbows in that little hospital room. The world's cruel irony rankled him. He felt the presence of an ill will invisible to the eye.

"I see."

He heaved a deep sigh.

"What do you think I should do?" Reiko asked.

"I want you to have it."

Saying this, Kaoru leaned forward. He hadn't just been playing when he started this relationship. If there was a child on the way, then he was prepared to raise it—he wanted them to live together.

"What are you saying?!"

Reiko took a newspaper from the magazine rack by the couch and threw it at him. It was this morning's edition.

He knew what she was trying to tell him without even looking at it. He'd read the article this morning.

The article accompanied a photograph of a stand of desert trees in Arizona, in America. The trees had been discovered by chance along US Highway 180 between Flagstaff and the Grand Canyon. According to the article, most of the plants, short trees and shrubs growing low to the brown earth were covered from their trunks to the tips of their leaves with strangely-shaped swellings. Of course there are relatively common

plant viruses that cause unnatural growth or withering, but these specimens suggested a viral infection on a scale never before seen. The very shapes
of the trunks, branches, and leaves had been
altered. All signs pointed to the work of a virus.
In fact, some were theorizing that the culprit was
a mutated version of the MHC virus. Not content
to ravage the globe's human population, it seemed
that the virus had extended its reach to encompass not only animals but even plants. The sight
of these grotesque trees seemed to signal the end
of the world. A gloomy article, ending on a
doomsday note.

Reiko was a carrier; she just hadn't gotten sick
yet. The probability was high that the child within
her would be born infected with the cancer virus,
too. And if that child were to be born into a
world in which the cancer threatened every living
thing . . .

It was all too easy for Kaoru to say that he
wanted her to have the baby. She lashed out at
him.

"You tell me, where in this world is there any
room for hope?"

In the Loop, the ring virus had come in the
end to have sway over every life-form pattern,
hounding them all to extinction. Kaoru was beginning to know how that felt.

It's starting. Reality is coming to take after the Loop.

"Just give me some time, okay?"

He was forced to beg. He couldn't come to any conclusions right now.

"Will a way open for us if we put off deciding? I'm sick and tired of this. Disgusted. I don't *want* to have an abortion. Can't you see that? It's like this child has come to take the place of the one I lost. Of course I want to have it, to raise and protect it. But I just can't, not when I think that this child might meet the same fate. To be born into the world only to suffer, to die so young . . . Help me, please. I don't know what to do anymore!"

He wanted to sit next to her, to let her whisper her pleas into his ear; he wanted to hold her and deliver her from her confusion. But he was afraid it was too soon for that. He fought down the urge.

"So you're not considering an abortion?" He pressed the point, and she slowly shook her head.

"I don't have the strength for that, even."

So she didn't mean to abort the child; still, that didn't necessarily mean she was determined to have it.

Kaoru searched as much of her soul as he could perceive from her eyes, and he thought he caught a glimpse of a decision. She wouldn't abort it, but neither would she give birth to it. Which must mean . . . was she on the verge of choosing suicide?

Kaoru had one wish now. He wanted Reiko to

go on living. In order to ensure that, he had to somehow prove to her that the world was worth living in, both for her and her unborn child. And not just for them, either: he had to learn the value of life for himself. How could he convince anybody else that life was worth living if he himself was willing to abandon the world to cancerization, to loss of genetic diversity, to doom?

I've got to prove it to her so that she can't possibly deny it.

There was only one way: he had to change the course of the world.

How much time would it take? Two, three months? If he hadn't settled things by the time Reiko's belly started to swell, there was every chance she'd choose death. Three months was about all the time he had, then: her nerves wouldn't let her hold out any longer.

"Give me three months. Please. I'm asking you to trust me."

"Three months?!" She gave a feeble scream. "I can't. Something's going to happen to my body, I know it."

"Two months, then."

She stared at him resentfully.

"I can't promise anything," she said at last.

"You *have* to promise me. For the next two months you can't kill yourself, no matter what happens."

Kaoru placed both hands on the table and

leaned toward her. Overwhelmed by his sudden intensity, she recoiled at first, but then a look of relief, of eerie lucidity, came over her. Her indecision seemed about to give way, in one direction or the other. If she could just settle on a direction for now, her suffering would be lessened, at least a bit.

He felt it best to distance himself from her for now, if only to redeem himself from the dishonor of being physically denied. Two months would be about right.

"Two months," she murmured.

"That's right. Let's meet again two months from now. Until then, you have to keep living, no matter what."

"Just stay alive?"

"As long as your heart keeps beating and your lungs keep breathing, and you think of me once in a while, that's enough for me."

She showed him a faint smile.

"I don't know about that last part."

It was the first flash of brightness she'd shown that day. It reassured him.

He needed her to trust him unquestioningly. If she started to inquire—if she asked him, for example, whether or not he was confident in what he was about to do, he wouldn't have satisfactory answers to give her. He felt he had several clues in hand. The unexplained fact that the number of bases in each gene of the virus came out to equal 2^n x 3. The fact—only a hunch, actually—that the virus had emerged someplace in the vicinity of Kaoru himself. If he could discover the secrets of its creation, maybe that would lead him to the means of its destruction. He had two months. He'd have to face this situation burdened with the knowledge that Reiko's fate, and his, depended on it.

17

In the elevator, on the way up to the twenty-ninth floor, Kaoru's ears began to ring. The elevator was designed to be unaffected by the change in air pressure, but today he felt a pressure on his inner ear that he'd never felt before. Simultaneously, an afterimage flickered before him.

The sound of Ryoji's bones cracking as his body hit the concrete still lingered in Kaoru's ears. He hadn't actually seen the boy falling; his impression was that he'd heard the body's impact as he himself was running to the window. It was nothing more than that, just an impression, but still the memory of the sound refused to fade away. Now, as the elevator climbed, something had triggered that memory, reviving images Kaoru had never actually seen.

In a somewhat depressed mood, Kaoru opened the door to the apartment and called out, "I'm home."

No reply. Thinking nothing of it, he took off his shoes and placed them in the cabinet by the door. When he looked up again, his mother Machiko had appeared as though out of nowhere.

"Would you come here a minute?"

She grabbed his arm and dragged him to her room before he could respond. Her eyes flashed with the excitement of discovery.

"What is it, Mom?"

Flustered, he offered no resistance, but let himself be dragged along by her intensity.

It had been some time since he'd set foot in his mother's room. Once the room was neat, but now it was piled high with disorderly stacks of books and magazines and photocopies. His mother's expression had changed, too. In fact, she looked like a changed person. Although they lived together, Kaoru felt it had been a long time since he'd really looked at her face.

"Would you tell me what's going on?" Kaoru's nerves were frayed, it being so soon after Ryoji's suicide. He worried about his mother's psychological state.

She seemed blissfully unaware of Kaoru's concern.

"I want you to take a look at this."

She handed him a magazine. *The Fantastic World*, the title read in English.

"What about it?" he asked in disgust. The title told him all he needed to know about it.

Machiko grabbed the magazine from his hands and flipped through it. Opening it to page forty-seven, she handed it back to him with uncharacteristic roughness.

"Read this article."

Kaoru did as he was told. The article was titled "Back from the Brink: A Full Recovery from Final-Stage Cancer".

Another one of these. He understood now. Lately his mother had been pouring all her energy and devotion into looking for a revolutionary way to treat cancer. But she was looking for it outside the bounds of modern medicine, in the "fantastic world" of myths and folk-tales. It was easy enough for him to dismiss it all as just so much alchemical nonsense. But she was his mother, and he had to humor her even if it was uncomfortable. He started reading the article.

Franz Boer, a retired surveyor living in Portland, Oregon, had been infected with the MHC virus several years ago. The cancer had spread throughout his body, and doctors had given him three months to live.

But he'd rejected the doctors' recommended course of treatment, instead embarking on a journey. As part of his trip he spent two weeks in a certain unnamed place. When he finally returned to Portland after a month, the doctor who examined him shook his head in disbelief. His inoperable cancer had completely disappeared.

Cells were collected from the 57-year-old man and tested to see how many times they had undergone cellular division. The result was a far greater number of times than was normal for a man his age.

In other words, Franz Boer had gained two things in that unidentified place: a reprieve from his sentence of death, and, not the same thing, longevity. But Boer, who lived alone, died in an accident before he could tell anybody where he'd obtained his miracle. Now everybody was frantically trying to figure out where he'd gone and what he'd done.

There was little to go on. One persistent reporter had learned that, soon after he'd been told he was dying, Boer had rented a car in Los Angeles. But there was nothing to indicate where he'd be going.

That was the gist of the article.

Machiko watched eagerly for Kaoru's reaction. Stories of miracle recoveries were everywhere these days. But he knew she was expecting something from him. He raised his head slowly with a quizzical expression.

"What do you think?" she asked.

Boer had probably taken a plane from Portland to L.A. Renting a car there, it was possible he'd been heading for the Arizona-New Mexico desert. It fit.

"I know what you're trying to say: Franz Boer was making for the longevity zone I've been talking about for so long."

His mother didn't bother to nod. She just leaned closer with her burning gaze. That gaze told him that she was sure of it.

"There's one more piece of evidence."

"And what would that be?"

"Look at this."

She brought out from behind her back a foreign book and handed it to Kaoru.

The title read *North American Indian Folklore*. Beneath the title was an illustration of the sun with a man standing beneath it on a hilltop catching the sun's rays full in the face. The man wore a feathered headdress, and his figure was blackened, silhouetted by the sun, as he stood in an attitude of prayer. The book looked to be old: its cover was faded and the edges of its pages dirty from handling.

As soon as Machiko handed him the book, Kaoru turned to the table of contents. It ran to three pages, seventy-four items. Each heading contained at least one word he was unfamiliar with. *Hiaqua*, for example—he'd never seen that word before, but he could tell at a glance it wasn't to be found in an English dictionary. He flipped through a few more pages, until he came to a series of photographs. One showed an Indian on one knee with bow and arrow.

Kaoru looked from the book to his mother's face, seeking an explanation.

"It's a book of North American Indian folk-tales."

"I can see that. What I want to know is, what does it have to do with that article you just had me read?"

Machiko shifted her weight. Her glee at being able to teach her son something came out in her body language.

"The Native Americans had all sorts of myths and traditions, but they had no written language, so most of them come down to us through generations of oral transmission."

She took the book back and paged through it.

"That means that most of these seventy-four tales were gathered and recorded by non-Indians. Look." She pointed to a page. "See? At the beginning of each story there's a notation by the title saying who collected it, when, and where. It also says what tribe the story was handed down in."

Kaoru looked at the title of the story Machiko was pointing to.

> "How the Mountaintops Reached the Sun"
> —the Shopanka tribe

Next there was an entry telling how a white man had come in contact with the Shopanka tribe, heard the story, and written it down. Only then,

at last, did the book go on to say how the moun-
taintops in fact reached the sun.

All seventy-four stories were short, mostly a
page or two, and had similar titles—lengthy
phrases, not single words.

"Kaoru, I'd like you to read this story."

She had the book open to what seemed to be
the thirty-fourth story: at least, it had the number
34 written above the title.

The title turned a light on in his brain.

Another coincidence?

The title was: *"Watched by a Multitude of Eyes."*

The title was in the passive voice. There was
no indication of who was being watched by what.

Kaoru stepped back, groped behind him for a
chair, and sat down. He started reading. Without
realizing it, he'd slipped into Machiko's world.

Watched by a Multitude of Eyes
—the Talikeet tribe

*[In 1862, at the height of the Civil War, a covered
wagon train was crossing the Southwestern
desert on its way west. A white minister,
Benjamin Wycliffe, got separated from the
wagons and was rescued by the Talikeet. He
lived with them for several days.*

*One calm evening, the Indians gathered around
the campfire to hear one of their elders speak. The
Reverend Wycliffe happened to be nearby, and he*

heard the tale. The flames reaching up into the night sky combined with the elder's singsong voice to make a powerful impression on Wycliffe's mind. He recorded this story that very evening.]

All living things were born from the same source, long long ago. The sea and the rivers and the land, the sun and the moon and the stars, are birth-parents to people and animals, and love them mercifully, but they themselves are contained within the womb of a being larger than themselves. Man feels the land to be filled with spirits because his heart is connected to the heart of this being. When man does something bad, this great being is pained in his heart, and this causes disaster to fall upon man.

Once when the stars were flowing across the sky on the stream of the being's blood, one of the stars came down to earth as a man called Talikeet. He married a lake named Rainier, and they had two sons. They lived together with their children happily on the land in the womb of the great being, never disobeying the will of the spirits.

The brothers grew up strong and were able to help their father and mother. They were skilled and courageous hunters, always bringing home game for their parents.

Then one day, Talikeet's leg began to hurt, and he told this to his wife and children.

They worried about him, but only Talikeet himself knew the reason why his body hurt.

Before he had drifted down to this land, he had been aware of being watched by a multitude of eyes. Men were permitted to hunt animals and eat them. Bigger animals were permitted to catch smaller animals and eat them. But they must not eat too much. And they must not store up too many animals they had killed. They must respect and honor the animals they hunted. To see that this was done, the great being who was also the father of all nature set a huge eye on a mountaintop. The eye which was set on top of the mountain was very large, but it was the only one, so it could not watch all men in all directions at all times. Eventually men began to hide from the eye and do things that went against the will of the great being.

Then the great being placed eyes within men's bodies so that they could not escape his sight.

"It is that eye which is causing me pain now," Talikeet explained to his wife and children.

"But, Father, I do not think you have disobeyed the will of the great being."

"I'm sure I did without realizing it," said Talikeet. Then he died.

The brothers and their mother were very sad, and they resented the actions of the great being.

Time passed, and then the older brother's waist began to pain him. Then the younger brother's back began to hurt. When they showed each other their bodies, they found fist-sized "eyes", one on the older brother's waist and one on the younger brother's back. They were surprised and asked their mother Rainier for help.

Rainier went down the river and visited the forest spirit. There she learned how to help her sons.

This was the forest spirit's answer. "Go due west and wait for a warrior to appear. Once you are sure of his true intentions, then follow his guidance." So she took her sons and journeyed due west, waiting for a warrior to appear. The "eye" on the older brother's waist grew larger, while the "eye" on the younger brother's back even wept great tears.

Finally a powerful man appeared astride a beast and guided the brothers to a pass in the mountains.

They crossed many rivers. The prairies turned to deserts, and the mountains stretching down from the north broke off. Going around them to the south, they

reached a high hill. Standing on the hilltop
looking west, they saw water flowing from
a mountaintop through a valley until it
became a river which flowed into the great
sea to the west. Looking east, they saw a
like river flowing into the great sea to the
east. They were on a bow-shaped ridge
connecting valleys on either side of the
mountains, at the source of two rivers
flowing into the two seas.

At the very highest point of the ridge the
warrior dismounted from his beast. They
walked to a waterfall and climbed up it. A
black cave gaped at the top of the waterfall,
and inside the cave lived the Ancient One.
The Ancient One told the brothers about the
creation of heaven and earth. He knew much
about the past, as if he had experienced it
all himself, so the older brother asked the
Ancient One his age. This was his answer.

"Look at me and decide for yourselves.
Tell me what you think."

But the answer came to neither brother,
so they could not tell him.

Instead of telling them his age, the
Ancient One said, "I have been here since
the birth of all things."

The brothers asked him to take away the
eyes on the older brother's waist and the
younger brother's back. He answered, "Very

well. But from this day you must keep watch here instead of me."

Then the Ancient One disappeared. At the same time, the "eyes" fell from their bodies, rolled over the stone floor, and turned into black rocks. The brothers became immortal, and watched over that land. With its rivers flowing into the sea east and west, it was a good land for keeping watch.

As soon as she saw he'd finished reading, Machiko spoke. "You understand what this means, right?"

Kaoru didn't much care for this kind of story. He wasn't a great reader of fiction to begin with, and he found folktales and myths in particular to be too incoherent, too lacking in reality. He had a hard time grasping them even when he did read them.

This one was like that. It developed too fast—what was it trying to say, exactly? The words sounded like they had significance, but they could be interpreted to mean anything. Kaoru felt that, no, he didn't exactly "understand what this means".

"Are the other stories pretty much like this, too?" he asked.

"Sort of."

"This 'Ancient One'. Are we to understand him literally as an old man?"

He imagined the Ancient One was a metaphor for something, along with the Multitude of Watching Eyes. Did the Ancient One represent a longevity zone? What did that make the Watching Eyes? It didn't make sense to him.

"Here's the problem," Machiko said, taking out the map included at the end of the book and unfolding it before Kaoru. It was a map of North America, showing the names of the major Indian peoples.

"Folktales and myths: are they completely made-up? According to some scholars, myths are based on historical facts from early in a people's existence. They contain that race's deepest wishes. Traces of the Great Flood, for instance, we find all over the world, and it's common knowledge now that the legend of the ark was at least somewhat based on fact.

"So let's assume that the story you just read, Kaoru, has some element of fact in it. Okay? Now the Talikeet were part of the Okewah people of western Oklahoma." She pointed with her pinky to a point on the map representing the current residence of the Talikeet tribe.

"It says in the story that the brothers went due west from here." She began to move her finger to the left of the page, but then stopped. "Where were they heading? According to the story the hilltop they stood on was at a southern gap in a great mountain range, at the source of two rivers, one flowing to the great western sea and one flowing to the great eastern sea. Geographically, those mountains have to be the Rockies."

She moved her finger along a north-south line, stopping at a point where the Rockies ended their long march down from Canada. The point was directly west from the Talikeet homeland, and just to the south of it stood a mountain of some twelve thousand feet. Which meant that the spot Machiko was pointing to was a huge valley supporting a bow-shaped strip of land. In the desert.

She traced an X over the bow-shaped rise with her finger. Just to the left of that spot could be seen the thin line of the Little Colorado River, which fed into the Colorado River, which flowed into the Gulf of California—the Pacific Ocean. Just to the right of that spot could be seen the uppermost reaches of the Rio Grande, which flowed into the Gulf of Mexico—the Atlantic Ocean. The sources of these two rivers flowing into the world's two great oceans came together at this point, divided by this ridge, part of the Continental Divide.

It was the Four Corners region, where the states of New Mexico, Arizona, Utah, and Colorado met. Site of the negative gravitational anomaly, where a longevity zone might, conjecturally, be located. Not far from the research labs at Los Alamos. Near where the deformed and swollen trees had been found. Right where Kaoru had drawn an X on his gravitational anomaly map ten years ago.

Kaoru felt dizzy. If he stood on that hill and looked west, he'd see water bubbling up from the side of the mountain that would eventually reach the Pacific Ocean; if he looked east he'd see a similar sight. Glittering water slicing its way through a desert wasteland.

The landscape presented itself before his mind's eye. He was standing unsteadily with one foot on either side of that ridge. He'd never been there, but from the contour lines on the map he could imagine it with clarity. But what shook him wasn't that. It was his own guesswork . . . The longevity zone he'd speculated about was now taking on the air of reality. Something was waiting for him there. The thought struck him with awe. Kaoru no longer cared whether the myth was just a made-up story. What was important was how much of his own hope and desire he could pack into the myth he himself was making. His father wanted it. Reiko wanted it. And now his mother did, too.

Machiko put her hand on Kaoru's knee and spoke to him. Her voice was a whisper, but it was full of assurance.

"You'll go there for me, won't you?"

But there were things he still wasn't sure of.

"You're positive this is where Franz Boer went, are you, Mom?"

Machiko grinned. "The article mentioned the work he'd been doing, didn't it? Do you remember what it was?"

"He was a surveyor, wasn't he?" *Franz Boer, a retired surveyor living in Portland, Oregon,* the article had begun.

"That was his day job, but he was also a member of the American Folklore Society. I bet you didn't know that."

"How could I?"

"This book," she said, taking up *North American Indian Folklore* again, "was actually compiled by several people. At the end it says who was responsible for which story."

In the back of the book there was a list of six editors, and beneath each name was a list of numbers corresponding to the stories in the volume each editor had been in charge of. The thirty-fourth story, "Watched by a Multitude of Eyes," had been edited by none other than Franz Boer.

"I see."

So with three months left before he died of terminal cancer, Franz Boer had headed to a certain point in the Southwestern desert to fulfill his last wish. He probably didn't care if he got his miracle or not—as a folklorist, he'd wanted to visit this place once before he died anyway. If he did nothing, he'd most assuredly die, so what did he have to lose by going? And, as it happened, he'd gotten his miracle.

"This story, 'Watched by a Multitude of Eyes,' exists in many variations, and the one included in this book is just the most basic. In one version, it's an older brother and a younger sister who meet the Ancient One and are granted immortality. In another version, Rainier has trouble recovering from childbirth, so Talikeet visits the Ancient One and brings back spring water which heals her. Some of the stories have different titles, too. But the description of the place is always the same. Right here. This place has the power to heal illness."

Machiko tapped the point on the map several times. "That's why Franz Boer went there."

"That place . . . "

"Kaoru, didn't you once show me a map of gravitational anomalies? You'd made a mark in the desert in Arizona or someplace. Can you show me that map again?"

Kaoru wanted to make sure himself. He knew without looking that it was the same place, but still he wanted to check. "Wait a minute," he said, and went to his room.

He hadn't looked at that map for years, so he imagined it would take him a long time to find it. He searched his bookshelves and desk drawers with no luck. It was just a scrap of paper—the proverbial needle in a haystack. But it wasn't a problem. All he had to do was access the same database that he had ten years ago and call up the same information.

He turned on his computer, realizing what an old model it was now. It was on this very screen ten years earlier that the gravitational anomaly map had been displayed.

Kaoru searched his memory for the exact paths he'd taken that night. First, he'd accessed the database on-line. But how had he searched it? First, the category: scientific and technical information. Then, gravity. Under that, gravitational anomalies. Under "area" he chose "worldwide".

Next it asked for a date: what year's gravitational anomalies did he want? He wanted the same map he'd seen ten years before, so he searched for the appropriate year.

Finally, a map appeared on the display. He enlarged the area he'd checked before, the North American desert.

His jaw dropped. The contour lines showed no anomalies in that area whatsoever. Ten years ago, when he'd looked, the negative numbers had gotten larger the closer they'd gotten to that point on the map. The gravitational anomalies had zeroed in on that very spot.

But the map before him now showed no such characteristic. His mother and father had both seen it, he was sure. All three of them had held the maps up to the living room light and seen for themselves that the low-gravity areas contained longevity zones.

Kaoru started again, repeating the same procedure as ten years ago. He did it over and over, but each resulting map held only an unremarkable arrangement of contour lines, a meaningless array of numbers.

He couldn't have misread the map ten years ago. That was impossible. His father's and mother's memories could not be doubted, never mind his own. Looking at that map had led his father promise them a trip to the desert. Kaoru still had the signed agreement in his desk drawer.

So where had that information come from ten years ago?

Kaoru got a pain behind his temples. What had his computer been connected to ten years ago? The thought made the blood rush from his head.

He turned off the computer and closed his eyes. His long-held vague image of the longevity zone in the desert began to rise again before his eyes.

It has to exist. I know it.

The world's outlines were fragile: one poke and it would all crumble into nothingness. But in the face of that fragility Kaoru found assurance. If he'd been able to call up the same information he'd found ten years ago, perhaps he wouldn't have felt this way—perhaps he wouldn't have been able to make up his mind.

He saw a bow-shaped hillock, and rivers swallowed up by the gentle rise of the land. In his imagination he could command the perspective of hawks circling overhead. The deep-carved valleys, the cool green of the trees cradled within them. Maybe the Ancient One still kept watch over the world, flanked by springs that fed into the Pacific and the Atlantic, water that circulated throughout the world like blood or lymph through the body. Incurable illness and ageless immortality; the rising and falling of the tides caused by fluctuations in gravity; life and death. All the contradictions fused into one and rose out of the desert sands. Everything suggested it. Everything whispered to him that he should go there.

Suddenly Machiko was standing behind him. Kaoru turned to look at her, and said, "I'll go, Mom."

"How will you go?"

"I'll have Dad's motorcycle flown to L.A., and then I'll ride out into the desert."

She nodded over and over.

PART THREE

Journey to the End of the Earth

1

Darkness filled his rear-view mirror. The eastern horizon was gradually brightening, but night still ruled the sky as a whole. At the moment, Kaoru was nothing but a figure making its way through darkness toward the dawn. The few clues he'd found had led him to this mission, this burden, to search out a way to combat the Metastatic Human Cancer Virus. All around was blackness, and he had to chase the faintest hint of light.

There were few cars on the interstate highway crossing the Mojave Desert at night, so for a long while he didn't need to glance in the rear-view mirror. But as signs of dawn began to press in upon him from the front, he checked it more frequently. The sky was definitely escaping night's dominion now, embracing the dawn. The landscape's transformation was beautiful to Kaoru's eyes. The brown earth received the corroding rays of the morning and in turn stained the darkness behind him red. On either side of the highway mountain ridges began to appear in silhouette.

Both hands gripping the handlebars of the XLR, the 600CC off-road bike his father had bought ten years ago, Kaoru turned his head to see his surroundings. He wanted to savor the landscape racing by with his own eyes, not through a mirror.

He'd been dreaming of this desert wasteland since he was ten. And now he'd come all the way to America and ridden six hours straight to see it.

It had been late yesterday afternoon when he'd picked up the XLR. He'd shipped it to America air freight. Then he'd had to pack for this race across the desert. It had been nearly ten when he'd finally left L.A. He'd considered getting a good night's rest in a hotel and departing the next morning, but when he contemplated the vast desert to the east of him he couldn't contain himself. He simply had to set off immediately.

But it was dark when he left, and had been dark ever since. Though he'd known he was traversing the Mojave desert, he might as well have been riding through mountain meadows for all he could see. But all he had to do was point the bike down the highway leading straight into the darkness and keep the handlebars steady. Now the sun was rising, giving him his first glimpse of the land.

Kaoru was glad he'd set off when he had, and

glad he'd kept going. This change in the landscape was not to be missed. That, and he'd avoided wasting a day. There wasn't much time left. Today was the first of September: he had to come up with some sort of conclusion within these two months, or it might mean the life of not only Reiko, but her newly-conceived child.

For six hours straight he'd been submerged within the thick hum and vibrations of the four-stroke OHC two-cylinder engine. The road was nicely sealed, but still he maintained perfect riding form, never loosening his knee grip. His father had drilled proper biking technique into him. Whenever he'd lapsed into an unsightly splay-kneed pose, his father would slap his knees and yell at him. *Keep your knees tight around the tank, kiddo.*

And he had, all the way. Shoulders relaxed, weight nicely balanced on the footrests. Kaoru's father had taken him riding even after his diagnosis, and on those trips especially his father's words of instruction had sunk deep into his heart. He tried hard to ride with precision.

The trip meter showed he'd come three hundred miles. The XLR's huge gas tank held thirty liters, good for three hundred and fifty miles of highway driving. Which meant it was about time to fill up: much farther and he'd risk running out of fuel. This highway had stretches of two hundred or more miles with no gas station, so he had to be careful. The luggage rack held a spare polyurethane gas can, but it was empty. He'd meant to stop at a hotel somewhere and lie down on a bed; now he might have come too far.

I'll stop at the next town and have some breakfast, he told himself. He knew if he didn't force himself to stop he'd ride his father's bike until it was out of gas. It frustrated him to have to stop. Watching the change from night to day had proven to Kaoru that the world was revolving on its own; he felt that if he stopped it would go on revolving without him, and he'd be left behind.

Just as the last traces of night disappeared from his rear-view mirror, leaving the land completely covered with light, a town appeared in the distance ahead. It should have a gas station and a place to eat.

Kaoru checked into a motel a little after noon, and then immediately showered and lay down on the bed. He tried to sleep, but the engine vibration had accumulated in his body to the point that his very cells were shaking: he felt itchy and restless. Even as he lay there his body felt like it was still on the bike. The flesh of his thighs in particular, where he'd been squeezing the gas tank, felt like it wasn't his own.

How long was I riding?

He counted on his fingers. Six hours from LA, then he'd dismounted and waited for the diner to open so he could have breakfast. He'd filled up the tank, then ridden for another three hours. Altogether, then, he'd been riding for nine hours. Another nine hours on Interstate 40 would get him to the vicinity of Albuquerque.

His plan was to turn north on Route 25 before Albuquerque, heading through Santa Fe to Los Alamos and Kenneth Rothman's last known address. Of course his final destination was the Four Corners region. But before that he figured it was best to find out what had happened to Rothman, and what his last words meant.

Kaoru reached for his rucksack by the bedside and groped around inside it for his billfold and the two photos he should have inside it. He took them out and studied the face they showed him. Still flat on the bed, he held them over his head and spoke to the beloved figure.

Needless to say, it didn't answer.

Before leaving Japan, Kaoru had visited his father's sickroom to tell him he was going to America. He'd explained why he needed to go, and his father had nodded and said:

"I see."

Kaoru had told his father everything, not even concealing the situation with Reiko. It was possible that his father might die while he was away from Japan: if he was going to tell his father at all, this was the time.

Hideyuki had laughed out loud upon learning that he had a grandchild growing within the womb of this woman Reiko.

"Way to go, kiddo." For a moment the old, healthy Hideyuki was back as he asked with an undisguised leer about Reiko's appearance. "Is she a good woman?"

"To me she's the best," Kaoru answered.

"Can't leave you alone for a minute!" Hideyuki trembled happily. Then he spoke earnestly. "I'd like to live to see my grandkid."

When he heard that, Kaoru was glad he'd told his father about Reiko.

He averted his eyes from Reiko's photographs and put them away in the rucksack again, by touch, not rolling over. His heart beat wildly. Just gazing at her seemed to increase his loneliness.

To distract himself he looked around the room without getting up. On one wall hung a garish round tapestry, and from the ceiling hung a fan, blowing lazily. The sound of the fan bothered him less than the noise of the refrigerator in the kitchen.

All of the furniture and appliances were old, just like the motel itself. He could hear something—a cockroach, maybe?—crawling around under the bed. He'd found one on the kitchen floor earlier. Maybe it was the same one.

Kaoru disliked cockroaches to an unusual

degree, perhaps because he wasn't used to them: he'd never seen one in their twenty-ninth floor condo overlooking the bay.

When he'd checked into this motel, he'd figured on falling asleep as soon as his head hit the pillow—he was that tired. More than the all-night ride, it was the sun beating down on him in the morning that had exhausted him. But unexpectedly, sleep eluded him. Maybe he was too excited: it was his first time in a motel outside of Japan.

It wasn't supposed to be like this, this trip. When he thought of the vacation he'd dreamed of ten years ago, the difference nearly brought tears to his eyes. His problems were too many. He had to save his dying father's life, he had to come up with answers for Reiko, he had to prove to his child that this world was worth living in—the child who was now just a cell starting to divide . . .

He listed his goals in order to bolster his courage. He felt excitement, sentimentality, fatigue, vibration, a sense of mission, fear, and heat all wrapped into one sensation; he felt as if an army of ants was crawling around inside his body. If he didn't find a way to calm his heightened emotions he'd never be able to get to sleep.

He suddenly remembered that there was a pool in the courtyard of the U-shaped motel. Maybe a swim would wash off this creepiness. He got up and changed into swim trunks.

He dived into the empty pool, and then turned over underwater and looked up at the sky. He loved the feeling of moving suddenly from air to water, from one medium to another. Looking up through the water at the sky, he could enjoy both layers at once. The blazing sun looked warped seen from underwater.

He thrust his head above water and stood in the center of the pool. The motel surrounded the pool on three sides, but on the fourth he could see the desert stretching out into the distance. Submerged in water as he was, he was even more struck by how parched and unforgiving the land looked.

He thought he could feel lumps of heat dissolving inside his body. When the last one had melted away, he got out of the pool and returned to his room. His body was telling him he could finally sleep.

2

The sun's rays just got stronger and stronger. He was wearing a long-sleeved sweatshirt and leather gloves, and his jeans were tucked into his boots, and the only skin on his body exposed to the sun was the back of his neck below his helmet. Even so, as he rode he could feel the burning sun all over his body.

He had no street address for the place he was headed. *Wayne's Rock, on the outskirts of Los Alamos, New Mexico*, was all he knew. Just before leaving Japan, he'd contacted Amano again and asked him to look up Kenneth Rothman's last known address. Amano said he'd been living in an old house that doubled as his work space. He had reason to hope that Rothman was still living there, and had cut off contact on purpose, for whatever reason. But even if Rothman was gone, the house at least should still be there in some form. It should at least furnish him with new clues.

On a desert highway with little traffic, it was possible to make travel-time estimates that were exactitude itself. He arrived at Albuquerque right on time, took Interstate 25 northward, and after a time turned onto a state road heading toward Los Alamos. Wayne's Rock should be this side of Los Alamos.

He stopped at a gas station not far from his destination. Not to fill up—he had plenty of gas—but to ask directions. Like seemingly all the gas stations on the state road, this one had a little convenience store attached, and so at the very least he'd find a clerk; if he passed it up, meanwhile, there was no telling when he'd meet another soul.

Since he was here, he topped off the tank, then went into the store to pay. A bearded, middle-aged man glanced a hello at him.

Kaoru hadn't even put in a full gallon, so it was a small amount of money that he gave the man. He then asked how to get to Wayne's Rock.

The man pointed northward and said, "Three miles."

"Got it. Thanks." Kaoru turned to leave, but the man stopped him.

"Have you got business there?" The man's eyes were narrowed and he was frowning at Kaoru. His question was certainly a blunt one, but there didn't seem to be any ill will behind it.

Kaoru didn't know quite how to answer, so he

kept it short. "An old friend of mine lives there. I think."

The man's lips twitched as he shrugged his shoulders and said, "There's nothing there."

Kaoru nodded that he understood, and repeated the words. "There's nothing there."

The man stared at Kaoru wordlessly. But what was he supposed to do, change his mind just because the guy told him there was nothing in Wayne's Rock? He had to go and see for himself.

Kaoru forced a smile and said, "Thank you" as he walked out of the store.

There was no one else around. Kaoru wondered, as he headed away north, just how many customers besides himself the gas station had seen today.

He wanted to check the time as he rode, so he lifted his left hand, the one he wore his watch on, from the handlebars. But he found his leather glove was in the way: he couldn't see the watch. He tried to pull his glove off with his chin, and in the process took his eyes from the road for a split second. When he looked up again, he saw, just beyond a rise covered with desert plants, a line of old trees stretching northward into the desert. Most drivers wouldn't even have noticed them, but Kaoru was paying attention. He was exactly three miles past the gas station.

He could see what looked like a dirt road

running alongside the line of trees. He stopped the bike at the entrance to the road. Up close he realized that what had looked like trees were wooden poles spaced dozens of yards apart; black electrical line sagged from some of them. Power lines, disused for what looked to be quite some time.

If he hadn't been keeping his eyes open, he probably wouldn't have realized there was a road here. It was little more than a slightly leveled-off space next to the power poles. The strip was the only place where cacti didn't grow, raising their gnarled arms skyward—proof that this was indeed a road, or at least had been at one time.

Kaoru scanned the northern horizon, wondering if following the power poles down this road would take him to the village of Wayne's Rock. The road disappeared over a hill. Wayne's Rock was invisible from the state road. But Kaoru had the feeling that distant ruins were calling to him.

At least I won't get lost: all I have to do to get back to the state road is follow the power poles, he thought to himself.

With that he grasped the handles, turned left, and sped off toward the middle of the desert. It was the first time since getting to America that he'd taken the bike off-road.

3

There was a dip in the road ahead of him; he could see it coming, but it didn't look that big. But when he went over it the bike flew more than he'd expected. He dropped his waist back and into the jump, and when the bike landed he wrestled with the violent motion of the handlebars until with precise timing he stabilized the bike. One mistake and he might have tipped over. He cursed himself for his recklessness, and did his best to avoid the craters in the road from then on.

After some initial ups and downs, the road flattened out and ran straight for a while. The dilapidated wooden poles still ran alongside the road, a dotted line linking civilization and wilderness.

"Aha," he said. He'd spied some broken-down buildings ahead, in a ravine cut into a hill. Both the road and the line of poles disappeared into the village. At some point, at least, this town had been connected to an electricity supply and phone service. He couldn't see any poles beyond the village. The lines seemed to end here.

He stopped on a hill maybe a hundred yards before the village. Still straddling the bike, he counted about twenty houses made of brownish stone. Even if there were some on the other side of the ravine that he couldn't see, the whole settlement probably held only a few dozen houses. He couldn't imagine what had led the first inhabitants to decide to dwell here. What had they been seeking out here in the middle of the desert? Judging from the way the houses were constructed, the first settlers had gotten here a long time ago. But the whole village was barren and windswept now. He couldn't see anyone. Even from a hundred yards away he could tell that the place was abandoned.

He remembered the words of the man at the gas station. *There's nothing there.* It looked like he was right. This was a ghost town, rotting away until only traces of its former inhabitants remained.

The sunlight was coming from the west now. A look at his watch told Kaoru it was past five o'clock. It wasn't quite yet time to head back to the state road and look for a town with people living in it.

So Wayne's Rock was a pile of ruins in the middle of the desert. The place filled him with a primal fear, and he asked himself why. Was it because the place represented for him such a fusion of unnatural contradictions? Why had Kenneth Rothman, a cutting-edge information engineer, chosen to live in such a remote place anyway? There were too many things Kaoru didn't understand.

But he'd come too far to back down now. He opened the throttle, gunned the engine, and was cheered by the extravagant noise he was able to summon forth. He sped down the road into the village.

On the way he spied a sign of the type common at the edge of American towns:

WELCOME TO WAYNE'S ROCK

It looked like a bad joke to Kaoru.

As he approached, netlike patterns on the walls began to stand out. Sand and gravel, probably blown by the wind, clung to spots where the stone of the walls was crumbling. Several cars stood abandoned on what looked to be the town's main drag. These, too, were covered in sand.

There was a gas station/convenience store here, too. A single pump stood on the cracked concrete apron; the nozzle was off the hook, and the hose lay on the ground, twisted and black like a cobra, the nozzle its head curled to strike. The store's windows were boarded up tight, and shards of glass were scattered over the ground.

He rode slowly down the main street, peeking at the empty houses on each side, searching for nameplates or the like.

There were more trees inside the town than in the desert surrounding it. Perhaps people had chosen to live here because there was water to be had. The trees thrived on that water, flourishing in and around the ruins. The street was lined with them, and at first they did indeed give an impression of health. But when the wind stirred their limbs and exposed their trunks, Kaoru noticed the strange lumps and pits in the rough bark. He approached one and inspected it to find that the bark on the swollen parts was a different color from the rest. The trunks were mottled in color like human skin peeling from severe sunburn.

The limbs were affected, too, and even the leaves, which looked so fresh, were covered on the back with ocher-colored spots. Only at first glance were the trees normal: scratch the surface and they were riddled with disease.

He'd only seen the cancerous trees of Arizona in a newspaper photo in which it had been impossible to make out the details of their deformation and discoloration, but from the looks of things these trees were showing the same symptoms. Virus-induced cancer, and pretty far advanced, too. It must have taken years for them to get this bad. This was no recent infection.

Kaoru hurriedly looked around him, apprehensive. If the trees here were so far gone, how bad was the damage to animals and humans?

He heard no sound but the wind, but still somehow he felt as if rattlesnakes, scorpions, or some other poisonous desert creature were burrowing under his feet. Some malicious life form, or its shadow, was hiding here, behind cliffs or cacti, under clods of earth, and it struck fear into him.

He had one foot on the bike's footrest and one on the ground. Both feet were encased in leather boots. No foreign object could penetrate to his feet, he knew, but still he shrank from touching the earth with them.

He was desperately thirsty. He had some mineral water in his pack on the luggage rack, but to get it he'd have to dismount the bike and place both feet on the ground. He really didn't want to do that, so he decided to endure the dryness of his throat and ride on deeper into the town.

Some of the houses had walls made of piled-up stone, but some had walls made of carefully worked dried mud. Most of the roofs had caved in: he'd probably be able to stand in the middle of any of these houses and see the sky overhead.

Kaoru actually steered the bike under the eaves of one of the houses and went inside to try. Sure enough, the setting sun was casting its rays slant-wise through a broken space in the roof; dust danced in the bands of light, clouds of dirt glowed with the same coloring.

Where had all the people gone? Were they all dead? Had the MHC virus gotten them all? Or had they escaped, moved to a town with a hospital?

"Hello?" Kaoru called into the depths of the house. No response; he hadn't expected any. He thought he saw the shafts of light quiver from the vibrations of his voice.

Through the crumbling wall he could glimpse a flat space like a plaza. It was surrounded by houses.

He dismounted, pointing the bike toward the edge of the village so he could leave in a hurry. He left the engine running. He reached into his pack for the mineral water and slaked his thirst.

He had a purpose in coming here, and he had to fulfill it. He needed to track down Kenneth Rothman, and to do that he first needed to find Rothman's residence.

On the ride in he'd carefully looked for names on the houses, but he hadn't seen Rothman's. It looked like he was going to have to leave the bike and check each one on foot.

He entered the house criss-crossed by the sun's rays and walked through it toward the plaza in the back. It looked to be some sort of communal space for the village. An old Spanish-style monument, made of plaster in the form of a woman and surrounded by a railing, stood in the center. It was the focal point of the village, which he could see now consisted of two rows of houses arranged in a semicircle; on the other side of the plaza was a hillside.

Kaoru stood in the middle of the plaza and imagined a view of this village from above. The double line of houses made a fan shape.

Behind the monument was a basin-like indentation in the ground, inside which gaped a circular rim. A well. So there was water here. That's why the village had grown up here. He peered in, and the stench of fetid water hit him. The whole village looked parched, and yet the well smelled like water.

The shallow-walled basin resembled a snail in shape. You came around from the outside and then down a set of stairs spiraling down to the rim of the well, as if you were tracing the snail's shell.

The well had no lid. The wind blowing over it made a flute-like sound.

Right beside the well's edge he saw some small black shapes, about the size of his fist. At first he thought they were rocks, but after staring at them for a while he realized they were dead rats, belly up. There must have been over a dozen in the plaza.

Kaoru's gaze naturally followed the trail of dead rats, until he realized the black forms were concentrated beneath a tree at the edge of the plaza, a tree that he could tell from here was cancerous. There was a bench under the tree. And sitting on the bench was a human corpse, the same color as the rats. With the sun at its back, the corpse was just a black shape.

Kaoru went toward the bench, stopping about ten yards from it. The corpse was male, and it looked half mummified. Its legs were spread, its arms hung down limply, and its head was thrown back against the back of the bench, jaw thrust forward. Several long strands of beard hung from the chin, a beard that Kaoru had once described as goatish . . . Only the gold chains around the wrists and neck hadn't rotted. They gleamed with an inorganic light.

Kaoru gingerly approached the man and examined his face. The Kenneth Rothman Kaoru had met—five years ago, when he'd stayed at the Futami house for several days during a visit to Japan—had an impressively narrow face, its most conspicuous feature being his long beard, and he used to wear gold chains around his neck and wrists such as those here. It seemed reasonable to conclude that this corpse was Rothman's.

He must have died here at home, without seeking treatment.

Kaoru looked all around, and something snagged his gaze. The hillside was covered with vegetation appropriate to an arid climate, and amidst it he could see flowers about the size of his palm, coming in and out of view as the wind blew the branches about.

A lone tree in bloom. Its trunk was thin, its branches slender, its leaves looked soft, but this tree alone displayed vitality.

All the trees on the hillside were cancerous: he could see the veins in the leaves standing out hideously. This tree and this tree only seemed to have retained its original coloring. And on the end of its drooping branches grew pale pink blossoms.

Some plants propagate through asexual reproduction, and some through sexual reproduction. Kaoru had observed that the ones covering the mountains in this area were of types that reproduced asexually. Blossoms, however, meant sexual reproduction. He'd heard of cases of asexually-reproducing plants suddenly shifting to sexual reproduction, blooming for the first time in their existence, before rapidly aging and withering away. Such a plant couldn't go on blooming forever, it seemed: the pleasure of producing flowers came in return for dying.

It occurred to Kaoru to pick one of the blossoms and place it next to Rothman's corpse as an offering.

Plants that reproduce asexually can go on living essentially forever, in the right environment. In the Mojave desert there are confirmed instances of such plants that have survived for over ten thousand years. Just like cancer cells in a Petri dish.

What Kaoru was witnessing now, though, was the opposite: only the tree which had gained the ability to reproduce sexually had escaped the cancer. And of course, before too long, this tree with its blossoms would follow the natural order of things and die.

A programmed death accompanied the pleasure of blooming, while a life form which had turned into cancer would go on living forever, unaging, but never producing flowers. It looked like a clear-cut choice between two alternatives. Which would Kaoru choose? A bright, shining mortality, or a dull life that went on forever? It didn't take him long to know the answer: he'd choose the life that bloomed.

Kaoru climbed the hill toward the flowers.

4

He snapped off a blossom and turned to descend the slope. As he did so, a sharp, narrow band of light glancing off one of the rooftops arrayed beneath him caught his eye. The roofs were made of stone of the same color as the land; they blended in dully with their surroundings. They shouldn't be able to reflect light, thought Kaoru, searching for the source of the flash.

A careful look revealed a black rectangle on the roof of a crumbling red-brick building. The rectangular object had a steel rim, and this seemed to have caught a ray of the setting sun.

The panel glowed there on the roof with an alien light. It looked altogether too new to be sitting on a ruined building like that. Maybe such a system was necessary precisely because the village was so far from the main road, but still it looked out of place.

He could tell even at this distance that the

black panel was part of a solar power system. It was quite big enough to produce enough electricity for a single household. If each house had possessed one, there would have been no need for the electric poles lining the road into town, but he couldn't see a similar panel on any of the other roofs in the village. This one seemed to have been specially installed on this house alone.

Rothman had installed his own private research lab at home. Maybe he'd used solar power.

Kaoru laid the blossom down on the corpse's knee and threaded his way between the houses, looking for the one with the solar panel. He'd marked its position from the hillside, but he quickly lost his sense of direction as though he were in a maze.

He wandered this way and that until he found the approach ahead blocked. He'd strayed into a house, and now he was in some sort of hallway.

The wind whistled as it blew in through gaps in the walls, but here it had no place to go, so it eddied around his ankles. He thought he could hear native American singing, a sort of call-and-response with the wind, or maybe it was the cry of a bird, or the sound of branches rubbing together.

Kaoru fell still and pricked his ears. His sense of hearing was confused: he couldn't tell what was near and what was far. One moment he thought he was hearing a human voice at a distance, and the next he experienced the illusion that it was whispering in his ear. It was a hoarse, male voice, muttering—he could hear it—by the wall to the right. It stopped, and when it started again the wind had wafted it over to the left-hand wall.

The voice and the whistling seemed to come from everywhere; the sound seemed to gain a vibrato effect as it slipped through the gaps in the walls.

Was it the dryness of the air that kept him from feeling afraid? Totally devoid of humidity, the air seemed to lack the little hands that would have grabbed him and given him chills. The moisture rapidly drained from any exposed skin; soon, he was afraid, he'd feel nothing at all.

He tried to ignore his other senses and concentrate on his hearing. Gradually he came to detect the source of the sound. Still concentrating on it, he ducked through a hole in one wall, then another, and then found himself in a somewhat different world.

There was a faint smell. He was in a two hundred square foot space with crumbling walls, where something he'd never encountered before, a man-made smell that couldn't possibly exist in nature, pervaded the air.

There was a pipe-framed bed in a corner of the room. It held no bedding, only an old mattress with several springs poking up through it. There was a sturdy-looking table next to it, and next to that two deck chairs, facing each other, looking more appropriate to a beach than a house. A floor lamp lay tipped over on the floor, and an old leather suitcase rested unsteadily against the table. There were shelves built into one wall, but some of them were broken, their contents leaning crazily. Several thick doorstop-like books sat on the bottom shelf.

Everything in the room looked precariously balanced. He suspected that if he took away just one of the shelves, or moved the bedside table just a few inches to one side, everything would collapse like a row of dominos.

From out of nowhere, the hoarse voice was back, breathing in his ear. Kaoru nearly jumped out of his skin. He looked around in every direction.

Nobody was there. The noise died away quickly, leaving an intermittent buzz in its wake. Kaoru glanced at the space between the table and the wall, and saw an electrical cord. Only then did he notice that there was a radio fixed to the table. It sounded like it wasn't receiving steady current.

Kaoru grasped the cord and moved it around a little. The buzzing decreased, replaced by a man's steady voice, accompanied by a sad-sounding guitar. A radio broadcast. The man was singing some kind of blues song. Kaoru was able to make out the lyrics: something about a love that had ended long ago.

Kaoru bent down and adjusted the tuner, reducing the static further. This was definitely the source of the voice he'd barely heard floating to him on the wind. For some reason this radio was still turned on, plugged in, and receiving signals. Playing music.

It was unthinkable that the power lines could still be supplying electricity to these ruins. The electricity would have been interrupted long ago.

The rooftop solar panel he'd seen must be providing the electricity. It was the only thing that could explain the radio still playing.

Kaoru followed the cord to the wall socket, then adjusted the volume again. No mistake, electricity was flowing from somewhere.

Press on, he urged himself. The knowledge that this house in the middle of the desert wore a crown of modern science gave him a kind of courage.

In one wall there was a door to the next room. He placed a hand on the knob. It opened easily.

Beyond the door was a short hallway leading to what seemed to be the entrance to a basement. The stairs led underground until they were swallowed in darkness. But on second look it wasn't total darkness: he could see a little light seeping out from around a door. There was a light on in the basement.

As he stood at the top of the stairs looking down, Kaoru felt like he was being guided.

There's a light on.

He pondered that fact for a while. Perhaps it had just been left on, like the radio.

A step at a time, he climbed down the stairs.

Stopping in front of the door, he pressed an ear against it and listened for signs of what was beyond. There was no sound, no sign of anybody. The light shining between the door and its frame was fainter than he'd first thought.

He was about to knock, but it came to him how foolish that notion was. In one bold motion he grasped the doorknob, turned it, and walked in.

A single fluorescent bulb hung from the ceiling, dimly illuminating the basement. But in the center of the room shone another light, a special one that meant civilization.

Spacious as the basement was, its purpose was clear. A computer had been set up in the exact center of the room, surrounded by associated cabinets. The monitor was flickering.

Kaoru went around until he was facing the monitor. Beside it sat a helmet, to both the inside and outside of which were attached electronic devices. Probably a helmet display: he'd used something like it as a kid to play virtual reality games. He hadn't seen one for so long that the sight of this one brought back pleasant memories.

A wired data glove sat next to the helmet, but Kaoru didn't touch either of them. He headed straight for the monitor.

As if cued by Kaoru's appearance in front of it, letters began to appear on the screen.

W...e...l...c...o...m...e

The word popped up one letter at a time. Kaoru found the idea juvenile in the extreme. Evidently the system was set up so that the display would sense when someone was standing in front of it and turn on.

He felt momentarily faint, and leaned on the chair in front of the screen. He eased himself into the chair, resting his elbows on the armrests, and caught his breath. Then he spoke to the computer.

"Who are you, anyway?"

The computer didn't answer him directly. Instead it showed him a scene.

A barren, windswept desert. An undulating landscape. The scene moved, so that the viewer felt like he was running across the desert. The view slid along just over the surface of the land, following a road up and down slopes, until a village appeared before it. Kaoru had seen it somewhere before.

Then he realized it was Wayne's Rock, albeit a different Wayne's Rock than the one he knew. The one he saw on the monitor was much smaller, with only a few houses visible, and those were made of wood, not stone. If it hadn't

been for the distinctive hillside in the background, he wouldn't have even realized what
he was looking at.

How long ago is this, he wondered. A hundred
years ago, maybe longer? He couldn't see any
people; there was no indication as to the era. The
scene screamed Old West, though.

Is this a movie? A natural question.

It didn't look like computer graphics. He
wanted to think it was a real filmic record, but
it was much too clear and well-preserved to have
been shot a hundred or more years ago. No, what
he was seeing was probably the result of the application of some special technology to recreate the
old town on shots of the present Wayne's Rock.
But it looked absolutely real.

He heard hoofbeats behind him. So real did
they sound that he turned around to look, only
to discover speakers attached to the stone wall
behind him.

The scene on the monitor was displayed in
only two dimensions, but the sound came through
in three.

He kept glancing at the helmet and glove next
to the monitor. He finally understood what he
was being instructed to do.

*If you want to experience it in 3-D, put on the helmet
and glove.*

So he did. And once he had the helmet on, a

turn of his head gave his mind's eye a 360-degree view of the landscape.

The hoofbeats behind him were no longer just a 3-D effect, they were utterly real, echoing in his brain. He could feel the ground shake with them. He should be wearing boots, but somehow he felt sharp pain as a cactus spine penetrated his foot. Human commotion overwhelmed him. A hot wind caressed the back of his neck, and he felt thirsty. Sweat dripped off him.

Kaoru ran on and on, trying to escape the figures bearing down on him from behind. Unable to bear it any longer, he looked back and saw a dozen or more mounted Indians, their feathered headdresses silhouetted against the sun at their backs.

I'm going to be trampled to death.

He tried to jump sideways, out of their path, but just then a muscular arm hooked itself under his armpit and pulled him up. The arm felt firm under his, real to the touch. He smelled sweat and dirt. Before he knew it the rough arm had slung him around and sat him astride a horse.

Kaoru told himself he was dreaming. He knew, or thought he knew, that this wasn't reality. But as he pressed his face against the Indian's muscular back and clung tight to keep from being thrown from the horse, he found himself eye-level with a bunch of scalps hanging like ornaments from the Indian's shoulder. One was still new, still wet on the underside, still smelling of blood.

His eyes swam and his head fell back, though his instincts told him that if he fell off the horse he'd die.

It was at that moment that the boundary between reality and unreality dissolved.

5

He couldn't figure out how long he'd been bouncing around on the horse. It might have been minutes, but if someone had told him it was hours, he might well have believed it.

They descended into a valley and stopped beside a river. Kaoru was a little surprised at the abundance of water snaking along at the bottom of the deep ravine. From the top of the gorge the river had looked minuscule—he'd never dreamed that it held this much water.

The water was far from clear: it was laden with dissolved brown earth. But in that arid land, just standing in the damp air beside the river was a relief. Kaoru found himself able to share in the group's consciousness enough to be aware of that.

They rode along the banks amidst the spray for a while until they came to a wide spot the river had carved into the valley. Here they halted. Several of the men looked up at the lip of the gorge and imitated the cries of animals. The rest separated into two groups, one keeping watch downriver, one upriver, guarding against pursuers or ambushers.

The brilliant sun scorched the earth: he could feel the heat through the soles of his feet. He could feel the passage of time.

A trembling disturbed the woods covering the sides of the ravine, and then from behind trees and rocks emerged small bands of women, children, and old people. The women and children outnumbered the men on horseback.

At first the women seemed afraid to approach. They looked at the men on horseback with mingled expectation and tension, joy and fear, and prayer. Then women who spotted the faces they were searching for began to raise scream-like cries, rushing to their men, while the men answered by alighting from their horses and embracing their women. The reunions were conducted with an urgency in direct proportion to the earlier display of caution.

All of the women's cries sounded like weeping, but a closer listen revealed two distinct types. Some wept for joy, and some for sadness. Those women who realized that the ones they sought were not among the riders fell to their knees, beating the earth with their fists and shouting imprecations. Some women clutched small children and looked up to the sky, and some held the hands of old people and sank down to the ground.

Kaoru suddenly caught on. A tribe of Indians—this area must be their home—had sent its warriors out to battle. How many had gone out? He judged the number of women embracing men and rejoicing over their safety to be roughly equal to the number of women wailing with lowered heads. So: twice as many men had left as returned. A woman who didn't find her man among those who returned had to assume he was dead. Every wife and family member was displaying heightened emotion—some positive, some negative.

Kaoru watched unmoved. Sizing up the situation he decided he was the only one able to look on as a bystander. He felt out of place, uncomfortable.

But a moment later his certainty as to which world he actually lived in was rocked. A hand grabbed him and dragged him sideways. He saw a weeping woman rushing up to him. Her earnest gaze denied his earlier scornful detachment. A ten-year-old boy grabbed him around the waist. Suddenly plunged into this vortex of emotion, Kaoru felt only confusion.

The woman had long hair that was braided down her back, and her broad forehead was exposed. Heedless of the infant she held at her breast, she threw herself at Kaoru. Kaoru felt suffocated. Still, he received the woman. Her passion moved him to an embrace.

The image of the woman before him merged with the picture of Reiko he held in his mind. They did look alike. The hair was different in length and style, but the shapes of their faces, the drooping eyes, were identical. Perhaps Kaoru simply wanted to see things that way, though. Ever since coming to the desert his desire to see Reiko had been stimulated to new heights.

As they held each other, crushing the baby between them, his hands and arms coming into direct contact with her flesh, Kaoru could feel the woman's emotions flowing into his own breast, just for a moment. He and this woman must be husband and wife. The boy clinging to his waist must be his son, the squalling infant squeezed between himself and the woman must be his newborn daughter. It came to him that he knew the kind of life he and this woman had led together over the years. Things he'd seen and felt growing up here came back to him. Sadness, but more than that, hatred. A desire to avenge his murdered father filled the depths of his soul.

New information kept coming to him. The woman had come from another tribe to live with this one. The marriage was her second. Her first husband had been killed far upriver. And not just killed. A band of white soldiers and ruffians had tortured him and then left him to die on the rocks.

The woman still nursed resentment over the way her first husband had been treated. The mechanism by which resentment goaded people to war was laid bare to his consciousness.

He now knew that the boy he had thought was his son was in fact the child of his wife by her previous husband. The only living people with whom he had ties of blood were his aged mother and his newborn daughter.

Kaoru tasted anew the suspicion that here was the real world casting its shadow over the virtual space. His relationship with this woman was almost exactly the one he had with Reiko. Except that Ryoji was dead. He'd thrown himself from the fire escape window, leaving behind only bloodstains on concrete. He'd gone to the other side. But the boy clinging to his waist now was weak and unreliable, just like Ryoji.

Kaoru realized that his own body and mind had started to go over to the other world, leaving him only half conscious. "The other world" was how he expressed it, unthinkingly, but he had no idea where it was located.

There was a brief interval of peace. He lived in a tent pitched on a gentle slope, surrounded by his wife and children and his aged mother. How long had they been together? Sometimes several years felt like a single moment to him, while sometimes a day lasted like a day.

It felt to Kaoru that time flowed, sometimes thick and sluggish, sometimes quick and nimble. The time that enveloped him was mottled, with patches of intensity and patches of attenuation.

His daughter, a newborn when first he'd met her, was a toddler now. His stepson showed not the slightest talent for fighting: a warrior he'd never be. The way he stood when using a bow made everybody laugh.

Kaoru was used to this body now. Crouching beside the river he saw reflected in the water a form totally different from his old one. Dark skin, thick neck and burly tattooed shoulders. He could touch this body and feel it react. Only, his facial features were obscured by ripples in the water: he couldn't get a clear view of them.

He made love to his wife many times, and each time he grew closer to her. His daughter looked at him differently now, too.

The tribe never lived long in one place: always they were forced to move. From the east and the south they were pressed by a tribe whose skin was a different color. West was the only way they could go. The most careful judgment was required on the part of their leaders to keep contact with the enemy to a minimum while securing food and water supplies. One miscalculation would mean the end of the tribe.

There was only one place they could aim for.

Fractured and factionalized though the tribe was, everyone's expectations focused on the same point: the old legends.

"You must head for a place at the southern edge of the great mountains, where rivers flowing into the western and eastern seas have their source. A place where no one has gone before. There you will find a great cavern with a lake in its belly. This will be the eternal dwelling place of the tribe. There the Great Spirit will watch over you so that none may threaten you, and you will live forever."

There was nothing left to cling to but legends. If they were to be pushed westward anyway, it was only natural to seek the place the legends spoke of.

Though much diminished, the tribe still numbered over two hundred. It wasn't easy to move all those people. Teams of agile scouts on horseback took turns patrolling the area ahead, and only when they had made sure the way was clear of enemies would they lead the main camp on. Hunters had to be sent out constantly to procure food.

At night families would pitch their tents in any handy place and gather around campfires to eat the meat of the beasts killed by the hunters earlier in the day. They could never eat their fill. Normally they would have preserved leftover meat by smoking it, but they were always too short of food now to even consider that.

Encountering water they would first wash themselves and then move upstream seeking cleaner water to drink. The most important element in their survival was water. He who discovered it would receive the thanks of everyone.

Now they had reached a place from where, by crossing two more peaks, they should be able to find the land the legends spoke of. Almost in sight of their goal, they camped in the woods, marshalling their last reserves of spirit. And chance blessed them with water.

It was children who found the spring. It was said that several of them had been at play, running around among the trees, when they had found a rocky outcropping peeking out from between tree trunks, with a pretty trickle of water running down its face. They called the news to each other, and several adults nearby set out for the spring with vessels in hand.

Here and there they stood, looking around them carefully. Kaoru counted the people climbing the slope of the mountain. Three in front of him, four behind: eight, including himself. The four behind were all women, with his wife and daughter among them. The three in front were all children, and his son was among them, suddenly eager to prove his worth. Only his mother was absent. She was down in the main encampment.

The child who said he'd seen water had spoken

truly. There it was, a thin line of water on the face of a boulder sticking out of the mountainside. It was so weak a trickle that they'd have trouble filling their vessels.

As they were debating climbing higher to search for a place where the water flowed more vigorously, the underbrush behind them rustled.

The men who appeared all of a sudden looked different. Many of them wore disheveled blue uniforms. Some wore white shirts with torn jackets tied around their waists, some wore black shirts with hide trousers. At a quick count the enemy numbered over a dozen. An organized platoon it was not. Several of the men held canteens, suggesting that they, too, had simply wandered onto the mountain looking for water. Others held firearms. Blood stained several of the white shirts.

A whisper arose among the band of strangers. The air crackled with tension. There was no time to wonder what to do. With women and children along there was no way to fight. If the strangers wanted a battle, Kaoru's group would have to flee. But it was best to make no sudden moves, in case their intentions weren't hostile.

The strangers exchanged words and worried expressions, but Kaoru couldn't understand what they said. His sense of time was going crazy again. It had only been two or three seconds since he'd seen the strangers, but he felt like several minutes had passed.

Suddenly the three boys started half-running, half-rolling down the mountain, yelling. Rifles had been pointed at their backs, but others brushed these aside, and as if on cue the men surrounded the boys and blocked their way.

The men didn't seem to want to shoot. The noise would alert the main encampment below, in which case they had next to no chance of surviving. They probably meant to silence every one of Kaoru's group.

Reaching that conclusion, Kaoru started to turn to face his wife. Then he saw his son's head split open by a rock as the men held him down.

Mouths covered by thick hands, the children were unable to raise a cry as their brains splattered onto the ground. The blood against the gray of the rock looked like the momentary blooming of a computer-generated rose. Behind him Kaoru could hear men's boots kicking at stone.

Violent pain shot through his Achilles tendon. It wasn't that it had been slashed—the bone itself had been crushed. He lost his balance and sprawled onto the boulder. He'd twisted as he fell, so he hit the stone with his side, but he no longer registered pain.

He reached out to try and touch his wife. But before he could, the men began lifting up the women and flinging them into the underbrush.

Kaoru summoned all his strength in an effort to raise himself, but the men held him down.

They even grabbed his hair and pressed his head back against the rock so that he couldn't move.

He heard the dull sound of something being crushed beside his head. He knew he shouldn't look, but his eyes rolled to the side anyway, following the sound of tearing flesh.

He saw that adorable little body he'd embraced so many times dashed on the stone from the height of a man's head. All his thoughts focused on his dying daughter, but his body wouldn't obey him. It wasn't pain he felt so much as a burning sensation. It was impossible even to know all the places he was injured. The pain was beside the point. He was prepared to die, and fear was a luxury he couldn't afford at this point. What he found unbearable was the violence being visited on those close to him, their unforeseen extinction.

He watched as once again his daughter's body was raised up to the same height and then slammed to the ground. She must be dead by now. And so her pliant, lifeless body was abandoned among the rocks.

The man who'd been tossing his daughter's body about had evidently found something else to entertain him, because he tramped across the grass into the trees.

Kaoru was able to follow his leisurely movements with his eyes. As he walked, the man was rubbing the backs of his hands on his shirttails, which hung down over his trousers. What was he doing? Blood streaked his once-white shirt. Not just blood: bits of flesh clung to the fabric. Was that his daughter's blood, her flesh? The man kept wiping his hands on his shirt as if shaking off something filthy; finally he rubbed them on his trousers.

He could hear his wife's voice, faintly. He could tell she was somewhere nearby. But no matter which way he turned his gaze, he couldn't find her. Perhaps she was sunk down in the under-brush. All Kaoru could see were the men standing or half-kneeling around her.

The hand holding his hair shifted its grip. It forced his head back even more powerfully, so that his throat was fully exposed to the sun directly overhead. He could see another sharp flash of light, not from the sun. This light moved quickly from right to left.

There was a gurgling in his throat, and then a whistling sound. He felt a hot liquid on his chest. His head seemed to have fallen even father back.

The sun's rays changed hue, gradually growing in intensity, until the background faded into monochrome and the darkness increased. The red sun gradually blackened, and his retinas were steeped in darkness. His hearing alone still seemed to be functioning.

He could hear his wife's cries. It sounded less like she was wailing in misery than that she was laughing weakly. His ears picked up her voice until the moment his consciousness disappeared. The woman he'd shared his time with, at least in this world.

His own death and the deaths of his loved ones had come at the same time.

6

Kaoru sat for a while slumped in the chair, immersed in darkness. To an innocent bystander he would have looked simply tired. But what Kaoru had experienced was death itself: his body was now just his soul's empty husk.

The sensations he'd experienced at the moment of death were not the same as losing consciousness. Even when a person has fainted, the brain continues to function. What Kaoru had known for a brief instant was the stopping of his heart, and the gentle sensation of time and space flickering out as his brain died.

He heard a voice beyond the darkness.

"Time to wake up."

It was a man's voice, powerful yet restrained.

"Come here," the voice ordered, before disappearing along with its echoes.

Kaoru shuddered, and then jumped up out of the chair. He sucked in great gulps of air, and unconsciously his body extended itself. He was like a drowning man seeking air, trying to force his head above water.

He tore the helmet display from his head and flung it onto the desk. He ripped off the data gloves and threw them down beside it.

He felt like his heart was being squeezed. He lowered his body into the chair again and tried to bring his breathing under control. The more his body reaccustomed itself to a real environment, the more violently his heart beat. The memories were still fresh and clear.

He realized he had tears streaming from his eyes. Waves of inexpressible emotion, not quite sadness and not quite pain, washed over him.

He collapsed onto the desk and wept. Telling himself it wasn't real didn't help to calm his roiling feelings. Looking at his wristwatch and calculating that he'd spent less than an hour and a half in the helmet was no comfort, either. When a minute corresponded to a year, time weighed heavily.

Kaoru had no idea who had made the virtual reality he'd just experienced, or how, but his feelings told him he'd lived a whole life in the other world. He'd loved a woman, had a child, fought for his people, and died, all in the other world. He'd lost his loved ones at the same time as he'd died—they'd been close enough to touch if only he'd been able to reach out his hand, but he'd been unable to save them.

"Laiche," he was calling. It was a name, his wife's name; he'd called her by it who knew how many times. He could remember them washing each other's bodies in the river, touching each other's skin. The sensations were still fresh.

"Cochise!" That was his daughter's name. How many mountains had he crossed with her on his back or at his chest before she'd learned to walk?

He could remember their names. But when it came to his own name, his memory was vague. He could remember their faces, but his own was hazy. The pain of the moment of death was now mostly gone from his memory, too. What remained were recollections of his loved ones—and those overwhelmed him.

Kaoru got up shakily, went to the wall, and rammed his shoulder against it. Pain shot through him. He wanted that physical pain, to help him forget the ache in his heart.

I must analyze what this means, he told himself, hoping reason would help drive away the sadness.

The experience Kaoru had gone through was nothing like watching a movie. The only way he could describe it to himself was this: he had been inserted bodily into a virtual space. And that virtual space reproduced reality exactly. How was that possible? The questions were only beginning.

The Loop.

The first idea he had was that this virtual space might be part of the artificial life project.

He knew that it was possible to be present for any moment in the history of the Loop simply by donning a helmet display like the one he'd just used and setting the time and space coordinates. One could be as a god to the Loop life forms, watching them from on high, or one could use the sight and hearing of a particular individual and live a virtual life.

The patterns of the birth and history of the Loop life forms were all saved in a huge store of holographic memory. It was possible to witness any moment in its history.

Which was what made Kaoru guess that the world he'd just visited was part of the Loop. What he'd experienced was a physical expression light years beyond computer graphics, possible only because the Loop contained beings evolved from the program's initial RNA life forms.

The bodies he'd touched, that he'd thereby grown to love, were real, not constructed. Just thinking back on them, Kaoru was moved.

The death and partings he'd undergone in the virtual world only strengthened his resolve. He couldn't lose any more loved ones. How much more painful would parting be in the real world? He didn't want to go through that again. He simply had to unlock the riddle of the MHC. He had to find a way to treat it.

The cancerization of the Loop is affecting the real world.

He was more convinced of that than ever. Just glimpsing a corner of the virtual world had shattered his emotions. The virtual world had affected him: why should it be strange that it was affecting the whole real world?

What did this room mean? Somebody had foreseen Kaoru's coming and left behind this elaborate system to greet him. He figured that it had to be Rothman, but he couldn't guess why.

But there had to be a reason. He couldn't shake the feeling that he'd been led here. And if he was being led, there was nothing else to do but follow whatever guidance was yet to come.

Maybe it was showing me where I should go.

His mother had shared with him that Native American folktale about a warrior guiding people westward. The tribe he'd belonged to in the virtual world had also believed in a place at the southern edge of the Rocky Mountains where they could live forever under the protection of the Great Spirit, and that belief had led them to move ever westward. The course they'd followed was still etched in Kaoru's brain.

Death had come unexpectedly upon them only two peaks from their destination, but he could clearly remember the path up to that point. Though they'd camped for months at a time, still the journey, that path, had been their life.

Kaoru grasped what he was to do. *I'm supposed to go the way the tribe went.*

But there was something he needed to do first.

He had to make contact with Amano in Japan. Connecting then and there with Amano's computer via satellite, he made a single request. *Send visuals of Takayama and Asakawa ASAP.* It was a request he'd already made once, before leaving Japan.

The Loop functioned on essentially the same scale as the real world. Billions of intelligent life forms living their lives, creating the histories of their ethnic groups. The amount of memory involved must be staggering. Amidst all that, Amano was trying to find the exact moments when the cancerization of the world began. No small task.

But if Amano could isolate that sequence, Kaoru would be able to use the helmet display and data gloves to conduct an investigation in real time. He'd first lock in on an individual in the Loop, searching for a clue as to why the cancer started. Who knew? Maybe that information would open everything up for him.

While waiting for Amano's response, Kaoru was assailed by an irresistible desire to hear Reiko's voice. What time was it in Japan right now? With seven hours' time difference, it should be nine in the morning there. Was Reiko up yet? After experiencing the death of someone he loved in the virtual world, Kaoru really wanted to feel Reiko's presence close to him. At the very least, he wanted to know how she was doing.

He dialed her number on his satellite phone.

It rang seven times before a drowsy voice said, "Hello?"

So evidently the real world was still there. Kaoru felt indescribable relief just to hear Reiko say "hello". It was like emerging from a treacherous swamp and finding oneself on firm ground again.

"It's me."

A pause, while she collected herself. When she spoke again, the drowsiness was gone from her voice.

"Is that really you? Where are you? How are you?" She fired questions at him, all her worry for him coming to the fore. Kaoru was gratified to hear it.

He answered her queries one by one, and then said, "It's alright. I want you to just relax and wait for me."

Then he ended the call. There was no reason to talk forever.

7

He decided to take a nap on the bed while he waited for Amano's response.

Kaoru figured he was the only one in the world to suspect the connection between the Loop and the cancer virus. It was of course possible that somebody else had arrived at the same conclusion differently, but he hadn't had any information to that effect, and besides, if it hadn't occurred to Amano, the man in charge of maintaining the Loop, then Kaoru felt that chances were he was the only person pursuing this angle. He hoped that by following his hunch, he might be able to shine some light on things that nobody had noticed before. He was sure that the Loop's demise had been investigated any number of times. But that was twenty years ago, before MHC.

The Loop had turned entirely cancerous. Not long thereafter, the real world had seen the isolation of the Metastatic Human Cancer Virus, which

was now starting to infect non-human popula-
tions, too. It certainly looked like it had spread
from the Loop.

Then there was the strange coincidence that
the nine genes which made up the MHC virus
all had base totals that came to 2^n x 3. This
suggested to Kaoru that perhaps the source of the
virus was a computer, something that thought in
binary code.

Just as he started to nod off, the computer came
to life. He went and sat down at the desk. Just
as he'd thought, a reply from Amano. The screen
displayed several steps for him to follow.

He followed the instructions, tapping on the
keyboard. Then it was simply a matter of letting
this computer access the relevant portion of the
Loop memory.

Access complete.

Kaoru donned the helmet display and data
glove, knowing this time what it meant.

The chronicle he'd been sent covered things
seen and heard by a certain individual beginning
in the summer of 1990, Loop time.

Everything was there for the viewing. If he
specified, say, a time of 1990/10/04/14:39 and a
place of 35.41°N/139.46°E, he'd be able to watch
everything that took place there and then. By
advancing the time coordinates while remaining
in the same place, the chronicle would unfold on

the display. There was a zoom function for a more exact location fix.

He could watch from a fixed viewpoint if he wished. He could specify, say, the fourth block of the Ginza district, and be able to observe any event taking place there in any age. The observer had the ability to look in absolutely any direction, could dart his gaze in between people on the street, could look around at everything like a ghost. The Loop inhabitants would be unaware of the observer, while the observer would be able to explore their world with the freedom of an invisible man.

Alternatively, the observer could lock into the perceptions of a single individual. This would allow the observer to meld his senses with his chosen character in the virtual world.

What Kaoru had in hand now were the memories etched in the brains of several persons. He wanted to observe the cancerization of the Loop from the perspective of someone intimately involved with it, just as he'd lived the entire life of a Native American man in a few minutes. He had at his disposal the experiences of several people, beginning with the one known as Takayama.

So what kind of life had this Takayama led? Kaoru was curious, but his fear outweighed his curiosity. He could be about to experience more unbearable heartache.

But by hesitating he'd only lose his courage. Kaoru started the program.

Of his own free will, Kaoru plugged into the Loop.

He seemed to be in a downtown coffee shop. Flashing neon signs outside the window cast brightly colored shafts of light into the shop. Takayama, the man onto whom Kaoru had locked, was seated at a table across from another man. The other man was the one known as Asakawa, Takayama's friend. Asakawa was haggard; the sight of him aroused Kaoru's pity. But of course he was haggard: the night before, he'd watched a videotape hideous like no other. Seeking someone to rescue him from the straits he'd found himself in, Asakawa had chosen Takayama. He'd called him here to the coffee shop today to explain the circumstances and ask for his advice.

Takayama took a piece of ice from the glass on the table, threw it in his mouth, and crushed it with his teeth. The chill spread through Kaoru's mouth, too.

Asakawa was scared and keyed up, and as he told his story he was prone to get the order of things mixed up. Takayama was forced to reorganize Asakawa's account in his own mind.

Asakawa's miseries all stemmed from a cab ride he'd taken with an overly talkative driver. The driver had related to him an incident he'd witnessed at an intersection.

The driver had been stopped at a light when a motorcycle next to him had tipped over. The rider had died on the spot from what looked like a heart problem. With the glee of a kid telling scary stories, the cabbie spoke of how the rider had writhed and struggled, trying to take off his helmet. Asakawa's life had changed forever as a result of this useless information.

On the basis of what the cab driver had told him, Asakawa had started looking into sudden deaths. He soon uncovered the fact that along with the motorcyclist, three other young people had died at the exact same time, with exactly the same symptoms, but in different places. One was Asakawa's own niece. His curiosity was aroused. All four deaths had been recorded as the result of sudden heart failure, but his reporter's instinct detected something untoward going on. Given the utter improbability of four kids dying of the same thing at exactly the same time, he felt there had to be a more convincing explanation.

He'd decided to look for commonalities between the four dead kids. It turned out that they were friends, and that exactly a week before their deaths they had been staying in a rented cabin in the mountains. Asakawa decided to check the place out: he departed immediately for the site, a members-only mountain resort, guessing that whatever had caused their deaths, they'd picked it up there.

Evidently Asakawa had initially suspected a virus. He thought they might have all contracted the same illness at the cabin, and thereby been scheduled for the baptism of death a week later.

But to his surprise, what Asakawa had discovered in the cabin was a videotape.

At that point, Takayama broke in and said, "First why don't you let me have a look at that video."

Asakawa looked to be stifling his irritation. "I told you, if you watch it your life might be in danger."

Takayama took another piece of ice from his glass, put it in his mouth, and bumped it around a bit. Asakawa seemed to think he was being mocked.

But in the end, mortal danger or no, nothing was going to get done if he didn't see the video. Takayama decided to go to Asakawa's place and watch the video he'd brought home from the mountains.

Takayama sat in Asakawa's living room, eyes glued to the TV screen. Through his eyesight, the images on the tape found their way into Kaoru's brain.

The images were chaotic and fragmentary. The tape started with an erupting volcano. Next up was a newborn infant's face in close-up. The sequence was fragmentary, and shifted quickly from one image to the next, but each scene left a strangely vivid impression, underlain by a baby's cries and other sounds.

The images were neither computer graphics nor the result of filming with a television camera. They were made some other way. One might think of them as shots of another, lower virtual world created by some sentient being within the Loop.

At length there appeared the face of an unknown man, shot from beneath at close range. A close-up of his shoulder showed blood streaming from it. His face was twisted in pain. He went away, and when he came back his face was transformed: the rage was gone, replaced by mingled fear and resignation.

The field of vision narrowed, until it was just a small round patch of sky, through which fist-sized black clumps were falling. They landed on something with a dull thud. Kaoru's body registered unexpected pain.

What's going on? he muttered.

No answer was forthcoming. The field of vision narrowed further, until it was perfectly dark.

As the tape came to an end, writing flashed across the screen. It looked like it had been written with brush and ink, but poorly: the characters were all of different sizes. This was what it said:

Those who have viewed these images are fated to

die at this exact hour one week from now. If you do not wish to die, you must follow these instructions exactly . . .

Then the screen switched to something completely different, bright images and voices. Fireworks on a riverbank, people in light cotton robes enjoying a summer's evening. The dark, creepy visions had been cut off, replaced by a healthful mundaneness.

A few seconds after that, the images stopped entirely.

Kaoru and Takayama looked up from their respective displays at the same time.

Boiled down, one thing became clear.

Those four dead kids had to have all watched this video. And a week later they were all dead, just like the video warns. So there's a video that kills people a week after they watch it, and the instructions for averting death have been erased. There was no saving those kids.

After watching that video in the cabin, Asakawa had been shaken, and now he was despairing, but Takayama was neither. He couldn't be happier than to be involved in this game, this death-wager. He was whistling a happy tune. Kaoru began to realize what a stout-hearted subject he'd locked onto.

He tried to take a step back from Takayama's consciousness so he could analyze things a little more rationally.

Common sense said it was impossible for an

intra-Loop life form to construct a videotape that killed anyone who watched it a week later. Of course, it was possible to introduce something from the real world into the Loop that took that form—a computer virus, for example. That would explain everything.

Kaoru put his own doubts on hold again to rejoin the bold and fearless Takayama.

Takayama had Asakawa make him a copy of the tape so they could each apply their intellect to analyzing it.

It wasn't long before Takayama was informed that Asakawa's wife and daughter had watched the videotape, which had been carelessly left for them to find. So now Asakawa was driven by the need to save not only his own life, but those of his family.

Takayama began by trying to figure out how the images on the tape had been filmed. His research and guesswork led him to an unexpected conclusion.

The images on the tape had not been created mechanically, by a television camera or any similar device. Instead, the individual responsible had utilized his or her own psychological power to project them directly onto the videotape. Psychic photography, "thoughtography". Psychic power had imprinted those images onto a blank tape that had been left in the VCR by pure chance.

The Loop was a closed world. Going strictly by

the physical laws that obtained there, such a thing was not possible. That wasn't the way the set-up worked.

Kaoru began to feel as if he were watching a movie—a well-made one, to be sure, but based on some pretty juvenile premises.

The two men investigated the identity of their paranormal thought-projector making full use of the information networks at their disposal. Finally, they settled on a name.

Sadako Yamamura.

At that point, based on what they knew, it was definite that the individual in question was female. They visited the island that had been her home, gathering as much data about her as they could.

What they learned as a result was that this Yamamura possessed power that far exceeded what was thought realistic. They ascertained her movements from birth through her graduation from high school and her move to the metropolis. But then Sadako Yamamura seemed to disappear—some twenty-odd years ago, Loop time.

It was time for a new perspective. They decided to shift the focus of their inquiry to the question of why those images had appeared on that video, in that mountain cabin.

Takayama and Asakawa decided to go back to the cabin, but on the way they took the opportunity of meeting someone. They had discovered

that before the resort was built the land was occupied by a treatment facility for a certain viral
illness, and that a physician who had worked
there was now in private practice nearby.

They called on him, and when they saw his
face, Kaoru himself gasped. It was the man from
the final scene of the video, the man with the
bleeding shoulder, the man with the expression
of terror and resignation.

Unable to withstand Takayama's interrogation,
the doctor confessed to having killed Sadako
Yamamura twenty-some years previously, and to
dumping her body into a well. These days, they
suspected, the cabin in question stood atop that
well. So Sadako Yamamura, supposedly twenty
years dead at the bottom of a well, had projected
her rage and resentment straight upward,
imprinting those mysterious images on a videotape inside the VCR inside the rental cabin. And
it turned out that the woman Sadako Yamamura,
in actuality, had possessed physical characteristics of both sexes.

Takayama elected that they crawl beneath the
cabin's floor, remove the well cap, enter the shaft,
and look for her remains. The idea was to give
her rest, in the hopes that it would release them
from the curse on the videotape.

In Loop time, exactly a week had passed.
Asakawa was still alive. The riddle had been
solved. Asakawa fainted with relief.

But it wasn't over yet. The following day, as Takayama's own deadline came, he began to experience inexplicable heart failure. It appeared therefore that exhuming Yamamura's bones and putting her to rest was not what the videotape was after.

Just before Takayama's death, Kaoru unhesitatingly switched subjects, locking onto Asakawa instead. Death, even in the virtual world, was a draining experience, one that he'd rather avoid if he could.

The news of Takayama's death plunged Asakawa back into worry. They hadn't figured out the mystery of the videotape after all.

Why was Asakawa still alive? There could only be one reason. Sometime over the course of the past week he must have fulfilled the video's wishes, unbeknownst to himself. It was something he had done that Takayama hadn't. But what? Asakawa racked his brain. He'd been spared, but unless he could solve the riddle, his wife and daughter would die. What did the tape want?

At that point, Asakawa received an inspiration.
A virus lives to reproduce itself.

He'd stumbled onto it. The videotape was behaving like a virus. What it wanted was to reproduce. He'd had to make a copy of the tape, show it to someone who hadn't seen it, and thereby help it to increase in number. It all made sense. Asakawa had made a copy of the tape for Takayama. But Takayama hadn't made a copy for anyone.

Arriving at his conclusion, Asakawa grabbed his VCR, jumped into his car, and sped off for his wife's parents' house. His plan was to make copies of the tape, show them to her parents, and save his wife and his daughter.

The dubbing and playback went off safely, but a trial that would prove too much for Asakawa awaited him on the drive back home.

He was about to leave the expressway ramp when he looked in his rear-view mirror to see his wife and daughter collapsed on the back seat. "We'll be home soon," he said. He released one hand from the steering wheel and reached into the back seat to touch them. They were cold. Wife and daughter had both died of sudden heart failure at the appointed time. Even making copies of the tape hadn't dispelled the curse.

In despair and grief, Asakawa forgot himself. Confused, he failed to notice the stopped traffic ahead of him: he rammed the car into it head-on.

As the shock passed through his body, in the instant that he lost consciousness, he was asking himself: *Why are they dead? Why am I alive?*

The twinned shocks damaged Asakawa's body and mind beyond hope of recovery.

8

Asakawa's eyes were open. His gaze was mobile, describing a slow circle around a point on the ceiling. Images passed from his retina to his brain, but he wasn't actively seeing. He was simply moving his eyeballs passively, randomly.

But even through those unwilled eye movements, Kaoru was able to guess at where Asakawa was now. The white curtain separating his bed from the next, the gleaming I.V. stand—the whole scene brought back painful, yet sweet memories for Kaoru. He was recalling the setting of his passionate exchanges with Reiko. Asakawa was in a hospital bed.

He must have been transported there right after the collision on the expressway. He must have been unconscious most of the time since: the display had been dark for long periods. Asakawa's retinas were covered in blackness most of the time, but occasionally, like now, he'd open his eyes and gaze vaguely around.

Through Asakawa's eyes Kaoru registered the faces of two men. One he'd seen hazily several times. From the white coat he wore it was likely that he was the physician attending Asakawa. The other face was new to him.

This second man came closer and peered into Asakawa's face.

"Mr Asakawa," the man said, placing a hand on Asakawa's shoulder.

Most likely he was looking for some sort of reaction to the tactile sensation, but it was no use. Asakawa was wandering in a pit so deep not even Kaoru's consciousness could reach him; no touch on the shoulder was going to rouse him from this.

The man moved away from Asakawa's bedside and asked the doctor, "Has he been like this the whole time?"

"Yes." The doctor and the other man exchanged a few more words. From what they said it was evident that the other man had a great deal of medical knowledge, too. Maybe he was a doctor also.

The man bent over again, peering into Asakawa's face. In an emotion-filled voice he spoke again. "Mr Asakawa." His eyes were filled with the charity of one who has undergone the same experience and can sympathize.

"I don't think he can hear you," the doctor said flatly.

The man gave up, leaving the bedside. "I'd like to ask you to notify me if there's any change in his condition." Kaoru found the man's expression interesting as he said this. He seemed particularly concerned about Asakawa.

He'd learn nothing more locked onto Asakawa's point of view. As long as he lay in bed in this in-between state, Kaoru's chances of being able to gather information were all but nil.

It's about time to choose someone new to lock onto.

Something told him that the man with the charitable gaze was the best candidate. He'd never seen his face before, but still he felt an inexplicable closeness to the man. Plus, his conversation with the doctor had showed him to be deeply involved with the case.

Kaoru typed some commands and de-assimilated his sense perceptions from Asakawa's, instead locking onto those of the visitor as he walked out of the sickroom. From that moment Kaoru was no longer bound into Asakawa's mind: instead, he was privy to the sights seen and sounds heard by his new subject, Mitsuo Ando. But there was no ease in Ando's heart, either. Kaoru looked to be in for more vicarious suffering. He sighed inwardly. He'd had enough of loved ones dying on him.

*   *   *

It wasn't long before Kaoru realized he'd chosen the right subject to lock onto.

Ando was the doctor who'd autopsied Takayama, and, just as Kaoru had suspected, he was deeply entangled in the affair of the video-tape. He belonged to the forensic medicine department of a university hospital, and together with a pathologist friend he was deter-mined to get to the bottom of things.

As far as they'd been able to ascertain, the number of people who'd died after watching the video was seven. In addition to the original four young people the total now included Ryuji Takayama and Asakawa's wife and daughter.

In each body they'd detected the presence of a new kind of virus. Ando was quite surprised when his friend told him about the virus; so was Kaoru. He was certain this virus was related to the one ravaging the real world.

Kaoru grabbed a nearby memo pad and started taking notes.

Need to analyze DNA of virus in Loop.

It was too much to hope that it might be the same sequence, but there could be similarities. It should be relatively simple to analyze the genetic information of a virus in the Loop world.

The world as seen through Ando's eyes was one of unrelieved misery. Kaoru didn't know why, whether it was simply due to Ando's personality, or whether there was another reason. Sometimes without warning his retinas would cloud over with tears. No, there must be some deep-seated cause, some incident in the man's past that had brought this sadness. Kaoru caught glimpses of it in Ando's present solitary life.

He was interested enough in the nature of the man's grief to want to search through his past, but there was no time for that now. Ando had just learned of the disappearance of a young woman he cared about, and he was searching for her.

The woman who'd disappeared was Mai Takano, a student of Takayama's. She lived alone in a studio apartment. He'd been unable to make contact with her for the past week.

She'd been connected to both Takayama and Asakawa, and now Ando suspected that something bad had happened to her, too. He decided to visit her apartment—there was always the possibility that she too was infected with the new virus.

Her apartment was empty. But the video, the one that killed its viewers in a week's time, was in her VCR. She'd evidently watched it. And all but a few seconds of it had been erased.

Ando wasn't sure how to interpret these findings. If she'd watched the video, there was no hope for her. She was probably already dead somewhere. It was just that her body hadn't been found yet.

So far the only person who'd seen the video and survived was Asakawa. He'd been spared because he made a copy of the tape. But his wife and daughter had died even though they'd made copies. Just what did the video want? It seemed utterly arbitrary about who it killed and who it let live. If there was a logical thread, it had yet to be found.

As he went to leave Mai Takano's apartment, Ando sensed the presence of a being he'd never encountered before. Something small and slippery that laughed like a girl.

Kaoru could feel it too, as he sat glued to the display. Something touched his ankles—he could feel something slimy against his Achilles tendons.

Impelled by fear, Ando opened the front door.
Something's here.

He felt sure of it as he stumbled out of the room.

Meanwhile, at the university, the work of analyzing the virus proceeded apace.

Ando was contacted by a newspaper reporter. He consented to meet because the man said he was a colleague of Asakawa's.

The reporter informed him of the existence of a floppy disk that contained an outline of the events of the case, written by Asakawa himself.

Ando had an idea of where the disk might be, and he managed to get his hands on it. There had been a word processor in Asakawa's car at the time of the accident. Asakawa's brother had it now. The disk was still in the word processor.

Ando opened the files on the disk and started reading. The document was entitled *Ring*, and it was well organized. Kaoru was already familiar with the events it recorded; its account matched up well with what he'd experienced through Takayama's and Asakawa's eyes and ears.

In effect, Kaoru was now able to confirm through the medium of writing the information he'd gained through Asakawa's sensory organs. The contents of the videotape had been transformed into the document called *Ring*.

At this point, Ando received a message that had been encoded in a DNA sequence.

Mutation.

This hint sent Ando's reasoning off in another direction. The videotape left in Takano's room had been erased. The other two copies had been destroyed one way or another. The video itself no longer existed. However, the first copy had been partially erased at the end by the four kids who found it. In DNA terms, part of the genetic material had been damaged.

It occurred to Ando to think of the videotape, in the way it made use of a third party's assistance to copy itself, as similar to a virus. Having suffered damage to its genetic material, he hypothesized, the video had undergone a mutation. It had been reborn as a new species. The old species, the videotape, had served its purpose. It didn't matter to the new species if the old one became extinct.

There were two essential questions at this point.

If the video has evolved, what has it evolved into?
And:

Why is Asakawa still alive?

Then another clue presented itself. Mai Takano's body was discovered at last.

She was discovered in an exhaust shaft on the roof of a rundown office building. It couldn't be determined if she'd died of hunger or of exposure. The autopsy turned up no signs of a heart attack: her death, then, was different in nature from the other seven. She'd simply wasted away. If she hadn't fallen into the exhaust shaft, she would still be alive.

Even more puzzling were the signs that she'd given birth immediately after falling into the shaft. This was proven by scars resulting from the placenta being torn out, as well as by fragments of umbilical cord found at the scene.

This all gave rise to a new question.

What did Mai Takano give birth to?

Ando, who had known her, was bothered. She simply hadn't looked pregnant the last time he'd seen her.

They attacked the problem from a variety of angles. The toll of the dead who had had some connection to that video was now eleven—a figure that now included Asakawa, who had died in his hospital bed without ever regaining consciousness.

Ando and his colleague determined that watching the videotape had caused the virus to appear in the victims' bloodstreams. They also discovered that the virus had some notable characteristics. There were two strains: one shaped like a ring, and one shaped like a thread, or a broken ring.

The thread type was more prevalent in the bodies of Asakawa and Takano, who had not died of heart attacks. In the other nine bodies, only the ring type was found. This, then, seemed to be the factor that determined whether or not the virus would kill a person. If the ring was broken the infected person would live, while if the ring was unbroken, death would follow in a week's time.

Ando was desperate to find a logical explanation. It was then that he discovered another odd coincidence.

The thread-like strain moves like spermatozoa.

There were signs that Takano had given birth. What if she'd been ovulating when she watched the video? What if the newly-created virus had headed for her egg instead of her coronary artery?

It seemed she'd been impregnated, and had then given birth to something.

But what?

Whatever it was, he'd encountered it in her apartment.

Ando applied the same logic to Asakawa. *As a man, Asakawa couldn't bear a child. What did he produce instead?*

That question would be answered for Ando very soon.

He received a visit from a woman who said she was Takano's older sister. He'd met her already, in the building where Mai had died. This time they became intimate.

She was in the shower, and Ando was flipping through a publisher's brochure, looking at the list of new books, when his eyes alit on a title of a book about to come out: *Ring*. To his surprise, Asakawa's report had been turned into a book, and was about to circulate in large numbers.

Ring: that was what Asakawa had given birth to. The videotape had evolved into a book, and was about to propagate on a massive scale. By writing it, Asakawa had played a crucial role in that propagation.

Just then, Ando received a photograph of Sadako Yamamura. One look sent him into shock. She looked identical to the woman who'd just stepped out of his shower, the woman who said she was Mai Takano's sister. What had Mai given birth to? *Sadako*.

Sadako, who was supposed to have rotted away at the bottom of a well in the mountains twenty-some years ago, had borrowed Mai's womb to effect her resurrection. But before that fact could sink in, Ando fainted.

When he regained consciousness, Yamamura asked for his cooperation. She confirmed that the videotape had evolved into the book, and was now on the verge of mass reproduction, and she didn't want him to interfere.

Ring would use its readers to change into all sorts of new forms. Ovulating women who came into contact with those forms would become pregnant and bear more Sadakos; the only other people to survive would be those who helped her to reproduce herself.

Ring would be a book, then a movie, a video game, an internet site—it would saturate the world through every branch of the media.

Ando's imagination couldn't fully grasp the disastrous consequences of this. In simplest terms, he guessed that the male-female compound that was Sadako Yamamura would go on being reborn with its singular genetic code, while the ring virus, constantly mutating, would eventually be left behind.

Variety is truly the spice of life: only genetic diversity allows a biological individual to derive any enjoyment from its existence. If all of that diversity contracted to a single genetic blueprint, life would lose its dynamism. Sadako may have achieved eternal life, or its equivalent, but every other life form would be chased into any corner it could hide in, and eventually be hounded into extinction.

Ando had to make a choice. He could either cooperate with Sadako, or be buried by her.

The reward for cooperating was simply too big.

The resurrection of my son.

The grief that dwelt in Ando's breast turned out to stem from the death of his young son two years previously.

Between the skills of Ando and his colleagues at the hospital and the unique womb of Sadako Yamamura, it was possible to effect the rebirth of Ando's son. At the moment the boy had disappeared into the ocean, several strands of his hair had come off. Ando still had them. His son's genetic information was well preserved.

He really had no choice. Life as the world presently knew it was going to end with or without his help. In which case, Ando would much rather it end with him reunited with his son—he'd prayed so hard for it.

Kaoru wasn't inclined to blame him. He could feel how badly Ando wanted to bring his son back to life. Kaoru wasn't at all sure he wouldn't do the same thing if he were in the same situation.

Ando's team removed one of Sadako's fertilized eggs and exchanged its nucleus for a nucleus from one of Ando's dead son's cells. A week later, his son was reborn from Sadako's belly.

Ando had sold Sadako the world in exchange for a life that had been lost two years ago.

Ring was published. Soon nearly twenty thousand of its female readers were pregnant. They all gave birth to Sadako. Collaborators helped *Ring* to move through form after form, infecting ever more people, allowing it to reproduce even more explosively. With the speed of a prairie fire, the world's genetic makeup became consolidated into a single pattern.

The ring virus was able to affect non-intelligent life forms as well, robbing the entire biosphere of its genetic diversity. The tree of life, formerly a giant with myriad branches and luxurious foliage, became a tall straight trunk. Its seeds all carried the same genes, and those seeds rapidly decreased in number. It was as if life was moving backwards, crawling back down the tree of life toward its primeval state.

What life gained in exchange for its diversity was immortality: driven to the brink of chaos, it achieved absolute stability. For life to progress means for it to scale steep peaks with a delicate sense of balance. Once those peaks had been eliminated, once Shangri-La had been discovered on the valley floor and claimed as a permanent home, evolution couldn't get a leg up.

The denizens of the Loop thenceforth lived repetitive, unchanging, boring lives. They stopped evolving. They had become cancer.

Kaoru typed the command that would unlock him from Ando. He was looking down from above now, as it were, on more and more territory, rather as if he were rising to heaven. He wanted to survey the Loop's squirming life forms. Individually they were tiny, wiggling about in a pack. The pattern they made was too monotonous to be beautiful.

He'd seen this somewhere before, though. He'd looked at a Petri dish full of his father's cancer cells under a microscope in the pathology department at the university hospital. He remembered how the cancer cells made ugly mottled clumps as they reproduced in their disorderly fashion. That was exactly how the Loop looked to him now, seen from on high.

Kaoru took off the helmet display and muttered to himself.

The Loop became cancerous.

He felt he finally understood what that meant, and how it had happened.

9

His sense of time was benumbed. He had no idea how many hours he'd spent sitting in front of the computer with the helmet display on his head and the data gloves on his hands. Time in the Loop moved differently from real time, of course, but then there was the fact that he'd been sitting in a basement where the sun couldn't penetrate. There was nothing to remind him of the passage of time.

When he stood up he was unsteady on his feet. He felt like he'd gone days without eating or drinking. His fatigue was extreme, his thirst was monstrous, and his hunger knew no bounds.

He looked at his watch to find that morning was drawing near. He climbed the stairs out of the basement. There was mineral water strapped to the luggage rack of his bike. His first priority had to be to rehydrate himself.

Dawn in the desert. The air was chill. Kaoru

found the bottle of mineral water, cleared his throat, and drank half of it down in one swig. What this gained him was the realization that he was actually alive. Peering into the Loop world for so long, he'd begun to imagine that the outlines of the real world were becoming fuzzy. The land on which he lived no longer felt firm under his feet. Reality and virtuality disengaged and re-engaged with alarming shakiness.

Kaoru leaned back against the seat of the motorcycle and drained the rest of the bottle. It brought his thirst under control. His body reacted honestly and straightforwardly. With no need to worry about anybody else, he unzipped his fly and urinated where he stood. Replenishing his body's water and then eliminating some had revived him somewhat. But it provided no proof that he truly existed in the flesh.

Still clutching the empty plastic bottle, he went back to the stairs leading to the basement and sat on a step halfway down. He'd just seen with his own eyes how the Loop had turned to cancer. But something about it didn't sit right with him. It felt like fiction. The images he'd seen were indistinguishable from reality, but still there was something faintly preposterous about the whole thing.

A videotape that killed its viewers in a week's time? Such a thing would be simple enough to concoct in an electronic environment. It would also be easy to rig it so that anybody who copied the tape would be spared. It was just a matter of setting the right parameters to produce a programmed death that would be disabled if the right action was taken within a specified period of time.

The problem was, all of this was beyond what the individuals living inside the Loop could accomplish relying solely on their own intrinsic abilities. In other words, the tape could neither be made nor neutralized without help from the real world.

Most of the deaths he'd experienced within the Loop had come as a result of watching the tape.

He felt he needed to confirm that, though. In spite of the heaviness he felt he forced himself to get up and sit in front of the computer again.

If the act of watching the video had functioned, within the Loop, as a trigger for those deaths, then it was worth taking a fine-toothed comb to the moments when future victims were actually engaged in watching it.

Kaoru began his search. One by one he called up scenes of Loop beings watching the video. He decided to observe them objectively, without locking onto an individual.

First to appear was a set of four young people, boys and girls, eyes glued in mingled terror and derision to a TV screen in the living room of what looked to be a mountain retreat.

One of the young people was stifling his fear, turning his adversarial laughter on his companions to get them to fall in line. It couldn't be more obvious that his high spirits were forced.

As the video ended, one of the females was deathly pale. "Eww," she said, before falling silent. The male who was trying to keep his spirits up was evidently worried that her single outburst would cast a pall of terror over all of them. He spoke up.

"C'mon, it's got to be a fake."

He kicked at the screen.

"Pretty scary threat at the end, though," said the other girl. Her expression betrayed no trace of fear. With a face like a mask, she puffed away on her cigarette as she rewound the tape. Then, as if it were the obvious course, while the other three watched she erased the bit at the end where the formula for avoiding death was written.

"Let's take it back and scare our friends," she said. But the other three held back. They didn't want to have anything to do with the creepy thing after tonight, no matter how much the girl dared them. Why should they take it back with them, inviting who knew what curse along for the ride? They said as much to her.

At that moment the phone rang. The other three gasped in surprise, while the expressionless girl picked up the receiver.

"Hello?"

Her reaction suggested that there was no answer on the other end of the line.

"Hello? Hello!" She sounded irritated, but a faint trembling could be detected in her voice. She swallowed once, then slammed the receiver onto the hook. She stood up and shouted, "What the hell's going on?"

To Kaoru, the space around the telephone, which had rung for no reason, seemed somehow warped.

The next to watch the video was Asakawa, followed by Takayama. Since Kaoru had already watched them watching, he skipped ahead to the next instance.

This was Asakawa's wife and daughter.

The tape had been left just lying around, and his wife had noticed it. She put it into the VCR, not even intending to watch it all the way through. Then it began.

She sat the child on a chair beside her and started doing her ironing. Then she glanced at the screen. Suddenly she couldn't tear her gaze away. It was the same with her daughter: she sat there unmoving, facing the TV.

As soon as it was over, the telephone in the living room rang. The video still running, Mrs Asakawa ran to the living room and picked up the receiver.

"Asakawa residence."

No response.

"Hello?"

For a few moments she stood there clutching the receiver. Just as before, the space around the telephone seemed to Kaoru to bend out of shape. Objects appeared ever-so-slightly doubled, straight lines wavered. The warping was barely noticeable unless you knew what to look for. Something was wrong here.

Kaoru figured that the next to watch the video would have been Mrs Asakawa's parents. But he was wrong.

The next scene was set in Ryuji Takayama's apartment. Checking the date and time, Kaoru realized he'd dropped in just before Takayama's death.

Takayama had been watching the video when he died.

Kaoru backed the scene up a bit. This time he could watch closely, with no distracting fear of death.

Takayama was seated at his desk, concentrating on a piece of writing. His head drooped, and it looked like he might be dozing off, when suddenly his shoulders shook and he jumped up. His neck muscles were taut and his hair stood on end. Seen from behind, he actually looked a bit comical.

Kaoru debated about which way he should orient the display. Should he keep it focused on Takayama's back, or should he synchronize it with Takayama's perceptions?

After wandering around behind Takayama for a little while, he decided to lock onto him. Kaoru's perceptions melded with Takayama's.

Takayama was gasping for breath. He knew intuitively that something was happening to his body. He was actually able to remain fairly calm in the face of his impending death, but he was trying to wrap his mind around a lot of things in a hurry. Questions raced through his head.

Did I not solve the riddle of the video after all?

Then why is Asakawa still alive?

Takayama glanced over at the VCR in the corner. The tape was still inside. He crawled over to the VCR. His heart was pounding. Moving caused him immense pain.

Kaoru knew exactly what was happening to Takayama's body. A sarcoma had developed in his coronary artery, and it was blocking the flow of blood. What he was experiencing were symptoms of the heart attack that was shortly to kill him.

Takayama removed the tape from the VCR and examined it from every angle.

Kaoru didn't know what he was thinking.

Takayama grasped the tape in a trembling hand,

looked at the top, looked at the bottom, read the title written on the spine.

Thinking Kaoru knew not what, he quickly ran his gaze over the ceiling, out the window, over the wall, to the bookshelf. He seemed to be searching for something.

Finally, Takayama's gaze came to rest again on the videotape he was holding.

He was clearly excited—not from the pain in his chest, though. The trembling in his hands was from an excitement that had made him forget himself.

Takayama inserted the tape back into the deck and pressed play.

He's about to die. Why's he watching the tape?

The now-familiar images began to appear before Kaoru's eyes.

Takayama looked at his watch, which he'd placed on the desk. It was 9:48.

He crawled toward his phone receiver, which lay on the floor. Kaoru could sense his desperation. Had he figured out a way to survive?

He picked up the receiver and hurriedly dialed. It rang four times before a woman's voice came through the line.

"Hello?"

Kaoru knew the voice. This would be Mai Takano. Takayama would die while on the phone with her. She'd hear his final scream.

With the phone pressed to his ear, Takayama

was still gazing at the television screen. Dice tumbling around in a lead container, flashing numbers, one through six.

Takayama shrieked. His voice traveled across the telephone wires to Takano's ear.

"Hello? Hello?"

Worried about Takayama, Mai kept waiting for an answer.

But Takayama hung up of his own accord. He placed the receiver on its cradle.

At that moment, he caught his own reflection in the mirror. Kaoru had the momentary illusion that he was seeing his own face in the display. Takayama's retinas were starting to lose focus, so Kaoru could no longer see the television screen clearly. His heart was racing, and the pressure on his blood vessels seemed to be stimulating random patches on his skin.

Takayama's vision, which was rapidly clouding over, remained fixed on the area around the VCR. A mist or smoke was rising there, forming into a slowly revolving cylinder. Space was twisting, like a dishrag being wrung out.

Takayama pushed the phone in the direction of the warp in space, dialing another number. Kaoru looked down, trying to see the numbers he was pressing.

But there was no need to look at the phone. The numbers were there on the TV screen. On the dice . . .

. . . 33254136245163423425413624516343432541 3 6245163413325413624516342342 5 . . .

All Takayama was doing was dialing the numbers that showed.

He's on the verge of death. Maybe he's losing the capacity for rational thought, was Kaoru's conclusion.

Just then Kaoru's satellite phone rang. He'd placed it beside the computer. It rang for several seconds before Kaoru noticed it—before he realized the sound was a real one, not one from Takayama's apartment.

Kaoru picked up the phone and slid the helmet display to one side so he could bring the phone to his ear.

He heard breathing, so faint it sounded like it would cease any moment. Labored, rhythmic breathing, in synch with what he heard coming from the display.

Kaoru couldn't believe his ears. What he heard next was a man's voice, its quality altered by passing through an automatic translation device.

"Are you there? Hey! Are you listening? I want you to do something for me. Bring me to where you are. I want to go to your world. I won't let you get away with this any longer."

Kaoru was confused. In the display he was looking at a close-up of Takayama's left hand, holding the telephone. It was definitely Takayama making the call. And it was Kaoru himself, in the here and now, who was on the receiving end of that call.

Of course he was confused. He felt like he was calling himself.

You can't call reality from the Loop!

Kaoru couldn't find his voice. And before he could rouse himself from his fugue, the line went dead. He could still hear Takayama's voice, though.

Bring me to where you are.

It was several minutes before the meaning of those words sank in.

10

Kaoru went over his chain of reasoning again and again. But finally, he knew there was only one way to test his theory.

The first thing he'd need to do would be to contact Amano with instructions: analyze the DNA of the ring virus and compare it to the genetic sequence of the MHC virus. It was a simple task, since the MHC virus had been sequenced. Kaoru had a copy of the results of that analysis. Once the ring virus was analyzed, comparing them would be easy.

He expected that somehow the ring virus's genetic sequence had been converted from binary code to the ATGC base code. A computer should be able to figure it out in a snap.

He decided to take a nap while awaiting a response from Amano. He took his pack from the back of the motorcycle, got out his sleeping bag, and spread it on the basement floor next to the desk. He rehydrated himself, took some sustenance into his belly, and then curled up in his sleeping bag like a shrimp.

In no time at all he was fast asleep. Unaffected by the stress of the day, Kaoru's youthful resilience pulled his consciousness down into slumber.

Two hours later, the computer came to life. The display flickered and the speakers emitted a signal.

Kaoru slipped out of his bedroll and sat down at the desk. Only two hours of sleep, but his body felt perfectly restored. He could face Amano's response with a clear head.

The display lit up with a comparison of the ring virus to the MHC virus. Commonalities between the two sequences were marked. The similarity was considerable—too much to be ignored. With this much overlap, they had to be considered essentially the same virus, or perhaps more exactly viruses that were originally the same but had mutated into somewhat varying strains. Kaoru felt safe in concluding that the Metastatic Human Cancer Virus had originated from the ring virus.

Having arrived at that confirmation, Kaoru stepped back from the computer with its display full of data.

Part of him thought it was an idiotic theory, even though it was his own. It militated against all common sense. The chain of reasoning was sound and allowed for no other interpretation, but still something nagged at him.

Be rational about this, he berated himself. Now was a time for flexibility, not for rigid adherence to fixed ideas.

Kaoru tried to put himself in Takayama's shoes and think about what had happened to him as a natural course of events. He'd been face to face with death. There's not a person alive who doesn't want to escape dying. What he was dealing with was a primal desire.

A bold analogy was starting to take shape in Kaoru's mind.

Takayama came to understand it intuitively, just before he died, didn't he?

That was the jumping-off point. The "it" that Takayama had come to understand included all manner of things. That was the key point.

Takayama, an individual within the Loop, understood everything.

He'd proceed on that assumption.

Takayama would have been wondering: why am I on the point of death while Asakawa is still alive? What did he do unknowingly this week that I didn't. At which point Takayama would have realized that copying the videotape was the key to evading death. Asakawa had made him a copy of the tape.

But that wasn't the only thing Takayama came to understand. Now he had a theory: watching

the videotape set one to die in a week, like one
might set a VCR, while copying the videotape
cleared the schedule. He wanted to advance his
theory to the next level: he concentrated on a
new question. What made the whole thing
possible?

"The world is an imaginary space."

It was a conclusion influenced by his
customary mode of thinking—that was pretty
much how he thought of the world he lived in
to begin with.

If the world was imaginary, a virtual reality,
then it was perfectly possible to set someone to
die a nonsensical death, and just as possible to
clear the setting. So who was doing the setting?
Whatever higher principle created the virtual
world.

God.

Maybe that word had flashed through
Takayama's brain; maybe it hadn't. But to create
the world and set it in motion was the work of
a god. From the perspective of the inhabitants of
the Loop, their creator was God Himself.

So Takayama, just before he died, had
attempted to hold congress with God. To that end,
he'd needed to find an interface between reality
as he knew it and God's world. He'd searched
desperately for that interface.

Which was why his gaze had wandered about
the room, over its ceiling, its walls—he'd been

looking for the tiny thread that connected his world to God's.

No doubt the videotape was the only possibility he could imagine. If putting the tape in a VCR and playing it had been enough to set him to die, then maybe that was the interface, or at least maybe it could lead him to it. He should be able to see a slight warping of space in the portal. If that wasn't the interface, then he was too late.

Takayama had decided to bet everything on the videotape.

He pressed play, started screening the images. His heart quavered—he wasn't sure if he had enough time to escape death even if he had figured it out. He called Takano. But all the while his eyes were glued to the screen. The television was showing him dice rolling around in a lead container. Numbers between one and six kept presenting themselves to his view.

Takayama emitted a cry, but it wasn't his death scream. He'd realized that the dice were repeating the same numbers.

. . . *3325413624516342342541362451634 3432541362451634133254136245163423425* . . .

If he took out the numbers 133, 234, and 343, he realized, the dice were persistently repeating a string of thirteen digits: *2541362451634*. Takayama, with his knowledge of genetic sequencing, had realized that those three numbers were stop codes.

He hung up on Takano and immediately started dialing the digits.

The call connected, the circuit was completed. It *was* possible to access reality from within the Loop.

As soon as he was sure he'd accessed the higher concept, Takayama blurted out his wish.

Bring me to your world.

It was a bold request, but one any scientist would have made. Not to escape death so much as to gain something greater. To move from within the world into the great outside from which it was created—to understand the workings of the universe.

That was Kaoru's own dream from of old.

Takayama's dream would come true if he was able to move from the Loop into Kaoru's world. He'd learn everything about the principles on which the Loop ran. He'd learn what lay beyond what was to the Loop beings the edge of the universe. He'd learn what time and space were like before the creation of the universe. He'd learn, in short, the answers to all questions.

Bring me to your world.

At first glance it might seem like a rather childish desire, but Kaoru could well understand it. In fact, he shared it. If there was a God who had designed the world, he'd love to go to His world and ask Him personally about a few things.

Now, then. In the Loop world, Takayama had

died immediately after the phone call. It had been observed on the monitor. One of the Loop's operators must have heard Takayama's request much as Kaoru had.

What had the hearer done, then? Had he or she granted Takayama's wish? Takayama's powers of intuition were amazing, to have not only figured out the riddle of the video but to have realized that his reality was only virtual. Maybe someone had taken an interest in those powers.

Kaoru began ransacking his medical knowledge for a way to allow Takayama to be reborn into the real world.

It would be impossible to recreate him based merely on an analysis of the molecular information that made up his body in the Loop. But since his genetic information was contained in the program's memory, it might be possible to use that to give him birth in the real world.

It was possible to manufacture sets of up to two thousand megabases. The genome synthesizers that allowed reproduction of their chromatin structures had been developed at the beginning of the century. This had been followed shortly by a technique known as GFAM (genome fragment alignment method), which enabled these fragments to be connected. As a result, it was possible to reconstruct all of a human being's chromosomes.

The first step would be to prepare a fertilized

human egg. Then they'd have to remove its nucleus and replace it with chromosomes they'd fabricated based on Takayama's genetic information. They'd replace the egg in its host mother. Nine months later, Ryuji Takayama would be born into the world. Of course it would be as an infant. But genetically, that child would be Takayama.

This could have been done. But then it would have involved a miscalculation. If someone had indeed recreated Takayama, then he or she had forgotten one key thing along the way.

Takayama carried the ring virus. When the genome synthesizer recreated his molecules, the virus would have been passed on, too. It was the only thing that could account for the resemblance between the ring virus and the MHC virus.

Looked at from another angle, that resemblance was itself evidence that Ryuji Takayama had been reborn into the real world. Yes, that was the most persuasive interpretation: in the process of rebirthing him, someone had loosed the ring virus in a subtly altered form.

So who summoned Takayama forth?

That he didn't know. Nor did he know what whoever had done it had hoped to accomplish by it. What was to be gained by bringing a virtual being to life in the real world?

Kaoru had played video games as a child. Not that he'd been hooked—he'd tended to tire of them rather quickly, as a matter of fact. He remembered the appearance of the princes and princesses in the games, rendered in supposedly 3-D computer graphics, with their somewhat clumsy planes. They were unmistakably different from real people, but nonetheless there had been a few female characters he'd considered beautiful. This was like bringing one of them to life. And unleashing whatever computer virus she carried into the world as a real, biological virus.

It was absurd, when he thought about it that way. But the Loop was the most sophisticated computer simulation the world had ever seen: given that, he couldn't rule it out. On the level of theory, at least, it was quite possible.

So where's Takayama now, and what is he doing?

He felt he was closing in on the truth now. He remembered Kenneth Rothman's last communiqué. *I've figured out the source of the MHC virus. Takayama holds the key.*

Kaoru was starting to believe it himself now.

11

As he climbed the stairs to the surface, Kaoru felt he'd spent years in front of that computer. The sun was directly overhead, its rays searing the earth. In terms of space and light, there was all the difference in the world between the basement and here.

He felt like his body had changed, perhaps because he'd lived so many more lives. But in reality he'd only spent forty-two hours at the computer. What he'd experienced was time concentrated.

The motorcycle's gas tank was coated with fine sand blown by the wind that whipped down the ravine and through the spaces between the abandoned houses. Dust was everywhere—the fact that the layer on the tank was still relatively thin showed how little time he'd actually spent in the basement.

Kaoru straddled the bike and started the engine.

He had a clear image of where he needed to go now. He'd follow the gorge due west, then pass over a hill with a spring, and then cross two tall peaks.

Kaoru knew that at the moment it was important for him to rely on a greater power and do as he was directed. Clearly, someone or something was intervening.

When had it started, this intervention? Maybe he'd known it would turn out like this for ten years, ever since the family had gotten the idea for this trip. Maybe all he was doing now was carrying out a long-prepared plan.

Let's go.

He grabbed the handlebars, made a U-turn, and went back the way he had come.

His plan was to head back to the main road and check into a motel where he could rest and replenish his gas and supplies. Then he'd start his traversing of the desert, on his road that wasn't a road.

Two days after leaving Wayne's Rock, Kaoru finally turned off the highway into the desert. He rode ten miles over flat country until a middling-sized mountain appeared, then he rode up its side.

The higher he went the stronger he felt the hush. The stream narrowed, and he could hear the sighing of the trees. There were as yet no traces of the MHC virus to be seen here. The vegetation was still healthy, the sight of it refreshing.

He could feel the plants' exhalations gently on his skin. He pressed on, higher, deeper into the stillness.

He'd never expected to find this much greenery in the middle of the desert.

When the valley had come into view, he'd been unable to accurately guess at its scale. But now that he'd ridden right up to it, it was no mere stand of trees, but a true forest, all contained within a huge ravine.

The trees only grew on the inner slopes of the declivity; the rest of the landscape was an unrelieved brown wasteland. Hidden in a valley this deep, he doubted the forest would be visible even from the air.

Jagged boulders pierced the sky and trees filled the spaces between them. Even with an off-road bike, he could ride no farther. The rocky outcroppings came together to shelter a creek which shrank the farther up along its flow he went. He'd have to dismount here.

He lay the bike down gently in the brush amidst some trees. He took what he needed from the back of the bike and slung his pack over his shoulders. He exchanged his riding boots for sneakers and then looked around, trying to memorize the spot so he could find it again.

He'd have to rely on his legs to carry him the rest of the way.

From time to time he would stop and gaze up at the vast gorge that the little stream had carved into the land. That stream alone marked his road now. How long had it taken to make this canyon, thousands of yards deep? Contemplating the time and energy required made him dizzy.

Endless years and ceaseless repetition. The high-rise in which Kaoru made his home in Tokyo would easily fit into this valley. It had taken three years to build. But the valley—it'd taken hundreds of millions of years, and the water was still working on it, bit by bit.

The sun was sinking in the west now. The rays that found their way into the valley were climbing up its side, licking the sides of the valley as if it were some huge organism.

He paused in his leaping from rock to rock to plunge both hands into the stream for a drink. The water was cold. He could feel its chill spreading from his esophagus to his stomach. It was a boon to have the stream alongside: he wouldn't suffer thirst. He scooped up more water, then sat down on a rock for a breather.

A hushed air hung over the secluded land. He stumbled across a memory. He'd once before breathed air that was otherworldly like this. It put him in mind not of the deep recesses of Mother Nature, but of a place with a much higher concentration of civilization. An intensive care unit.

His father went into the ICU every time he had to have more cancer removed. In that sealed-off space, where the only sound was the rhythm of the respirator, the patients' flesh became so enveloped in stillness that it was hard to tell if they were alive or dead. Every time he visited his father there, Kaoru came away with the impression that it was only the machines that were really alive in that place—the people had sunk to a level below the inorganic.

He got chills as he remembered the tubes sprouting from his father's face and head, the pain he must have been in—the greater the number of tubes the more they seemed to speak of the ebbing of his father's life. There was something in the silence of this valley that reminded him of the ICU.

I wonder how Dad's doing.

Now that his thoughts had arrived at memories of his father's condition, he felt he couldn't rest any longer. His father just had to hold out until Kaoru returned—otherwise, he would have come all the way here for nothing.

He worried about his mother, too. Was she still obsessed with Native American legends, praying for a miracle to save his father? Kaoru wished she could deal with things a little more realistically.

And what about Reiko?

He felt his chest tighten at the thought of her. He took the two photos of her from his breast pocket. One had been taken in the cafeteria at the hospital. In the photo, Kaoru was holding his head up high, while Reiko rested her head on his shoulder. Ryoji had taken the picture. What had gone through his mind as he'd captured this image? His mother's affection for Kaoru was revealed in her pose. She had more of a womanly aura in this photo than a motherly one. Ryoji couldn't have enjoyed seeing her like this. What he saw through the viewfinder had to have bothered him.

Every time Kaoru thought about Reiko he took out this photo and looked at it, but the sad memories of Ryoji it brought back were always stronger than any recollections of Reiko that it held.

He looked at the second photo. In it, Reiko was sitting alone on the floor of what was probably her living room at home. She sat casually, legs bent to one side, hands behind her, on a thick carpet. Her hairstyle was different. The photo was probably two or three years old, but as to whether it had been taken before or after the onset of Ryoji's illness there was no clue.

Not long after their relationship had turned physical, Kaoru had asked Reiko for a photo from her younger days. It had been a bad choice of words. "Are you trying to say I'm old?" she'd scowled, poking him in the ribs. But the next day she'd brought him several photographs.

One had been taken at a party at her home. She was surrounded by friends, and she was holding a glass. Her face was flushed from drinking.

In another she was posing with one hand raised and the other on her hip. In another she was wearing an elegant orange kimono and standing nonchalantly beside a chrysanthemum doll.

In yet another, she was standing at the kitchen sink washing dishes. It was a perfect shot, catching her just as she turned around in response to someone calling her from behind.

Kaoru imagined that Ryoji had taken this one. He'd sneaked up behind her, called "Mom!" and then clicked the shutter. The reaction on her face was unfeigned—surprise mingled with laughter to create a most unusual expression. A valuable photo, capturing a side she usually didn't show.

Kaoru was particularly fond of that picture, but he'd decided to leave it behind when he departed for the desert. He'd elected to take only two photos of her, the one of the two of them together and the one of her sitting on the floor. He kept them safe in his pocket.

In that second photo she was wearing a knit wool one-piece dress. From the waist up, it looked like a sweater; in fact, it was less a proper dress than a really long sweater. The U-shaped neckline was modest to a fault, providing not the slightest glimpse of the swelling of her bosom. Not that her breasts were that large to begin with. They were just big enough to fit in the palms of Kaoru's hands. Their perfect volume and firmness fascinated him, though.

The dress material didn't accent the lines of her waist, either. Instead, his gaze was drawn to her legs.

Because of the way she was sitting, the hem of the dress had hiked up to just above her knees. She was leaning back, knees raised slightly off the carpet. In the space between them there was a darkness that extended far back. Time after time, Kaoru had buried his face in that soft valley.

Day after day they'd waited for Ryoji to be taken away for his tests. Then in the brilliant light of day Kaoru would lay Reiko down on the bed, hike up her skirt, pull down her panties, and examine her sex organ. It was no more than one organ of the many that made up her body, but he found it inexplicably fascinating. His love for her had endowed it with inestimable value.

When he'd raise his head from between her legs he could see the almost too-bright light pouring in between the open curtains. The full rays of the sun made him feel that he was doing something terribly immoral. But this was a temptation he could not resist. He'd lower his face again, avoiding the sunlight, praying that this moment would last forever as he received her fluids with his tongue.

And now, as a result of moments like those, she had conceived his child.

Kaoru glanced at her slender waist in the photograph.

I wonder how big it is now.

He could guess: the embryo was probably about three quarters of an inch long now, looking something like a seahorse. At the moment, his affection for this new being that inherited his genes was not as strong as his affection for Reiko, who was carrying it.

But he had no more time to lounge on the rocks. All the faces passing through his mind were now urging him to hurry. Kaoru stood up and set off for the peak.

12

The sun was going down behind the ridge. Kaoru quickened his pace. He'd have to find a likely place to camp before it got completely dark.

He came to a flat spot surrounded on three sides by huge rocks. Looking around, he decided it wouldn't be a bad place to spend the night.

He'd been here before. As an Indian, as the man whose point of view he'd assumed via the computer in the ruins of Wayne's Rock. The tribe had passed through a place that looked exactly like this.

The Native American legend his mother had shown him had said to follow the warrior's guidance. No warrior would be appearing to him in reality, but the place to which he would have guided Kaoru had he appeared was already stored in Kaoru's memory. All he had to do was follow the strands of memory, comparing them one by one with reality, and he'd find his route.

There was no longer any doubt. The place would appear to him somewhere up ahead. Tonight, though, he must have rest. Kaoru unshouldered his pack and rested his legs.

Every step on the road thus far had further awakened Kaoru's senses. With no rhyme or reason, sensation after sensation had flooded his consciousness. He felt terror, jealousy, exultation, with no grounds for feeling them—they just came over him, stimulating his senses. He suspected that if he persisted in tracing their source back into the past, he'd eventually arrive at the moment of his own birth.

He spread his mat out on a flat rock and then curled up in his sleeping bag. It wasn't all that cold yet, but he knew that as the night wore on the temperature in the desert would plummet. In his bedroll he nibbled on some bread and sipped at some whiskey.

Suddenly he sat up and looked around. He had felt, or imagined he'd felt, something's breath on the back of his neck.

He could feel the chill of the stone through the mat and sleeping bag. The breathing was regular, rhythmic, like the working of a respirator, or the breathing of a predator eying its prey, trying to calm itself, body and spirit.

From the same direction, Kaoru could feel something gazing at him. He could plainly sense the will behind it. The gaze bored into the base of his skull, quickening his pulse.

He couldn't bear it any longer. He looked behind him. There he saw, maybe ten yards away in the shadow of a tree, a naked man on one knee training a bow and arrow on him. The man's skin was dark, so dark that he could have blended in with the night, but somehow Kaoru was able to make him out.

The man's long hair was tied back simply; he wore no feathers or other headdress. He looked to be of medium height and build, and his muscles hardly bulged, but he held the bow with the air of an expert.

Kaoru tried to move, and found that he couldn't. It was as though he was in one of those half-waking states where the mind is aware but the body is immobile. All he could do was stare at the arrow.

The man's right thumb was bent where he was pulling taut the bowstring. He was aiming at Kaoru's head. The arrowhead was of gleaming obsidian. Kaoru knew at a glance that this was no rubber toy.

The man's face was expressionless. Kaoru could detect there no hatred, but no charity either. No rapture. Only the stare of a hunter determined to faithfully perform his allotted part.

Kaoru stared dumbfounded at the slowly receding arrowhead. He felt no fear. Somewhere in the back of his mind he knew this was not real.

But when he could see that the energy accumulating in the bow had reached a certain peak, suddenly the image of himself transformed into a beast burst into Kaoru's head. Reflexively he tried to duck. But the arrow had already been released. Its silently revolving tip grew to dominate Kaoru's field of vision. Kaoru leaned forward, as if throwing himself at the arrow, and then consciousness receded.

He was only out for a moment. When he awoke, he just lay there for a while, staring at the trunk of a tree that towered over him. He thought he'd fallen forward, but now, somehow, he was lying on his back. He brought his hand up to his right eye, the one the arrow should have pierced. It was unharmed. He stood up and looked around for the man with the bow. Gone. He'd disappeared without a trace.

Kaoru realized he must have been hallucinating. Maybe it was because of the peculiar atmosphere of the valley—maybe a memory imprinted on his brain long ago had been resurrected. The brown-skinned man had vanished, leaving the strong sensation of death in Kaoru's mind. He felt as if he'd absorbed death directly, like some kind of radiation.

Phantom it may have been, but the image of

the revolving arrow digging into his eye, leading him into darkness, was something he couldn't chase away. It was a dry run for the death that was dogging his footsteps. More than the pain, more than anything, he found that it was the emptiness of death that filled him with bottomless horror.

Every time he experienced death he found a renewed appreciation for the fullness of life. Life and death brushed up against one another, inter-mixed. For the first time, Kaoru had a premon-ition of rebirth.

His breathing gradually came under control. As he regained his calm, he lay down again on the earth and looked up at the sky, head pillowed on his hands. Through a gap in one rim of the valley the full moon had appeared. Men had stood on the moon once, decades ago. As a result, the actual existence of the moon was something that was now within the realm of human knowledge. Most likely the sun, too, was really there, at the center of the solar system.

But the Loop's sun and moon were real to its denizens, too, while Kaoru and others knew that they weren't, not in a spatial sense. Beings in the Loop were merely programmed to perceive time and space.

This train of thought reminded Kaoru of some-thing his father had repeated to him once, a remark of one of the astronauts who'd landed on the moon.

It was just like in the simulation, the man had said when pressed for a comment.

That had stuck in Kaoru's memory. Before going to the moon, of course, the astronauts had been through any number of detailed simulations of the moon's gravity and other physical conditions, many of which had taken place in the deserts of America. Only after they'd experienced the moon walk virtually a number of times did they experience it as reality. What this astronaut was saying was that the reality was exactly like the virtual reality. No matter how fine the calculations, though, there should have been some differences.

Kaoru remembered the Bible's words about God creating the world in His own image. What exactly did it mean that the Loop had ended up looking just like the real world? In the Loop's primeval state life had not arisen naturally. Then the researchers had introduced RNA life forms. And these had become the seeds of all life in the Loop—they'd developed into a tree of life just like the real world's. Given that the Loop and the real world shared the same physics, it wasn't, perhaps, all that surprising that life should have taken the same form. But, to take a hint from the astronaut, shouldn't there have been at least a few differences?

Is this an epiphany?

He couldn't shake the thought that the real

world itself was only a virtual world. Logically, the idea couldn't be disproved.

A god. A higher principle. There was nothing to stop Kaoru from accepting life as the creation of such a being. If this was simply a virtual world, then it was after all possible for the Holy Mother, as a virgin, to give birth to the son of God. Or for the son of God, having once died, to rise from the dead in a week's time . . .

With humanity on the brink of extinction, now would be a good time for God to come. If things went on like this, the whole world would turn cancerous. God had to be watching somewhere, invisibly.

Kaoru stared unseeing at the starry sky, pondering the advent of God.

13

He'd used up half of his food supply, but he'd made his way out of the deep ravine and onto the ridge. He was about to head northward, toward the mountaintop.

The scenery was locked away in his memory. Once in a while he would hallucinate seeing the tribesman, and that would call forth recollections, letting him know which way he should go. Kaoru emptied his mind and went where he was led.

Sometimes this tribal guide would appear standing on a rock ahead of him. He'd stare at Kaoru until he'd fully caught Kaoru's attention, then wave to him before disappearing up ahead. He never drew his bow anymore. His gesture was easy enough to understand: *Follow me*.

Sometimes Kaoru would see things drawn on the brown arcing rock faces deep in cul-de-sac ravines, things that filled him with foreboding. He imagined they'd been drawn ages ago by the

Native Americans who had settled here, animals and human faces expressed with varying degrees of abstraction. Geometric patterns that, depending on how you looked at them, resembled the double-helix structure of DNA. Kaoru realized he was nearing his destination.

He pictured the elders living in a huge cave, preserving a more natural way of life. He'd come to imagine the place he was heading to as an unexplored region, veiled in mystery. There the elders lived as naturally as plants, dressed in hempen robes. Their mission was to impart to seekers the knowledge they'd stored up over the course of thousands of years . . .

But Kaoru's expectations were betrayed. He walked for a day and a night without finding any ancient cave filled with relics.

It was getting to be time to wonder about his food supply, whether it would run out and with it his strength. Now was the time to turn back if he was going to. He still had a little food left, and if he could just make it back to where he'd left the motorcycle, he should be alright. The bike had nearly a full tank of gas, and the nearest town was about twenty miles, an easy ride. Maybe he ought to go back there and replenish his supplies.

He'd have to do what the situation demanded, he told himself, in an effort to calm his thoughts.

He couldn't let himself be trapped in a blind alley.

He'd been mentally referring to the beings that lurked here as "the Ancients". The question was how to meet the Ancients and learn from them how the world worked. His father's life, his mother's life, Reiko's life depended on it.

Somewhere along the line, Kaoru had started to see the Ancients as some kind of gods. But he told himself that he needed to consider the opposite possibility, too. What guarantee was there that they bore good will toward men?

As if to second that notion by allowing him a glimpse of malevolence, clouds raced across the sky. Since coming to the desert, he hadn't paid much attention to the sky. Day after day of clear, bright weather had lulled him.

From where he stood on the ridge he had a three hundred and sixty degree view of the landscape—he felt he could see to the ends of the earth. Now in an instant his vision was cut off by roiling clouds, and the sky was a thick ashen color.

The clouds were moving in layers, hanging low in the infinite sky, until they seemed like they'd come crashing down on his head. The pressure was suffocating.

Expecting rain at any minute, Kaoru began searching for a particular spot on the ridge. The trees up here were short and their foliage sparse—

he knew he'd find no shelter under their limbs. He was looking for something like a crevice between boulders. He'd seen several small openings while following the river upstream, but they were too far down the mountainside. Up here on the ridge near the peak, it wouldn't be so easy to find a suitable cave, he was beginning to fear.

A drop of rain hit him on the cheek. He tensed his body, ready to dash for shelter, but there was none to be found, only rubble. A few more drops spattered on his head. Then the rain let loose with an earth-shaking roar of thunder. The scene was so changed that its previous appearance seemed to have been an illusion. At first the parched ground drank up the rain, but soon it could absorb no more, and rivulets of water began to appear.

Kaoru had no option but to huddle where he stood. There was no escaping nature's wrath. For the first time in his life, he was afraid of the rain.

He had plastic bags in his rucksack, but only a few, and of what use would they be anyway? He had no tent, nothing to keep himself dry with. And even if he had brought a tent, it wouldn't have done him any good. He was soaked to the skin in a flash.

His sneakers were waterlogged and heavy. Each step squeezed out a little flow of water. Waterfalls ran down his back and belly under his heavy jean jacket. He couldn't see where he was walking anymore, and he began to be afraid he'd stumble into one of the torrents that had appeared from nowhere. All he could do was find slightly higher ground, firm footing, and crouch there.

His last bread was in his rucksack, wrapped in plastic, but he knew he hadn't wrapped it very well. It was bound to get wet and dissolve. But he couldn't eat it in this downpour. He was forced to stand there helpless while his food supply was destroyed. Then again, he thought, at least he'd have enough water. He opened his mouth wide to take in as much of it as possible.

But the rain was falling too mercilessly: it hurt to stand there with his face exposed to it like that. He had to squat on his heels again.

Looking down, however, exposed the back of his neck to pain. He couldn't leave any skin uncovered, it seemed. He moved his pack so it covered his neck, then hugged his knees and waited for the rain to pass. He had the impression that rainstorms in the desert never lasted very long.

But this one did. The raindrops did get smaller and smaller until they seemed to turn to mist, but then, instead of stopping, they returned to their former size and force, pelting the ground. It was as if the storm was mocking him.

His fear grew. The rain had robbed his body of all warmth, and he was chilled through and through. On top of that, it was getting late. Darkness, cold, and hunger. He thought of this rain continuing all night, and it nearly paralyzed him.

The temperature of the air was falling, too. The dimness of evening turned into pitch blackness, and the rain sounded even louder. He couldn't see, but he could feel someone close at hand, striking him on the back and the head. He was surrounded by people kicking and hitting him. He felt like he'd been cornered by a lynch mob.

But even worse misfortune awaited him. Suddenly muddy water was flowing around his feet, and when he jumped in surprise, he dropped his pack. He lost his footing, twisted and fell, and as he did so he lost his sense of direction. Based on recalled sounds, he groped around for his pack, but to no avail. He touched the ground with both hands, feeling out a circle around where he lay on his back, but found nothing. It could be just a little ways away, or it could have been carried off by the current. It was all the same to him: the pack was gone.

Kaoru stayed still in the midst of the darkness, unable to move freely. He'd have to rely on his sense of touch and his hearing now. If the water eddying around his feet rose to cover his ankles, he decided, he'd have to move, but to where? He'd have to hear and feel his way to where the water wasn't as deep.

He was a worm, squirming in the mud. He'd seen worms that had crawled up out of cracks in the asphalt after days of heavy rain, only to be caught and dried up by the burning sun. Why did worms crawl out of the ground after the rain anyway? One theory was that they were trying to escape the carbonic acid gas dissolved in rainwater; Kaoru didn't know if this was right or not. Poor creatures—they finally crawl out of the dirt and get out of the rainwater, only to be dried up by ultraviolet light. Was it the light that drew them, despite their weakness to it?

Kaoru would settle for even the tiniest bit of light at the moment. He'd been in utter darkness for hours now. How many hours, he didn't know, as he'd lost all sense of time. He couldn't even see the hands on his watch.

Without being sure of the lay of the land around him, he couldn't walk anywhere. On the way up he'd seen numerous hundred-yard drops. If he wandered off now he might step right into a yawning crevice.

He thought he heard the sound of falling rock somewhere close by. He stiffened with fear. Several boulders rolled by, shooting pebbles when they hit them—he could feel the air move with their passage. The rain must have softened the ground enough to start a landslide. But then the rumbling abruptly stopped, right in front of him. There could be only one explanation: there must

be a ravine directly in front of him. As the falling
rocks pitched into empty space, they ceased
making any sound. He was sure of it. He was on
the edge of a gaping maw.

He backed up, sliding along the ground on his
back. He had to put some distance between
himself and this pit whose depth he couldn't
know. It was an instinctive thing. His feet slipped
once, and he slid back down a couple of feet, and
even that was enough to set the muscles of his
buttocks trembling.

He was taking the rain full in the face now,
and by and by he was becoming oblivious to the
drops pounding his cheeks. No doubt tears were
coursing down his face, too, but the Kaoru that
wept seemed like somebody else.

Illusions crowded in on him with frightening
force. He saw himself clinging to a rocky outcropping amidst towering waves, waist washed by the
sea, and then again he saw himself being sucked
into a bottomless swamp, sinking deeper into the
ground the more he squirmed.

And then every time he managed to shake off
the delusions, to recover his grip on reality, he
was left with an overpowering consciousness of
death. His body was nearly frozen, and his senses
were about to give out.

I'm going to die from rain.

He'd never, not once in his life, worried about
rain. It had simply never occurred to him that it

could kill him. It was comical, really. Here the whole world was about to die of cancer, and meanwhile he was going to die of a little rain.

He realized it had been quite some time since he'd been rained on enough to get wet. He remembered a late afternoon shower about a month ago: he'd stood by the window on the top floor of the hospital and watched it. One moment the clouds beyond the thick pane of glass were changing color, and the next moment the streets below were wet. That pane was all that separated him from the outside, but it looked at that moment like another world.

Reiko had been with him. Shoulder to shoulder they'd stood in the air-conditioned hallway; Kaoru had been glad for the shower, as it hadn't rained for a while. He'd looked on it as a blessing then. Ryoji was still alive, and new life had just begun in Reiko's womb.

Rain was rain, but what had once seemed like heaven now felt like hell.

He tried to drive away negative thoughts with memories of Reiko's face. He thought of his father and his mother; He tried to muster some courage. But he was too weakened. The moment he let his guard down, the shadow of death crept back over him.

All he had to do was go to sleep and it would all be over. The cold would take care of him, the darkness would carry him off.

Kaoru strove to retain his grip on consciousness.

He was fading fitfully in and out now. When he came to, he sometimes didn't know where he was. If he stayed out for longer, death would take him.

As he shivered from the cold, he longed for the dawn. Once the sun came up, the temperature was bound to rise. Then, if nothing else, he'd be delivered from this fearsome darkness.

As it was, the unrelieved blackness was a breeding-ground for delusions. He thought he sensed somebody nearby. Not the familiar Indian, but somebody whose scent was far stronger as it wafted past his nose. Voices of indeterminate gender whispered back and forth. There had to be at least two of them, shadows in communication.

"Is somebody out there?" Kaoru yelled as loud as he could, loud enough to be heard over the rain, loud enough to chase away evil spirits.

But the shadows didn't recede. Instead they increased—there were three of them now, four, five. They surrounded him, muttering. Kaoru couldn't make out what they were saying, couldn't even identify what language they were speaking. They sounded like they might be sympathizing with him, but then he thought he caught a mocking undercurrent. Maybe they were laughing at him after all.

At length, the rain began to lessen and the darkness started giving way. He could gradually make out his surroundings. Everything was gray as of yet—that distant peak that poked up like some sort of religious monument should be brownish-red, but instead it was just a black shape. A monochrome world was better than an invisible one though.

Watching the scenery around him change for the better should have given Kaoru courage. The dawn had come. The rain was stopping. But he was feverish now, his mind dazed, and he was still chilled and exhausted. Budding doctor though he was, Kaoru had trouble explaining his condition.

He hoped he'd simply caught a cold, but he could feel a tortuous rasping in his lungs. He'd never experienced these symptoms with a common cold. Pneumonia? He put his hand to his forehead, his chest, under his arm, trying to gauge his temperature. He seemed to be running a considerable fever. He couldn't make himself move.

The rain had stopped and morning had come, but he was still curled up in the mud. He wiggled like a shrimp, trying to get to someplace out of the standing water.

What he wanted now was sunlight. He wanted to bask in it, to dry his body and his clothing. His waterlogged clothes were warm now, but from his fever, and he couldn't stand the feel of them.

He took them off and wrung them out. Even that was a hard task in his present state of weakness. When the wind hit his bare skin, he shivered so much that he almost fell over. Still, he managed to get rid of enough water that he felt lighter.

He crawled into a space between the rocks to get out of the wind whipping up the ravine. There he rested for a while. He'd have to husband his strength by staying still until the temperature rose.

As he lay there among the rocks, fighting his fever, the world around him continued to transform. Colors appeared, and distant objects became clearer.

He watched it all, waiting for the clouds to part.

Hours passed. As the temperature climbed, Kaoru was able to sleep for short periods of time. Every time he opened his eyes he gazed vacantly at the movements of the clouds. Still the sun hadn't broken through.

He awoke to a roar. Reminded of his sufferings of the previous night, he sat bolt upright in terror.

He saw something hovering in the sky. Right behind it, the sun was finally emerging. The clouds split apart and rays of sunlight shone on the floating object. Kaoru squinted against the brightness, staring at the heavens beyond the gleaming black thing.

This thing that had appeared was not what Kaoru had imagined. He'd expected to find ruins that bespoke the very beginnings of time, a group of people shrouded in mystery. Instead, what hovered there in the sky backlit by the sun was the product of the most cutting-edge modern science: a jet helicopter. And, just like the Indian's bow had been, the antenna projecting in front of it was aimed straight at Kaoru.

The wind from its rotors buffeted him. Appearing like this, it was almost as if it had been waiting for him to arrive. For a time the helicopter stayed in one spot in the middle of the air, bombarding his ears with its noise. Then it turned, showing him its underbelly, and climbed.

Its rotors rent the clouds, enlarging the hole through which the sun shone. The light that came through now looked to Kaoru like a halo.

PART FOUR

The Space Underground

1

The first thing he saw when he opened his eyes was the whitish ceiling. Kaoru next turned his gaze on all four walls in succession, then on anything else that came within his field of vision.

The room was perfectly sealed off, with no windows. There was a rectangular grating in one corner of the ceiling, most likely a vent for the climate control system. That had to be what kept the room at such a steady, comfortable temperature.

There were two cracks in the walls, each tracing the shape of a rectangle. Doors, of course, but since they were exactly the same color as the walls he wouldn't have noticed them had it not been for the cracks. One had a sturdy-looking doorknob. He guessed this door connected to a hallway. The other door only had a little handle, and looked like it couldn't be locked from either side; probably it led to a bathroom or something.

The walls were covered not with wallpaper but with leather. At first he'd thought they were white, but as his eyes got used to what they were seeing he realized the walls were actually a light beige.

Over the course of these observations, Kaoru was able to confirm that his consciousness was in good working order. He was still alive, or so it seemed.

Still lying on his back, he stopped looking at things for a while, instead concentrating on each part of his body in turn. He commanded his chest to move, then his belly, his arms, his legs, and finally his fingers and toes. He was relieved to note that he could feel them all move.

It was easy enough to explain to himself the situation in which he'd been placed. He was in a little room with leather-covered walls, lying on a bed. It was that simple. Kaoru was the only person in the room.

Naturally, he was put in mind of hospital rooms, which made it even harder to figure out where he was.

He'd traveled to America alone and ridden a motorcycle to a point in the desert—or had he? Had he done all that in reality, or in a dream? He wasn't sure he could say. At the moment it would have been easier for him to believe he was in his father's hospital room, and that the whole thing had been a dream.

He'd been walking along the ridge in search of the cavern containing the long-lived ones, along the way glimpsing rock-paintings done by ancient Indians on the walls of little caves, illustrations that created an irresistible sense of mystery and perhaps foreshadowed the underground space that he believed was soon to manifest itself to him. But then had come the rainstorm, casting him into the depths of terror, pummeling him half to death.

His head still echoed with the sound he'd heard at dawn, just before the sun came out. That thunderous roar, that strangely out-of-place object hovering in space. An ultramodern jet helicopter painted gunmetal black. It seemed to him now that he'd lost consciousness just as it had flown up and away, showing him its underside.

He could string together the recollections, alright, but there was no way of verifying them. Reality and virtuality had become so confused that he didn't trust his memories.

The only way to confirm things would be to wait for the testimony of a third party. But he'd been awake for an hour now, and he'd been left alone the whole time.

Maybe I'd better get up and leave the room on my own . . . Kaoru sat up slowly. He felt no pain, but the difficulty with which he managed to raise himself told him that his body was still exhausted. He sat there on the bed trying to bring his breathing under control—he felt a rasp in the back of his throat. Sitting up was one thing. Moving around was another thing altogether.

He looked down to find a pair of sandals waiting for him beside the bed. They didn't belong to him. Somebody had put them there. Huge sandals. They'd dwarf his feet.

In the end it seemed that those sandals were urging him into action. He summoned all his willpower and lowered his feet over the side of the bed and into the sandals. They felt just as oversized as they looked, and they were heavy as well.

He tried walking across the room in them. He made for the room's single point of interface with the outside: the door.

But his feet were tired, and the footgear was bulky and heavy. His feet dragged. The hem of his white gown parted and he saw his thighs. He suddenly realized that he was wearing no underwear beneath the gown. He was buck naked except for this flimsy white gown he'd been dressed in.

The door was right in front of him now. He had no idea where he'd go once he opened it; he just wanted to know where he was. That was his only motive. What kind of place was this? He wanted to see what was outside. And if there was somebody, anybody, there, he wanted to hear what they had to say.

Kaoru placed a hand on the doorknob. Up until that moment it hadn't occurred to him that the door might be locked, but as he touched the knob, his intuition told him that it was. He turned the knob, pushed and pulled, but the door wouldn't budge.

So now Kaoru had achieved a deeper understanding of the situation into which he'd been placed. He'd been confined.

Even standing up was tough. He felt he'd better give up on going out and go back to bed instead. He released his hold on the doorknob and turned around.

At that moment, though, he sensed somebody on the other side of the door. Kaoru froze in place and listened to the *click* as the door unlocked.

He took a couple of steps backward and waited for it to open. He'd been denied any information about the person or thing about to appear. The person could walk through that door and introduce himself as a Martian and Kaoru wouldn't have been surprised.

The door opened quietly. He'd been expecting to see someone standing there. Instead, he saw someone sitting there: an old man in a wheelchair, staring straight ahead.

"I see you're awake," the man said in English. Kaoru nodded reflexively.

"You're Kaoru Futami. A pleasure to make your acquaintance. My name is Cristoph Eliot."

The old man held out his hand for Kaoru to shake. Kaoru glanced at the hand: it was abnormally large.

As were the feet that stuck out in front of the wheels of the wheelchair. Even seated as the man was, Kaoru got a good idea of his size. Overall, he was on the small side for a foreigner, but his hands and feet were disproportionately big.

Kaoru then wondered at himself and the way he was remarking on the irregularity of this man Eliot's body. Shouldn't he be in shock right about now? *Why does this old man know my name?* All of his identification, all his papers, had been lost with the rucksack.

He shook the man's hand, observing him closely. He had a head like an egg: not a single hair grew on it. His skin was porcelain-white and lustrous. Judging by the hue of his skin, it was probably unfair to think of him as an old man. At the same time, he had a dark spot on his neck and left cheek, the kind of mark peculiar to old age. It contrasted sharply with his pale skin.

From Eliot's grip, Kaoru realized the man bore him no ill will, so he decided to ask the question that had been on his mind.

"What is this place?"

Eliot's grayish eyes narrowed and a smile played over his lips.

"The place you were trying to get to."

But the place Kaoru had been trying to get to

was supposed to be a huge cavern with a village
of very long-lived people in it.

He looked around the room with new eyes.
The little sealed room, the beige leather walls—
no, it couldn't be. This was too different from
what he'd imagined.

Eliot seemed to pick up on Kaoru's perplexed
expression. He raised one great finger and asked
a question of his own.

"What do you think is above us?"

The ceiling, and beyond that—what? How was
Kaoru to know?

Seeing he couldn't answer, Eliot answered for
him.

"A thick layer of water." Not a "tank". A "layer
of water".

Kaoru couldn't figure out what he meant. Was
he using some sort of symbolic expression for
rain? After his experiences of the last few days,
Kaoru found that idea plausible.

Next Eliot pointed down with the same finger.

"And what do you think is below where you're
standing?"

What could be beneath this little room? Earth,
of course. But Kaoru wasn't about to give the
obvious answer. He remained silent.

Eliot provided the answer to this question
himself, too.

"A vast space."

Kaoru realized what he was being told: that

he was suspended between water and space. But it still didn't make sense to him.

It would, however, explain some things. If what Eliot was saying was true, then the force of gravity in this area should be abnormally low. Gravity increases in spots with great mass underneath, and decreases in spots with low mass underneath. A vast empty space beneath his feet would account for the gravitational anomaly. It was persuasive.

Kaoru still couldn't believe it, though. Had he really reached his destination? If he had, if this was the place indicated on the fictional gravitational-anomaly map, then he shouldn't be surprised that Eliot knew his name.

The old guy's trying to tell me that gravity is lower here. He knew I was trying to reach this place.

Confusion overwhelmed Kaoru, and he had to put his hand on the wall to steady himself. He was gasping for breath, but he finally managed to force out the question.

"Did you know I was coming?"

Eliot reached out a huge hand to keep Kaoru from toppling over, and said, in a voice full of charity, "Yes. You were meant to come here."

Kaoru felt hot. His fever must have come back.

"The only thing that wasn't predicted was that record-breaking storm."

Kaoru couldn't even tell any longer if he was burning up or freezing. He felt feverish, but chills were running over the surface of his body. He couldn't stay on his feet. Eliot's words were indistinct in his ears.

He brushed Eliot's hand away and tried to walk back to the bed under his own power. Halfway there he collapsed.

2

For the next three days Kaoru's task was to recover his strength. This expenditure of time, Eliot finally gave him to understand, wouldn't have been necessary had it not been for the rainstorm. Once his strength had been restored, Kaoru would be given the answers to all his questions. Until then, he was forced to recuperate in that little room, in ignorance of his real situation.

Eliot poked his head in once in a while, but mostly it was the nurse, Hana, who looked after Kaoru's health and other needs.

Kaoru thought Hana was a cute name: in Japanese, *hana* means flower. He asked her if it was her real name, but her only response was laughter. "You can call me that, at any rate." And it was easy to call her by it, once he got used to it.

Hana . . . It reminded him of delicate wildflowers blooming in a meadow—an image that fit the nurse to a "t".

Once Eliot had left them alone, Kaoru would barrage her with questions. *What kind of facility is this place? Who is Eliot? Is there a purpose to all this?*

He delivered himself of every question that occurred to him, with an effect that must have been overwhelming, but Hana simply smiled and held her peace, shaking her head to show that no answers would be forthcoming from her.

In face and body, Hana looked like a child. She couldn't have been more than four foot ten, and she had plump cheeks and big round eyes. If she'd worn her lustrous black hair down, sweeping back from her forehead to cover her whole back, she might have looked more grown up. As it was, she wore it tied tightly back, exposing her smooth, arcing forehead in a way that emphasized her youthfulness, obscuring her true age. The swelling of her breasts, too, was that of a half-grown girl, but he doubted she would get any bigger. Her small breasts, however, went well with her delicate Oriental features.

Kaoru was taken in by her childlike appearance, at first. He assumed that she wasn't answering any of his questions because she herself hadn't been let in on the truth. The innocence in her face seemed to indicate ignorance, so that even though she supplied none of the information he asked for, he felt no suspicion, no anger, tow ard her.

But Hana's skills as a nurse turned out to be such as to belie her appearance. Kaoru could recognize a good nurse when he saw one, having virtually lived in hospitals for almost as long as he could remember. It was as though she knew how to scratch him exactly where he itched. She was perfectly efficient, with not a movement wasted.

She had him hooked up to I.V.s, taking antibiotics, and trying to get sufficient sleep.

She was fairly taciturn as she went about her work. He thought he detected in her gestures an unnecessary briskness. He wondered, although it was unfair to her, if she was trying to minimize contact with his body. She had manual dexterity in line with her competence as a nurse, but sometimes her hands seemed to hesitate when it came time to touch him. And occasionally he caught her stealing glances at him, observing him as if he were something unnatural, alien. He noticed it more as time went on.

It was two days after he first met Hana. He heard the sounds that meant she was about to enter the room, and he pretended to be asleep, leaving his eyes open just a slit. He watched her gaze at him with curiosity as she quickly changed the I.V. bottle. It was almost a morbid curiosity he saw in her eyes—she was afraid of him and intrigued by him at the same time. This in turn piqued Kaoru's interest. What was she reacting to in him when she got that expression on her face?

She finished changing the bottle, and then bent over him, hips thrust back, observing him nervously. Surely she was convinced he was sleeping. But then why didn't she let down her guard?

Kaoru snapped open his eyes and grabbed Hana's arm. He hadn't intended to startle her, but that was the effect. She tried to let out a little scream, but couldn't find her voice. It died in the back of her throat, and all that escaped was a gasp.

"Why do you look at me like you're seeing a ghost?" Kaoru spoke slowly and distinctly. He wanted to calm her down, first of all. Her hand, the one Kaoru wasn't holding, was pressed to her cheek. She wasn't putting up any resistance worth the name: she didn't try to shake loose, didn't turn her head away from him. She swallowed her scream and looked down at him vacantly. She looked like she was about to burst into tears, a look that was a fine complement to her childlike features.

"I want to know. Why do you look at me like that?"

She shook her head sadly. "I'm sorry." The words seemed to come from the bottom of her heart, but they didn't answer his question. He could interpret them one of two ways. Either she was saying she was sorry for looking at him like he was a ghost, or she was apologizing for not being able to answer him. Or maybe it was both.

He let her go.

Her job was just to nurse him back to health. She'd been forbidden to open her mouth about anything else. Any explanation about the way she looked at him would necessarily involve explaining the whole situation he was in, and she couldn't do that. As Kaoru came to understand this, he decided to quit pressing her.

She remained standing next to his bed even after he released her.

"Isn't it difficult for you to talk?" Her sense of duty was showing through. Her first impulse was to check on her patient's condition.

"It's difficult for me *not* to talk. It's driving me crazy."

"Well, then, why don't you tell me about yourself?"

"What do you want to know?"

"Let's see . . . How about everything, starting with your birth?"

"And what good would it do you if I told you?"

"At the very least, I probably wouldn't look at you as if you were a ghost anymore."

In other words, she knew nothing about him. If she knew more, maybe she'd be able to look on him as a fellow human.

"I want to know just one thing about you first," Kaoru said.

Hana composed herself, without answering.

"If it's not too forward of me, I'd like to know how old you are."

Hana laughed. No doubt she'd been asked this any number of times.

"I'm thirty-one years old. I'm married and have two children. Both of them boys."

Kaoru's jaw dropped open in amazement. She looked no more than a girl, and yet she was telling him she was thirty-one. And a mother of two! An unexpected response, to say the least.

"I can't believe it."

"Everybody says that."

"I was sure you were younger than me." At twenty, though, he was eleven years her junior.

"How old are you?"

He told her. She furrowed her brow and in a low voice said, "Really?"

"I look older, don't I? But I'm really twenty."

Kaoru put a hand to his cheek. He hadn't shaved since arriving in the desert, so he figured he might look even older than usual.

He couldn't quite get over the shock that this woman was in fact older than him. It was bound to make him act differently with her.

Learning each other's true ages seemed to change something between them. After that, whenever Hana looked in on him, Kaoru watched for the chance to tell her a little more about himself.

Hana was a good listener. She only came by the room a few times a day, and they only had a limited time to talk, maybe ten minutes at a time. But she made good use of it, never getting off track, always eliciting more about Kaoru's past life.

And Kaoru found he enjoyed talking to her, telling her things. It allowed him to make sure of himself as he was now. Of course, doubts did come to mind, but he shunted them aside and he spoke haltingly of himself.

He told her of his childhood, what he'd thought about, the kind of dreams he'd had. Bits and pieces of life with his father and mother. Their plans to go off to America together, to the desert . . .

There were things that were hard to talk about. Most of all, his father's cancer: how it had dashed their travel plans, how their lives had revolved around hospitals ever since. How after several years his cancer had been identified as coming from the Metastatic Human Cancer Virus, and how there was essentially no hope of him recovering. How Kaoru's mother refused to give up, but had immersed herself in Native American legends until she found hints of a miracle cure, belief in which had allowed her to go on undaunted. How Kaoru, forced to balance his father's illness and his mother's headlong rush into spiritualism, had abandoned his early desire to study astrophysics for medical school.

As he spoke, Kaoru began to feel a nostalgia for it all. Over a period of four days he spoke to her for a total of two, maybe three hours. He certainly couldn't tell her everything about his life in that amount of time; he had to cut out a lot of things. But he remembered a lot of things too. Sometimes he'd have to fight back tears, and then sometimes he'd burst out laughing as he told her about some crazy thing his father had done.

A life that could be told in a mere two or three hours—could it be real? As he talked, his more distant memories began to cloud over.

"Haven't you ever been in love?"

Her question was perfectly timed. At that very moment Kaoru was wondering whether or not he should tell her about Reiko. He'd been leaning toward avoiding the subject, and if Hana hadn't spoken, he very well might not have mentioned her.

Telling her about his affair with Reiko would

naturally involve telling her about Ryoji. The experience still filled him with sadness, and more than that with pain. Regrets always came to mind first, shame for his ill-considered actions. He realized that the room where he and Reiko had taken their pleasure and the room he was in now were rather similar. Of course, Ryoji's room had boasted a west-facing full-length window overlooking the green of the park and admitting the rays of the setting sun, while this room had no window at all. But that aside, in terms of size and the color of the walls, the rooms were very much alike.

No matter how hard he tried, he'd never be able to communicate to Hana the carnal joy that Reiko had given him.

Kaoru confessed his feelings honestly. Now and then Hana looked at him disbelievingly, shaking her head and saying, "Oh, no," in a commiserating tone. Then when Kaoru revealed that Reiko was carrying his child, Hana's expression froze.

"And this child—it's going to be born?"

A strange way to phrase the question, he thought, but he didn't stop to worry about it.

"Of course, I want her to have it. That's why I came here."

Hana closed her eyes. Her lips were trembling and she seemed to be praying, although he couldn't hear her words.

In this windowless room, the only way to gauge the passage of time was by his watch. If it was to be believed, this was the evening of the fourth day. After he finished telling her about his and Reiko's child, Hana said, "That should do for today." She seemed not to be permitted to do whatever she wanted with her time; she was always cutting their talks short when she found the right moment.

"I want to hear the rest tomorrow, though." She spoke with kindness. This woman whom he'd once thought of as a child had now become a merciful mother-figure.

She placed a hand on his arm and contemplated him for a while, and then walked to the door. Once there, she stopped, glanced back at the bed, and then went out into the hallway.

The expression on her face as she looked back at him burned itself into Kaoru's mind. He'd seen it somewhere before.

He thought about facial expressions, deciding that they usually fell into a finite set of categories. People generally made the same sort of face placed in the same sort of situation: hearing a piece of good news, for example, or jumping from a high place. He tried to figure out what category Hana's expression belonged to.

Something came to mind immediately, something that had always stayed with him.

The situation had been almost exactly the

same. A woman, dressed in white like Hana, walking out of a sickroom, turning around for a last look at the patient. A nurse.

Once, his father had been moved to a larger room, as a temporary measure. He'd just had surgery to remove the cancer from his rectum, and seemed to be making good progress. It had been a four-person room, and every bed held a cancer patient.

One of the nurses who frequented the room had been particularly popular with the patients. She was no great beauty, but she was attractive enough, and more than that she was the type of woman who just radiated goodness. She was always long-suffering toward her patients, listening to their demands with never a look of complaint. Kaoru's father had liked her, too. He'd joke with her and touch her bottom, all for the pleasure of being admonished by her like a child.

A time came when she left the hospital, albeit temporarily. She was in her second year of marriage, and in fact was seven months pregnant. She'd put in for a year's maternity leave.

On her last day at the hospital, she came by Kaoru's father's room to say goodbye. Kaoru was visiting his father at the time. She told the patients that she expected them all to be happy and smiling when she came back in a year, to which one of the patients joked, *By the time you get back, honey, I'll have checked out of this place.*

Kaoru seemed to remember the other two patients, but not his father, saying similar things. It was impossible to tell how sincere the patients were being. In any case the nurse just nodded in agreement as she made the rounds of each bed to say her goodbyes.

Then, as she left the room, she turned back to glance at the patients in their beds, exactly as Hana had done just now. The look in the nurse's eyes had not evaded Kaoru's notice then: it had been one of certainty that there were those among the patients she would not see, could not see, when she returned in a year. And not because they'd have checked out. Her look was a wistful one of final—for this life, at least—farewell.

The patient in the bed next to Kaoru's father had just learned that his lung cancer had spread to his brain. The next patient over had just lost his manhood to prostate cancer. Kaoru's father was the only one with some vitality left. All the rest were proceeding steadily toward their dates with death.

Awareness of that had informed the nurse's gaze. And now Kaoru had seen that same gaze directed at himself.

Why did Hana look at me like that?

It made him uneasy. He'd ask her directly if he could.

But as it turned out, Kaoru was never to see Hana again.

The next morning, at the usual time, there was a knock at the door. Kaoru opened it expecting to see Hana, but found Eliot instead, his huge feet sticking out in front of his wheelchair, his huge hands resting on the wheels.

Seeing that Kaoru was recovering smoothly, Eliot gave a satisfied nod. "How are you feeling?"

Kaoru's endurance was at its limits: he had so many questions, and all of them had been put on hold for so long. Hana's cuteness had helped him to bear it for a while, but facing Eliot he knew he couldn't keep them back much longer.

How am I feeling? You've got to be kidding. Why am I always the one who's got to answer questions? My physical strength is back, but at this rate I'm going to turn into a nervous wreck. How am I feeling, indeed!

He bit back his anger, but not all that effectively. His voice shook as he said, "Knock it off already."

Eliot evidently noticed the tension in Kaoru's voice. He held up his hands as if to tell Kaoru to hold on a minute, then paused. At last he spoke. "I get it. I think I understand your feelings. It's about time we get underway with our plans."

Plans? What plans? And what have they got to do with me?

With a hard look on his face, Kaoru began to press Eliot for answers. "First I want you to tell me where I am and what you're up to."

Eliot pressed his palms together.

"First I want to ask *you* something."

Kaoru waited silently for him to continue.

Eliot's voice was grave when next he spoke.

"Do you believe in God?"

3

Eliot showed him into a room with no windows. Why was this whole place sealed up like this? Kaoru disliked windowless rooms. This room was bigger than the last, though. There was a leather living-room set in the middle of it.

Eliot invited Kaoru to have a seat on the couch. Kaoru did as he was directed. Then Eliot got out of his wheelchair. He stood up, rear end thrust backward, and without using a cane hobbled over to seat himself opposite Kaoru.

Kaoru couldn't help but stare. Since Eliot used a wheelchair, Kaoru had naturally assumed he couldn't walk. But he could: somewhat awkwardly, but fairly steadily.

Noticing Kaoru's surprise, Eliot flashed a triumphant grin. "You must learn to look at things without preconceptions. Trust nothing."

But Kaoru was already quite accustomed to suspecting everything. One thing he'd learned crossing the desert was how to keep his balance as he walked the hazy line between reality and virtuality. It was the one thing he'd most wanted not to lose during that rainstorm on the ridge.

"When are you going to answer my questions?" Kaoru said sulkily, ignoring Eliot's words. Eliot raised his hands in a gesture that seemed to say, *Any time you want.*

There were so many things Kaoru wanted to ask. He decided to lay aside his basic questions for the moment, and instead to start by exploring something Eliot had said earlier and which had been nagging at Kaoru ever since.

"I was fated to come here, from long ago. That's what you told me, correct?" Kaoru wanted to know why he'd said that. Doubtless he'd been speaking figuratively, but the way he'd said it troubled Kaoru deeply.

"It's a little early yet to explain that. If we go out of order, you're liable to end up screaming."

"In that case, you're going to explain things to me so that I understand, so that I don't end up screaming—right?" Kaoru was on edge again. Eliot's roundabout way of speaking rubbed him the wrong way. Kaoru got the feeling that this man held his life's rudder, and was laughing at the mother and father who'd brought him into the world.

"This was the only way to do it. I decided I would never be able to force you here. You had to come of your own free will. And looking at you now I can see that I was right about that." Eliot spoke as if to himself, then smiled. He spoke as someone who'd intervened in Kaoru's life. At that moment, Kaoru wanted to wring the old man's neck.

Eliot was unfazed by Kaoru's violent glare. For a time they were both silent.

It was Eliot who resumed speaking. "How much do you know about the Loop?" His hands were clasped in front of him, and there was something boyish in his upwards glance at Kaoru.

"It's an extremely well-designed computer simulation."

Eliot frowned, not content with that answer.

"Well-designed? That doesn't even begin to cover it. When I made the Loop, I made a world perfect in every respect."

"You made it?"

"I should say 'we,' I guess, but really, I was the one who had the initial idea for its structure." Now that he was discussing the Loop, there was a perceptible note of pride in Eliot's voice. The words came like water from a burst dam now; at times something like ecstasy was visible on his face.

"I was still a student at MIT. That's right, I was about the age you are now—this was nearly seventy years ago. The world was in love with astronauts—we'd just landed on the moon—and everybody was convinced that before long science would bring us space stations and space tourism. But I wasn't interested in outer space. My gaze was turned on another world, one I was trying to build myself."

Having said that much without pause, Eliot ducked his head and pursed his lips.

"Incidentally, do you know what makes the world go round?"

"The real world, or the Loop?"

It was easy to see what made the Loop go round: electricity. But the real world, that was a different story.

Eliot laughed at Kaoru's question.

"In this case, they're a lot alike. They move according to the same principle. The thing that makes the world go round—both worlds—is funding."

Eliot waited a few moments for the import of his words to sink in, then continued. "If the gargantuan project that was the Loop hadn't been funded, then that world would never have come into being. Neither this world nor that one will move without money."

Kaoru was listening closely now, eager to see what Eliot would say next, and how it would all connect to himself.

If only there had been funding, we might all be aboard space stations now. Eliot was right. Science, Kaoru knew, did not progress along a straight line in a vacuum sealed off from social conditions. Instead, it changed direction from time to time in response to the situation. Budgets were controlled by the opinions of societies and governments—priorities were determined according to what people wanted most at a given time. Seventy years ago, outer space was the canvas on which the future was expected to be drawn. Everybody imagined that humanity would make colonies of the moon and Mars, that shuttles would make regularly scheduled trips between the planets. It was the stuff of novels and movies.

But by Kaoru's day, not only had man not been to Mars, he hadn't even returned to the moon. In the end, man's presence on Earth's satellite had been limited to that one brief, shining moment. Since then plans for space exploration had moved along at a snail's pace, if at all. And for one simple reason. *No funding.*

In hindsight, it seemed odd that nobody had been able to predict that grinding halt.

Eliot, however, was saying that he had, in fact, predicted it. He was boasting of his foresight in turning his prodigious talents in another direction entirely.

He'd chosen as his academic fields computers, which at that time were unbelievably primitive compared to the ones Kaoru was familiar with, and molecular biology, which had just been revolutionized by the discovery of the double helix.

Eliot had had the uncanny intuition to combine these two emerging fields. His first research project had asked the simple question of whether or not it was possible to create artificial life within a computer.

He'd pursued this question through highly original means, and at length, his work began to bear fruit. Just as Eliot had foreseen, society's interest began to shift from space exploration to the creation of a user-friendly world of information. Computers were the stars of the age, and Eliot suddenly found that he had venues in which to present his work, and listeners to present it to.

With new wind in his sails, Eliot proceeded to develop the first self-replicating program, and then the first software that could evolve on its own. All without losing sight of his initial question. *Is it possible to create artificial life in a computer?*

He first realized his goal sooner than even he had expected, in the final years of the twentieth century. He'd never expected it to happen before the end of the century, he said; he'd shocked even himself. Of course, the beings he called life at that point were quite simple in structure, moving around onscreen in a way that resembled nothing so much as parasitic worms.

Then he caused male and female to appear, and at the beginning of the new century, new life had appeared within the computer of its own accord. The new cells divided again and again, and eventually they crawled around in the display just like their parents. Eliot called it a sight worthy of the new century.

Things accelerated after that. The basic process was much the same for all kinds of life forms. Producing fish or amphibians was all a matter of accumulating adaptations.

Having accomplished that much, Eliot allowed for an evolution in his ultimate goal. The question now became: *Is it possible to create in a virtual space a biosphere on the scale of the Earth's?*

This was the germ of the Loop project, an idea that at this stage was already pretty clearly defined.

At Eliot's invitation, scientists the world over began working toward a single goal. Computer scientists, medical doctors, molecular biologists, evolutionary theorists, astrophysicists, geologists, meteorologists—people from every branch of the sciences were involved. But interest wasn't confined to the hard sciences—economists, historians, political scientists, and social scientists of all stripes were paying attention, too.

Because it turned out to take more than just science to create a virtual Earth. It took an understanding of the humanities and social sciences as well. For this reason it was expected that the results of the Loop experiment would contribute to all fields. In addition to the basic evolutionary and biological mysteries, it was hoped that creating intelligent life forms in a virtual world would help provide clues to social problems such as wars and population increase, even fluctuations in the stock markets, areas in which it had been impossible to find definitive governing principles. Leading scientists in every field recognized the importance of the Loop project.

So the Loop started to function formally, in reality, with a budget equivalent to that of a full-fledged country.

Due to the reservations of certain government actors, the project couldn't be conducted in the open at first. Nobody could predict what might come of it—some new strategy for world domination, perhaps—and so it was felt that it should be carried out with the greatest circumspection. In the end, with no great ceremony, the project was launched as a joint effort by the U.S. and Japan.

The next name Eliot mentioned was one dear to Kaoru.

"Hideyuki Futami . . . Yes, he was a brilliant researcher. Young—fresh out of grad school—but he made the biggest contribution of anybody on the Japan side, I think." Eliot's phrasing tickled Kaoru—as was Eliot's intention, no doubt. Hearing one's father praised like this would make anyone feel good. Certainly that was the effect it had on Kaoru.

"Have you met my father?" Kaoru asked enthusiastically.

"Not face to face. But I heard about him, from my assistants."

Hideyuki had never talked much about the Loop. Kaoru was curious as to just what role Hideyuki had played in the project. He resolved to ask next time he saw him.

Eliot went on, interrupting Kaoru's thoughts of his father.

"I think you know what happened to the Loop after that."

"It turned cancerous."

"In the end, yes. But up to that point it was simply incredible. We'd never expected it to go so far."

He gave Kaoru a portentous look, as if urging him to ask the question.

"There was something you hadn't predicted?"

"Does it not surprise you? After all, you've seen a part of the Loop with your own eyes."

"So many things surprised me that I'm not sure what I should be surprised at."

Kaoru wasn't replicating Eliot's excitement, and this seemed to take the wind out of Eliot's sails: he sat there with his mouth half open, spittle dribbling from a corner of his lips. When a drop of drool began to descend on a clear string, Eliot finally noticed and wiped his mouth on his sleeve.

"We'd expected that with physical conditions the same as on Earth, we'd get roughly the same sorts of life forms. We didn't dream that they'd be *exactly identical*. In those days everybody thought that the course of evolution was guided by chance. It couldn't happen the same way twice."

That was indeed one of the things that had surprised Kaoru. The course of evolution in the Loop had been exactly the same as on Earth, down to the last detail, and it certainly mystified him.

"So what did you conclude from that?" he asked.

"We didn't see life naturally emerging in the Loop at the very beginning. So we introduced it. We introduced RNA, thought to be the earliest form of life. Sowing seeds—that was the metaphor we used, but it was no metaphor. That RNA was in all reality a seed, destined to grow into a certain, specific tree of life."

Kaoru had taken part in a discussion like this before, he remembered. With Ryoji. Reiko was dozing nearby while Ryoji and Kaoru debated evolution. And the point Ryoji had been trying to make then was more or less the same one Eliot seemed to be making now.

"What are you trying to say?" Kaoru tried to keep his tone cool and rational. If he broke in too unnaturally, the old man might start drooling again, and Kaoru had no desire to see that.

"The Loop matched up perfectly with reality. Life didn't emerge naturally in the Loop—that's why we sowed the seeds. Don't you realize what that means?"

It hit Kaoru. He remembered what Eliot had asked him at the beginning of their long conversation. *Do you believe in God?* That gave Kaoru the answer.

"That reality is only a virtual world, too, right?"

"Indeed. Life didn't emerge of its own accord on Earth, either. So why are we here? Because somebody sowed the seeds of life here. Who? The being we call God. God caused there to be life on Earth, and He made us in His image. The Bible was right."

Kaoru wasn't particularly shocked by this. He'd had the same thought many times on his journey to this point, but he hadn't been able to prove or disprove it. This was mere reasoning by analogy. It had no bearing on reality. It could not be verified. In the end, it would be, as it always had been, a question of belief or unbelief.

"But that doesn't change anything, does it?"

Eliot sank into his couch as if pushed there by Kaoru's logic. "Even if reality was created by a god, I'm not saying it was made in the same way as what we created in the computer."

Before Eliot could finish the sentence, Kaoru was saying, "I guess God's world must be controlled by funding issues, too."

Eliot's eyes narrowed and flashed coldly. "You're making fun of me." His sternness didn't last long, however. He immediately resumed his former calm expression.

Kaoru glanced at the clock on the wall. This conversation had gone on for three hours already. He was getting hungry, and with no end in sight he was getting tired as well.

Eliot seemed to guess Kaoru's thoughts. "You must be fatigued. Why don't we take a break, watch an old movie or something. I'll see to lunch." His face was expressionless, betraying neither anger nor excitement. He produced a remote control, and a screen descended in front of one wall. He pressed *PLAY*.

Then he stood up slowly, returned to his wheelchair, and went to leave the room. Kaoru followed him with his gaze. When the door shut behind Eliot Kaoru heard it lock. The sound told Kaoru everything he needed to know about his current situation. He was still incarcerated. He'd have to find out why.

On the screen an old movie was playing, one he'd seen before. It was a sci-fi flick his parents had taken him to see when he was ten. He knew the theme song by heart—he'd liked the movie so much that he'd gotten his mother to buy the soundtrack, and he'd listened to it over and over.

A large black man dressed in white appeared and placed a sandwich and some tea with milk in front of Kaoru.

As he ate, Kaoru closed his eyes and listened

to the music divorced from the images. It brought back more memories when he turned it into his own private movie projected onto the backs of his eyelids. Images of his family from the peaceful days before his father's cancer had been detected.

Kaoru didn't notice he was weeping until the tears creeping down his cheeks reached his lips. He wondered again about coincidence. Had Eliot chosen this movie at random, or had he put it on in full knowledge of the many memories it held for Kaoru?

If it was the latter, then things went a lot deeper than simple confinement. *Maybe Eliot's been watching me all along.*

He'd often felt, as a child, like somebody was watching him from behind. He'd always dismissed it as his imagination, but now the feeling came back, and it felt real this time. Kaoru lost his appetite.

4

Eliot returned about the time Kaoru finally finished his lunch.

"My, you certainly had an appetite," Eliot said, looking at the empty plate. "Good, very good."

"Can we cut the crap? I can't even tell you how this is making me feel." As a result of their talk this morning, Kaoru had accumulated even more questions than before. He couldn't wait to put an end to this farce. Why had he come here, anyway? To find out how to combat the MHC virus. He couldn't afford to kill time like this.

"Well," said Eliot, as he lowered himself onto the sofa, "our theme for the afternoon is you and your mission." Once again he seemed to have seen right through Kaoru. Now he couldn't leave even if he wanted to.

"My mission?"

"Yes. Why have you come here? To find a way to combat the Metastatic Human Cancer Virus, no?"

Kaoru and Eliot stared at each other for a while.

Kaoru felt a deep nervous annoyance. Eliot seemed to know all kinds of information about him, while he'd been provided with no knowledge about Eliot. It wasn't fair. He had a reasonable understanding now of the man's place in the history of science. But what Kaoru wanted to know was more private things. Maybe if he had a clearer idea of Eliot as a person, he wouldn't feel so uncomfortable.

"How about a pop quiz?" said Eliot, breaking in on Kaoru's thoughts. He extended his right index finger, pointing at the ceiling. He seemed to be thinking of himself as a teacher now.

"In what year was it discovered that when a neutrino interacts with another object its oscillation goes out of phase?"

Kaoru was familiar with neutrinos, a kind of subatomic particle. If he were asked their main characteristics, he'd be able to answer with three: they move at the speed of light, they have no electrical charge, and they're composed of energy. Looked at in that way, they're quite similar to light. The decisive difference is that even though they have energy they can pass through anything. Neutrinos given off by the sun pass right through the earth, coming out the other side and heading straight off into the darkness of space.

But what did that have to with anything?

Kaoru's answer came automatically. "2001."

Kaoru hadn't even been born yet, but he'd read the information in a history of science textbook, and he remembered it clearly.

"That's correct. In fact it was only at the end of the last century that the neutrino, which had always been considered massless, was discovered to have mass after all."

"Yes, and?" Kaoru's irritation was rising, and he tried to interrupt. Eliot stopped him.

"Just wait. Hear me out. Everything's organically interconnected, and this affected our plans. You're probably not going to understand what I mean when I say this, but if the neutrino's phase shift had not been discovered, you would most likely not exist."

"Give me a break. Enough with the jokes already. What could the nature of the neutrino possibly have to do with my existing or not?" Neutrinos are said to comprise ninety percent of all matter. They're everywhere. But what did that have to do with Kaoru? He wouldn't be able to take much more of this.

"Alright, alright. I'll just ask you to keep that idea in a corner of your mind, and to stay with me for another three minutes while we talk about neutrinos."

Then Eliot proceeded to explain what could be done using the neutrino's phase shift.

It turned out that by shooting neutrinos at an object, measuring their phase shift, and then recomposing them, it was possible to create a detailed three-dimensional digital picture of an object's structure. Neutrinos could be projected through inorganic and organic objects alike. But it was the fields of medicine and pathology that expected to see the greatest applications of this discovery, because suddenly it became possible to have a digital record of an organism's entire molecular makeup. This was different from a mere DNA analysis. Sequencing an organism's DNA simply meant analyzing one cell out of the nearly infinite number of cells in a single organism. Using neutrino oscillation made it possible to record everything about a subject, from brain activity to the state of the heart, even memory.

"Not long after the inception of the Loop project, another team of researchers began to construct a piece of equipment known as the Neutron Scanning Capture System, NSCS for short. This would allow us to instantaneously capture an organism's molecular structure. Needless to say, their project too had a huge budget. I myself had no direct connection with the NSCS project, although of course I offered whatever advice I could."

Eliot paused there.

"How about some tea? You'll need some time to digest this information."

Kaoru obediently raised his teacup to his mouth. The tea was cold. Kaoru had heard a fair amount concerning neutrinos in his lifetime, but this was the first he'd heard of the NSCS.

"I'm sorry if this has been confusing to you. It's time now to bring the discussion around to the MHC virus, which threatens us all."

"Finally, we're getting to the point."

The news came as a relief to Kaoru. He was starting to be afraid that this, too, would lead nowhere.

"What do you know about the Human Metastatic Cancer Virus?" Eliot asked.

"I know that its genome has been sequenced. I've seen the results myself."

"And yet there's still no treatment for it, no progress on a vaccine to prevent it."

"Why is that?"

"It can take a long time to figure out where a virus came from. In the case of the MHC virus, an *extremely* long time."

By now, Kaoru felt he could guess where the virus had come from.

"The Loop, right?"

Eliot opened his eyes wide and stared at Kaoru. "How did you figure it out?"

Kaoru enjoyed the look of sincere amazement on Eliot's face. He felt like delaying his answer to prolong this pleasure, but he hadn't the patience. "The MHC virus isn't very large. It's only got nine genes, each of which ranges from several thousand to several hundred thousand bases in length. But the total number of bases in each gene comes out to equal 2^n x 3. That can't be a coincidence."

Eliot groaned. "Nice catch."

"Not to brag, but I have something of a sixth sense when it comes to numbers. It didn't take much to figure it out."

"And from that you were able to guess where the virus had come from?"

"Well, why did they equal 2^n x 3? That was the question. The times-three part was fairly easy to understand, since three bases together make one codon specifying a single amino acid. But what about the other part of the formula, the 2? No doubt I never would have gotten the idea had I not known about the Loop project. The 2 had to come from the binary code used by computers. The virus must have leaked out of the Loop somehow. That was its birthplace."

"Exactly." Eliot gave a weak smile and clapped his hands. Whether or not the applause was sincere, it sounded like mockery to Kaoru.

Kaoru lowered his voice in an attempt to sound calm. "So we know where it came from. Does that help us find a cure?" A cure for the virus— that was the main thing.

Eliot ignored the question. "When did you figure this out?"

"Huh?"

"When did you figure out the origin of the virus?"

"About a month ago."

"I see. For me it was about six months ago."
He didn't seem to be trying to brag. He was
counting on his fingers like a child, a look of
unguarded remorse on his face.

"I want to know what you think about it,"
Kaoru said, pressing him.

Eliot's response was dilatory, as he started
making excuses.

"It's too bad that it had to be cancer—such a
common disease. Had it been something more
distinctive, maybe we could have done something
at an early stage. But it was able to blend in with
normal cancer as it laid its groundwork. It was
like the wanted man realizing the best place to
hide is in the big city. Precisely because cancer is
such a common illness, the virus was able to use
it as camouflage. Think about it. Who would raise
a fuss just because a researcher on the Loop
project died of cancer? Whereas, if one of us had
died from an unknown illness, we would have
been quite active in looking for the virus that
caused it. But with cancer . . . we mourned the
loss of another colleague, but didn't suspect
anything. It was able to sneak in and do away
with us one by one."

Kaoru could sympathize. It had been a mere
seven years since this cancer was definitely proven
to be viral in origin, and therefore different from
normal cancer. And it had only been a year since

scientists had first successfully isolated the virus. And all that time, the virus had been laying the groundwork for an explosive spread.

Kaoru imagined that Eliot had lost people close to him to the virus. His gaze, one of hostility and regret, was focused on the past.

This was Kaoru's chance to find out more about Eliot as a person, but instead Kaoru brought the conversation back on track.

"Have you been able to figure out precisely how the virus escaped from the Loop?"

"Eh? Oh, yes. Of course."

"Will you tell me?"

"We froze the Loop twenty years ago. Time has stopped inside the Loop. All of its inhabitants are frozen in place. Do you know why we put an end to the project?"

"You're going to tell me you ran out of funding."

He didn't mean it as a joke, but Eliot, after a moment's shock, laughed heartily.

"That's absolutely right. We used up our budget. We'd gotten scholarly feedback from all directions, about as much as we were going to get, and the results had been quite good, at least valuable enough to justify the expenditure. But a project like that can't go on forever. Do you have any idea how many massively parallel supercomputers we buried in the New Mexico desert? Six hundred and forty thousand. And we put another six hundred and forty thousand in the ground underneath Tokyo. We needed our own power plants just to keep them running. They ate up a staggering amount of electricity, and it took massive amounts of money to keep them running. It couldn't go on forever. And then the Loop started turning cancerous."

Kaoru felt he knew all he needed to about how that had come about. Back at Wayne's Rock he'd witnessed for himself, with his own eyes and ears, the key scenes in that chain of events. He informed Eliot of this, and Eliot nodded twice.

"So you've seen it. Or, I should say, you've experienced it. But you don't know why it began to turn cancerous. Let me say right up front that I don't know, either. The making of that odd videotape, the spread of that new virus—these are things that the individuals within the Loop couldn't help but find impossible to explain. You're thinking that even if they couldn't explain it, I should be able to, as the one who made the Loop. But I have to be honest with you: I can't explain it. Not all phenomena in the world can be explained. We've always got problems that need solving; the world is always coming apart at the seams. There's no world anywhere without its internal contradictions. Maybe the real world's internal contradictions infected the Loop; alternatively, it's not inconceivable that it was the work of a computer virus. Our security was supposed

to be perfect, but as long as the Loop was
connected to the outside world, there was at least
the possibility of it being breached. If it was a
piece of mischief, it was an extremely well-
wrought one. But what interested me most was
one of the individuals within the Loop: Ryuji
Takayama."

Eliot stopped there and turned on Kaoru a gaze
that seemed to be searching for agreement. Kaoru
obliged.

"Yeah, he's a pretty interesting guy, alright."

"He's unique."

"He must hold the key to the MHC virus."

Now Eliot's eyes narrowed, as if he were trying
to peer into Kaoru's brain. As if it wouldn't do to
take his eyes off Kaoru for a second now.

Slowly, with suspicion, Eliot said, "Did you not
see Takayama on the monitor?"

"I spent most of my time seeing things from
his perspective, actually." Kaoru answered carefully, each word given special weight, in imita-
tion of Eliot; at the same time he was checking
his own memory to make sure he wasn't making
any mistakes. No, that was how he remembered
it: he'd made full use of Takayama's senses as he
reexperienced the event.

Eliot made an awkward sort of cry and blinked
rapidly several times. "Oh-ho. That explains it."
Uneasy, Kaoru watched Eliot's eyes as they darted
around.

"Explains what?"

"Eh? Oh, nothing. It's just that the conversation begins to move in an interesting direction. Anyway. So that means that you heard Takayama's scream just before he died as if it were your own voice."

"That's right."

He could recall it all clearly, everything he'd seen and heard through Takayama's eyes and ears. On the brink of death, Takayama had found an interface with the real world, and he'd called it. Kaoru could hear Takayama's voice echoing within his body.

"What did Takayama say to you?"

Kaoru repeated the phrase, in as close as he could come to Takayama's intonation.

"'Bring me to your world.'"

"What do you think it means?"

"I think he deduced the existence of the Loop's maker, a god from his perspective, and he wanted that god to bring him back to life in that god's world—in other words, in the real world where you and I live. At least, that's what I took it to mean."

And Kaoru could sympathize with that request. How many times had he confronted his father with a desire to understand how the world worked? But it turned out that this world's working was a little too complicated to be fully comprehended. Every time he thought he'd chased down the answers, they receded a little farther into the distance, like an endless game of cat and mouse. He felt like he was chasing his own shadow, something he'd never ever be able to catch. If it turned out that the world had a maker, then going to that maker's own world would answer all his desires. It would surely tell him how his own world worked.

Eliot spoke calmly. "I understood Takayama's feelings completely. His request came not out of fear of death. What moved him was an insatiable thirst for knowledge. His curiosity about the world exploded in that instant, and it brought about what was to him a miracle."

"A miracle?"

"That's what it was to him. On the brink of death, his greatest desire was to cross over into this world. If the NSCS plans hadn't been in my head, I doubt the idea would ever have occurred to me. In fact, I'm sure it wouldn't have. But as I say, things are connected, organically. I believed I could see twenty, thirty years into the future, and based on what I saw, I made up my mind to grant Takayama's wish."

Kaoru cried out in surprise.

Grant Takayama's wish?

It was just as he'd suspected. Somebody had been rash enough to bring an entity over from the virtual world into the real one. Kaoru was speechless.

Eliot, though, was calm as he began to explain how he'd gone about bringing Ryuji Takayama into the real world.

It was impossible to bring him over as an adult, possessed of his current state of consciousness and all the memories it held. The only thing Eliot could do was extract genetic information from one of Takayama's cells, and based on it, use a genome synthesizer and the genome fragment alignment method to create DNA that would be valid in the real world. Once he'd analyzed Takayama's DNA sequence, it was essentially a matter of chemically synthesizing it.

The next step was to prepare a fertilized human egg, extract its nucleus, and insert the manmade Takayama nucleus in its place. Then all he had to do was return the egg to the mother's body and wait for Takayama to be born. The process wasn't all that different from the cloning procedures that had been developed in the last century. Nor was it all that difficult.

In short, the only way to bring Takayama into the real world was to allow him to be born here as a baby, a new human carrying all the genetic information of the virtual Ryuji Takayama.

"This was a grand experiment, to say the least. We were all quite excited at the prospect of bringing something from the virtual world into the real one. But we had to act in the utmost secrecy. I'm sure you can see why. If the media had gotten wind of it, they would have had a field day, saying we were playing God, ignoring the sanctity of life, that sort of thing. We'd seen the furor that had surrounded the first successful human cloning at the turn of the century, and we wanted no part of that. I doubt you can imagine what things were like then . . . Anyway, the plan was kept secret even from most of the scientists involved with the Loop."

"Not even my father knew about it?"

Eliot nodded once. "That's right. He didn't know. It was more convenient that way."

"So he was left out in the cold, is that it?"

"It wasn't like that, exactly . . . But, well, I guess you could say that . . . "

Eliot seemed at a loss for words. But Kaoru thought he could guess what came next. "So anyway, you mean . . . ?"

"Yes, it's just what you're thinking. We collected Takayama's genetic data from a point just before he died. A point at which he was already infected with the ring virus. When we brought Takayama into the real world, we brought the ring virus right along with him."

"In other words, the ring virus that took over the Loop world was the basis for the MHC virus that's taking over our world?"

"That's what we think. Careful comparisons of the genetic sequences of both viruses reveal too many similarities to be explained away as mere coincidence. The ring virus seized on our plan to resurrect Takayama in this world as a chance to escape. We think the virus's RNA must have invaded an intestinal bacterium, as luck would have it, and thus made it into the outside. And then it mutated with frightening speed, as viruses are wont to do. The result was the MHC virus."

The sequence was essentially what Kaoru had guessed. What to do about it, though, remained a problem.

He leaned close to Eliot's face and said, "Let's clear something up right now. Have you or have you not figured out a way to conquer the MHC virus?"

"You said it yourself: Takayama holds the key."

"So Takayama is alive. Where is he now?"

Eliot rested his chin on his hand and gazed into Kaoru's eyes for a while. Then he snapped his fingers. "The eyes play tricks on one, don't they? What we think we know can affect our judgment."

Shaking his head, Kaoru leaned back on his couch. Eliot always evaded the important questions. He began to be suspicious of the old man again—what was he up to?

Eliot, meanwhile, was punching buttons on the remote control, ignoring Kaoru's nonplussed gaze. From one wall appeared a large computer monitor.

"You saw it all. You even put on the helmet

display. But you failed to notice it. I suppose that's liable to happen. Your preconceptions got in the way, I suspect."

Kaoru thought Eliot was talking to himself; he was speaking as one might speak to a bird that's landed in one's yard. So Kaoru swallowed his annoyance and waited for Eliot to play his next card.

Eliot had called up on the screen the last moments of Takayama's life. He'd probably prepared this ahead of time—he had the scene up and ready to play with only a few commands.

"Let's go through it like you did, locked into Takayama's perceptions."

And they began to go through the same sequence of events that Kaoru had lived through already amid the ruins of Wayne's Rock. It was a week after Takayama watched the video, and he began to see signs of his impending death. Spurred by his final wish, he put the tape into the VCR and pressed play. Those mysterious, fragmented images danced across the TV screen. Dice rolling around inside a lead case. In the middle of a phone call, Takayama noticed the ever-changing dots on the dice and made a sound like a scream.

Just then it happened. A reflection appeared in a mirror at the edge of the monitor. A man with a telephone receiver held to his ear and a look of utter shock on his face. It was Takayama. While on the phone, Takayama's glance had momentarily settled on his reflection in the mirror.

Eliot paused the playback there and zoomed in on Takayama's reflection.

"You were locked into Takayama's perceptions, but your own preconceptions clouded your vision. Your mind's reaction was that you couldn't be seeing what you were seeing, and so it simply wouldn't let you see it. It happens. Take another look. Don't you recognize that face?"

The face in the mirror was slightly blurred. Eliot sharpened the image.

Kaoru sat face to face with Takayama's reflection. His jaw dropped. His nerves were buzzing, as if they didn't want to recognize the face.

Takayama's features were distorted by his expression of astonishment. On top of that, the imminence of death seemed to have abruptly aged him. But even so, there was no mistaking the outlines of his face, the muscular line of his jaw. Kaoru did indeed know that face. He'd known it all his life.

"This man holds the key to the MHC virus." Eliot poked Kaoru in the chest with a huge finger. "Kaoru, you're Ryuji Takayama."

Kaoru tried to block the words from reaching his brain, but their truth seeped into his body anyway. He felt the world collapse around him. His body, the flesh that he'd always thought of as his, had betrayed him.

"It can't be." Kaoru turned his face toward the ceiling, eyes shut tight.

"We need your help. You must cooperate with us."

Kaoru saw nothing. Eliot's words entered his ears, but he couldn't grasp their meaning. All he knew was that the world was falling apart.

5

Kaoru sat on a boulder hugging his knees. From the flat edge of the ridge he could see a deep valley carved over the course of billions of years. Here and there he saw whitish mottled places on the rust-colored earth. Strangely shaped rocks stood out against the horizon, looking like creations not of nature, but of man. But man had not touched the landscape that stretched before him.

He hardly remembered the scenery from his hike along the ridge—the storm and what came after felt like events in a dream. When he'd huddled alone in the dark, had he been here, in the midst of this vastness? He gazed on it now as if for the first time, following with his eyes every wrinkle and furrow in the land. They reminded him, quite naturally, of the furrows on the surface of a brain. Kaoru's own brain was engraved with many memories, but its history was still comparatively short, only twenty years. Its origins, however, were utterly out of the ordinary. It had been born not of biological reproduction, but digital recomposition.

In the distance he could see a yellowish river flowing in a near loop. A strange sight. A manifestation of the synchronicity between the real world and the virtual?

He turned around, but there was no one there. Only the building housing the elevator that connected the underground laboratories to the surface, and next to that the heliport. A helicopter, painted gun-metal black, rested motionless on the heliport. This was the jet copter that had carried Kaoru's helpless body here after the storm.

Midway between the elevator building and the heliport was a dark hole, the entrance to a huge limestone cave stretching deep into the earth. In the cavern was a vast bowl-shaped depression filled with clear water.

Eliot had been telling the truth. Pointing to the ceiling and the floor, he'd spoken of a great layer of water above them and a great space beneath them. Both turned out to be actual.

They'd dug down into the earth to a depth of three thousand feet, and there they'd found this spherical hollow space, six hundred feet in diameter, floating there like a bubble. The layer of clear water was like a shield, keeping external radiation from getting into the hollow space. The natural landscape had been put to good use in installing the Neutrino Scanning Capture System in its underground shrine.

Kaoru still hadn't seen the apparatus, that machine that would decide his fate, be it the electric chair or . . . what?

He'd spent nearly a week in those labs underground. Now, finally, he was getting his first look at the place from the outside. His wish to go to the surface had finally been granted. Evidently Eliot had been kind enough to admit that he wasn't about to run away or hide.

The weather was calm. Kaoru was soaking up the afternoon rays after a week without sunlight. As long as he was in the sun, he was warm enough in just a T-shirt. He shifted his arms, still folded in front of him, rubbed his upper arms, and tried to pull his thoughts together, but it was no use. He couldn't even decide what there might be for him to decide. What was he to think of his life up to this point? There were no precedents to guide him. He was deeply troubled.

It was easy enough to doubt Eliot. That might even be the simplest solution: just deny everything he said. After all, who would believe he'd been created from genetic information taken from a virtual reality program anyway? That was like denying his very existence. Maybe Eliot was simply making up a story because he wanted to experiment with the NSCS. Kaoru should deny him that: he ought to leave this mountain of his own free will, after cursing Eliot with curses the likes of which the world had never known. And then . . . then what? Kaoru didn't know. Certainly nothing pleasant remained for him. He was going to lose the ones he loved. All he'd have left would be regrets.

He kept going back to the starting point. Monozygotic twins share the same genes and look virtually identical. If Kaoru and Takayama shared the same genes it would certainly explain their faces looking alike. Then there was the curious sensation Kaoru had experienced the first time he'd heard Takayama's voice directly, the same queer feeling he felt when he heard his own voice on a recording. So face and voice matched. But that alone was not sufficient proof. Those could be easily manipulated by computer.

Kaoru had pointed this out to Eliot. As if he'd anticipated Kaoru's doubts, Eliot merely held out a satellite phone.

"It's your father. I think you should talk to him."

Kaoru took the receiver and heard his father's voice from where he lay in his hospital bed. And once he'd heard what his father had to say, Eliot's story began to seem credible at last.

The most convenient way to raise Takayama's clone, it was decided, would be to choose one of the participants in the Loop project and have him raise the clone as his own child.

At the time, Hideyuki and Machiko Futami had been married for four years. They had no children. In fact, a gynecologist had recently confirmed Machiko's infertility.

But still they wanted a child. Eliot and his colleagues got wind of this, and through several intermediaries they approached Hideyuki about the possibility of adoption. Both Hideyuki and Machiko were receptive to the idea of bringing a newborn infant into their home and raising it as their own child.

Events progressed swiftly, and soon Eliot, through a devious route, delivered to Hideyuki and Machiko the newborn Kaoru. They were told nothing about the child's birth or lineage, under the pretense of avoiding future trouble. There was no telling if they would have been willing to accept the child had they known he came from within the Loop.

And so they brought Kaoru up lovingly as their own child, never telling him he was adopted.

As they spoke, linked by the satellite phone, Kaoru could picture Hideyuki lying in bed, weakly grasping the receiver.

"Kaoru?"

It was a joy to hear his father's voice, though it was weaker than he remembered it.

Kaoru and Hideyuki reported to each other on their recent doings. On hearing that his son was well, Hideyuki seemed happy. "I seem to be doing better myself lately," he said, although Kaoru had no way of knowing if it was true or not. Judging from his voice, it had to be a lie. He felt that his father's time was fast approaching.

Then, calmly, off-handedly, Kaoru asked his father about his origins. Hideyuki was sincerely surprised at first that Kaoru had discovered he was adopted, but then he seemed to decide that the boy was bound to find out sooner or later, and proceeded to tell him honestly how things had been twenty years before.

As he listened to his father's explanation, Kaoru had his eyes closed and said something like a prayer in his heart. Who had approached Hideyuki—where had he gotten Kaoru from?

Kaoru's prayer was in vain. His father's explanation matched Eliot's in every detail.

"Weren't you at all hesitant, Dad, to raise a child who wasn't carrying on your genes?" Kaoru asked quietly. Even if his mother was infertile, it wouldn't have been difficult at all to create a child who inherited their genes.

"Whether or not you had our genes wasn't what mattered. Parent-child bonds come from being together, from how they act toward each other. Think about our relationship over the past twenty years. You're my son, Kaoru."

These words etched themselves into Kaoru's cells.

Kaoru said goodbye and broke the connection, feeling that he'd never speak to his father again.

He watched Takayama's life over and over on the computer. As he went through episodes in the man's childhood when he displayed his rare talent for science in general and math and physics in particular, Kaoru couldn't help but feel that they were the same person. Even his gestures when absorbed in a book or deep in thought were identical to Kaoru's.

It was a strange experience to watch Takayama onscreen. Here was an individual with the same genetic makeup as Kaoru himself, growing up in a different environment—a different universe, no less. A man with a different personality from Kaoru, a different consciousness, but exactly the same features. An identical twin.

Kaoru got to his feet and strolled toward the end of the ridge. A downward glance showed him the edge of a sheer cliff, at the bottom of which could be seen a stream in its snakelike course. Its surface was green, either from a trick of the light or from the composition of the dirt dissolved in its water. Even now, the river continued to carve out its canyon, bit by tiny bit.

He realized he'd have to accept the facts. He was in this world because somebody had constructed him based on Ryuji Takayama's genetic information. It fit, and he'd better deal with it. He could deny it all he wanted, but he couldn't escape his fate.

Kaoru was destined to return to the Loop.

The wind had picked up. He took a step back from the edge of the cliff. It wouldn't do to be blown off the cliff and dashed on the floor of the canyon. That would mean the loss of valuable information—the end of two worlds.

Eliot's plan was a devilish one. He had indeed seen twenty years into the future, just as he'd averred.

Why exactly had Eliot felt the compulsion, twenty years ago, to grant Takayama's wish and bring his clone into the real world? Perhaps he'd seen it as an experiment in cloning, but more than that, it had to be because Eliot already had a clear vision of the NSCS. He'd already gotten the idea for a complete digitalization of a human being's molecular structure using the as-yet-unconstructed apparatus. Indeed, he'd already settled on a trial subject.

Nobody could be expected to volunteer for neutrino scanning, but without a volunteer, the machine couldn't be tested. The days when test subjects could be drafted against their will were long gone. Without a young, healthy, willing volunteer, this elaborate apparatus would simply go to waste.

Eliot put it best himself. "If we plucked somebody out of the Loop and kept him around long enough, then we'd have a legitimate reason for using the NSCS on him: to send him back. If he wanted to go home, we'd be in a position to send him there. Cloning is the only way to bring someone from the Loop into the real world, but things are different when it comes to sending someone from the real world into the Loop. Using the NSCS, we can reconstitute you inside the Loop as you are this very minute—your consciousness, your thoughts, your memories."

If he wanted to go home.

That was the condition, but that was also the rub. Why would he want that? He'd never see his father, his mother, or Reiko again. And his child . . . Kaoru had already planted his chromosomes inside Reiko's womb—he had a child on the way, via old-fashioned biological reproduction, and if he went into the Loop he'd never see the child's face.

If that was the only factor, he'd never play along with Eliot's scientific game. Not a chance. His genes may have come from the virtual world, but at the moment he was very much alive in this one. Home? This was his home now. No matter what he'd been before, since his birth here he'd lived his own life, chosen his own course. He liked it here.

But luck was conspiring against him. Kaoru was in a no-win situation.

During the process of reconstituting Takayama, the ring virus had escaped, eventually mutating into the Metastatic Human Cancer Virus. That was a fact. The ring virus had been embedded in Takayama's genes, and sometime during the operation of the genome synthesizer, something had gone wrong: a fragment had become embedded in an intestinal bacterium. Which was not to say that the ring virus had been cleanly extracted from Takayama's genes, returning his DNA to its pristine, uninfected state. No, it was likely that the ring virus was still there, a part of him.

As soon as Eliot told him this, Kaoru started to wonder. *If this virus is embedded in my genes, why haven't I come down with MHC myself?*

Not only had he never come down with the cancer, but every test he'd ever undergone for the virus came out negative.

Eliot had an explanation for that. "Somewhere in the RNA-DNA transcription process, a mutation must have occurred, inserting a stop code. It didn't show up in tests. You see, the MHC virus causes a mutation in gene P53 of the infected cell. The virus itself has a telomerase sequence. It inserts the sequence TTAGGG into the DNA of the infected cell. This makes the cell immortal, but cancerous.

"As soon as we realized that the MHC virus came from Takayama, we obtained a sample of your cells and started analyzing them. I hope you don't mind. You may remember an unexplained blood test a while back . . . In any case. We were surprised to find that the telomere sequence in your cells was not TTAGGG. It seems that in your case, although the MHC virus produces a telomerase and attaches the TTAGGG sequence to DNA ends, it's unstable and soon breaks down. Your cells' lifespan doesn't increase, but your cells don't turn cancerous. You may be a new type of human being, one with true immunity to the MHC virus."

Eliot's explanation made a certain amount of sense to Kaoru. His immunity probably came from a slight discrepancy between Loop genes and real-world ones. All things considered, maybe that was only to be expected.

As Eliot's words flashed through his brain, Kaoru thought he could see the course of his past life stretched out in the canyon below him, trailing a tail of light. The course that light would travel in the future seemed to have been foreordained.

Kaoru wondered when the suggestion that he come here had first been implanted in his mind. He was ten when the gravitational anomaly map had made its way onto his computer screen, despite the fact that the information it contained was nowhere in the database he'd been using. Of course Eliot had sent it. No doubt he'd seen to it somehow that Kaoru come across the information on longevity zones, too. Eliot needed to keep Kaoru perpetually intrigued by this spot in the desert, but he couldn't be open about it. He had to continually feed Kaoru hints to keep his curiosity aroused. Eliot had allowed Kaoru to think that everything was his own discovery, one coincidence on top of another, while at the same time he'd carefully emphasized the mysterious possibility of salvation that this point in the desert seemed to offer them all.

Kaoru was sure that Eliot had been behind his mother's stumbling across the right Indian legends, and the article about the man who'd miraculously recovered from cancer. Such stories had been on the increase over the last six months or so—no doubt Eliot had sent out a lot more clues than the few that Kaoru and his mother had picked up on. But even those had been enough: Kaoru was here now.

He'd come here on his own, of his own free will, out of a sense of mission. That had been Eliot's ultimate requirement. The procedure wouldn't work if he'd captured Kaoru and brought him here by force. The NSCS would reproduce his exact mental state at the moment of scanning. If he'd been forced here, his mind would have been filled with fear and hostility, and those emotions would have gone with him. He'd need to go willingly, with a goal clearly in mind and a calm acceptance of his fate.

"It's not my style to use force," Eliot had said, but Kaoru knew what that really meant. The project would fail if the participant was unwilling.

Willingness and a sense of mission: Kaoru had showed up with exactly what Eliot required of him. And the carrot Eliot held out to him was quite enough to satisfy that sense of mission.

"The key to conquering the MHC virus is within you. Unless we can analyze your genome in three dimensions, your mitochondria, your metabolic cycle, your secretion factors, we're not going to be able to solve this. Simply analyzing your DNA sequence isn't enough. We need to digitize your entire body. We think that a special gene insertion method might prove to be a powerful treatment, but in order to understand the full effects of insertion, we need to run detailed simulations, and we need data on you for that. Do you understand what this means? The things we learn from you will have imme-diate application. Your father, your mother, your lover will be the first ones to benefit. It's only proper that you be rewarded for laying your life on the line."

Eliot's expression was earnest as he offered this promise.

The longevity zone Kaoru had imagined he'd find out here in the desert had proved to be a mirage. Its only vestige was this decrepit old scientist, Kaoru reflected bitterly. But what Kaoru had hoped to find in his longevity zone—a cure for MHC, something to save the lives of his loved ones, something to prevent the entire spectrum of life on earth from falling victim to this cancer—that was about to be granted him, in a most unexpected way. As long as he was willing to trade his body for it . . .

His body supposedly contained something that completely blocked the effects of the virus, and the best way to instantaneously and exactly lay bare that mechanism was to neutrino scan him. The things they learned would have immediate application. The terror of the cancer virus would disappear: life on earth would learn to coexist with the virus.

Kaoru understood the logic behind it. There was no time to pursue this knowledge by traditional methods. Long before they arrived at a cure, time would have run out—at least for his father. His mother would probably lose her mind, while Reiko might kill herself and the baby inside her.

He may have come from the virtual world, but he felt that this life had value, and was worth living. He'd been alive these twenty years—the hunger he'd satisfied with Reiko was proof of that. If it hadn't been for her, he might not have ever felt so alive.

I exist, right here, right now.

Beaming with confidence, he stood at the end of the ridge like one of those peculiar rocks visible on the horizon. He gathered all his courage and expressed it in a shout, as loud a *yawp* as he could make.

The sound of his voice echoed in the canyon, flew across the land toward the horizon, disappearing in the distance. He imagined that was how he himself would disappear, leaving only echoes behind.

His feelings toward Eliot were complicated, needless to say. They went beyond straightforward hatred. After all, it was thanks to Eliot that he had a physical body. All the pleasure and pain he'd experienced these last twenty years he owed to Eliot's ingenuity. If someone had asked Kaoru whether he'd wanted this life, he would have answered with a resounding yes. But then, if he'd never received this bodily existence, the cancer virus would never have been loosed upon the world.

Kaoru knew he bore no responsibility for that. But as a fact it was undeniable, and it weighed on his mind.

However, this was no time to be caught up

in resentment, hatred, or the pricks of conscience. It was time for him to steel himself and pay the price. It was time to look to the future. Always to the future.

Kaoru turned around and strode purposefully away from the cliff.

6

It took another ten days to make everything ready. Kaoru spent the time going through the record of Takayama's life in the Loop, experiencing it until he knew it all, up to the moment of his death. He made it all his own, from the man's relationships with parents and friends to his scholarly learning, his habits of thought, the way he spoke.

By the time Kaoru got so that he could understand the language they spoke in the Loop without a mechanical translator, he'd essentially finished committing the man's life to memory. Perhaps because they shared the same genes, Kaoru found it felt rather natural to become the man in this way. In fact, the more he found out the less he considered Takayama a separate person. At certain moments Takayama's life seemed to overlap with his own.

On the morning of the big day, Eliot accompanied Kaoru down in the elevator. As they descended three thousand feet below the surface, all of Kaoru's misgivings melted away. He was about to cross over to that distant shore, but strangely he felt no fear. The special atmosphere of the place actually lent his mood a touch of solemnity, of grandeur.

The elevator doors opened. He could see a section of the NSCS control center. Surrounded by thick security walls, the computers' lights were flashing. But they weren't inside the NSCS yet. Kaoru would go in there alone.

Eliot kept pace with Kaoru. He refused to use a motorized wheelchair, telling Kaoru that he preferred to propel one himself, to keep his muscles in shape. The old-fashioned wheelchair looked out of place here, surrounded by the latest technology.

Panting faintly, Eliot said, "I need to ask you something before we begin, so that we have no misunderstandings. You don't think I let loose the MHC virus on purpose, do you?"

The thought had crossed Kaoru's mind, but all his doubts on that score had been settled.

"Why would you do that?"

Kaoru went behind Eliot's wheelchair and tried to push for him, but the older man waved him away as he would a fly. "Don't interfere," he said, but kindly, renewing his grip on the wheels. "Why would I do it, you ask? Isn't that obvious? To ensure funding for the Loop."

True enough, if Eliot could make the case that restarting the Loop was a necessary step toward defeating the MHC virus, then he'd get a massive amount of funding. A cure for the virus was the top priority worldwide—if one were developed, it would bring huge profits all around. The return on investment would be phenomenal, to say nothing of what it would contribute to society. And with that funding, Eliot would be able to achieve his dream of reactivating the Loop, a dream that had been on ice for twenty years.

"You wouldn't do something like that."

"And why wouldn't I?"

"Because there'd be no way you could foresee how the virus would behave. That, and I have a hard time believing your hatred of the virus is feigned."

Eliot swallowed and made a queer sound in the back of his throat. He, too, had lost several intimates to the disease: it was obvious what fueled his animosity toward it.

"I'm glad you understand. The virus's getting loose was an accident, pure and simple. Had I known the virus was this wily, this nefarious, I would have been much, much more cautious . . ." His words of frustration carried the weight of truth.

"I know. If I didn't believe that, I wouldn't be down here."

Eliot stopped his wheelchair and gazed vacantly up at Kaoru. His wide eyes were wet with tears.

"So you don't . . . hold a grudge?"

"For what?"

"For taking it upon myself to bring you to this world, and then saying, 'Time's up, back you go.'"

"But I wouldn't be here, as a human being, if it weren't for you. The last twenty years haven't been bad at all. In fact, you've given me a lot of great memories. I don't have any grudge against you."

Kaoru was trying to view things philosophically. He felt that if he failed to affirm the present world completely, then all that would be left to him would be fear of the world to come. Unhappiness had dogged him. He'd seen his father, his mother, and his lover infected with the MHC virus; he'd witnessed Ryoji's suicide. But he could still state unequivocally that this life had been a good one. It was the only thing that allowed him to remain composed as he walked down that hallway.

"Stop and talk with me for a moment." As ever, spittle hung at the corner of Eliot's mouth.

"Alright."

So the two of them stopped to shoot the breeze there in the middle of the long hallway leading to the neutrino scanner. Kaoru leaned back against the wall, and Eliot propped his head against the back of his wheelchair. They each laughed at the other's casualness.

"I'm sure I've already told you this, but we wouldn't have arranged for your birth here had there not already been plans for the NSCS. Everything's organically interconnected. If just one element had been missing, things would have turned out entirely different."

"So it's a mere accumulation of coincidence?"

"Certainly it's coincidence that's led us to restart the Loop—to be forced to restart it. But the Loop and the real world correspond to each other on some level."

Kaoru had begun to notice that himself. It was almost as if the virtual world, cancer-ridden and frozen in time, was reaching out to move the real world, to use it.

Eliot changed to a new metaphor as he continued his explanation. "There comes a point when a child—even one not particularly precocious in science—notices that the structure of the atom resembles the structure of the solar system. The child sees the atom and its component particles as constituting their own universe, and wonders if life exists on those miniature 'planets' just as it does on ours. That's the circle of life. That's why I named it the Loop."

"I think I said something like that to my father when I was in elementary school." And to Kaoru it seemed that it wasn't just the microscopic realm that might work like that. Maybe the solar system was but an atom, and the Milky Way an aggregation of atoms, a molecule. The surrounding universe was a cell, and all of existence a huge organism. A being that held within it a smaller being, which held within it a smaller being—like a series of nested boxes. Certain ancient religions took such a view, just as they saw life cycling through a series of existences, past, present, and future.

"What do you think happens if the circle is broken? The microscopic and the macroscopic are connected, interlocking—if part of the cycle is arrested, it's going to affect the rest of it."

"If the circle gets broken . . . well, it just has to be reconnected."

"That's right. But not simply by going back to the beginning and doing it over. We have to overcome the calamity that has befallen the Loop, and then reconnect it."

"So what happens to the Loop's historical trajectory? Its cancer?"

"The same thing that happens to any species that runs into an evolutionary dead-end: it goes extinct. Records will remain in the Loop's memory banks, but the events will be surgically removed from the real world's history, just like we'd cut out cancer cells. The history of the Loop will be shunted onto a side road. It will start again from a new page."

It reminded Kaoru of a river carving out a landscape. Water follows the shape of the land as it flows ever downward, but sometimes it finds itself trapped, and then it swells into a pool. Even then, the water is always searching for an escape, probing weak places in the ground until it succeeds in making itself a new path. It's easy to tell where a river ran into dead ends on its way to the sea: the tale is told by a river's oddly acute angles, its occasional islands.

The Loop was like a river in that respect. Right now it was stalled, its way blocked. But left as it was to stagnate, it was bound to find a way to overspill its containment and exert a negative influence on the real world. The real world corresponded to it, after all. While it was necessary to find real-world ways of dealing with the cancer virus, it was just as necessary to change the trajectory of the Loop, its history of cancer. Until that was done, there would be no fundamental solution.

It was Kaoru's job to overcome the blockage in the Loop, to make a new way for it to flow.

Eliot spoke again. "Sometimes the world needs divine intervention. So God is born of a virgin. And reborn. All the arrangements have been made."

Kaoru realized what he was being told: he was to become a god. It didn't feel real to him. He felt too vividly the sense of being pushed along this path.

He started down the hall again, and as he walked, he thought. *That Indian's life I was shown at Wayne's Rock: what was the meaning of that?*

Eliot had prepared that experience for him, of course. Kaoru had yet to ask why. Kaoru's own interpretation was that it had been a dress rehearsal for death. But another possible meaning had just occurred to him.

The Indian had seen his wife and child die before his very eyes. The cruelty, the loss, and his own inability to do anything about it had been much harder to bear than thoughts of his own death. Right up until the veil of darkness closed around him, his thoughts had been ones of pity, rage, fear at having been unable to save them. Those negative images had swirled around in the blackness of Kaoru's helmet display, and after taking it off he was determined not to ever have to feel that way again, in the virtual world or the real one. The Indian's story was not one of a man who had sacrificed his life for those of his wife and daughter. It was incomparably worse than that. It was the story of a man who'd been forced to look on helplessly while they perished.

Why was it necessary for me to see that—to experience it?

In view of subsequent events, the experience's effect on him seemed to accord with Eliot's plan. Kaoru's desire to never go through that again motivated his decision to sacrifice himself to save his loved ones. But now what planted itself in Kaoru was the idea that he'd been manipulated, trapped, into doing just what Eliot wanted him to.

He strode down the corridor with profoundly mixed emotions. Eliot chased him in his wheelchair.

"Don't you wish to make a phone call?"

Kaoru stopped. "A phone call?"

"Yes. Is there no one you wish to speak to?"

He'd already spoken to his father, not long before. He would have liked to hear his mother's voice, but he didn't know what he'd say to her. How was he supposed to explain what he was about to do? She'd lose it for sure.

Reiko. There was nobody else he could talk to.

Eliot showed Kaoru into a small room off the hallway and handed him a telephone receiver.

Kaoru dialed, praying she'd be in. Eliot gestured wordlessly to a monitor, as if to ask, *Would you like video?* Kaoru refused the offer. There was no need to make it a video-phone call. He had the feeling that hearing her voice alone, with no extraneous information, would better allow him to hold on to the memory.

A connection. "Hello?"

First contact with Reiko's soft voice had the unexpected effect of reducing Kaoru to tears.

Waves of emotion buffeted him. Memories overcame him, aural and visual. It was an explosion,
triggered by her voice. He couldn't control himself.

"Hello? Hello?"

Kaoru realized he never should have called
her.

7

The hallway ended at a black door. This was where Kaoru said goodbye to Eliot.

Eliot held out a gargantuan hand for Kaoru to shake. Kaoru returned his grasp, although not very strongly. The last words he'd exchanged with Reiko still occupied his brain—his heart had been shattered into a thousand pieces—his gaze was elsewhere.

"I seem to have lived too long."

Kaoru snapped back to reality. He looked down at Eliot and saw a man who had, indeed, grown too old for his own good. A man who had a precise grasp of how much longer he had to live.

I'll be following you eventually, he seemed to want to say, but in fact they were headed to different places altogether. Eliot would never go where Kaoru was about to.

"Don't forget your promise," Kaoru said. He'd

extracted another pledge from Eliot, in addition to his promise to use the data from Kaoru's body to help his parents and Reiko first of all.

"I won't. Trust me."

Kaoru listened carefully for Eliot's response, then turned and opened the door. Only he could go beyond that point. He slipped in, and the door shut behind him automatically.

An odd smell. Ions, perhaps. From this point, he'd receive instructions via loudspeaker. The metallic voice coming through the speakers was the only sound that came in from the outside. Kaoru was utterly cut off from the external world.

Following instructions, Kaoru took off the gown he was wearing, and then his sandals and his underwear. He went into the next room naked. According to what Eliot had told him, he was to pass through several clean rooms.

He had a pretty clear idea what was going to happen. He was going to be suspended in the center of the huge sphere that was the neutrino scanning capture system, where he would be bombarded with neutrinos from all directions. But there was a procedure he had to follow first.

In the next room he saw a stretcher. A voice instructed him to lie down on it. He lay down face up, and the stretcher began silently moving down a narrow, dark hallway. It took Kaoru through an air shower, and then a shower of purified water. Together these cleansed the surface of his body of all contaminants.

As he passed each station on the line, he could see a digital meter with a reading flashing in red, numbers approaching closer to one hundred with each stage. *99.99 . . . 99.999 . . . 99.9999 . . .* The gauges showed the degree to which the rooms, and thus their occupant, were free of impurities.

The stretcher conveyed Kaoru into a clear oblong container. Purified water, slightly warmer than body temperature, began to engulf him. The container was shaped not so much like a bathtub as like a slightly oversized coffin.

Kaoru was fixed firmly in place, floating in water. Next he was transported into the neutrino scanning capture system.

The water had a calming effect on him. Gradually he became unable to tell where his body left off and the water began, as his ego began to dissolve into tiny bubbles and joined the water.

Reiko's last words came back to him again, in what might have been his ego's last attempt at resistance.

I felt the baby move this morning.

She'd sounded so happy to be able to report on the baby's growth. The thought of the fetus in the embrace of her amniotic fluid allowed Kaoru to see his own situation as a bystander might. Come to think of it, he was in the same state as that baby, right down to its will to be born.

This place was a universe unto itself, ruled by utter darkness. Gravity had disappeared: his body felt weightless. He knew he was inside a sphere six hundred feet in diameter. His eyes should have been able to see its inner surface. But in the darkness the space surrounding him felt infinite.

As a child, he'd often gone out onto the balcony of his family's high-rise apartment to stare up into the night sky. Seeing the stars and the moon always strengthened his desire to fathom the universe.

What a different situation he was in now. Back then he'd stood on a height overlooking the ocean; now he was in a three-thousand-feet deep hole in the desert. Back then the air had been filled with the scent of the sea; this space was filled with the artificial smell of ions.

He thought he saw a blue light flash for an instant in the emptiness above him. Had the neutrino bombardment begun? The flash reminded him of a star twinkling.

Any moment now he would be bombarded with neutrinos from points on every part of the inner surface of the sphere. Each would penetrate his body and reach the point on the sphere wall opposite its point of origin. Molecular information about him would accumulate gradually, until Eliot would begin to get a three-dimensional digital image of his body's minutest structures. The more neutrino radiation he received, the sharper that image would become. He'd been told that the first rounds would simply pass through his body—he wouldn't feel much if anything. But that level of irradiation wouldn't provide enough information for their purposes. They would need to expose him to so much neutrino penetration as to actually break down his cells. Kaoru tried not to think about what would happen to him then.

There were more blue lights now, and they flashed more quickly, blinking energetically in the darkness. They was beautiful. They tore through space like shooting stars, glittering, leaving white trails behind.

Kaoru stared peacefully into the night sky. He felt like a child again . . .

He wondered if this was what astronauts felt like. They said that seeing the Earth from space brought one closer to the territory of the divine. If so, then it was a little different from Kaoru's situation after all. What he was aiming at was godhood itself.

Something was pressing rhythmically on his eardrums—strange, as he should be cut off from all sound in here. Someone or something was speaking loudly into his ear. Whatever it was, it couldn't be human. Maybe a digital signal from the virtual world?

Suddenly, an image was inserted into his mind. It was as if a Chagall painting had been forcefully placed inside his head. He wasn't seeing it with his eyes—it was like a cord from a video deck had been connected directly to his brain. Brightly colored, impressionistic images flashed through his mind, disappearing as abruptly as they had appeared.

The bluish-white lights connected into tangled threadwork now, an infinite number of bands intersecting in the middle distance. The lines of light now filled the darkness. He could hear the sounds of their collisions, sounds he shouldn't have been able to hear . . . Digital signals whirled around him, caressing his earlobes.

His body was cast into the gravity-less universe. He felt as if he were floating up out of the tank of water and into the vortex of light. His mind wandered from his body, becoming clearer all the time.

Kaoru was entering the final stage now. Every second brought him closer to the end of this journey which had begun as a trip toward a point in the desert and had become a pilgrimage to death and rebirth.

The images were slipped into his brain, images composed of rough particles. Mosaic-like images, with indistinct edges. Try as he might he could no longer summon smooth, natural images as before. There wasn't enough information to analyze properly.

The neutrino bombardment intensified. His molecular structure began to take digital shape. As its resolution increased, the mosaic filter was removed from the images in his brain. Now they were reproduced before his mind's eye as perfectly natural images.

Vision was back to normal now. He thought he glimpsed, at the far end of a corridor of light, a Hades indistinguishable from the here-and-now.

His journey ended. His body disappeared from the real world and was reborn into the Loop.

The procedure had concluded. The tank in which Kaoru had been floating now contained no human form. Instead it held the liquefied remains of his destroyed cells. As his ego had melted into the water, so too had his body broken down into its smallest components, dissolving into the purified water. The water was no longer pure. Thanks to the bluish-white light it didn't look bloody, but it was a noticeably thicker liquid than before.

His body was defunct. But Kaoru's consciousness still existed. Neutrinos had captured the state of his brain on the brink of death, the positions of his synapses and neurons, chemical reactions in mid-reaction, and had recreated them all digitally.

He was not to be reconstructed directly from this final blueprint. Rather, he would be reborn according to the information captured by the NSCS. The growth process would be carefully controlled, and after approximately a week of Loop time, the infant would grow to the physical state the subject had been in when he'd entered the NSCS. He should regain his original consciousness, as well.

Kaoru had a pretty good idea where he was now. Inside a womb. A real one, not a metaphorical one. He was inside a virgin womb, bathed in amniotic fluid.

He could hear his mother's heartbeat as if over a great distance. The sound echoed in the dark, sealed sphere, getting louder and louder.

Kaoru did not know whose womb he was in, but he knew he was about to be born.

He stretched out his body, filled with a desire to get out into the world.

The light was too bright: it hurt his eyes. But this wasn't the bluish flickering anymore. The light was steady and white, artificial. It seemed to come from overhead fluorescent light fixtures, the kind you find in hospitals.

In the light, he could see his umbilical cord, the grotesque thread that alone connected him to the mother. He reached out a hand and tried to sever it himself, and let forth a loud cry. A cry just like any normal baby's.

"Wah! Wah!"

It was the beginning of a new journey.

PART FIVE

Advent

1

The day was so clear it was hard to believe it was the rainy season. Walking along on the embankment that separated the beach from the road, he set his sights on the horizon: the other side of the bay was obscured in haze. A sea wall extended out from the beach; several anglers stood on it, lazily casting their lines into the sea. It was still early in the summer, so there were no bathers yet, but a couple of families had spread sheets on the sand and were picnicking.

Gazing at this peaceful seaside scene he could forget that this was only a virtual reality. Six months had elapsed since his rebirth into the Loop. He'd adapted to this world completely, body and mind.

The previous October, Ryuji Takayama had died, once. His death had been confirmed, and an autopsy had been performed by a friend of his from medical school, Mitsuo Ando. Notwithstanding that, in

January of this year Takayama had awoken from his three-month sleep, due to the combined efforts of Ando, his pathologist colleague Miyashita, and others. He had crawled out of the womb of a maiden named Sadako Yamamura, had torn the umbilical cord with his own hands, and in just a week's time he'd grown into the body Kaoru had possessed when he'd entered the neutrino scanner. Ando and Miyashita, unaware that the Loop had been created by a higher power, could not be expected to understand the true mechanism behind Takayama's resurrection. The three months Takayama had been dead corresponded to the twenty years of Kaoru's lifetime. And now the consciousness that had once been Kaoru had taken on Takayama's flesh in order to live in the Loop.

His living conditions were rather inconvenient—a dead man couldn't very well walk around in public—but he was in a perfect environment for research. Takayama had spent most of half a year in a laboratory lent him by Miyashita, researching the virus. This meant unraveling one by one the clues hidden within his own cells. It had taken half a year to finish the greater part of the research and to perfect a vaccine for the ring virus.

This was his first time out in a long while. He could feel the gentle wind cleansing his heart as it played over his skin. In his days as Kaoru he'd enjoyed the nighttime breeze on the balcony of their apartment; evidently his tastes hadn't changed.

He could see the small form of a boy beyond the picnickers, standing where the waves petered out. The boy would creep hesitantly up to the water, and then dash back so as not to get his feet wet. Then he crouched and started digging a hole and making a sandpile. His body was bare from the waist up, and below the waist he wore a swimsuit, making his aversion to the water all the more conspicuous. His movements were quite careful. The boy wore a tight bikini-type swimsuit, and no swim cap.

The watcher thought about the first time he'd seen Reiko, at the pool. He remembered the queer impression her son Ryoji had made with his plaid shorts, not meant for swimming, and his swim cap from which not one strand of hair poked out. The touch of Reiko's skin, the last words they'd exchanged—these images and sounds remained clear in his memory. What was she doing now?

He was walking along the narrow embankment with a plastic bag full of canned drinks, carefully balancing so as not to fall onto the sand or the road. Unlike the ridge he'd walked in the desert, the embankment was only a couple of feet wide. As he walked he felt as though he were traversing the thin, fragile boundary between this world and the next.

The boy ran away from the waves toward the embankment—he was heading toward a man seated on the embankment about a hundred yards ahead. The seated man was the boy's father, the man he himself had come to talk to.

The man had eyes only for his son, and so was utterly unprepared for the visitor. Thinking it best not to startle him, Ryuji Takayama called out his name.

"Hey, Ando!"

Hearing his name called, the man looked up and all around. Then he caught sight of Takayama walking toward him, and his expression became one of dumb amazement.

"Hey, long time no see."

Takayama hadn't had any contact with Ando these six months. After assisting in Takayama's rebirth, Ando had left the university. He'd disappeared.

Takayama sat down next to Ando and leaned closer so that their shoulders touched. But Ando quite openly avoided meeting his eyes, instead returning his gaze to his son, still running across the beach toward him.

Nonplussed, Takayama took a beverage out of the bag he carried and quickly drank it down. Then he took another can out and offered it to Ando. "Thirsty?"

Ando accepted the can silently and popped the pull ring, still not looking at Takayama.

"How did you know I was here?" Ando asked calmly.

Takayama simply said, "Miyashita told me." Knowing that today was the anniversary of Ando's son's death, Miyashita had guessed that this was where he'd be, and he'd told Takayama.

A curious thing it was, though, that anniversary. Two years ago today, at this very spot, Ando's son had drowned, and yet now here the boy was. Forgetting his own situation for a moment, Takayama could not help but smile.

"What do you want?" Ando asked, in a voice thick with tension. He didn't seem very happy to see Takayama. Takayama had made a considerable effort to get here—he'd had to sneak out of the lab, then take a train and a bus. He felt he deserved a bit warmer a welcome. There seemed to be a misunderstanding of some kind.

Eliot had told him that everything was arranged for his rebirth. In any world, the idea of a dead man coming back to life would be pretty hard to accept. The stage would have to be set.

And set it Eliot had. He'd singled out Ando as someone who could be of use and sent him hints in code, all so he could arrange in as plausible a way as possible for Takayama's rebirth. Bringing Ando's dead son back to life was bait to get him to assist in bringing Takayama back.

In the case of Ando's son, an inhabitant of the Loop, there was no need to go through a neutrino scan. It was an intra-Loop transfer, a simple matter of reconstituting the boy's genetic information.

The Loop had been reset, six months ago, to the point where its cancerization had been triggered, and then restarted. Takayama's advent had been timed with the utmost care so as to enable him to conquer the calamity whose seeds had been sown. If he were to do nothing, the Loop would proceed along the same path, turning cancerous. He needed to construct for it a new history, make a new channel for its dammed-up waters. If he succeeded, the world he'd lived in before, too, would retain its genetic diversity.

"Listen, I'm grateful to you, I really am. You worked out just as I expected."

Takayama was indeed grateful to Ando. Just before coming to the Loop, he'd committed Takayama's life to memory. He knew of his school days with Ando, and he knew of Ando's brilliance. Without the help of such a friend, he doubted he ever would have been able to make his entrance in such a reasonable way as via virgin birth.

But Ando, it seemed, simply felt used. Or worse—maybe he suspected Takayama of being in league with Sadako Yamamura, of coming back in order to destroy the world.

If that was what Ando thought, then Takayama had no way to defend himself. The one thing he couldn't do was reveal his true identity. Sometimes it depressed Takayama to think of the lonely life that awaited him. The only thing that kept him going was the desire that he kept hidden in his breast.

Down by the water's edge again, the boy stood up and waved at Ando. Ando returned his signal, and the boy came closer, kicking sand as he came.

"Daddy, I'm thirsty!" Ando offered his son the beverage that Takayama had given him. The boy took it and drank it down.

Takayama watched the boy's pale throat. He could almost see the cool liquid coursing down the little throat. Living, moving flesh and blood, brought back to life by only slightly different methods. A product of the same womb—a brother, almost.

"Want another one?" Takayama said, fishing around in his bag.

"Nope," the boy said to Takayama, then turned to his father, raising the half-finished can as high as his head. "Can I have the rest?"

"Sure, drink up." The boy went back to the water's edge, swilling the can. Takayama figured the boy wanted to play with the can after it was empty, maybe fill it with sand. Ando yelled after him. "Takanori!"

The boy stopped and turned around. "What, Daddy?"

"Don't go in the water yet, okay?"

The boy grinned in acknowledgement, and turned his back to him again.

The child was still afraid of the sea—he remembered drowning. He'd have to overcome that fear before he could get on with his long life.

"Cute kid," Takayama said. He was thinking of his own child, still growing, no doubt, inside of Reiko.

Ando ignored his comment, instead saying, "Tell me something. What's going to happen to the world now?" He glared at Takayama as if to say, *You ought to know.*

And he did know. Or at least, he had a better idea of it than Ando did. But he could never tell him.

"What do *you* think's going to happen to it?"

Ando answered by sketching out a future that closely resembled the final cancerization of the Loop. The ring virus would spread throughout the world. The videotape would transform itself into various forms of media, and would itself spread worldwide. Women who came into contact with it while ovulating would give birth to children with the same genetic makeup as Sadako Yamamura; everyone else would be eliminated. The same would happen with men: a very few on whom the new media depended would survive, while the rest would be destroyed. You didn't have to be a doctor to predict the results of this. All life would be assimilated to a single genetic pattern: Sadako.

"And you're okay with all that?"

Ando's gaze was brimming with animosity. He definitely misunderstood Takayama.

Without changing his expression, Takayama reached into his pocket and pulled out an ampoule. He handed it to Ando. "I want you to have this."

"What's this?"

"A vaccine."

"A vaccine?" Ando accepted the tiny glass vial and examined it carefully.

After six months of research, Takayama had succeeded in developing a vaccine for the ring virus, based on hints found within his own cells. He'd only just perfected it. Animal trials showed it to be effective.

"Take that and it'll take care of the virus. Your worrying days are over."

"Did you come all the way here just to give me this?"

"What, can't a guy go to the beach once in a while?" Takayama gave an embarrassed laugh. Ando's expression seemed to soften a little.

As he put the vial in his breast pocket, Ando repeated his earlier question, but more calmly this time. "Can't you tell me what's going to happen?"

"I don't know." Takayama's reply was blunt.

"Don't give me that. Together you and Sadako are going to redesign the world and everything that lives in it—aren't you?"

At that, Takayama had to laugh. There was no point in staying here any longer. He got to his feet, muttering, "Well, I guess I'll be off now."

"Are you leaving?" Ando looked up at him from where he sat on the embankment.

"It's about time I took off. What are you going to do now?"

"What can I do? I'll find a deserted island someplace out of the media's reach, and raise my son there."

"That sounds like you. Me, though, I've got to see things through to the end. Once it's gone as far as it can go, who knows, maybe a will beyond human wisdom will exercise its power on us. Wouldn't want to miss that." Takayama was speaking vaguely on purpose, trying to say something without saying it. *Relax. The world's not going to turn out like you think it will. It already did end like that, once, but this time it won't. I came back to see that it doesn't.*

He started walking away along the embankment.

"Bye, Ryuji. Say hi to Miyashita for me."

Takayama stopped at the sound of Ando's voice.

"Before I go, I want you to remember something. No matter what disaster strikes, we've got to meet it head on and overcome it. Only by accumulating that kind of experience can we change the world, you see. So . . . yeah, it'll be alright."

Takayama waved and walked away. He was sure Ando hadn't understood. But that was okay. Someday he would.

He glanced behind him from time to time as he heard Ando's voice and his son's.

"Daddy, you promised, right?"

"Yes, I did." Ando again told the boy what would happen once he overcame his fear of the water. "I'll take you to meet Mommy."

Ando and his wife had separated over the boy's death.

"Mommy's going to be so surprised."

Listening to these scraps of conversation, Takayama imagined the Ando family's happy reunion.

He was jealous. That was something he'd never have.

2

He reviewed the longitude in his head, although he had no trouble remembering it exactly. The time, too. There was no way he could forget the appointment he'd made with Eliot.

From the seaside town where he'd met Ando, Takayama headed due south, arriving at the appointed place slightly ahead of schedule. It was on a hillside with a nice view across the water to a cape. The gentle pine-covered slope continued right down to the water's edge.

Takayama sat down on the grass and waited.

June 27, 1991, 2:00 pm exactly, Loop time. That was what Eliot had told him. There was still a half hour to go.

Six months had passed for Takayama since the Loop had been restarted, but time moved somewhat slower in Eliot's world. The Loop would be moving even faster if they'd been able to mobilize the same number of supercomputers as before, but they hadn't. As a result, the Loop would only move five or six years for every year the computers ran. Six months to Takayama would correspond to about a month where Eliot was.

He'd made contact with his father and with Reiko just before going into the scanner. A month had elapsed for them since then. He'd made his crossing to this world without being able to explain things to them. They probably thought Kaoru was lost somewhere in the desert, when in fact, he'd disappeared completely.

At the very least, there were things he still wanted to tell them. And how else could he fully explain his actions but with his own mouth, his own body?

It was easy to call Takayama up on the computer monitors over there, a simple matter of specifying time and place. So he'd made Eliot promise to show his parents and Reiko that he was safe and sound.

Takayama looked at his watch. Almost time.

Then, as if to proclaim the arrival of the appointed moment, the clouds parted in front of him and sunlight shone on the surface of the ocean. It was as if a window had opened in the sky, an interface. Takayama wouldn't be able to see anybody through it—no faces, no expressions—but they would be able to see him.

Two o'clock on the button. He should be in

view for them now. Takayama raised his head slightly and smiled at the people who would be watching him.

He called them each by name, speaking to them, telling him about what he was up to.

There were so many things he wanted to ask them, but he knew he couldn't. Had they been able to use the digital information they'd gained from his body to combat the MHC virus? He wanted to think they had: he wanted to think that his father's life was saved. His child with Reiko would be farther along now than when he'd spoken to Reiko on the phone. Had Reiko found the hope to go on living in her world? Takayama hoped that seeing him like this, she'd make up her mind once and for all to live.

He had every intention of dealing with the ring virus and the mutated-video media that carried it in this world. If coming in contact with those media programmed one to die in a week's time, it should be simple enough to devise a de-programming system. He had absolute confidence. He'd come all the way to this world from the other one determined to overcome. When it came down to it, he was godlike. He knew how this world worked. What cared he for viruses or mutant media?

As he spoke these thoughts to the sky, he tried to imagine that other world recovering as the course of Loop history normalized.

He remembered the hideous desert trees, disfigured by cancer. He remembered the dead rats he'd seen in Wayne's Rock, swollen bellies upturned.

He remembered the single pink blossom on the hillside, the one tree that had escaped the cancer. Takayama concentrated on that tree, allowing it to expand in his imagination.

He wished with all his heart for the moment when those trees would cast off their tumors and reassume their fresh greenness. He imagined those withered limbs heavy with beautiful blossoms. If the Loop recovered its biodiversity, those scenes would be reality.

A breeze widened the gap in the clouds. The observers' faces flickered in and out of view.

Takayama nodded. "It's going to be alright," he said.

That hope was likely to be heard.

Only Forward
Michael Marshall Smith

A truly stunning debut from a young author. Extremely original, satirical and poignant, a marriage of numerous genres brilliantly executed to produce something entirely new.

Stark is a troubleshooter. He lives in The City - a massive conglomeration of self-governing Neighbourhoods, each with their own peculiarity. Stark lives in Colour, where computers co-ordinate the tone of the street lights to match the clothes that people wear. Close by is Sound where noise is strictly forbidden, and Ffnaph where people spend their whole lives leaping on trampolines and trying to touch the sky. Then there is Red, where anything goes, and all too often does.

At the heart of them all is the Centre - a back-stabbing community of 'Actioneers' intent only on achieving - divided into areas like 'The Results are what Counts sub-section' which boasts 43 grades of monorail attendant. Fell Alkland, Actioneer extraordinaire has been kidapped. It is up to Stark to find him. But in doing so he is forced to confront the terrible secrets of his past. A life he has blocked out for too long.

'Michael Marshall Smith's *Only Forward* is a dark labyrinth of a book: shocking, moving and surreal. Violent, outrageous and witty - sometimes simultaneously - it offers us a journey from which we return both shaken and exhilarated. An extraordinary debut.'
Clive Barker

ISBN 0 586 21774 6

Spares

Michael Marshall Smith

Spares – human clones, the ultimate in health insurance. An eye for an eye, but some people are doing all the taking.

Spares – the story of Jack Randall: burnt-out, dropped out, and with a zero credit rating at the luck bank. After five years lying low on a Spares Farm, looking after inmates that can't even spell luck, he is finally faced with a chance at redemption . . . if he, and the spares, can run fast enough.

Spares – it's fiction. But only just . . .

'Comic, cruel, twisted and surreal' *Empire*

'Witty, hard-edged and coruscatingly imaginative . . . compellingly off-kilter' *New Scientist*

'Smith masterfully moves the whodunit toward the future, opening up refreshing vistas for a genre rooted in the present'
People Magazine

ISBN: 0-00-651267-4